PRAISE FOR *THE FIVE*

MW00511944

"Through the classic lens of a youn̲ in a new land, George Weinstein deftly brings a fascinating bit of lost history to life. Tense, tender, and ultimately hopeful, Weinstein offers a vivid picture of the Great Depression from an entirely fresh angle, wrapped in a beautiful love story that will touch your heart."

— Joshilyn Jackson, NYT bestselling novelist

"George Weinstein's *The Five Destinies of Carlos Moreno* is the gripping story of illegal deportation of Mexican-Americans from Texas during the era of the Great Depression. Told through memorable characters splendidly created by a skilled and gifted writer, it achieves what important literature ought to achieve—a sense of awe from the discovery of a grand experience. Few books shadow me after the reading; this one does."

— Terry Kay, author of To Dance with the White Dog *and* The Book of Marie

"Though George Weinstein's *The Five Destinies of Carlos Moreno* is set during the Great Depression, its concern for what happens to those living in the margins is just as urgent today. A love story wrapped inside a classic game of cat-and-mouse, this book is both a pleasurable and a highly relevant read."

— Susan Rebecca White, author of A Place at the Table,
A Soft Place to Land, *and* Bound South

"Echoing themes from *Les Misérables* and *The Grapes of Wrath* of discrimination and injustice, Weinstein tells the story of a young Mexican challenging bigotry, restricted opportunity, and the threat of deportation during the early years of the Great Depression. Carlos Moreno finds his destiny in a tale that will keep readers up late at night, reluctant to wait until the next day to read what happens next in the life of this remarkable young man."

— Abraham Hoffman, author of Unwanted Mexican Americans in the Great
Depression: Repatriation Pressures, 1929-1939

"Weinstein's second novel establishes him even more firmly as a remarkable and gifted writer, with a sure eye for historical detail, a powerful, authentic voice, and a compassion for the marginalized and dispossessed that is compelling without ever condescending."

— Man Martin, author of Paradise Dogs *and* Days of the Endless Corvette

"Like a love ballad, this story resonates on sweet and tender chords; yet there are disharmonic relationships, melodic, but bitter journeys, and collective intonations, all which crescendo in the multiple possible lives of one hero dancing along to the damned and lovely music. Weinstein has written an unforgettable story."
– *Doug Crandell, author of* The Flawless Skin of Ugly People *and* They're Calling You Home

"With *The Five Destinies of Carlos Moreno,* author George Weinstein has accomplished two tasks. The first is obvious—*Destinies* is one helluva read. Of greater relevance, however, Weinstein has given not only a voice to the everyday Hispanic 'illegal' in the U.S.—whether it be in the book's 1920's Great Depression setting or amid today's political insanity—but he's also presented this noble race of 'hard-working wanderers' with a heart and soul, not to mention love and compassion. A must read for anyone who desires to look behind today's headlines."
– *Jedwin Smith, author of* Our Brother's Keeper, Fatal Treasure, *and* Let's Get It On

The Five Destinies of Carlos Moreno

Gail —
Thank you for your support.
May you and your overcome every Tower!

The Five Destinies
of Carlos Moreno

George Weinstein

Deeds Publishing | Atlanta

Published by Deeds Publishing | Marietta, GA
www.deedspublishing.com

Library of Congress Cataloging-in-Publications Data is available upon request.

ISBN 978-1-937565-71-8

Books are available in quantity for promotional or premium use. For information, write Deeds Publishing, PO Box 682212, Marietta, GA 30068 or info@deedspublishing.com.

10 9 8 7 6 5 4 3 2 1

DEDICATION

For Kate,

When I consider the countless improbable actions that needed to have occurred at exactly the right moments since the
dawn of time so that we could be together, it's obvious we
were destined for each other.

PROLOGUE

Ask your question.

Now cut the deck three times and spread the seventy-eight cards of the Tarot before you. Seventy-eight cards whose origins are shrouded in mystery. Twenty-two are the familiar Major Arcana: The Fool, Death, Justice, The Lovers, The World. Fifty-six are the suits of the Minor Arcana: wands, cups, swords, and coins—fire, water, air, and earth. Elements as old as time, each as vital to life as the others. The cards all lay face down, yet some of them call to you more than others. Can you see each one? Can you hear them? Your fingers tingle and your palms itch. You are anxious to make your choices before you lose track of the ones that cry out.

Proceed.

You select your first card. The Self—who you are at present. Then come five prophecies. Your destinies. Choose the card that predicts how you will manage obstacles. The third pick will be the opponent in your quest; the fourth your ally. Your fifth choice contains a message your intuition whispers. Will you now listen? The final card answers your question. You may have thought this the most important, but your other selections tell me even more.

Shall we unveil the truths that came straight from inside you? You hesitate. Do not worry—many who come here are un-

comfortable at glimpsing their future. I will tell you something to intrigue you: the story of another seeker.

Hear me.

CHAPTER 1

A brown moth struggled to free itself from the white-painted burial cross. Carlos checked the smaller cross beside it on the table of scarred oak. Nothing on that one. He knelt and used his thumbnail to pry the hair's-width legs from entrapment, one by one, as the moth tapped him with its fluttering wings.

Carlos cupped his hand over the moth as its last leg came free and carried the insect across the weathered shack. Sticking his hand out an open window, he spread his fingers. The moth hesitated, shifting its painted feet. Wings tickled his palm like a soft breath. "Fly!" he whispered in Spanish and brushed it with his other hand. The moth fluttered toward Galveston Bay.

He listened to the cries of seagulls perched on a small dock behind the workshop, hoping none of the sleek white birds spotted the moth. He knew he wouldn't need a push if given the chance to escape. Only duty to his father held him in place.

Isaac Shapiro apologized for the bugs as he brushed wood shavings aside with his liver-spotted hands. He lit his pipe and said, "It's five dollars for the pair."

Despite a steady breeze, the air smelled of warm sawdust, sweat, and tobacco. Carlos inhaled the familiar odors of work and tried to make his English reply flawless for the handyman who'd created the sturdy crosses. "My father just has pesos left. You will take them, sir?"

"Sure, but they're not worth as much as they used to be. Call it eighteen pesos. I told Gerardo I'd carve the dates for free."

"Thank you, sir." Carlos' lips moved as he counted. He tried to smooth the creased, sweat-stained money before handing it over.

"Your father told me to engrave 'Elisa Esmeralda Moreno.' Make sure I spelled her name right. Gerardo didn't remember your mother's birthday, just the year."

Carlos leaned down and peered at the three groups of letters on the crosspiece. He said, "That's fine, sir." The dates, 1890-1928, seemed to have been carved deeper, with more confidence, after her name. He slid his finger along the serpentine grooves of the final 8, getting lost for a moment in the pattern that had no beginning or end, just endless looping. All of his brothers and sisters had perished in their infancy, and Papá had nearly died several times, but in all his nineteen years, Carlos had never imagined losing her. When he straightened, he saw that streaks of white paint had stained his fingertip.

Señor Shapiro puffed on his pipe as they stared down at the monuments. He asked, "Are you sure Gerardo didn't want a name on the baby's cross?"

Carlos looked at his sandaled feet and murmured, "No, sir, he will not give him one."

"I went ahead and carved October 26th, the date your father mentioned." The handyman shook his head and said, "Bad luck to be buried with no name. His soul might not get into heaven if they don't know who he is."

"Yes, sir." He bit hard on the inside of his cheeks; the pain overwhelmed his urge to cry.

Sr. Shapiro gestured toward the window overlooking the bay. He said, "Gerardo mentioned that he'd hire me to row you both over to Galveston after the funerals."

Carlos asked how much.

"Six bits apiece. Say four pesos."

He paid the money and pocketed a half-dozen remaining bills. Wanting to show some appreciation, some concern for any inconvenience, he mentally practiced his English before offering, "I cannot say how long the funerals will take."

"As much time as they need to." Sr. Shapiro shrugged and said, "I'm not going anywhere."

Carlos lifted the crosses, white paint still tacky against his hands, and said goodbye.

*

A narrow beach led him toward the colored cemetery. Carlos tried not to despair at Mamá's death. He still couldn't quite believe it was true—everything seemed to remind him of her vibrancy. The air whistled in his ears like her songs; waves broke as steadily as the rhythms she'd taught him. All around him, the vigorous world suggested that she lived as well.

A strong wind from the west pelted him with grit, so he turned his face toward the bay. Distracting himself, he looked across the briny water at the long, pale hump of Galveston Island and the blue Gulf of Mexico beyond. A fellow *estibador* on the wharf had told him of the thousands of deaths on the island and the east coast of Texas from a storm in 1900, twenty-eight years ago. He tried to imagine standing against a hurricane and wondered how he'd fare.

The gusts rippled his green work shirt; the color had faded to that of the lichen clinging to scraps of driftwood along the shore. Carlos judged the musical suitability of each board and branch that had washed onto the beach: a stick that could be whittled into a *flauta*, a hollow log that could be beaten like a *tambor*. Making music, dancing, and telling stories had been the only entertainments his family could afford at the end of their long days in the fields and along the railroad tracks.

Carlos swayed as small mounds of earth gave way beneath his sandals. With a cross in each hand, staying upright on the shifting sand provided another distraction. The frayed cuffs of his tan trousers, his best pair, collected the crystal grains like keepsakes as he crossed the low dunes. His mother had often praised his balance as she taught him to dance on a blur of dirt and warped wood floors in all the shacks and rooming houses of his youth. Carlos still could recall the secure grip of her callused hands the first time he danced with her around their rented room.

In 1911, when Carlos was two years old, Mamá and Papá had taken him across the border, fleeing Mexico during *La Revolución*. He had earned a full day's pay from age six, working alongside his parents in the brutal heat as they had traversed south and east Texas to follow the farm and railroad work. While picking cotton and endless rows of beans, peas, lettuce, and more, he would daydream of escape by joining the hawks overhead and flying on broad, brown wings to the mountaintops. During his adolescence, he'd notice instead the teenage girls picking and chopping nearby. He fell in love with every one of them and fantasized about life beyond his duty to family. When he grew even taller and stronger, he caught the young women looking at him. Work and constant moving, though, had always gotten in the way.

The cemetery was in view. Carlos ruefully considered another migration, but with Papá alone. He knew his father was devastated by Mamá's death in childbirth—Papá had been anxious and irritable for months, as if he'd had a premonition. Papá had worried aloud about how they would afford food for the baby. He had also pointed out Mamá's advanced age, thirty-eight, saying, "You're too old for such foolishness." Wounds that had nearly killed him two years before—deep cuts from a Klansman's knife—seemed to hobble him again, as if fresh blood had been spilled. It made sense that Papá had chosen an island for their new home, a remote place to heal.

The resurrected city of Galveston would offer no comfort to Carlos, however. Disasters haunted his dreams. His friends on the wharf had warned him that Galveston promised few good jobs for *tejanos,* and there was talk of Immigration agents starting to deport undocumented workers. An island would leave him with nowhere to run.

He neared the cemetery, and Papá met his gaze from among the clusters of burial crosses, wooden grave markers, and other monuments. Carlos' father stood knock-kneed, a hand over his abdomen, as if trying to hide the Klansman's legacy. They both were scarred by the attack; the same man had kicked Carlos in the forehead after carving up Papá. Only a miracle had saved them.

The priest from Galveston's diocese and the mourners—four women and one man—waited for Carlos as well. They were the Morenos' neighbors from the town of La Marque, fellow *tejanos* who were born in Mexico but had lived for decades in Texas. The wind forced the women to tighten the black scarves around their heads and made the men keep one hand on their *sombreros.*

Pedro Rodríguez, the broad-shouldered, middle-aged man from La Marque, had helped Carlos prepare two graves that morning. Pedro bore long scars on both cheeks; a broken nose further disfigured his face. His hat couldn't conceal a vertical groove in his forehead, and his wilted shirt collar didn't quite cover the deep furrow that appeared to circle the base of his throat. Carlos guessed that Pedro had escaped a lynching, since violence remained a constant threat from policemen, Anglo mobs, the Klan, and Texas Rangers. Pedro had mentioned his intention to set out for Houston later that day; Carlos wondered if he was still fleeing.

Father Vignaud held up his hand in greeting. Carlos had missed the priest's Funeral Mass so he could dig the graves. He regretted not hearing the prayers, though Papá had once instructed that only women were responsible for participating in the Church—they prayed for the whole family. Carlos wondered who would pray for him and his father now.

He stepped over the stone ring surrounding the cemetery. Wind blurred the sand where the women had weeded and raked. The children's section stood apart from the graves of the adults. Carlos had counted four times as many plots for *los angelitos* and felt gigantic as he walked past the diminutive crosses and small piles of rock. Over the years he'd helped to bury his five brothers and sisters—stillborns and infants who'd died in the night without warning—and wished all their resting places had looked so well-kept.

Mamá's cross bumped against Carlos' leg as he reached Father Vignaud. The young Cajun priest stood beside the two enshrouded bodies lying on the ground. The clean sheets rippled against them and his black cassock flapped.

Carlos set down the crosses and eased himself into the larger grave. He wiped his hands and examined them for paint smears and dirt, then slid his palms against his trousers again. His father knelt above him with Mamá's body and leaned over, grunting. She felt surprisingly light in Carlos' arms, like a plaster statue. He lowered her to the smooth floor and tucked the shroud tight. Dirt fell and smudged the winding sheet as he climbed out of the hole. When the priest moved toward the pit, Papá and Pedro removed their hats. Carlos stood between them and bowed his bare head. He fought the urge to reach into the grave to clean the shroud.

Father Vignaud led them in the Rite of Committal. The priest's small hands tried to hold the riffling pages flat as he recited in Latin. Carlos knew the prayers would help his mother's soul get to heaven, but he couldn't guess their meanings.

Papá took a fistful of dirt from the pile beside the grave and dropped it toward the center of the shroud. Keening air carried away the sound of the impact. Carlos sifted loose soil over the lip of the grave so that none of the dirt clods touched Mamá. Windblown grit stuck to his face where tears had made his cheeks wet.

The priest led the mourners to the infant's gravesite. Papá wouldn't touch the body, so Carlos carried the well-wrapped bundle. He knelt and lowered his tiny, unknown brother into the much shallower hole. During the pregnancy, his mother had patted her abdomen often and, seemingly oblivious to Papá's grousing, thanked him for their "miracle baby."

Carlos edged the small sheet under the delicate skull and shoulders and the curled legs. The stillborn boy received the same burial rite from Father Vignaud, and Carlos added handfuls of dirt around the body. He paused over the grave, head down and eyes closed, and forgave his father for hating the soul who'd caused Mamá's death.

Pedro filled both graves and, working with the wind, rounded off the mounds. Papá held the crosses as Carlos tapped them into the earth with the back of Pedro's shovel. The clink of iron against wood startled a pair of seagulls nearby. The birds squawked and ascended, white and black against the heavy cloud cover. They flew toward the island.

Papá shuffled to the graveyard's edge and faced the shoreline and Galveston across the bay. Hands on hips, he stretched his back. A proud man who never rested until he'd picked ten full rows or laid a quarter-mile of rails, Carlos' father could no longer stand erect.

Carlos thanked the women, shook the priest's hand and Pedro's, and led them to the stone border of the cemetery. He returned to his father's side.

"God only punishes the wicked," Papá said, facing the water. His thick mustache had gone gray. Carlos wished his father wouldn't blame himself; as far as he could tell, the man had done nothing wrong.

Papá continued, "We have to make peace with His judgment—maybe we'll come to understand the reasons." He made a fist and tapped it against his only clean pair of pants. A decade earlier, three fingertips on his left hand were cut off in a machete accident, leaving them only as long as his little finger. A fellow worker had tied a kerchief to stanch the blood so Papá could keep chopping sugarcane and get paid for the day. The resulting infection cost him weeks of lost work and almost killed him. He rubbed the three nubs against his trouser seam and said, "Time to start over again, son."

"I paid Sr. Shapiro for our trip." Carlos handed the leftover money to his father, who counted it before putting the cash in his pocket. A police patrol boat cut a wake across the bay; he wondered if any Immigration officers were on board. He said, "Did you hear the rumor that *la migra* is checking documents?" His father grunted and Carlos continued, "Mamá wanted me to visit one of our neighbors—a forger who sells citizen-papers. If we have enough money—"

Papá thrust his right index finger into the air for a moment, an old habit. "Not even twenty years old but you're ready to become a criminal. I've never done anything illegal in my life—I paid the fees the Anglos charged after we came across." He continued to raise his voice, almost shouting, "Your mother should've known better."

The sudden flash of anger startled Carlos. He kept his voice soft. "We never got any papers to prove we belong."

"If you're scared, then run."

"No, sir. I won't abandon you."

A man behind them called, "It might be a good idea to run."

Carlos pivoted and looked at Pedro Rodríguez. "*¿Perdóneme?*"

Pedro pushed his fedora down as the wind tore at the feather in his gold hatband. The brim almost covered the deep scar in his forehead. "I thought it proper to wait until after the funerals to mention this: the man I rent my room from said a ranger had been through town a few days ago, asking about two men named Moreno."

Carlos' father glanced back toward the bay and the now-distant patrol boat, his knees pressed together. "Did your landlord say why?"

"No. He only overheard the sheriff talking to another Anglo."

Carlos wondered if his father shared the panic that made his heart race. He doubted Papá would be able to outrun a lawman. Hiding seemed like a better bet. "Sr. Rodríguez, you'd said you were leaving for Houston?"

"That's right. The *barrios* there would be good places to disappear. You'd have to go all the way to San Antonio to surround yourself with more *tejanos*. And I hear the jobs pay better than around here."

Carlos asked, "How far are we from Houston?"

"About fifty miles. I figure a long three days' walk."

Papá spit in the sand between his well-worn boots. "I bet we can do it in two."

"You won't make it," Carlos said. "The trip would kill you."

"You think this ranger won't?" His forehead now gleamed with sweat.

"We just buried Mamá. I don't want to dig a grave for you, too." He glanced at Pedro, whose face was a mask of scars. Only the man's dark eyes looked alive as they seemed to will Carlos to join him. He took a slow breath and rubbed the boot mark in his forehead. "We'll go to Galveston. Maybe *el rinche* won't look there. Maybe the Anglos will let us be."

Pedro shook his head. "You'll have a much better chance in Houston."

"Standing here isn't helping our chances at all," Papá said, taking a shuffling step toward the cemetery. "We'll get our things and start walking."

Carlos put a restraining hand on his father's shoulder. He'd never fought with Papá before or even raised his voice in anger. His determination seemed to surprise the man as much as himself. Another plan occurred to him. "You're going to the island. If you went with us, you'd slow us down and you'd probably die. If we both stay, we'll get caught."

His father failed to pull Carlos' hand away with both of his own. "Damnation! Let me go."

Carlos grasped Papá's other shoulder. He lowered his head to stare into his father's eyes and hoped he didn't betray his fear. Not just about what he was doing now, but what he was committing himself to do. "No, sir. I'll lead the ranger away from here. Sr. Rodríguez's friend can tell the sheriff next week that you and I left for Houston." His father pushed at his arms until Carlos shook him a little. "I can beat you if I have to."

Papá's eyes narrowed and he clenched Carlos' shirt, knuckles hard against his chest. "You'd hurt your father?"

"To save you, I would." At last Carlos felt his father relent. He let Papá go.

Pedro said, "Any *gringo* spotting us would just remember seeing two Mexicans—we're all alike, right? That'll be enough to support my friend's story."

"It's the only way you'll be safe, Papá."

Some of his father's old gentleness crept into his voice. "And what about you?"

Carlos looked from one to the other, both men butchered by the Anglo world but unbowed. Pedro gave him a slight nod, a signal he'd seen often among men to encourage one another. He let out his breath, a long sigh like the wind, and said, "I'll be fine."

Papá rolled his shoulders and resettled his hat. He spit on the sand again. "Go on then. You never wanted to live on that island anyway."

Carlos had to smile at his father's bravado. "That's right, Papá—looks like I found a way out. I'll keep giving you half of the money I make. I'll mail it to the boardinghouse until you send your new address."

"If you send more than a dollar or two at a time, I'll mail the rest back. You need to start saving for a family of your own." One end of his mustache rose with the corner of his mouth. "Just be as brave when you fight with your wife."

The muscles tightened in Carlos' throat as he said, "I'll come back someday, Papá."

His father shook his head and touched Carlos' cheek with his foreshortened fingers. "Never backtrack, son—especially when someone's following you. But never forget where you came from either."

Carlos hugged Papá hard and kissed both of his cheeks before he walked away next to Pedro. He looked at the fresh graves and then back at his father, one last time.

CHAPTER 2

C arlos thought about the last image he'd seen of his father—caught between the cemetery and the expanse of the Gulf—during the five-mile walk through the tall prairie grass to La Marque. With the wind no longer blowing, the humidity loosened Carlos' pores even as it strangled his breath. His shirt clung to his back and chest.

Pedro spoke about the fifty-mile journey to Houston, hands hidden in his pockets.

Carlos asked, "Are there many more Anglos than *tejanos* in Houston?"

"There are more of them everywhere in America. But they're as afraid of you as you are of them." He smiled, pushing out the scars in his cheeks.

While Pedro crossed the oil-spotted concrete road to reach his room, Carlos greeted the *tejana* who ran the colored boardinghouse, one of the mourners at the funeral. He accepted her condolences again and asked her to write down her address so he could mail money back to Papá.

In his tiny bedroom with the low ceiling that seemed to press down more than ever, Carlos rolled up a spare set of clothes, his only possessions besides what he wore. The bare mattress, sunken in the middle, was the room's sole furnishing. He went into his parents' room, aware of the rusty stench and a spoiled sweat odor that wouldn't dissipate in spite of the open window. Their mattress partially covered the pine boards where Mamá's blood had soaked in and dried. The large stains looked black in the dusty rays of sunlight. He tried not to stare at them as his breath seemed to echo in the quiet upstairs. A three-drawer bureau remained shoved into a corner. Atop the chest, Mamá's small, battered statue of *Madona y Niño* lay on its side, the hollow, cobwebbed underside exposed.

He sorted through a pile of his mother's cooking gear in another corner and set aside a tin pot to hold drinking water, and a frying pan. He held the clay pot dyed black inside from simmering beans, and the griddle that had cooked thousands of corn *tortillas* on its cast-iron ridges. The mill still had cornmeal lodged among its gears. Carlos wondered who would buy these things from Papá, since only women ground corn kernels and made *tortillas* by hand. He smelled the yellow dust trapped in the mill and thought of his mother's puddings and her cornbread cookies she'd called *panochitas*.

The last time Mamá had baked *panochitas* was in Port Lavaca, the night she told Carlos that she and Papá would be having another baby. Her smile when she said this looked as fragile as the edges of the thin golden wafers. Shortly thereafter, they'd moved up the coast to La Marque—his father's idea—to look for higher paying jobs.

Only after Mamá told him about her pregnancy did Carlos realize why both of his parents had seemed increasingly miserable; the likelihood of losing another baby was probably more than either of them could bear. The depression and spurts of anger Papá displayed since the Klansman's knifing had become worse—his tone was never less than razor-sharp. When Carlos had asked Mamá if she was happy, a melancholy smile lifted his mother's lips and she said, "No, but I'm in love. I don't think about happiness anymore."

His mother's cries and the midwife's instructions to her had been the only sounds heard on the second floor on the evening of October 26. Carlos, Papá, Pedro, and the others who would later attend the funeral, sat in the dark hallway as the midwife worked and Mamá screamed within the closed room. Her voice weakened in time, the shouts no longer rattling windows. Then she fell silent.

Carlos jumped up first and opened the door. A kerosene lamp on the floor barely lit the scene: Mamá's legs awash in blood, dark as endless night, one arm across her chest and the other above her head. Her face was turned away; sweaty black hair hid her profile. The midwife knelt in the large pool of gore, muttering as her fingers tried in vain to untie the cord from the dead baby's throat. She kept saying she'd never lost both as her fingers picked at the mottled garrote around the narrow gray neck. Never lost both.

*

Carlos met up with Pedro in the street, and they walked northwest along the shoulder of the road. Pedro gripped a small satchel. He'd given Carlos a shoulder-pack to tote his gear and had filled two large canteens with water. With his hands freed, Carlos picked at a loose thread on his shirt, his mind still back in that room.

The sun-bleached concrete cut a swath through grassy prairie. The road looked as smooth and bright as a machete in the shimmering distance. Occasional salt flats dotted the pale landscape. Cattle in hues of cinnamon and clay fattened themselves on grass within and around these ponds. Anglo cowboys astride horses called back and forth as they kept their herd together.

Blasts of air from passing cars and trucks buffeted Carlos and Pedro as they walked along the shoulder. Hiking far from the road through waist-high prairie grass had slowed them too much—the chance the ranger would drive past seemed remote. Still, Carlos watched each vehicle with suspicion. He feared a sudden stop and doors swinging open like rodeo gates, releasing dead-eyed lawmen with stars on their chests and guns in hand. If a car slowed down, red lights flaring, Carlos edged back onto the prairie.

"Fear just attracts your enemies," Pedro said. His voice sounded gentle, coaxing rather than critical. "Your scar goes deeper than the mark on your forehead, doesn't it?"

"You've been through a lot more than me, Sr. Rodríguez. Don't they worry you?"

The man pushed his hat back. Late-morning sunlight brightened his face, and the scars seemed to lose their depth, creasing his skin like mere wisdom lines. "Call me Pedro. It's too long a trip to waste your breath on '*señor.*' You think some *gringos* did this to me, but I got these wounds back in Mexico."

"I didn't know Mexicans did things like that." Carlos peered at the leathery face softened by sunshine and the man's faint smile. The wounds were older than he'd first thought, the heavy scarring burnished in the light.

"And even worse than this," Pedro said. "But far better, as well. Just like the people here and everywhere else. Unfortunately, God didn't order His world so conveniently that we can say all of those people—" he pointed at a truck shooting past "—are bad and all of our people are good."

Carlos shrugged. He hoped the man didn't plan to lecture him for fifty miles.

"What I say may not be so obvious if you thought Mexicans couldn't do this. They murdered my wife and children as well." He pulled the brim of his fedora down again, shading his eyes. "When Death stole into your parents' room and snatched those two lives, I knew just how Gerardo felt as a husband and father."

"Did you ever marry again?"

"I couldn't bear the thought of losing another. Actually, witnessing your father's pain without being able to offer any real comfort helped me decide to go to the seminary in Houston." He smiled and said, "Don't you think my preachiness will come in handy as a priest?"

*

Ten or so miles of prairie and highway separated small towns, a dozen one- or two-story wood-frame buildings and outlying cabins with farmland. Carlos and Pedro refilled their canteens and purchased food where Anglo shopkeepers would sell to tejanos. In the places where they wouldn't, Carlos admired the dignity with which Pedro thanked them in spite of their hatred, as if bestowing his blessing on those in need of guidance.

As they hiked the two-lane road, he expected Pedro to ask about the ranger, but the man inquired about his parents instead. Carlos related conversations from the many instances when they wandered the old U.S. Army trails and the paved roads, following rumors of work. Papá would have immediate, unchallenged explanations for everything, from cars backfiring to Carlos' stomach when it was upset. Mamá had sung to help pass the long hours of walking, the same folk tunes she would hum while doing chores. She'd taught him to whistle two notes at once, a trick Carlos demonstrated for Pedro. The overlapping tones had the sorrowful quality of wind blowing through pines as he whistled a grim *tragedia*.

"Right now," Carlos said, "I can only think of Mamá's favorite songs, the saddest ones."

"You're in mourning. That's only proper."

"But it's not just that. I remember the way my parents used to be, before the trouble a few years ago with some Klansmen and a Texas Ranger—probably the same one looking for us now." He touched the mark on his forehead. "They killed my father's spirit, even if they left his heart beating."

Pedro dabbed a red kerchief at the base of his throat. "Can you tell me what happened?"

Carlos took a long draught of water. He began walking again as he described the attack of two years before, when he was almost eighteen.

The encircled five-pointed star on the ranger's crimson shirt reflected moonlight, in Carlos' memory. The lawman stared at the night sky; his tan skin and dark hair showed clearly in the blue-white glow. He'd appeared on the path leading from the *hacienda* to the town of Victoria. Three white-robed Klansmen, peaked hoods as sharp as gator teeth, joined the ranger and beat Carlos and his father. The robes made soft, rippling sounds while their fists and boots crashed down. Each blow landed like a railroad hammer. They left Carlos and Papá curled up on the path.

"Tell the other illegals what's in store," *el rinche* said, his voice soft and deep. The lawman's dark eyes didn't reflect any starlight.

But the Klansmen weren't through; one of them drew a knife. Carlos struggled to sit up as his father screamed, pinned by the two other laughing Anglos. The serrated blade and the Klansman's hands and sleeves soon dripped with Papá's blood. The white-clad *monstruo* then approached Carlos, who couldn't get his legs under him.

The Klansman's eye-holes looked as empty and pitiless as the ranger's stare. Rivulets of Papá's blood dribbled down the white cassock. The Anglo's boot slammed into Carlos' forehead and knocked him senseless.

Pedro touched his own brow and ran a finger up the crease that disappeared under his hat. "They did other things?"

"No. They never got to finish. Someone interrupted them."

"Did you see who?"

He shook his head. During the remainder of the night of the attack, he had drifted in and out of consciousness. After the Klansman kicked him, he awoke looking down at his outstretched arms and fingers. The man who shouldered him also carried Papá in his arms.

Carlos had raised his aching head. He winced at the pain in his neck; the bruises on his ribs and stomach throbbed. The ranger and the three Klansmen twisted on the ground twenty yards behind him. He could hear them cry and groan. He heard too, and felt, his rescuer's breathing: steady, reassuring. Then, a pitiful wail from his father broke Carlos' heart. He squeezed his eyes shut and passed out again.

When Carlos had blinked his eyes open later, he lay sprawled across a pallet on the floor of his parents' rented room. A damp cloth on his forehead failed to soothe the sharp ringing that stabbed inside his ears. His father lay in the bed while a man stood over him, his broad back to Carlos. Mamá knelt on the floor and cried as she rinsed blood-soaked bandages. She couldn't get them clean. Red-tinged water slopped onto the planks near Carlos' head, soaking into the wood. He whispered, "I'm sorry, Mamá. I wish I could've stopped them."

She wiped her eyes with her forearms and pushed the long black hair from her face; her fingers dripped with Papá's blood. "You did all you could. Rest your head now." The rose-colored puddle grew, touching the stranger's boot at one edge and Mamá's knees at the other. When Carlos had woken again, the floor was mopped and the man was gone.

Pedro asked, "Did you ever see him again?"

"No, never. My mother said he gave his name as Rafael Bernal. She described him as a hulking, moon-faced *tejano* with a drooping mustache."

"You've had trouble with other lawmen?"

Two trucks raced past, blasting Carlos with hot air and dust. "No."

"Then that ranger from two years ago must be the one who passed through La Marque," Pedro said. "Maybe he's really looking for Rafael Bernal, to avenge himself."

Carlos said, "He's not after me and my father?"

"*El rinche* somehow found out your names, probably because he could give a description of you."

"He looked right at me."

"But maybe he didn't get as good a look at the man who injured him and his *maleantes*. He'd assume you two know your savior's identity, right? So, he wants to use you to get to the other man."

"But I can't tell him anything. Neither can Papá."

"You'll be safe from him in Houston." Pedro began to follow the road north again.

Carlos stayed in place. "What'll he do to me if he doesn't like my answers?"

"It's best not to think about it. Come along."

*

They made it to another town to refill their water and purchase supper just as dusk slipped into evening. The café owner wouldn't let Mexicans use the same crockery or utensils as the white customers who dined on his beef stew, so Pedro produced two bowls and spoons from his satchel. Carlos followed Pedro outside the diner, the wooden bowl in his hand warm with sloshing broth. They camped on the prairie beyond the town and faced west. A pale blue glow rimmed the horizon; the azure twilight above it gradually deepened to blend with the night.

Pedro shared half the bread he'd saved from their last meal. Carlos sopped up greasy soup that lacked flavor; no chilies relieved the monotony of diced carrots, potatoes, and stray bits of stringy meat. Still, he was grateful for the warmth, as the humidity had changed from stifling to clammy. He told Pedro that, after sundown during his family's earlier travels, they would lie on the dry grass and pebbled earth to watch the sky. "My father once said stars were like the sun but very far away. Shooting stars were God's way of moving one from place to place. But Mamá insisted: 'God lets the angels peek through the sky at us. They make holes so they can see. What we call stars are the bits of heaven that shine through.'"

He waited for Pedro to comment on one of his favorite memories of his parents. However, the man merely laid there, hands beneath his graying hair, starlight gleaming in his liquid eyes. Carlos continued, "I asked her, 'Are my brothers and sisters watching us?' 'Oh, yes,' she said. '*Los angelitos* love to gaze down on their families.' Do you think your children are looking down, Pedro?"

"Your mother was right. I've always felt them watching out for me."

Carlos considered his parents' words again as he counted shooting stars and gazed at the twinkling lights. His extra clothes made a pillow behind his head. He could smell chimney smoke from the town, and he tucked his hands in his armpits for warmth. Crickets chirped and cicadas droned in the waving prairie grass around him as he looked for two new holes in the sky.

Pedro murmured to himself and perched his hat brim against his shattered nose, covering his eyes.

"What did you say?" Carlos asked.

"Something my wife taught our children. She taught me too since I used to listen in. Did your mother say a bedtime prayer with you?"

Carlos recited:

> *Con Dios me acuesto*
> *Con Dios me levanto*
> *Con la Virgen María*
> *Y el Espiritu Santo*

He sighed, his breath ragged. A warm tear escaped from one eye, slid along his temple, and caught in the hair beside his ear.

"Nighttime," Pedro said, "is the hardest when you've lost someone. You grow up sleeping easily because the people who love you are nearby. But one day, you lose a parent or a wife, or children who slept well because you were near to them. Then, they're sleeping forever and you have to relearn how to sleep at all." He lifted his hat and met Carlos' gaze. "That's why God made a way for your loved ones to look down—so you can sleep as you did when you knew the next day would be your best ever. *Buenas noches,* Carlos."

Carlos said goodnight and returned his attention to the stars. He felt Mamá, and his brothers and sisters whom he never got to know, look down and fill him with hope that something good awaited him in Houston: a better life, a wife and family of his own, maybe his best day ever. God moved a star across the heavens, and Carlos made his wish.

CHAPTER 3

On the third day of the journey, a large, dark shape that had been waving in the heat coalesced into recognizable forms beside the highway. Carlos asked, "Should we cross the road to go around?"

"No," Pedro said. "I see a few *tejanos*."

A bus was parked twenty feet from the edge of the road. A dozen Anglo women in dresses and bonnets and girls outfitted like their mothers stood in the shadow of the bus on the side closest to the concrete. They pressed against the dusty steel hull, clustered in the diminishing shade as the sun rolled directly overhead. A few women stared at Carlos and Pedro and then they all sidled into the brightness toward the front of the bus and disappeared from view. On the other side, Anglo boys in overalls threw baseballs to one another, their arms, chests, and heads bobbing above the prairie grass. The men stood in a semi-circle, felt hats tilted forward, long-sleeved shirts and creased pants glowing in the sunshine. They smoked and offered advice to another man—probably the bus driver—whose legs stuck out from beneath the vehicle.

At the back end of the bus, a solitary *tejano* family stood together. The father, in a wide-brimmed Stetson, and the mother, holding a black umbrella above her, were dressed like those at Mamá's funeral, probably their best clothes. The man looked at Carlos and Pedro, said something to his wife, and stepped closer to the bus. He placed a hand upon it, as if to convey that they belonged inside: he had enough money for them to travel by motor-coach.

When he moved, the man revealed an adolescent daughter he'd been blocking from Carlos' view. She had her parents' pine-straw coloring, with even features and a pretty smile, which she directed toward Pedro and him. The young *tejana* said in accented English, "Mami, maybe they can help."

Her mother peered over her shoulder, tilting the umbrella aside to reveal a suspicious expression creasing her face. She replied in Spanish, "That kind cannot help themselves." She lowered her voice, but Carlos was close enough to catch the word "filthy" as the mother drew her daughter beneath the umbrella's black dome.

Pedro called a greeting, his Spanish drawing the attention of the Anglos. Some of the boys mimicked the sounds like mockingbirds, repeating them and laughing. Carlos held up his canteen to the father and kept his voice low. "*Señor*, does your family need water?"

"No, we're fine."

Carlos only glanced at the daughter and her mother a moment, to avoid a misunderstanding. The girl's lips curved up, while her mother's mouth collapsed at the corners. He told the father they'd alert someone in the next town about the broken-down bus.

"Good." The man gave them a nod of dismissal.

Pedro leaned close to the father and whispered a few sentences, his gaze searching the man's face. The *tejano* slid his hand off the bus and adjusted his hat and shirt cuffs, staring at the ground between them.

Carlos waited for Pedro to join him and edged into the grass, drawing closer to the arc of men who continued to give advice to the one under the bus. Some stared at Carlos, but most appraised Pedro, light-colored eyes shadowed beneath their hats, hands on hips. Loosened ties flapped like strips of cowhide. The men stopped their chatter, and their sons quit bantering as well.

Pedro opened his mouth to speak, but a hard object thumped between his shoulder blades as loud as a striking fist. A baseball rolled into the grass while the boys laughed. Their fathers joined in, and the man beneath the bus asked what was going on. Pedro lifted his chin a little higher and walked past the men. Carlos swallowed and stayed close behind. He wanted to run, but knew Pedro would maintain his dignified pace. He also knew the pretty *señorita* was watching. He murmured in quavering, appeasing English, "At the next town, I will tell them about the bus."

One of the men tipped his hat and whined, "Eh-thanks, seen-yor."

A few men chuckled, and Carlos walked by them as quickly as he could. He held his spine erect, hoping to match Pedro's bearing while bracing for another baseball. Or worse. Something hot flicked the back of his neck. The men laughed, and Carlos heard "Mex" and "greasers" among the comments. Maybe one of them had tossed a cigarette. He wouldn't turn to look or rub the tingling patch of skin.

When the bus and its passengers had become a vague, wavering shape behind them, Carlos asked Pedro what he'd said to the *tejano*.

"Just an old proverb my grandfather told me: 'Don't look for your reflection in those who hide their skin with silver, nor spit on others to clean the dust from them.' Maybe it won't make a difference, but perhaps it'll change his life. Or his daughter's."

"Do you think there's any chance of that?"

Pedro shrugged. "If I didn't say anything, there'd be no chance at all."

*

The early afternoon air was sticky and the autumn sun blazed. Sweat stains on Pedro's shirt looked like tree rings beneath each arm. Footsore and weary, Carlos and Pedro passed a plantation supporting hundreds of acres of cotton, beans, and vegetables where tejano men, women, and children stooped over the crops. Farther north, a road led them away from the highway, becoming the main street of a town that ended in front of a train depot. Carlos' stomach growled as they approached a long row of two-story wood-frame buildings behind which ran a double set of railroad tracks.

At a filling station Pedro told a greasy mechanic about the bus, his accent less pronounced than Carlos'. The Anglo loaded toolboxes in the bed of his pickup, and Carlos and Pedro crossed the street through dust raised by the departing truck.

They walked into the general store. Carlos wondered if they'd receive a greeting or an angry shout this time. He was prepared for more of the latter. Hazy sunlight shone through the front windows, illuminating amber bottles of tonics and cure-alls. Barrels of food staples, tack, and farm implements crowded the floors; clothing, canned goods, and tools sat on shelves. The smells of sun-warmed grain and leather competed with sweet and medicinal aromas. Two ceiling fans turned in lazy circles, stirring the air and delivering each scent.

He looked for the shopkeeper. A teenage girl with deeply tanned skin and sun-streaked hair turned to stare at him from her stool at a soda fountain. She wore a creamy linen shirt with the sleeves rolled back and jeans over dark boots. Her bright, green-eyed gaze never left Carlos as she sipped from a bottle of cola. Behind the counter, a tall Anglo man set glasses on a high shelf. Sweat darkened his blue shirt across the back, and damp white-blond hair stuck to his scalp. He turned and said in a hoarse voice, "Yes, what is it?"

Pedro said, "May we use your pump to get some water, please?" He held up his canteen.

The man said, "Sure. It's out back. Help yourselves."

"Thank you. What town is this, sir?"

"It's called Casson." When Pedro asked the distance to Houston, the man said, "Y'all look fit—it'll probably be just a day's walk."

Pedro asked about the price of the apples in one barrel.

The man wiped his face with a small towel and said, "Nickel apiece."

"Two, please, for each of us."

Carlos hesitated, wondering if the man would mind him touching the produce, but the Anglo returned to stacking glasses. Carlos took two nickels from Pedro and stacked ten pennies beside them on the counter. Pedro made his selections, and Carlos picked out two large apples, heavy and sweet-smelling.

The man said, "Jacinda, bag those up."

"Yes, Dad." Jacinda reached over the counter and produced two flattened sacks of brown paper. The girl snapped her wrists, and the bags filled out with twin cracks, like tree limbs being broken for a campfire.

Carlos handed one apple to her and then the other, making sure his fingers didn't touch hers. While the girl put Pedro's apples in the other sack, she continued to examine Carlos' face. The girl's father leaned on the counter and watched them.

Carlos gave his thanks, and he and Pedro walked out the open back door to a hand-pump in a sandy patch of earth. Beyond, two rows of houses hunkered within a sea of prairie grass. The areas around the homes had been mowed or reduced to bare, raked soil. A large cemetery near the houses looked as thoroughly swept. The sun had bleached a few dozen tombstones. Wooden crosses appeared no grander than the ones Carlos had set above his mother and infant brother; smaller monuments nestled among the rows of adults' graves.

The splintered wood siding behind the store scratched Carlos' back as he leaned against it. He drank from his canteen, allowing the cold water to wash over his chin and soak the kerchief around his throat and the front of his shirt.

A delicious chill spread over his skin. To keep from staring at the graveyard, he closed his eyes and listened to the freshened wind rattle windows in the store and swirl down the street. His hand covered the mouth of the canteen as dusty air blew over him and Pedro.

Carlos wanted to complete the journey to Houston that day. He needed to lose himself in pursuing work and exploring his new surroundings. Since they'd left La Marque, so many things reminded Carlos of all he'd lost. The Anglo girl's hands had looked like those of the Cajun priest as he'd managed the prayer book's ruffling pages. The *hacienda* south of town took the shape of the many plantations where his family had toiled. A railroad crew they'd passed resembled one on which Carlos and his father had worked side-by-side; the bang of their hammers sounded like the shovel on Mamá's cross.

He was grateful for Pedro's companionship; his new friend provided a welcome distraction from his sorrow. Carlos tried not to think about losing Pedro, too, as soon as they reached Houston's seminary.

Pedro took small bites of fruit, reminding Carlos of his own hunger. He tried to eat slowly, to savor the sweetness, but he devoured his first apple—core and all—before Pedro had finished half of his.

They tried to keep within the narrow band of shade granted by the afternoon sun, reminding Carlos of the Anglo women pressed against the bus. He asked, "What were you about to say to the *gringos* when that ball hit you?"

"I have a talent for engine repairs, used to have my own shop. So I was going to offer my help."

"If our *compatriotas* hadn't been stranded too, would you have told the mechanic?"

Pedro finished his apple before answering, "What do you think?"

Carlos nodded. Rather than invite another lecture, he said, "I haven't told you about the one time I rode on a bus."

He could still summon the memory of the wind and the motor both roaring in his ears on the bus trip from Port Lavaca to La Marque. Carlos sat on the smooth wooden seat, the one farthest back, and felt the tires rumble on the road beneath him. He stared out the open window, a leather shade fastened above the rectangular hole. His mother looked out her window from the bench in front of him. Her loose black hair blew over the seatback in dark streamers. Papá sat beside her but looked out the window across the aisle. They'd all dressed in their best clothes, though Carlos still felt ragged whenever he watched the stylish Anglos in the seats up front.

Two days before—when Mamá baked her last batch of *panochitas*—Papá had insisted they leave Port Lavaca. He told Carlos they would have to find better jobs up the coast as soon as possible. Carlos couldn't imagine how much the bus fare cost, but was sure Papá had used up most of the family's savings to take them over a hundred miles away.

On the bus, Mamá thrust her fist out the window and opened her fingers. Dozens of fireflies appeared to leap from her palm and scatter in the wind. Carlos peered over her shoulder. She had in her lap a box containing her small, battered statue of *Madona y Niño*, the centerpiece of the *altarcito* that she created in every new home. The statue nestled in a cradle of ancient, shredded newsprint. Mamá pulled out some more strips of paper and tore them into tiny squares. She put her hand out the window again. Carlos envisioned the yellow bits settling, leaving a trail behind them.

"I almost told her the *estatua* could break if she threw away its padding," Carlos said as Pedro scattered apple seeds before him, "but Mamá seemed to be in a trance. From the look on Papá's face, I thought he'd take the box and break the statue himself, but he didn't say a word. The bus carried us to our new home—our last one as a family it turns out."

They stood, stretched, and gathered their packs to finish the journey. Heavy footfalls inside the store approached the back door. Knuckles rapped on the wood doorframe, drawing their attention. The shopkeeper with the rasping voice said, "Do either of you gents know a Texas Ranger named Donati?"

Pedro glanced at Carlos. "No, sir. Is there a problem?"

"Not with you. With him." The man pointed at Carlos.

"I have done nothing."

Pedro held up a palm, silencing Carlos, and asked, "Was there a law broken?"

"Look, all I know is Donati has been through here a number of times with a couple of sketches of a father and son, last name of Moreno. He's way off-base with you," he indicated Pedro. "But he's got your son down cold, except for the scar on his forehead. He has the right description, too, tall and strong, 'a real bruiser' in his words."

Sweat raked down Carlos' ribs. He touched the slight indentation above his eyebrows. *El rinche* seemed more real than ever, now that Carlos knew his name.

Pedro said, "But the ranger said nothing of what he wants?"

"Right. Just asked me to tell the sheriff if I see y'all. Donati stops by every month or so."

Carlos thought he knew the answer, but still asked: "Will you tell him you saw us?"

The man gazed at Carlos with dry-looking eyes that were tinted red. A smile flickered over his lips. "Saw who? These peepers of mine haven't been the same since the German artillery found me at Armentiçres." He pulled a folded sheet of paper from his pocket and handed it to Pedro. "If y'all get tired of the city, come back this way. We can always use more hands at the farm you passed. Just give that to whoever's at the plantation house." He pointed at the homes beside the graveyard and said, "Not everyone in town was gassed in the Great War, though, so you best be on your way."

Pedro extended his arm. "Thank you, Mister…"

"Webster. Tom." He glanced at Pedro's hand and shook it. "Some Mexican doughboys rescued me over in France," he said. "Fierce men—wouldn't back down from the devil himself. The more the Krauts shot them, the harder they fought. It was the damnedest thing you ever saw." He nodded to Carlos. "Y'all watch yourself with Donati. He got crippled a couple years back—walks with a limp—but he's a tough nut all the same." Tom offered his hand.

Carlos had never shaken hands with a white man before. He hesitated a moment before clasping Tom's cool, dry palm. He glanced away and found himself looking at the man's teenage daughter who stood at the window. She gave him a thumbs-up and smiled.

CHAPTER 4

꧁

Jack Donati stood at the foot of the fresh grave. He took a pack of Lucky Strikes from his breast pocket, jostling the badge pinned there: a five-pointed star encompassed by a circle into which was stamped "Texas Ranger." The taste of tobacco eased the throbbing in his left knee. Useful as a barometer in the years since an attack had left him lame, the mended bones also seemed to forecast when he drew nearer to his assailant.

The ranger read aloud in his soft, deep voice, "Elisa Esmeralda Moreno." *Moreno*—brown, like the skin of the men he hunted. He tried to picture the *tejano* who'd ambushed him and his hirelings that night two years before, but still couldn't visualize the man's face. A steady breeze carried dust away from the mound of earth covering Gerardo Moreno's wife, the mother of Carlos.

Jack removed the stub of cigarette from his mouth. A wisp of smoke escaped between his thumb and forefinger as he pinched off the end. He glanced around the well-tended cemetery and dropped the butt into his pocket.

He considered Galveston across the bay, but chose to follow a tip about two Mexicans heading north along the highway. Jack limped toward his Model A Ford and spotted the other fresh grave, this one nestled among the dead children's plots. On the way to his car he murmured a Spanish prayer for *los angelitos*.

*

Carlos and Pedro arrived in the southern outskirts of Houston at sunset, both men panting after the twenty-mile hike. They looked for a place to refill their canteens, but were clearly in an Anglo suburb. White pedestrians on the sidewalks forced them to walk in the road, where they had to watch for cars and trucks. Pedro murmured that the Anglo wards must have a curfew for the colored. Fortunately, they appeared to be heading in the right direction.

Well-kept houses and shops gave way to factories, stockyards, mills, warehouses, and sprawling railroad yards. The Anglos were gone, and Carlos and Pedro walked among a mix of blacks and *tejanos*. Large homes nearby had been cut into tenements. Trash littered the ground, and the air was filled with swarms of flies and billows of smoke. Sagging lines of tattered laundry hovered like fog. Side streets of unpaved clay and gravel supported huddled *jacales* made from discarded tin and wood. Carlos breathed through his mouth as he smelled the familiar, choking stench of manure and outdoor privies.

Pedro knocked at one home and removed his hat when a black woman answered the door. She pointed toward the west as she spoke, her teeth bright in the fading light. After disappearing inside for a moment, she returned to her doorstep with a porcelain jug and refilled their canteens. The woman apologized as water overran the lip, wetting Carlos' hand, but he rubbed his face and neck, sighing dramatically and making her laugh. They thanked her, and Carlos followed Pedro a half-dozen blocks toward the vanishing sun. The water she'd given him cooled his mouth and throat. He felt the liquid spread inside his stomach, rewarding him with a pleasant shiver.

Pedro said, "The seminary should be somewhere around here."

Carlos turned in a circle, looking at the peeling or unpainted doors of homes and businesses and the blacks and *tejanos* walking on the narrow, cracked sidewalks or in the road where no cars drove. Pedro touched Carlos' arm, halting him.

"What kind of priest will I be," he said, "if I can't even think to look up to heaven?" Pedro pointed skyward. A few streets to the south, a small cross on a peaked roof stood silhouetted against violet clouds.

They cut through an alley cluttered with pallets and trash and stinking of urine. The next block looked cleaner, just cigarette butts littering the ground and newssheets blowing against parked cars. Roadsters and sedans with their headlights on rumbled along the boulevard, and black men in suits and women in dresses window-shopped with well-groomed children in tow. Pedro led the way down to the next block, another street of a prosperous Negro neighborhood.

The avenue on which the seminary stood was segregated for whites. Women, who all traveled in pairs and trios, walked in wide loops around Carlos and Pedro. One man asked if they were lost, but moved past without waiting for an answer. A car passed them and honked its horn, an ugly squawking sound that drew the attention of two Anglo priests chatting in the archway of the seminary. Pedro raised his hand to them and they waved their arms, summoning him.

Carlos walked beside Pedro, looking up and down the canyon of buildings, all two stories or higher, and the shiny cars with white-rimmed tires and the men in their crisp suits and sharp hats. Carlos made sure he never let his gaze settle on anyone, but each person's outfit and swagger fascinated him. Women in high heels wore skirts that bounced well above their stocking-clad knees. Tight-fitting blouses barely concealed the rest of their figures. Those who wore shawls against the cool air draped them over their elbows, leaving bare shoulders exposed.

Pedro spoke with the priests who shook his hand after a short conversation. He introduced Carlos to the *padres* and said, "You're safe now, but if you need help, you know where I'll be." He removed from his pocket a number of dollars folded together in a rectangle and handed the cash to Carlos, explaining, "My vow of poverty begins today." When Carlos tried to refuse it, Pedro said, "You talked about finding a wife and starting a family like a good Catholic. This'll help. And treat yourself to a hotel room tonight—you've earned it."

Carlos shook his friend's hand. He said, "You'll come find me again as soon as you can?"

"You are not lost—you're home. Now go make a life for yourself." Pedro gave him a nod and followed the two priests under the archway.

*

Carlos watched the tall wooden doors close behind Pedro. He wanted to count the money, but was conscious of standing in the Anglo neighborhood with American dollars in hand. He slid the cash beside his savings in a secret pocket his mother had sewn into his trousers. For the first time in his life, he was on his own.

The street was clear of traffic for the moment. Carlos trotted across to the other sidewalk and through an alley, leaving the Anglo world. He yawned and his body creaked and popped as he stretched, reminding him of how good a bed would feel. With no one nearby, he counted Pedro's gift, his lips moving in time with his fingers: twenty-four dollars. He folded the money together with his own four dollars. He could afford a month's rent at a boarding house, decent meals, and some new clothes. He imagined himself in a starched shirt and pressed suit with dress shoes on his feet, and wondered how he would look to young women in the *barrio*.

He focused on finding a room for the night, one with a soft mattress atop a sturdy frame. All of the buildings nearby looked like storefronts and homes. He walked north, past more factories and rail yards. His sandals began to drag on the street as his legs tired.

A child turned a corner and walked a few blocks ahead of him, a girl with long, tightly curled dark hair. The lavender dress she wore over her stocky frame looked almost black in the gaslight. Carlos found himself mesmerized by her lurching walk, the way her body pitched right and left with her steps.

She glanced back and he stopped following for a moment. He wondered if he was asleep and dreaming. The girl's face was almost monkey-like, dark with downy hair and featuring a broad mouth and prominent brows. Her violet eyes flashed as a flivver rumbled past her. He'd seen a freak show once when a carnival swung through southern Texas. He recognized that the girl ahead of him was an adult midget, perhaps the World's Hairiest Woman.

Hearing a faint song his mother had loved, he wondered if the *enana* hummed it. The music sounded whisper-soft, just like Mamá's voice long ago when she had stroked his hair at bedtime, easing the wear of day-long labor. The woman resumed her unsteady walk, and Carlos followed her over the broken sidewalks, passing darkened stores and houses. He now recognized the sounds of violins and guitars playing the same song, keeping him moving.

The crossroad ahead blazed with firelight. Overlapping *mariachi* melodies flowed out to him. The woman glanced back at Carlos again before disappearing around a corner. He trotted after her, willing his tired legs to lift higher.

Carlos found himself on a main thoroughfare where a *fiesta* overwhelmed his senses. Flames leaped up from dozens of large barrels placed at intervals along the street. Men and women swung each other in circles and danced in lines, weaving among the fires. Children cavorted with cloth dolls that had been painted in swirls of black and white. Vendors sold breads, candy, and other treats—the sweet smells of food made his mouth water. The midget who'd led him along the streets had vanished in the crowds.

Two *mariachi* violinists and a guitarist played the familiar melody on the nearest corner. A woman swayed, her back to Carlos, facing the street festival. Straight, dark hair fell over her back and shoulders. Her rising arms turned to copper in the firelight. Far above, a brilliant moon glowed.

Dazzled by the waves of music and her movements, Carlos let the pack slip from his shoulder. The clatter of the pot and pan was lost in the cacophony of melodies and voices. The woman turned. Her face was painted as white as a skull. Deep black ovals shadowed her eyes, a triangle of black covered her nose, and black lips parted to reveal gleaming teeth. Her body shimmied in a tight dress that glittered with bands of orange, purple, green, and gold, writhing and shifting like a serpent's coils.

The musicians' faces shone with white and black paint, too, and cloth skeletons bounced within the children's arms and dangled from shop windows and lampposts, entwined in hand-cut streamers of skeletal *papel picado*. Pails of marigolds and cockscomb—yellow for death, purple for pain—littered the sidewalks. Musicians played on a corner of every intersection, creating a glorious maelstrom of noise. Over the chaos of instruments, whistles, bells, and the howling of street dogs, a corn gruel vendor shouted, "*¡Atole aquí!*" while the man who sold sweet rolls topped with the shapes of bones and skulls advertised his *pan de muerto*. Everyone had dressed for the final Day of the Dead celebration, November 2, the Vigil for the Adults. Carlos realized he'd lost track of time—it was his twentieth birthday.

The woman reached for him. She seized his wrists and he grabbed hers, the skin hot under his palms, her pulse fast like the music. She moved to her left with startling strength, spinning him toward the road, and they twirled together.

Carlos held tight against the momentum. He barely felt his sandals touch the road as they spun each other down the street. Fires whipped past on one side, then the other, and costumed revelers blurred into colorful streaks. She opened her black mouth to laugh, and Carlos heard a brass blare, a joyful shout that called to him as much as her body did. He led them in a whirl toward the new noise.

A giant of a man stood on one street corner, stripped to the waist, surrounded by a skeletal band on strings and guitars. A painted, grinning skull masked the bandleader's features, but the cheeks looked alive, compressing and inflating. Before his black-rimmed mouth, a golden trumpet glowed. Its bell took in the light from a dozen barrel fires in swirls of orange and yellow and blew out that energy as crescendos of sound. Stylized bones streaked his muscular chest and arms. A glaze of sweat swirled the white paint on his cinnamon skin just as his trumpet blended firelight with luminous brass.

Under the spell of the music, Carlos danced a reel with the woman. She grasped his shoulders and drew him closer while his fingers strayed over her behind, feeling the rhythmic clenching of her muscles. Rolling her head, she lashed his cheeks with wet black hair.

A dozen other couples danced nearby and clapped with the quickening tempo of the melody. Carlos stared into the hazel eyes that gleamed from his partner's painted sockets. Sweat soaked him and heat pulsed from his face and hips. Her hands traveled over his broad back and descended below his waist. She seized his buttocks, jolting him as the music climaxed.

Carlos closed his arms around her, dizzy and weak, while the crowd cheered. The woman exhaled hard, black nostrils flaring. She leaned her chest against his wet shirt, and brought her face to his. Her eyes closed, and he gazed into black ovals. The woman pressed her painted lips to his and separated them with the tip of her tongue. She caressed the inside of his mouth.

Her hands eased around to the front of his trousers. She tilted her head back, breaking contact. He saw her teeth again as she found what she was doing to him. She put those fingertips to her lips and blew a kiss over her palm—cool air against the sweat that beaded his face. The woman backed away, serpent coils still shifting. A black wave of hair flung around as she turned and disappeared among a throng of dancers.

The band started another song. Carlos pushed through the revelers and staggered to the narrow sidewalk, scanning the crowds. He couldn't find her. Whimsical skeletons dangled nearby in a shop window, staring out at the celebration of death and life. In the glass reflection, he noticed a lavender dress among the costumed frolickers behind him. He leaned his back against the brick of the storefront and slid down until seated on the concrete beside a few pails of flowers. Carlos watched the trumpeter and dancers until his eyes drooped. The revelers' shadows swept over him. Then he slept.

CHAPTER 5

Carlos did not need my guidance the first time I saw him. He would have found la fiesta *on his own. But my visions compelled me to behold the young man who had made himself so familiar through my cards. Since late October the images had conveyed what I knew inside: a seeker had begun his journey. My purpose would be to show him what he already knew as well—the significance of events often needs to be distilled so their meanings become clear. I would set before him a cup that brimmed with this essence. He would then have to choose whether to drink.*

The Tarot suit of cups figured prominently for Carlos. The water contained within symbolizes emotions and intuition, relationships and love. This was his quest.

We know about water: Houston is the Bayou City. We know how it gives life and brings death. The relentless surge of water over Galveston in 1900 decided the economic contest between our rival cities. Water solidified our hold on commerce: the Houston Ship Channel connected our Buffalo Bayou to the coast and the great cargo vessels and tankers came. Oil and water mix quite nicely in Houston.

The bayous help segregate Houston and its people into wards. Just south of the Buffalo Bayou is where many of us live, a mile of homes and shops close to the railroad and factory jobs. This is where I led Carlos: the Second Ward—El Segundo Barrio—or what the Anglos call "Little Mexico."

There are only 15,000 of us in a city twenty times that large, but it feels even lonelier than that. "Jim Crow" laws keep all the colored out of Anglo businesses and public buildings. Even the thousands of us who were born here are still referred to as "Mexicans": alien and unclean.

Despite the obstacles, we endure. Parents pray their kids will do a little better. They hope their grandchildren will live in fine homes, wear nice clothes, and drive to good jobs, that their faucets will grant an endless supply of nourishing water, hot and cold. That is why seekers journey to Houston. But such a destiny is not always in the cards.

CHAPTER 6

C arlos awoke at dawn, his mouth dry with thirst. He was one of two dozen *tejanos* who slumped against the buildings or lay curled on sidewalks amid the trash and pots of flowers. He pushed himself up the wall and, stretching out his sore back, glanced in the shop window. The skeletons stared out at him. They looked childish and tattered in the morning light, their magic gone for another year.

He noticed his reflection and touched his face where the woman's kiss had left his lips smudged black. He wet the back of his hand and slid it across his mouth, staining the skin over his knuckles with two dark streaks like railroad tracks. Carlos recalled the music and his dance with the woman, the way she controlled his body. He slapped his hand against the window to still a sense of vertigo. When he pushed away from the glass, he left a handprint as large as the life-size cloth skull that grinned from the other side.

His shoulder-pack, with the canteen inside, nearly tripped him. Someone must have put it beside him while he slept. He thought of Pedro first, but then remembered the *enana* in the lavender dress, the way her violet eyes flashed when she'd looked his way.

He finished the water, drinking and then washing his face with the last of it, grateful for her kindness. Liquid sloshed in his empty stomach; he'd forgotten to eat supper. He reached into his pocket, within the secret pouch his mother had sewn, but the twenty-eight dollars were missing. His fingertips slid along the fabric and touched the smooth edges of a few coins. Only thirteen cents remained.

Cold sweat mingled with the water dripping from his face. Carlos looked at the pack near his feet and almost kicked it in frustration, but he thought of his mother using the pot and pan it held. He'd never been robbed before, never had so much money to lose. He needed to take the first job he could find.

Crumpled newspapers, spilled food buzzing with flies, abandoned toy skeletons, and barrels still radiating heat obstructed his path down the street. He recalled the warehouses and rail yards he'd passed on his way through the city and turned south. After a few blocks, he arrived at a large intersection. Cars and trolleys carried Anglo businessmen dressed in suits and hats; Carlos joined a crowd of black and *tejano* laborers in shirtsleeves, dungarees, and jumpsuits walking alongside the streetcar tracks, heading in the opposite direction.

At the first two warehouses he went to, he failed to get noticed by the foremen picking workers for the day. When he stepped over the last of the rail spurs and sidetracks that crisscrossed a massive rail yard, he counted two dozen *tejanos* and blacks already waiting outside a large dock door. He had just decided to try another warehouse in the vast complex, but then chains were drawn against metal and the dock door rattled upward.

A short Anglo man set a long board in place to hold the door, and stepped out onto a concrete apron. He turned the cuffs of his shirt back over brawny arms. "I only need ten today," he announced. Muffled Spanish translations followed while he started pointing. "You, you, you." The *tejanos* clambered onto the loading platform and went inside the warehouse. Five more followed, two blacks and three *tejanos*.

The Anglo peered at the labor pool and pointed at one more. "You."

Men anxious to be seen raised their hands and jostled Carlos out of the way, making him stagger. The movement seemed to catch the foreman's eye. "And you, the big one there in the back," he called, pointing at Carlos, who exhaled the breath he'd held and followed the last man inside.

The warehouse was enormous, with rows and rows of wood crates and oily metal shapes illuminated from above by bright lights. Carlos had never worked in an electrified building. He stopped and squinted at the lamps suspended from the ceiling before joining the other nine men selected.

The foreman's hard-soled shoes thumped double-time against the concrete floor as he caught up to Carlos. "You speak English?"

"Yes, sir, I do."

"I'm Mr. Glickman. I need a big guy to load and unload the trucks. Job pays three dollars a day for ten hours' work. There're two trucks waiting for that cargo by the bay doors. Heavy crates on the bottom, lighter ones on top of them, and make sure they all fit snug. These other guys will be packing and bringing parts to you." He clapped his hands together. "Get to it."

The job required strength and planning, but only in spurts. Carlos assured himself periods of rest if he could stay ahead of the crew who packed the machine parts and the truckers who backed in to be loaded or emptied. In the fields, where he had to go as fast as he could all day, he didn't depend on others, but forever raced the weather, the continual ripening and spoiling of the crops, and the relentless sun. He found it much easier to stay ahead of people.

*

Mr. Glickman paid him with three creased dollar bills at the shift's end. He said, "Come back tomorrow. We can use a guy like you six days a week."

Carlos thanked him. He folded the money into his pocket and strode north through darkening streets toward the *tejano* community. He reminded himself of his promise to eat a decent meal and sleep in a bed.

At the edge of the rail yard, he passed abandoned boxcars with *tejanos* sitting within, sleeping or just staring out the open door, shoulder to shoulder. The line of slumping men probably went all the way around the inside: a ring of men in an airless box.

He finally found a vacancy in a rambling two-story house in the east end of *El Segundo Barrio*, fifteen blocks from the warehouse. The rundown tenement crouched in a neighborhood of shabby homes beside the oily, opaque Buffalo Bayou.

The landlady required two dollars and fifty cents per week, but provided supper each night. Carlos followed her, a thin candle flickering in her hand, up the creaking stairs and along hallways of sagging floors, water-stained walls, and ceilings that had rotted through in many places. Behind closed doors men conversed in low tones or sang in loud, drunken voices.

She opened the door to her last vacancy. A mildewed sheet hung from a clothesline that had been nailed above the center of the doorway and extended across to the opposite wall. A loud snore came from one side of the bisected room. The landlady indicated the empty bed on the other side, the only furnishing. A west-facing window yielded just enough twilight for Carlos to detect movements on the floor, walls, and ceiling. Cockraoches. She said she had some supper left over, still warm, all his.

Carlos cursed losing Pedro's money, but knew he could be even worse off. He listened to the grating snores from the other side of the curtain and watched two cockroaches scurry under the thin pillow of the empty bed. He said, "I'll take it."

CHAPTER 7

❦

The bed frame beneath Carlos' mattress lacked an adequate number of slats. That first night he felt as if he and the pad beneath him were folding inward and would soon collapse atop the skittering cockroaches on the floor. The next day he amended the frame with some boards reclaimed from a trash bin; after that, only dreams disturbed his sleep. Every night, the dancer spun in his arms and seduced him as musicians played. The trumpeter seemed to control the pace of the fantasies. Whenever Carlos woke up, jangled and bleary, he recalled the music as much as the woman.

His fellow workers had assured him the same musicians from the *fiesta* gathered to play every weekend. After work on Saturday, he ate supper quickly and walked to the business district within *El Segundo Barrio*. Carlos stayed close to other *tejanos*, remaining vigilant for the Texas Ranger named Donati.

He forgot his fear, though, when he heard the songs from his youth and saw the rollicking street fair. A *mariachi* band stood at one corner of each block playing folk songs. They all dressed in loose white *camisas* and baggy *pantalones*, with broad *sombreros* and leather *sandalias* to complete their peasant costumes. Most of the bands consisted of two violins and two kinds of guitars. One of the guitarists invariably led the singing, his expressions exaggerated according to the lyrics, head tilted back and lips peeled away from his teeth. Some bands had a fifth musician whose sharp plucking of a handheld harp stressed the song's rhythm, helping the dancers land their steps with more emphasis.

Dancers crowded the street. The men dressed in dark trousers and white shirts, with suit coats and matching ties if they owned them. They wore sandals or boots at the least—many had dress shoes—but their bare ankles revealed that none had adopted the Anglo convention of socks. Men smoked between dances, since their hand-rolled cigarettes didn't hold together through stomps and spins. The women wore long, colorful skirts and blouses or bright print dresses. As they moved, stockings added sheen to their pulsing calves. After a song, the women tightened the ribbons with which they tied back their raven hair. Some lifted their feet from the high-heeled dress shoes they all wore and leaned against their girlfriends, laughing as they massaged their toes and insteps. Children wore their best clothes as well; they danced with their parents and each other.

Carlos drifted from corner to corner, listening to the songs but also looking for the mystery woman who ruled his dreams. The bands specialized in the particular styles of dance from different regions of Mexico and each had enthusiastic followers who surrounded them. Dancers before one band formed in a loose semi-circle of couples, while at other corners they made long parallel lines and gaily dressed women flirted with their somber-suited partners across narrow corridors of pavement.

The *mariachi* band with the largest number of dancers and stomping audience members hailed from Cocula, in the state of Jalisco. The wife of the bandleader explained this to Carlos as she taught him the syncopated pounding of the *zapateado*. "*La vihuela,*" she shouted, her red mouth close to his ear as she pointed to the round-backed guitar, "provides the rhythm, and *el guitarrón* gives us the base. Drive your heels into the ground as you pound railroad spikes!" She stamped in rapid syncopation with the *vihuela*, grit leaping from beneath the heels of her shoes like sparks.

Carlos danced with her, mimicking the thunderous stomps. His body shuddered as his heels slammed against the paved street. After a half-hour, he quivered like the loose strings on the *guitarrón*. He hadn't seen his dancer in the crowd and needed to keep looking.

The musicians with roots in Veracruz played more complicated melodies, but simpler rhythms. Two rows of dancers faced each other for the *huapango*, holding their heads and torsos still while quickly shuffling their shoes. Carlos rested his heels as he balanced on the balls of his feet and twirled his legs in response to the pretty woman shimmying across from him. She was not the one from the *Día de los Muertos fiesta*, however. Carlos bowed when the band took a break and continued his search. He scanned the dancers farther down the avenue for his tall, voluptuous *sirena*.

At the edge of the street fair, he found the least popular group. *El Mariachi Santa Cruz de Guadalajara* boasted the largest ensemble, with three violins, harp, *vihuela*, *guitarrón*, and the only trumpet among the bands. The latter seemed to be too untraditional for older *tejanos*—only a dozen young couples and the wives of two of the musicians gathered at their corner. Though the man playing the *guitarrón* led the singing, the trumpeter clearly led the band, and Carlos recognized the barrel-chested bandleader as the massive skeleton from the celebration that haunted his dreams. The trumpeter tipped the horn down as he bowed to Carlos and sent forth a brass crescendo in greeting.

El Mariachi Santa Cruz poured out exciting and sensuous *jarabes* that combined *zapateados*, *huapangos*, waltzes, polkas, and other folk dances, reminding Carlos of the various styles his mother had blended when she taught him. The mystery woman was nowhere in sight, but he could at least have the music. In fact, while Carlos partnered with the musicians' wives and the others, he forgot his guilty desires. Melodies propelled gentler fantasies of making music, while rhythms sparked his body merely to dance.

The trumpet sounds captivated Carlos. Some of the notes reminded him of hawks' calls as they circled the fields he'd worked in as a child. He recalled their cries and the coarse dirt and slick plants as his thumb automatically pressed into endless hillocks of plowed soil and his other hand deposited a limitless supply of onion stalks. He would look up to straighten his sore back and lose himself in the vast blue sky with the gliding hawks that called to each other. Now, Carlos watched the trumpeter and imagined himself soaring with the power of the horn and calling to his avian *amigos* with melodic fanfares. He'd coaxed some complex tunes from flutes he used to make from hollow wood but wondered if he could master a real instrument.

Each dancer reeled around the bandleader's straw fedora lying on the street, high-stepping or quickly tapping their feet to *el jarabe tapatío*, the hat dance. The trumpeter's rapid fingering and the tremulous pulsing of his cheeks so captivated Carlos that he missed his turn. *El Mariachi Santa Cruz's* song-set ended to the dancers' applause. One of the wives handed the bandleader his *sombrero*, and the man held out his trumpet to Carlos as if inviting him to try it.

The silent instrument looked impossibly complex in the bandleader's loose grip, a vast array of cylinders and loops, slides and valves. Carlos decided he'd be foolish to try to learn such a thing. Worse, the experience would be humiliating. He shook his head and waved goodbye. He walked home in the shadows, buffeted inside by anger at his fear of failure.

*

For a few nights, his dreams replayed that scene. Sometimes he took the trumpet from the bandleader, but other times he couldn't reach it or it slipped from his grasp and disappeared, startling him awake. In those instances when he did take the horn, the brass cylinders and curves and flared bell looked absurd, like a skeletal fish plated in gold. He wondered what had made him think he could go from playing a whittled flute to this complex machine. And then the trumpet would writhe and thrash in his hand. His eyes would snap open in the darkness and he'd listen to his roommate's snores, like a giant saw cutting through the floorboards toward him.

Though the mystery woman was supplanted in his dreams, at least temporarily, Carlos still looked for her during his journey to and from the warehouse. In the early evenings, he'd study the *tejana* pedestrians as he explored *El Segundo Barrio* after supper. Almost a week after the street fair, he spied the dwarf again in a steady downpour. She stood on the corner *El Mariachi Santa Cruz* had occupied on Saturday night, again wearing the lavender dress, holding a black umbrella against the rain that had long since soaked through Carlos' clothes. He stepped onto the curbing near her as men and women walked around them like water parting for jutting rocks.

"Carlos Moreno," she said. He'd expected to hear the squealing voice of the carnival *enanas,* but her tone sounded deeper than some men's. The fact that she'd named him struck him with more force a moment later, and he took a step backward, almost toppling into the street. As he opened his mouth, debating what to say, tasting the rain, she added, "I am called María."

The rain sluicing over her umbrella made a curtain through which he couldn't see her expression or features. Only her eyes and the left hand supporting the umbrella were clear. He counted, and recounted, five hairy fingers and also a thumb grasping the walnut handle.

"You found my shoulder-pack during the *fiesta.*"

"I thought you might be thirsty when you woke up. You had traveled far." Her Spanish was formal and had an old-world music of its own, perhaps the way people spoke a hundred years ago or longer.

"Thank you—you were right." He shielded his eyes from the patter of rain and added, "You've been right about everything." Carlos towered over María physically, but he didn't feel a need to hunch down, hands on his knees, to talk to her—rather, he stood straighter, as if he needed to look up.

"My cards and intuition have led me well in your case. You are not seeking me, but I have seen you searching for another."

Carlos didn't hear himself voice his question, but he must have asked María who she was, because she answered, "Your guide when you need answers. We will find them together." She gave him directions to her address and turned on her heel. María lurched ahead, rocking from side-to-side; the lavender skirt billowed, briefly revealing wide, dark feet encased in sandals. Her umbrella swayed and bobbed below the level of most people's shoulders. Though *tejano* pedestrians crowded the sidewalk, they parted as María drew near to them and came together again after she passed, shielding her from Carlos' view.

*

His dream with the trumpet turned friendlier after that. No longer did it squirm in his grip. The brass radiated warmth through his palm and fingers. The same energy came from the bandleader. Carlos asked him why the horn had tried to escape before. The man replied in Pedro's voice, "It was as afraid of you as you were of it. Now you show no fear." He smiled, pushing out the scars that had appeared in his cheeks, and said, "We'll go just as soon as you're ready."

Before Saturday's *fiesta*, Carlos dressed in the navy-blue secondhand suit he'd bought so he could look like the other dancers. The patent leather shoes included in the five-dollar purchase pinched his feet as he trotted to María's blood-red door with purple trim. It stood out from blocks away among the drab wood-frame row houses. He knocked twice and heard her call his name, beckoning him.

He came through the front doorway and smelled roasted pecans and cinnamon as María entered from a dark back room. She wore a satin robe patterned with golden eyes that were rimmed in heavy-lidded scarlet. The small front room was unadorned except for a round wood table with four chairs, one of them higher than the rest. The smooth tabletop held a cluster of lit yellow candles of various heights and six tall, worn stacks of oversized playing cards. The candle glow didn't extend to the corners of the room or the dark walls, and the light and noises from the street somehow didn't penetrate the open windows.

She said, "I am pleased you decided so quickly." María climbed into the chair with the higher seat. "Join me." She moved the candles away from the center and reached for a deck, her gaping sleeves sliding back to reveal dark brown, scrawny arms dappled with black hair.

Carlos sat on María's left, trying not to stare at her monkey-like face. Small hairs curled around her swarthy neck and chin and over her upper lip. Dark fuzz crossed her cheekbones and blended into kinky hair that fell to her shoulders. Heavy brows arched above María's very large violet eyes. Where the robe opened beneath her throat, hairs bobbed against her *prieto* skin like tiny springs. She gave off the warm, homey smells that scented the air.

"My reading costs one dollar," she said. When he hesitated, María looked at Carlos—into him, it seemed. "It is just a third of a day's wage. You have a dollar forty-one in change in your pocket." Her eyes closed, but the lids were translucent pink, so that she appeared to stare at him through stained glass. "And a quarter hidden inside each shoe."

With a shake of his head, he stacked the coins in a tower beside María's arm. This had to be a dream. Rolling his tense shoulders in the confining suit jacket, he said, "Do I ask a question?"

"Yes, though I recommend you do not make it too limiting." She smiled and exposed four gold canine teeth. "The cards will tell you things you did not know to ask about."

María shuffled the deck. Her left hand had the extra finger he'd noticed, while her longer right hand's four fingers and thumb each possessed an additional joint. The paper edges looked soft, but she made the cards crackle. She put the deck facedown in front of him. "Ask your question and then cut the deck three times. Spread all seventy-eight Tarot cards in front of you, so you can see a bit of each card's back."

A breeze disturbed the candle flames and stirred the hair over his forehead. He said, "I want to ask, 'What will happen over the next few years?'" and looked to her for approval. She nodded and repeated the question and her instructions. The cards felt fleshy, like living things, as he separated them into three smaller stacks and then rejoined them. Carlos fanned the long line of cards in front of him. Though all the backs had the same intricate swirls and crosshatched black lines over yellowed paper, some of them seemed to call to him more than others. He itched to start picking them before he lost track of the ones that felt right.

María said, "Please choose six cards. The first card is your self, who you are at this time. The other five represent destinies: people and events and actions." As he picked the cards, she placed them in a pattern on the table in front of him: the first one in the center, second to the lower right of it, third to the lower left, fourth to the upper left, and fifth across the first one. He hesitated over the last card, edging one from the row but then pulling out another. María put the sixth card to the upper right of the center.

She slid the first card from under the crosswise fifth and turned it over. "This is your self: the Page of Cups." The card depicted a young man dressed in a Gulf-blue tunic; a round hat sported azure feathers. His fawn boots were planted on sand with water lolling behind him. A gentle smile curved the page's lips as he gazed at what he held: a bright golden cup from which a blue fish emerged.

"Water is a theme that runs through the suit of cups, representing emotion and intuition," María said. "This card says you are sensitive, kind natured. Your feelings are easily hurt, but you always strive to trust again."

"Why is he smiling at the fish?"

"The emerging fish is your artistic gifts that are about to be realized. You chose this card to remind yourself to follow your hunches, express your talents, and to love and love again. You have a desire for intimacy with the one you seek?"

"I can't stop thinking of a woman from the *fiesta*."

María smiled, tapping the card with the yellowed nail of her four-knuckled index finger. "Love affairs and loving friendships are the Page's other gifts."

"Will I find her?"

"Let us see." María touched the second card. "This tells us the way you deal with challenges—the way you live—and predicts the way you will continue to face obstacles." She flipped the card to reveal a night scene with huge, multicolored, eight-pointed stars crowding the sky. A slender, nude woman, tanned with black hair bobbing at her shoulders, knelt and poured out a pitcher of water from each hand, one into an azure pool, the other onto the pine-green land where it separated into five streams.

"She's beautiful," Carlos whispered.

"The Star," María said. "The maiden—who is unclothed because she has nothing to hide, nothing to fear—pours a balanced amount on the land to nourish it and the water to replenish it. The five streams are the five senses the Page of Cups needs, to complement his intuition. You go through life balancing desire and work, hope and effort, love and expression. The Star points seekers to optimism, joy, and a sense of purpose. The card predicts you will continue to be guided in the night by these inspirations."

"Does she have something to do with me?"

"*La doncella* is a symbol, but you are clearly drawn to her. You may be seeking to balance yourself with such a woman, just as she is balancing the health of water and earth."

Carlos hadn't realized he'd been staring. He blushed and set it back in place. Still, his gaze returned to the golden maiden who, he sensed, was altogether different from his dancer.

María pointed to the third card. "This is your opponent during the next few years." She turned it over and said, "The King of Swords." A crowned man dressed in a purple cape over red robes stared straight out of the card, sword upright in one hand while his other hand was curled into a fist. Storm clouds gathered behind his throne, swelling above distant cypress trees. The man's jaws were set, his face expressionless. "Purple is the color of wisdom; red means action, desire. Cypress trees are symbols of strife and sorrow. In this position, the King is an intrepid enemy, because he is confident in his sense of justice. He judges harshly but, in his mind, fairly. The truth might sway him, but the King of Swords does not yield to pleas of mercy."

Carlos bumped the table, upsetting the tower of coins. He looked at the hard line of the King's mouth and the dark eyes—Ranger Donati's stare—and asked what he could do about him.

"Stay ahead if he is in pursuit. You are not alone, though." She touched the upper leftmost card. "There are things or people in your favor." She overturned the fourth card, which depicted a man with one ankle tied to the crosspiece of a tree. He hung upside-down with his hands hidden behind his back. A halo shone around his head and his expression looked surprisingly peaceful. "The Hanged Man," she said, "can teach you sacrifice, wisdom, and surrender to a higher power."

"Who hanged him?"

"He hangs there by choice, sacrificing himself for his own *redención*. He is a mysterious figure, a keeper of secrets— notice his hidden hands? He has much to teach, if you are open to it."

Carlos said, "He looks helpless. Can he really save me from the rang—the king?"

"This is a symbol, like the maiden. He's not as helpless as he appears. You will have to save yourself, but the Hanged Man can give you the lessons you'll need."

María continued, "The fifth card is a prediction from deep inside. It is a message you have been trying to tell yourself." She slid the crosswise card from under the Page of Cups and dropped it face-up.

The Five of Coins showed a night scene: two scrawny beggars, one hobbling on makeshift crutches, trudged over ice and snow. They passed beneath a church window lit with five golden coins in the stained glass, each crisscrossed with a five-pointed star like the badge on Donati's shirt.

María said, "You are warning yourself about physical suffering, financial hard times, spiritual decay, valuable things you stand to lose. If you do not pay attention, maybe even more will be lost."

He stared at the pitiful men staggering in the wet and cold. He'd felt a snowfall once during a freak blue-norther that froze the mild air and poured sleet and snow over the fields. Feelings of helplessness had lasted longer than the ice. "Will I lose everything?"

"As in all predictions, if every player continues to behave as before, the outcome grows likelier. If you are displeased by the road you are on, take a new path. One may argue whether you change your destiny that way or put yourself in the way of what has been your fate all along."

"Which do you think?"

"I think you were at such a crossroad deciding what to select as your final card, call it your fifth destiny. A prophecy about the next few years." She turned over the upper rightmost card, revealing a storm and a lightning bolt blowing the top off a tall building. María snapped the card down. "The Tower," she said. Flames shot from the windows and screaming men plunged toward the moonlit cliffs below.

"Another night card symbolizing fear and uncertainty: more trials under the moon. The Tower can be a sudden event that destroys trust. It can signal calamity, adversity. Ruin. It also holds the promise of new ways and new life after the old, rigid structure is gone." María pointed at the Hanged Man. "It may be that you do not follow his teachings, or the King of Swords executes his vision of justice without mercy. The Tower may relate to the Five of Coins—your warning from within—or many of your paths may lead to such Towers." She folded her deformed hands and said, "I know this is a lot to ponder. Have you any questions?"

Carlos began to reach for the card he nearly chose from the long row, but then pulled the shirt collar from his damp, overheated neck. "Can a man like the Page of Cups, an artist maybe or a musician, survive all this? It looks impossible."

María indicated the Star. "Remember to be true to yourself. Follow your intuition and your heart. There can be peace and beauty under the stars. We have all been taught to wish on them, right? Perhaps if you find *la doncella* your dreams will come true."

She turned over the card he'd touched before choosing the Tower. A man and woman stood together, each with an arm around the other's waist. Their free hands stretched toward a rainbow that contained ten golden cups. The colorful arc hovered above a lovely valley and cottage. Beside the couple danced two children, a boy and a girl.

"I almost picked that," he said.

"Learn to trust your instincts. The Ten of Cups is the ultimate prize of love and happiness: lasting contentment and a blissful family."

"That's what I want. Why did I pick the Tower?"

"Maybe another message from deep inside. You had to see the Tower first to make the danger seem real."

"And the only way to avoid the Tower is to get the King of Swords to change?"

"It may be one of the ways. Some think everything affects everything, and would say each event is random. In my experience, people do not change very often, so I view life as a river: you can choose to row from shore to shore and may even stop on an island, but eventually the current takes you where it will. The Page of Cups with the Star as his guide will have to survive the Tower—maybe more than one—and make a new start each time, wiser and hopefully closer to his true goal." She tapped the Ten of Cups.

Carlos wiped his hands on his trousers, leaving long, damp stains. He said, "*Gracias, señora.* Looking downstream on this river, what else should I know?"

María's eyelids slid closed, and she looked into him again. "Lust is not love, though each has important lessons to teach. You have been told fear attracts your enemies; it also drives away your allies. Do not be afraid—the Ten of Cups is still within your reach."

"Can you tell me more?"

She opened her eyes and smiled with her gold teeth. "That will be another dollar."

"I don't have enough," he said.

"None of us ever do."

CHAPTER 8

❦

C arlos reached *El Mariachi Santa Cruz's* corner just as the bandleader began the frenetic *jarabe tapatío*, his straw fedora lying in the street. This time, Carlos took the final turn at the hat dance: arms overhead, hard-soled shoes stamping rapidly around the *sombrero*. When the song concluded, Carlos dusted off the fedora and approached the man with the glittering trumpet.

The bandleader thanked him and tapped it onto his large head. He said, "Welcome back—I'd wondered if I scared you away last week. I'm Oscar Santa Cruz."

"Carlos Moreno." They shook hands, and Oscar introduced him to the other musicians: the four Herrera brothers who played the trio of violins and the small harp, Hector Tolores with his *vihuela*, and Sergio Limón on the *guitarrón*. A bottle of *mezcal* got passed among the musicians and dancers during the introductions. The liquor burned Carlos' throat. He hated the taste, but didn't want to offend, so he drank again as it made another round. Oscar led him beyond the ring of musicians and admirers. Carlos' face flushed as the alcohol burned his insides. He loosened his tie and collar and said, "I'm sorry you don't have a bigger following. You sound so different from the others…so much better I mean."

Oscar rubbed the mouthpiece with a yellowed handkerchief and then wiped his face. "'Sound so different' is the key. The trumpet hasn't caught on yet in *mariachi*, but it's the only instrument I play well, so we'll keep trying. There're other styles of music, too, but *mariachi* is the crowd favorite."

"I love the trumpet's sound. The only other place I've heard it is in the air."

Oscar smiled. "Flights of angels? Gabriel?"

"Hawks. Your music can sound a little like them. I used to dream of escaping across the sky instead of working the rows."

"I grew up doing farm work too, but never noticed that." He laughed and said, "I like the comparison. Are you getting homesick for a plantation?"

"I hope I never go back to being a *peón*. I'm making Houston my home."

They swapped stories about growing up on farms and railroads camps. The alcohol made Carlos talk fast and repeat himself. In the middle of one of Oscar's anecdotes, Carlos blurted, "Will you teach me to play that?" He quickly lowered the hand he pointed, wincing at his rudeness.

Oscar said, "So you can make a home with *El Mariachi Santa Cruz*? From your dancing, I could tell you've got a good ear for melody by the way you used your hands and shoulders, and your feet maintained the rhythms perfectly." He took Carlos' arm and drew him farther away from the other musicians. "I enjoy singing even more than playing. Nothing against Sergio there, but he plays *guitarrón* much better with his mouth closed. I'd do the vocals if I could find someone to play this." He waved the trumpet in the air. "You sure you're interested in harmonizing with the hawks?"

Carlos reached out with both hands and cradled the warm brass, just like in his dream. He tapped the valves and peered into the bell, swaying on unsteady feet.

Oscar continued, "It's just a few miles to our practice spot in the countryside, out where we'll only bother armadillos and coyotes."

Hector handed his *vihuela* to his wife and approached Oscar and Carlos, his calloused hands clamped onto slim hips. Carlos put his age at about forty, the oldest and sourest member of the band. He'd noticed that even when Hector played he grimaced and frowned. The man said, "What's this about?"

"Looks like I found a student."

"Oscar, you've finally got the sound you wanted."

"And I'll be teaching Carlos that sound. It's the only way to keep it alive, right?"

"People are just beginning to appreciate us—why wreck that?"

"I don't want to cause any trouble." Carlos handed the trumpet back.

Oscar crossed his arms, refusing it. "Of course, he won't play in public until he sounds as good as me."

Hector seemed to relax a little. "You're going to stir things up too much one day." He shook his head and returned to the small gathering. However, his scowl kept drifting back to Carlos and Oscar.

The bandleader patted Carlos' shoulder. "You could use a walk to clear your head."

*

Carlos focused on picking up his feet as he matched Oscar's long strides. They passed a few bands whose large audiences implored the musicians to keep playing. Oscar waved to the leader of El Mariachi Mendoza de Cocula and his wife and stomped his boot heels a few times along with the crowd.

They followed the railroad tracks south through the neighborhoods. Carlos tried to memorize the route, since so many rails ran together and then diverged, but his mind drifted back to María and her prophesies. Whichever path he was on with Oscar, it felt right. His attention returned to the present when Oscar talked about his job repairing and maintaining steam engines. Though Carlos hated laying track, he was fascinated by the trains that thundered along those rails. A barrel-shaped locomotive chugged past them, giving him an excuse not to say much in reply to Oscar's question about his work. He'd love to do an important job such as working on trains, but seemed destined for nothing but menial work.

Oscar pointed out the electric lights of bungalows and larger homes half a mile away on either side of the rails and the dark, seedy shacks nearby where moonlight reflected dully from rusted tin roofs. "If you stay near the tracks, you don't have to worry about the Anglos and their curfews. They never come close to the noisy, smelly trains, except to ride them and eat the food delivered by the boxcars, the stuff we used to pick."

"I hope I never go back to that life."

"Who knows? Maybe you'll wear a tuxedo and play for the mayor one day. Whatever happens, it was meant to be."

Carlos yawned. The heat had left his face, but his feet felt heavy.

Oscar said, "You're not taking in enough air. Breathe deeper and lay off the *mescal*."

His face flushed. "Everyone else was—"

"You didn't see me drinking. If you're concerned about appearances, put your thumb over the mouth of the bottle when you tip it back."

The tracks led them out of town and onto the prairie. Oscar stopped at a patch of dirt and flattened grass and pulled off the trumpet mouthpiece. "Rule number one of trumpeting is to be clean. That goes for you and your instrument." He blew out the accumulated saliva before rubbing it again with his cotton rag.

Rule number two was to breathe properly. Carlos spent long minutes relearning how to expel and take in air. He found his head clearing as he used his diaphragm and the muscles in his back. He could smell the grass and earth again, sweet and dry on the balmy breeze. Overhead, the stars came back into focus. His face burned as he considered that Mamá had watched him drink liquor from her heavenly perch.

"Rule number three," Oscar said, "is never play without properly seating the mouthpiece. The word I was taught for this is '*embouchure*.'" He explained how he positioned his lips and tongue to create a perfect seal and control the flow of air. He told Carlos to try it.

Carlos took the horn from the bandleader and placed the metal circle against his mouth. Oscar put his hand on the bell. He pushed gently toward Carlos' face until Carlos lowered the trumpet and wriggled his lips. "That hurts."

"You've got to make a tight seal to force all your air through that end if you want to get music out the other." Oscar took the horn from him and demonstrated the sound with the metal resting against the front of his lips: as much breath blew back at him as peeped from the bell. Then he pursed his lips and locked them against the mouthpiece.

Air flooded through the loops of brass like water through a hose and shot out from the bell in a blast of sound. He used the valves to change the notes and his tongue to slur them and then create a staccato patter and kept playing and playing on one breath. Oscar's shirt drew inward against his stomach as he pushed the wind from his lungs. He lowered the horn, taking in a normal breath through his nose.

Oscar resumed talking, nonchalant about what he'd just done. "Don't kiss it like some girl at a dance. Pretend it's a reed and you're hiding from someone under water. If you kiss the reed and blow out, you'll get a lot of bubbles and you're caught. If you clamp your lips against it, you can breathe pure air and stay free."

Carlos took a full breath through his nose and tried again. He blew and a sound emerged from the bell—not music but close. The note flared and then wavered as he got excited. He exhaled too quickly and lost his breath, killing the tone.

They practiced until Carlos panted. He wanted to sit down and continue, even at the risk of his blue suit, but

Oscar forbade it: "No one ever sits in a *mariachi* band. Don't be impatient. This is the most important thing to get right. You'll feel stronger because you'll use your air better. You'll even become a better kisser."

Carlos took a few more deep breaths. He said, "That's the second time you mentioned kissing."

The bandleader grinned. "I remember you dancing in front of my corner with that *caliente monada* in the tight dress."

Carlos jolted, full of energy again. He asked if Oscar knew who she was.

"None of us had seen her before, but lots of people come into town for the holidays, from partygoers to whores and thieves."

Carlos remembered her hands on his trousers and his discovery that his money was gone. "I'll bet she picked my pocket."

"But she also led you to *El Mariachi Santa Cruz*. She was like one of the spirits of the season. A trickster and a guide, full of contrasts, like the music itself." Oscar cleaned the mouthpiece again. He said, "I don't think people meet by accident, Carlos. She was supposed to lead you to me and now I'm supposed to teach you."

"Do you think I'm supposed to find her again?"

"Maybe next year." He looked at Carlos' dour expression and laughed. "I think she stole more than your money."

"How did you know that?"

Oscar held up the trumpet. "Son, when you get to playing this just right, it's like having a giant third eye to see the world in a new way. And peer into people's souls."

CHAPTER 9

🔥

Despite the cooler weather, Jack Donati sweated and tossed in his sleep. Burial crosses haunted his dreams. The nightmares always began with him in a small boat that rocked as his hired thugs finished weighting a body, a rabblerousing *tejano* union organizer who'd annoyed one too many politicians. Jack sat in the stern. He looked at the night sky and reordered the constellations with new figures and new names, setting things right. An old habit. He glanced down at his chest, admiring the glint of moonlight on the badge pinned there.

When the two men heaved the Mexican into Christmas Bay, Jack expected a splash, but heard nothing. One of the roughnecks lifted and dipped the oars to row them back to Freeport. The boat merely rocked in place. Jack leaned over the gunwale to see what held them, but the water shone like a wavy mirror, reflecting a billion flashes of starlight. He ordered the men overboard to investigate, but saw he was now alone.

He lowered himself into the corpse-cold bay, took a deep breath, and descended. Dozens of ropes were attached to the boat's underside. Jack followed a line down through the murky green. Beneath him, ghostly squids drifted among schools of grotesque bottom-feeders with snapping jaws and long fins. As he drew closer, he recognized Klansmen in their peaked hoods and billowing robes and the other ruffians who did his dirty work. They all swam above burial crosses planted in the sand like anchors. The ropes led up from the crosses and held his boat fast.

Jack looked up but couldn't see the keel anymore. The line he held now seemed to hold him. He panicked and tried to rise. He could not. As usual, before he awoke, Jack realized he'd been breathing water all along, just like the others who'd glided over the forest of graves.

No, he was different from them, Jack told himself in a ritual that followed the dream as his consciousness surfaced. Sometimes he even had to remind himself of his last name. He'd legally changed it from "Diego" after his mother died in a TB epidemic, leaving him with no one. "Donati" came from astronomy books he'd stolen from the library where he worked—they didn't give "Mexicans" a library card, not even half-breeds like him. The Comet Donati captivated Jack with its majestic, curved tail of stardust and twin gas-trails as straight as rapiers. The drawings of the comet sweeping over Paris in 1858 depicted what he'd often fantasized: reordering the heavens, filling the night with shooting stars. Setting things right.

He wiped the sweat from his face with a clammy bed sheet. Linda moved beside him, murmuring and then settling herself against his damp back. Jack sat up and swung his legs out of bed, his left knee aching, and found his pack of Lucky Strikes on the nightstand. His hands moved automatically in the dark room, putting the cigarette in his mouth, igniting the matchstick, bringing the fire close, and ending with a game. He dropped the flaming match, watched the comet fall through black space, and swooped down to squeeze it in his palm. It was a trick he'd invented as a child, a diversion whenever he'd gotten bored with grinding lit cigarettes into his too-dark skin.

Idle pastimes. Something to do after school while waiting for his mother to race in and check on him before dashing to her next ten-hour sweatshop confinement south of town, on the border. He couldn't go outside and play with the other boys, white or Mexican. Neither side would have him.

One time she almost caught him playing the game. He sat on the warped planks of their one-room apartment, ten years old, smoking and staring at her *altarcito* for *La Virgen* in the corner. The cracked and soiled plaster statue of *Nuestra Señora de Guadalupe* was a foot tall and leaned against the adjoining walls, the base and feet broken off and lost long ago. Flowers his mother had laid before the icon slowly disintegrated and added to the dust on the uneven floors. He would steal votives from the church so she could say her prayers in candlelight. Food was scarce, but they always had a supply of matches.

His mother had swung open the door and trotted into the rented room, a blur of sweaty black hair, swarthy skin, and dirty clothes. She sniffed and looked at him. In the northern accent of her native village near Piedras Negras, she said, "We can't afford cigarettes, Jackson."

"I found them." A half-truth: he'd found them in a teacher's drawer.

She looked at the blood-stained rags tied to his forearms. "The bullies at school hurt you again?"

He said they had. Smoke curled between his slender fingers.

She kissed his forehead and stole a quick puff of tobacco. "I can't look after you during the day. If you can't protect yourself, you better make friends with the bigger boys. Pay them with your *cigarrillos* if you have to. I need to go."

The door closed and he looked at his arms again, darker than his Anglo classmates'. They'd learned some Spanish to insult him. The Mexican boys in the neighborhood had eagerly taught them the right words. "*Prieto*," the Anglos would shout at him and call him a half-breed. Young Jack said it aloud, "*¡Mestizo!*" and puffed the cigarette to make the tip glow. When the wounds healed, maybe he'd be whiter. Maybe no one would notice him.

Now, with Linda snoring softly behind him, Jack held out his scarred arms in the darkness of his bedroom. Invisible. Perfect. He pulled on the pair of boxer shorts he'd discarded earlier and edged over to his desk, feeling ahead of him. His fingers grazed the back of the chair and the smooth leather of the gun belt hanging there. Jack felt the walnut grip, the long holster, and the ranger badge stuck into the leather. The encircled star always was fastened over his breast or beside his revolver. In the fifteen years since he'd earned it, Jack kept it nowhere else.

He clicked on the green-shaded lamp and sat down at the table, the chair seat smooth and cool beneath him. A sketch pad lay on the leather blotter. His habit was to start at the back and fill up the pages in reverse so he didn't ruin the earlier works by constantly folding them over. The Comet Donati was the first subject he'd ever sketched, copying from the library books he'd always returned. Now he drew those he hunted and the way they ended up. Drawing always put him at ease after the guilty were jailed or killed. He immortalized them, Jack often told himself, with a dignity and grace few of them had displayed as free—or living—men. A hand-built cypress bookshelf beside the desk held dozens of volumes of his work. He had room for plenty more.

A storm commenced outside, rain pounding the windows and lightning outlining the shade in blue-white pulses. The thunder came several seconds behind the flashes. He surveyed the earlier drawings in the sketchbook in front of him. Starting at the back, he saw bootleggers, thieves, rapists, gangsters, murderers. What they'd looked like at their trials or how they had died. Jack tried to use only the best strong-arms he could afford. He preferred not to dirty his hands or waste his own bullets. Still, he always memorialized the guilty with lead from a pencil.

He turned more recent pages, every face shaded darker. Illegals, agitators, and petty crooks. His knee ached as the rain rapped on the glass. An image from his dream stretched into his consciousness like the smoke climbing from his stubbed-out cigarette. There—the sketch of the burial cross, made after a tip had led him to the Mexican cemetery south of La Marque a few months before. He'd dated the drawing November 2, 1928, All Souls' Day and *Día de los Muertos.*

Elisa Moreno. Two loose, tattered drawings lay on the desktop: Gerardo and Carlos. That was the last time Jack had used Klansmen. They weren't professionals, didn't follow orders. Two of those idiots were probably still learning to walk again and the third one had eventually died. And Jack's knee had been ruined, along with any chance of advancement. He'd given sketches of the Morenos to a few other rangers and sheriffs he could trust, but he largely worked alone to find the father and son, the only link to his assailant.

Jack turned to the next clean sheet on his pad. Once again, he tried to capture the Mexican with the axe handle who'd ambushed him and the Klansmen and carried the Morenos away. The side of his pencil point brushed hesitantly over the page, like a flutter of wings against a windowpane. The moon had been near-full that night and the stars bright, even in their disorder. Why couldn't he recall that man's face?

The storm drew closer, the booms sounding just a beat behind the flashes. Jack crumpled the paper and fired it into his wicker wastebasket. Linda stirred and pushed dark bangs from her eyes. She squinted into the light from his lamp and said, "Jack, what time is it?" She spoke English with only the faintest accent.

He looked up from a fresh page at her. "Linda" was Spanish for "lovely" and well-suited the *prostituta.* She rose onto an elbow and the sheet slid aside, giving him a view of her golden arms and breasts and brown areolas. Jack said it was late. He apologized for the noise. More thunder rattled the casements and she laughed at his joke.

"Come back to bed." She flicked long black hair across one breast and said, "You paid for the whole night. I don't need another picture of me."

He'd arrested her a year ago and negotiated a schedule of payments. After she'd worked off the fine, he still brought her to his place. She charged Jack her best-customer price and he always tipped. Sometimes, they gave each other gifts.

"Go back to sleep," he said. "No more work tonight." He looked at her for a few moments as she tucked an arm beneath his pillow and resettled herself, her breast almost white where the mattress compressed it. His left hand held the pencil tip just above the paper, and he resumed his struggle to remember that fleeting glimpse from years ago. Crooked nose, something wrong with the cheeks—Flat? Sunken? He couldn't get the eyes either. Jack rubbed his knee as he tried to summon the Mexican with the length of wood that struck like a lead pipe. It was useless. The pain of the impact had obliterated his memory, like heat searing through acetate film at a picture show.

Jack focused on his favorite whore instead, sun-kissed and raven-haired. Pencil lead caressed the paper. She appeared to be a simple beauty—symmetrical, delicate features—but he noticed the small details that had first caught his eye. The curves of her upper lip, the smooth bridge of her nose, a shadow of a cleft in her chin.

When he completed his gift for her, he signed it as always, with a curve like a comet tail, intersected by two straight slashes, under his name. Jack lifted his wristwatch from the table, checked the time, and wound the spring. He hadn't given a gift to himself for a while and decided one was overdue.

He limped into the living room. Flashes of lightning lent brief glimpses of his progress toward the phone on the wall. He gave the Houston operator the number and waited while she routed the call to the local exchange in Brownsville. Finally, the phone buzzed at the Hanson house.

After the fourteenth tone, a man grunted an exasperated, "Yes?"

Jack said, "It's me."

J. Bainbridge Hanson—J for Jackson—said, "I thought you'd gone away."

"No, you'll never get rid of me. Time for another visit to Western Union." He'd intended to slaughter his Anglo father after tracking him down. However, stepping onto the deep, wraparound porch of the man's mansion, Jack had decided payments without end would be a better punishment. Reparations for the life the man had stolen from Jack's mother and now owed to him.

Hanson asked how much and moaned when Jack said, "Two thousand." Jack replied, "Stocks keep going up. You're a rich man—Dad." He gripped the receiver tighter, thinking of his mother crying late at night and talking in her sleep as she relived the months Hanson had abused her while she worked as his maid. "Peccadilloes"—that's how the man had defended his rape of Jack's mother and untold others, like it was just a bad habit. Ironically, the word came from the Spanish *pecadillo*, a little sin.

Jack kept his voice soft and low. "My friends in Brownsville could visit tonight. You know how much those guys love to work in the dark." Once, Hanson had hired bodyguards and refused to pay. None of those men had survived the evening.

"No, I have it. I'll wire the money in the morning."

"Get Phoebe on the line." He'd forced Hanson to hire a black live-in maid, a woman as big as a football linebacker. Someone Hanson couldn't intimidate. When Jack had brought her over with his ultimatum, he only half-joked, "Even I'm afraid of her."

In a few minutes, Phoebe bellowed into the phone, "Yes, I'm still happily employed here, numbskull. Did Mr. Hanson pass the test? Can I go back to bed now?"

"He did and you may. Put him back on." Jack told his father, "Also give Phoebe fifty bucks. Don't let the bedbugs bite, old man." He hung up, fingers trembling with rage. He could've changed his first name, too, but he liked the all-American sound of it. He just hated that his mother couldn't help following her traditions. Did she ever regret having that man's child, let alone honoring Hanson by passing on his first name? As a kid, he often cursed both of her choices; the other boys had made him wish he'd never been born.

The storm had moved away, leaving dripping eaves and the echoes of distant thunder. Jack limped into the bedroom, needing to shed his pent-up energy before he exploded. He woke up Linda and put her to work again.

CHAPTER 10

Early in his life, Carlos had learned he could will his body to perform like a machine: bending, chopping, hoeing, picking, pounding, stacking. After half an acre or twenty yards of track—or, now, after filling and unloading a few trucks at the warehouse—he would turn his brain to fantasy. He dreamed while his body moved with precision. Carlos had the satisfaction of doing a job perfectly and knowing he'd be chosen the next day to do it again. Secretly, though, the aches and pains lingered longer than before, a hint of the damage being done to the machine that would break down in time and for good. His work habits gave him little cause to smile.

However, on the prairie south of Houston in the cool night air, Carlos grinned with bleeding gums and bruised lips as he flexed his aching fingers against the trumpet. His torso, front and back, cramped as he forced his body to breathe as instructed, but he knew the pleasure of devoting his entire self to something he loved. He focused his mind on the bandleader's words and demonstrations, reveling in the pains that meant accomplishment.

He studied the trumpet with Oscar every evening, Monday through Friday. On Sundays, the bandleader spent the day with his girlfriend Marguerite and her mother, starting with Mass at Our Lady of Guadalupe Catholic Church. Oscar tried to coax Carlos into joining him, saying he and the priest were the only adult male regulars. Carlos imagined Pedro one day standing in the pulpit, facing pews full of mothers and children but few men. He knew he should attend, but Mamá's piety didn't save her life or the lives of her other children; her *Madona y Niño* was hollow and powerless. He decided his time was better spent elsewhere.

Neither did he follow the path of some other laborers and musicians who spent their wages on drinking, gambling, whoring, or all three. Instead, Carlos chose to practice his music alone on Sundays and work odd-jobs for spending money. Since his lessons honored the Page of Cups' artistic desires, and he'd begun to search for the maiden under the Star as well as his dancer, Carlos felt optimistic that he was on a better course now. No Towers were in sight, and no King of Swords either.

On Saturdays after work, Carlos had the Texas Mercantile Company, a private postal service, mail a two-dollar money-order to his father in care of the La Marque boardinghouse. He increased the amount to three dollars when the warehouse foreman upped his wage by a nickel. Carlos only received one piece of mail in reply, a new address in Galveston scrawled on a narrow sheet of paper he left with Texas Mercantile for future mailings. As soon as he'd pay for the money-order and postage, Carlos would walk five blocks to take in the weekend *fiestas.*

When *El Mariachi Santa Cruz* played or rehearsed, he was on their corner before the first instrument was tuned and lingered after the last dancer strolled home. The other band members got used to Carlos' role as Oscar's *protegido fanático* and began to treat him as their good-luck mascot. In time, Oscar's trumpet piqued more audience interest. Even *tejano* clergy from churches and the seminary came to listen and dance the occasional *jarabe,* but Carlos didn't spy Pedro's scarred face among them.

Work and music practice should've given him dreamless, exhausted sleep. But two images now haunted him: *la sirena* and *la doncella*. His dancer tried to dominate his dreams, her sensuality becoming bolder, while the Star's golden maiden— though naked— balanced his desires with a purity of spirit, a light he wanted to take into his own body.

As the days grew longer, he often strolled through the City Market in the Third Ward after work. The crowds concealed him from Ranger Donati, he hoped, while permitting his observation of others. The produce was so familiar to his senses, the tender skin of tomatoes swollen with juice that smelled of their crisp green vines, slick and brittle layers protecting the pungent onions, waxy *jalapeños*, and the reptilian texture of yellow squash. As he explored with his fingers and inhaled the remembered scents, he watched dozens of lovely young *tejanas* attired in the brazen Anglo styles. The women shopped alongside modestly dressed mothers and *ancianas* cloaked in nineteenth-century shifts with dark *rebozos* over their shoulders, whose crow's feet deepened as they passed judgment on the short skirt and revealing bodice of someone's grandchild.

The palette of skin tones appealed to Carlos as much as the curves that the spare clothes accented. His instant attraction to the lighter-skinned women reminded him again of the maiden beneath the Star. Ever since he'd begun to notice girls, the golden-toned ones captured his immediate attention even though both of his parents were dark, as were his dancer and himself, dusky skin varnished in leathery hues.

He would linger in the market until the time to meet Oscar for practice. Though he flirted with a few of those fawn-colored beauties who tempted him, they weren't his *doncella* and his instincts told him to wait until she came along. If the *sirena* crossed his path first, he wasn't sure what he'd do.

*

By August 1929, Carlos had memorized the band's unwritten play-list of popular songs and numbers Oscar had created with a trumpet in mind. On the last Saturday fiesta of that month, Oscar motioned for Carlos to step out of the audience—twenty couples and a dozen bystanders—and join the band while they rested between song-sets.

Hector tuned his *vihuela*, muttering to himself. Oscar went to him and whispered something. Carlos heard Hector say, "This is just what I mean—you're always trying something, stirring things up. That boy hasn't even practiced with us." Hector glared past the bandleader at Carlos, who cleaned the trumpet's mouthpiece and glanced from the musicians to the restless crowd and back again.

"He shows up to rehearsals before you do and pays more attention than me." The dancers began calling out requests. "It's time." Oscar clapped Hector on the back and stood in front of the band. He moved Carlos to the center of the group, and called out, "*La noche y tú.*" The audience cheered for their favorite of Oscar's love ballads.

The trumpet felt warm in Carlos' hands, against his mouth. He followed Oscar's count and played on cue. Carlos almost forgot his place when Oscar began to sing in a rich bass voice that sounded even purer than his playing. The bandleader patted Sergio's shoulder and stepped in front of the band, his hands emphasizing the lyrics. Sergio's mouth closed slowly and the guitarist focused on his strumming.

Carlos played well enough not to disrupt the band's tempo or distract the dancers from their *jarabe*, and the crowd applauded for a long time afterwards. Oscar signaled for him to stay in place, and *El Mariachi Santa Cruz* finished the set with their new trumpeter and vocalist.

After the *jarabe tapatío,* around Hector's wide straw hat, the *vihuela* player picked it up and passed it around, collecting almost seven dollars in change. He swirled the coins around within the crown of his hat and winked at Oscar. "We've got a big crowd now. *El Mariachi Mendoza* asks for donations to replace broken strings and so on. Why not us?" He pounded Carlos on his back and said they should use some of the money to buy their new band member a beer.

"No," Oscar said, before Carlos could reply. "Alcohol is no better for his pipes than mine."

Hector rubbed his mouth and said, "I'm glad I only play *vihuela* with my hands. Why did you keep your singing a secret?"

"If you went to church, you'd know it wasn't a secret."

Carlos felt stung, while Hector laughed and said, "You planned this all along. Now you can sing and still have the trumpet lead."

"A good plan, it turns out. Carlos is a natural—I was holding you back. Did you hear Sergio's *guitarrón*? He sounded great. Now, the whole band's better." He addressed Carlos. "Hector's right about you practicing with the band, though. Everyone needs to get used to my singing and your playing."

"I've learned," Carlos said, "you always have two reasons for doing everything. What's the second?"

"On the other hand, maybe you shouldn't be around Hector so much." Oscar laughed and put up his hands. "Well, yes, there's Marguerite—she wants me to spend my free time on voice lessons with her. I thought a woman singing duets with me and maybe some of her own solos with the band would be interesting. Another new sound for the old music, and some new songs for me to create."

Hector shook his head. "You've got out your big spoon and you're stirring again."

A man leaned into their circle and offered compliments in a familiar voice. Carlos turned and smiled at the priest standing beside him. He'd seen him in the crowd that night along with some *padres* he recognized from previous *fiestas*. A full, graying beard covered the priest's cheeks and jaws and obscured his Roman collar. He wore his salt-and-pepper hair long, as well; locks curled around his ears and over his forehead. The skin that showed was the brown of saddle leather; it creased at his temples beside cocoa-colored eyes and formed deep crevices alongside the broad plane of his nose.

After Carlos introduced himself, the priest said, "You've come a long way from just whistling two notes at once." Pedro Rodríguez's smile gave him away as much as his comment.

Carlos nearly dropped the trumpet as he grabbed Pedro's hand and shook it. "I'd left word with a few *curas* at the seminary, but they always said you couldn't be disturbed."

"They had to work hard beating the demons out of me. Just now they're letting me set foot in the world again. I have a while to go, but they allow me to masquerade." Pedro stroked his beard with an apparently practiced motion. "My instructors thought I should cover up anything that could distract my future congregation. It might be a handy disguise—they have something interesting in mind for me."

"I didn't recognize you at all. Your hair's more silvery than before."

"When you see the Light, it's bound to bleach you a little. And singe you around the edges, like your mother's *panochitas*."

Carlos introduced Pedro to the musicians as an old friend, to which Pedro added, "And the world's oldest seminarian." When Hector offered to buy Pedro a drink along with the others he was treating, Pedro said, "Thanks, but I'm also the world's most insufferable prude since I 'bound myself to the service of the altar,' as they say. If Prohibition ever ends, though, I'll lift a glass with you—something besides sacramental wine."

The bandleader remained behind when Hector led the rest of the musicians and some dancers to a nearby social club that harbored an illegal cantina in the back. Carlos said, "Oscar never drinks either. He's also the only other man I know who goes to church."

Pedro smiled. "Besides you?"

"Besides you," Carlos said. Heat rose in his cheeks and scalp as his compliment to the bandleader became a criticism of himself. He rubbed the trumpet's mouthpiece and murmured, "Oscar's a much better Catholic than I am."

Oscar said, "Maybe we can work together, Father Rodríguez, to get this young man back into the fold." He led Carlos and Pedro down a sidewalk, passing barrel-fires that added to the summer heat. Performers mingled with celebrants in the street. Musicians cleaned their instruments with kerchiefs and then wiped their faces, always in that order. Many of them—not just the single men—handed colorful, folded linens to young ladies who perspired, like peacocks lending their feathers.

"It's rare to find a man who's so devout," Pedro said. "Would you be interested in the priesthood?"

Oscar tipped back his fedora and shook his head. "I have a *novia* named Marguerite. The courtship's slow, but I'm not that pessimistic." As Carlos and Pedro laughed, he said, "Carlos might be on a bleaker romantic path than I am."

"The reward will be worth it," Carlos said. He was glad to have Pedro's attention deflected from his errant faith, but his pursuit of two women—one of whom he'd never seen— didn't bear scrutiny either. He told Pedro, "I was careless after leaving you at the seminary. I went to the Day of the Dead *fiesta* and heard Oscar and his band. It was my twentieth birthday—"

"*¡Bueno!*"

"But someone ruined it by picking my pocket. I lost your gift and my money, too."

"My vow of poverty has taught me having money makes one vulnerable because something can be taken away." Pedro nudged Carlos with a cassocked elbow. "When you have faith—confidence in yourself and the Lord—it's like having an impenetrable shield none can steal."

"Of course, you have to be able to afford food," Oscar said, waving to some other musicians who lounged against a storefront chatting and drinking bootleg beer.

"God provides abundance. The city makes us weak, I've learned. A man forgets how to look at nature with a survivor's eye. So, Carlos, you have your eye on someone?"

Carlos shook his head, disappointed but not surprised that Pedro hadn't been derailed from either of the topics he wanted to avoid. "No, not really. There was a woman at the *fiesta* who I might like to see again."

Pedro grinned and said, "It does sound bleak, Oscar."

"Not hopeless, though," Carlos interjected before the bandleader could poke fun again.

Pedro's expression turned somber. "Have you seen Donati or heard anything more about him?"

"No, thank God." He'd already given Oscar a brief account of the night he and his father were wounded and the ranger's subsequent manhunt. "With the scattered *barrios* here, maybe he doesn't know where to look for me."

Pedro said, "He's probably much too busy with other things. I mentioned I met some priests through the seminary who have an interesting assignment. Not the usual clerical duties, but I'm not the usual seminarian. They told me *la migra* is recruiting from the police departments and the Texas Rangers to help them with deportations."

Oscar said, "There was a man from Immigration at the rail yard yesterday with some deputies. They got the supervisor all worked up; my boss asked me if anyone in my crew was an 'illegal.' I said a Hail Mary last night as penance for lying."

"They're declaring a war on us. America used to love the Mexican, but not anymore."

Carlos couldn't help looking up and down the street, anticipating Donati's reappearance. Only *tejanos* and a few blacks strolled or clustered in voluble groups. He asked, "What do the priests want you to do?"

"Stop them."

CHAPTER 11

Melting pot. That is what everyone calls America. All of us go into the same olla *and we melt and we blend, giving away our culture as we take in theirs.*

This is why we try to hold tight to our language and our ways. Our newspapers proclaim, "Once a Mexican, always a Mexican!" But we came across the border because American culture intoxicates, and we melted and we blended. Now we walk around with holes inside us, gaps where things do not fit right anymore.

The moment we complain, we are un-American, un malcontento. *They say, "If you don't like it here, go back home." As if this is not our home. And then they say: "We never wanted you here anyway."*

Except they did. The businessmen, the soul of America, wanted us here when crops needed picking and tracks needed laying. They wanted us here when they were making so much money off our cheap labor they demanded more of us. "No one will work as hard for so little," they told los políticos. *And we came across the border at America's beckoning. Anglo mobs, the Klan, and* los rinches *couldn't discourage us because men with money promised steady work and better lives. We weighed the risks, and we came across. We saw our parents and brothers and sisters beaten, tortured, and murdered, so we watched each other's backs, and we came across.*

We had always planned to return when things got better in Mexico. Except things never got better there, never good enough to lure us away from the jobs and the promises of this culture of freedom. So we stay. And we melt.

Our children are Americans from birth. Not just legally—it is in their blood. They do not have the empty places inside. They say "hotsy totsy" and "whoopee" and strut in the current American fashions. Mexico is "the Old Country," a place that holds no nostalgia, no encanto for them, only disdain: the motherland has become the "bogeyman."

Now, the mighty American economy is faltering. Their políticos taunt, "Once a Mexican, always a Mexican!" They brag about how little they pay to ship the undocumented and the destitute "home." At only fifteen dollars a head, transportation is cheaper than charity. Our wealthy and middle classes don't want the poor around any more than the government does. So los indigentes hear the message of return everywhere.

What comes out of the melting pot when the government reaches in and grabs us by the fistful? Americanized men and women are told they no longer belong north of the border, but neither are they Mexican. And our American children who think life is "hotsy totsy"…What will become of them?

CHAPTER 12

❧

Jack Donati leaned against a crumbly brick corner and watched three large trucks converge from the east and three more from the west. Ropes secured the large doors in the back of each truck to the side panels. The sun had just broken the horizon and the air still smelled fresh. By evening, each hot breeze would carry smoke, grease, urine, and sweat, the stench of his childhood.

Two police sedans already waited on the broken street where loose newspapers drifted like tumbleweed. Moisture from the humid dawn had misted the windows, silhouetting the four officers in each car. The trucks pulled up with a screech of brakes. Jack pushed away from the wall and pointed at the block of East End slums. No one moved inside the vehicles.

The passenger door of one of the trucks opened, and a florid-faced man in a tailored olive-drab uniform stepped out. Immigration Agent Guy Lebrun motioned to the others. The car and truck doors opened immediately. Immigration officers and Houston police clambered out of the sedans and the shadows of the truck bays. Lebrun smirked at Jack.

Lawmen swarmed into the buildings. From the street, Jack could hear them pounding on doors and giving orders in English. Some shouted the few Spanish words they'd evidently picked up.

Jack thought he should give a class to teach the officers more than crude slang. It would reduce panic to tell a starving family of ten, "We're taking you where there's plenty of food and clean water. You'll have a better chance there." Of course, breaking down doors would undercut that message.

Lebrun wiped a truck fender with a handkerchief before leaning against it. He said, "This'll get my September numbers off to a good start. They keep raising my quota. I know it's early for you cowboys, Jack, but this is the hour when we professionals go to work."

As he'd done repeatedly over the past few months, Jack resisted his urge to shoot the Immigration agent. He also withheld the petty reply forming in his mouth, instead pretending to ignore the *culo*.

The first of the illegals emerged: men and women in filthy clothes trailed by half-naked children, either emaciated or bloated, with at least one mother at the back to make sure no one got left behind. Most of the women carried mewling babies, but few of *los tejanos* had possessions to take with them. Jack recalled a childhood insult, *chivo*, for dirty ones who smelled like goats.

Two officers with holstered revolvers escorted the brood to one of the trucks. Adults boosted up their children and then clambered inside, disappearing. A guard laughed when Lebrun pounded on the metal side panel with the butt of his gun and asked if everyone was comfortable. The babies and young children caterwauled, their voices echoing within the truck.

Jack limped into one of the tenements. He stood aside as lawmen led away more families. The bowed stairs groaned under his boots as he gimp-walked to the second floor.

He'd first worked with Guy Lebrun in May 1929. The Labor Department assigned Lebrun to the Houston region to begin repatriating as many illegal and poor Mexicans as possible. The police chief had asked Jack to work as a go-between with Lebrun, citing his ability to act as the state's buffer between city officials and the federal government's agent. Jack figured this logic occurred to the chief after he'd met the man from Washington, D.C. In the chief's office, Lebrun first greeted Jack by saying, "You're going to help me lasso some Mexicans, huh, *amigo*? I guess it takes one to know one."

Lebrun had a nose for gossip and seemed to know all about Jack. The agent joked about the hearsay in Washington that Texas Rangers helped the Mob and bootleggers in exchange for services or cash, possibly alluding to Jack's contacts in Brownsville. When he quizzed Jack about attending Texas A&M using the Donati surname, Lebrun asked if that was in preparation to run the family farm in Tuscany, and took to calling him Giuseppe. By the end of July, he'd returned to treating Jack like a broken-down, half-breed deputy in a one-horse town. Jack took it all without comment, as he always did to those who could hurt him. He even laughed sometimes—Lebrun could be clever when he put his half-Frog, half-Mick mind to work—and so far he'd kept his gun holstered. Who knew, maybe one of Lebrun's raids would net the Morenos.

Jack moved past the apartments being emptied, and knocked on a door. The knob had no lock, and the hinges creaked as he pushed the door inward. He delivered a helpful message in Spanish to the four men, their wives, and fourteen children huddled in the tiny, reeking space. He smelled their fear.

"Where are you taking us?" one of the men said, buttoning and straightening the grease-marked cuff of his frayed cotton shirt.

"You're going to Mexico." Jack whistled down the hall to summon some escorts.

"But we're *americanos*. We were all born here."

Two Immigration officers came into the room and began to collect names and ages on a clipboard thick with paper. Jack shook his head at the man and, rubbing his thumb and fingers together, said, "If you have money, you get to be *americanos*. If you're living like this—" He shrugged and stuck his thumb over his shoulder, pointing south. "*Repatriados*."

CHAPTER 13

The *fiesta* on September 16, 1929 closed Congress Street
in the business district to celebrate the *Diez y Seis* Mexican national holiday, the declaration of independence
from Spain. During the afternoon parade, Carlos had to march
while playing trumpet, a constant struggle to keep the mouthpiece locked tight against his lips while rhythmic steps on the
pavement sent vibrations through his hands and face. For this
occasion, he and the other entertainers had traded their loose
peasant costumes for ill-fitting rented tuxedos. Still, he loved
every moment as the trumpet sent forth its music.

Tejano children and adults crowded the sidewalks and
spilled onto the street. Everyone waved tiny Mexican flags
and cheered as each band passed. Hands emerged above
heads, wrists snapped, and long spools of green, white, and
red confetti unraveled in the air, sailing among the musicians
like shooting stars.

Behind the last band, *El Mariachi Santa Cruz*, the crowd
poured into the street and followed the entertainers along
the route. The spectacle swept through the Anglo business
district as well, where white children and adults waved
empty-handed and applauded as the bands marched past.
Some Anglos joined the long trail of followers, and the parade
route curved back through *El Segundo Barrio*. The pageant
ended with the bands being led to their traditional corners by

streams of excited dancers. Father Pedro Rodríguez clapped Carlos on the back and joined the crowd of dancers. As the other bands began their performances, Oscar called out the first tune to his musicians over the cacophony of voices. The Herrera brothers' bows struck their violin strings in unison and the celebration continued.

When Carlos lowered his tired arms between song-sets, sweat that had soaked all the way through the armpits of the jacket cooled his ribs and biceps. A woman in the throng of dancers stepped forward with a tall paper cup, extending her hand to him. Beads of water dripped from the sides, as if it had sprung a hundred pinpoint leaks. He thanked her and tipped the cup back, seeing the blur of her red dress and then thin, wind-torn clouds in the late afternoon sky. Ice chips bumped his upper lip as a chilly flood filled his mouth and then sluiced down his throat while he gulped. The base of his stomach filled like a subterranean lake being replenished by a cascade.

Carlos couldn't conceal the belch that vibrated in his frosted throat after draining the cup. He lowered his face to thank her again, but his voice lost its power.

This time his *sirena* wore a tight crimson dress with short sleeves, a mandarin collar, and a pleated, abbreviated skirt. Long, bare legs gleamed like molten copper above matching red pumps. Damp bangs stuck to her forehead and black hair disappeared behind her shoulders. From the faint lines around her mouth and eyes that the *Día de los Muertos* face-paint had disguised but regular makeup could not, he guessed her age as thirty, almost ten years older than him. Still, she was so attractive he couldn't look away. She smiled wide, her rounded cheeks and narrow jaw forming a heart-shape. A wide band of sweat darkened the red fabric from her throat to her breasts, where the silk was stretched even more by her nipples.

Oscar asked the band to reassemble, and then called Carlos, who glanced away from the woman momentarily to acknowledge the bandleader's stare. He turned back, quickly introduced himself, and asked for her name.

"Paz." Her voice thrummed with a deep, melodic timbre, like Sergio's *guitarrón*.

He had to smile, since she brought him anything but peace. He said, "Don't leave this time."

"I didn't think you'd remember me." Paz took the empty cup from him as her other hand grazed his groin. She grinned as she stepped back and said, "How nice—you do." Her index finger aimed skyward and then descended as her arm came forward until she pointed a red fingernail at him. "I'll be right here when you want me, Carlos."

The crowd absorbed Paz as Oscar called out the next song. Carlos resisted the urge to check his pockets, to see if she'd swiped his cash again. He watched her long hair and crimson dress weave through the pairing-up dancers, men and women smiling and interlacing fingers. She reached a rail-thin man, all angles and bone; he was perhaps two or three years older than Paz and dressed in a white dress shirt and pressed pants. As Carlos raised his trumpet, he expected her to partner with the man, but they merely talked. Her friend flashed a humorless smile at Carlos, his skin taut over a pointed chin and bony face, his mouth brimming with sharp-looking yellow teeth.

Carlos concentrated on his breathing and his accuracy. To clear his mind, he sacrificed style for technical perfection. Oscar turned before singing the next verse and winked at him, and Carlos relaxed. The dancers responded with more energy and cheers, unaware of his mistakes, appreciating what he gave them.

The man with Paz took the cup from her and gestured with his chin at an un-partnered *tejano*. Paz began to polka. She grabbed the startled man's hands, flashing her smile and swirling her hair and short skirt. Paz's partner picked a money-clip from now-unguarded trousers, dropped it into the paper cup, and moved along the edge of the crowd. He left Paz to free herself, which finally required stomping on the man's sandaled foot.

She circulated through the dancers, her hands sometimes visible while passing into her partner's pockets a stolen wallet, money-clip distended with cash, or—much more often—a thin fold of dollar bills. Carlos kept his face lowered a bit so he could watch her over the trumpet's bell. As busy as she was, her gaze often met his.

At one point, Paz smiled at him, lifted her arms above her head, and spun. Sweat stains darkened her armpits. Her skirt swirled and rose nearly to her waist. His breath caught for a moment, killing the trumpet's voice, as she revealed curves outlined by her red panties edged with lace. Her partner clapped and whistled as she twirled, drawing part of the crowd's attention. Carlos could no longer see Paz as men and women encircled her. Her partner brushed against the people stretching to catch a glimpse.

Was her seduction of him once again just a distraction for theft? He slurred a few notes to catch up to the band. It bothered him that he could still swoon for the bait even as he saw the traps being sprung. What kind of people would steal from the poor, he wondered. And what kind of person was he for still desiring one of those thieves?

Oscar rolled his eyes at Carlos before stretching his mouth wide and raising his hands dramatically with the song's climax. When the bandleader turned his face back to the audience, Carlos did the same, but could no longer see Paz. The scrawny thief had disappeared as well.

Another man moved around the edge of the crowd, studying the dancers with dark eyes as the music reached its finale. His tan face and hands were streaked with dirt, and he wore battered work clothes, the shirt tails hanging down well past his waist. Despite the grime, Carlos recognized the face. The man limped on a weak left leg.

Carlos knew the reason the thieves had gone: They'd sensed Ranger Donati. Birds hunting mice in the field had fled from the raptor that would feed on them. As the crowd applauded, Carlos kept the trumpet as a shield in front of his face and waited for Oscar to call the next tune. His fingertips trembled against the valves.

He played with his eyes half-closed, hoping *el rinche* would move on; he willed him to disappear. Donati did, in a way, as Pedro intercepted him. The broad, cassocked shoulders and mane of graying hair blocked Carlos' view. A much younger priest with steel-rimmed spectacles, who Carlos recognized from Mass at Pedro's *Misión Católica*, joined the conversation.

As they talked, Pedro's right boot cocked back slowly, like a bow being drawn. The pointed toe sprung forward, and Donati crumpled. Even with the celebration at its peak and playing a crescendo, Carlos still heard the man's cry as Donati pitched to his left. Dancers turned to look as Pedro caught him. The other priest supported Donati's right side as Pedro held up his left. They carried the ranger away to the north, in the direction of the Mexican Clinic on Canal Street. The ranger's eyes squeezed shut and his head lolled back, lips pulled away from clenched teeth.

Carlos considered bolting, but knew he wasn't the one in immediate danger. True to his word, Pedro had sacrificed himself: the ranger would come looking for the Hanged Man.

Within minutes, Paz returned to Carlos' corner but without her partner. She stayed, dancing with some men but mostly by herself, until the end of the *fiesta*. Carlos told himself he watched her every move only to see how many pockets she picked: none, this time.

After the *jarabe tapatío*, the band accepted the crowd's ovations. The mouthpiece made a wet whistle as Carlos turned from the dancers and blew out the accumulated spittle. Droplets flew toward the pavement, looking like sparks in the firelights set at twilight. He rubbed his linen kerchief over the mouthpiece, cleaned the valves, and buffed the rest of the horn as Paz slipped through the large group of *mariachi* fans who always remained after any *fiesta*.

As Oscar and the other musicians chatted with their fans, Carlos talked with some trumpet enthusiasts and swiped at the sweat trickling down his face. He had a second, clean handkerchief ready when Paz breached the final shoulder-to-shoulder obstacles with the ease of a shadow appearing beneath a locked door. Carlos excused himself and handed Paz the folded square of white cloth.

Her fingers slid over his as she said, "What's this for?"

"I thought you might like to wipe your face. It's hot and—"

"I like to sweat." She shook her head, flinging watery beads against Carlos' shirt and chin. "It's like *salsa:* the wetter you get, the better it is. Thanks, though, you're sweet." She reached out to return it.

"Keep it. Would you like something to eat?"

"Very much, but I have no money."

"Lots of people out tonight with that problem." He held her gaze as she appraised him and then he glanced lower at the swells of her breasts, circles within circles. He checked his pocket and confirmed the folded money was still there. Eyeing her, he said, "I have a few dollars."

Paz waved her hand at darting mosquitoes, the kerchief fluttering like a captive bird. "That's unusual for a musician. Can I bring Jorge?"

"Your partner?" Carlos watched the man walk toward them, his angular face turning to seek out easy marks.

She paused for just a moment. "That's right. I'm sorry we didn't get back to Houston for so long. We travel around a lot—don't we, Jorge?"

The man drew up beside her, slid an arm around her waist, and looked Carlos over. Jorge's white dress shirt was still crisp with starch, unblemished by sweat despite the stifling humidity and his activities. His voice sounded high and tense, a *vihuela* string close to snapping. "Yes, it's good to leave a place before they get used to your face. It's also good to finally meet you, my friend." He introduced himself as Jorge Flores and shook Carlos' hand with a rail-hard grip, still holding Paz tight with his other hand.

"Carlos offered to buy us supper."

"Excellent. Paz had mentioned your generosity."

Though annoyed that she invited Jorge, Carlos was flattered she'd told her apparent lover about him. Maybe he still had a chance. He said to Paz, "You've talked about me a lot?"

She lowered her gaze to take in all of him. "You make a good impression."

Heat rose in Carlos' face. He needed help to keep her from overwhelming him. "Oscar," he called, "do you want to get something to eat with us?"

The bandleader stood beside his willowy girlfriend, Marguerite, and her parents, who regarded Carlos' company with disapproval. "No, thank you. Enjoy yourself, but don't overdo." Oscar tapped his pockets. "You have to go to work in the morning."

The dense night air created yellow nimbuses around the gaslights and glowed orange beyond the barrel fires. Far above them, a corona surrounded the moon, like the explosion from a rock hurled into a still pond. Carlos led Paz and Jorge to an *enchilada* vendor. They ate as they leaned against a storefront, listening to a few musicians showing off for hangers-on, sawing rapidly on violins or strumming *guitarrónes* with a blur of fingers. The trumpet bell-down at his feet, Carlos nibbled on the spicy blend of beans, chilies, and pork baked in a corn *tortilla*. Fresh sweat pricked at his scalp, but he enjoyed the food's zest and heat in spite of the sweltering air. He drank from a large cup of water, a bargain from another vendor whose ice block had melted, and asked, "Where's home?"

Jorge bit his meal in half, his sharp teeth tearing through the tender wrap. Steam escaped his mouth as he spoke. "We're from Matamoros—grew up on the streets. I met Paz when I was eight and she was six. We made our way together after that."

"That town has a bad reputation."

"Well-earned. We learned a lot. When it didn't have any more to teach us, we crossed into Brownsville and have been giving lessons in Texas ever since."

"You must be doing well." He gestured to take in Jorge's pressed black trousers, large silver belt buckle, and dress shirt.

"You have to spend money to make money, my friend."

"Except for what I send to my father, I save every penny I can."

Paz finished her *enchilada,* grease shining on her chin and lips, and finally spoke, "Thank you for spending your pennies on us tonight. May I have one more?"

As they ate a second round and then a third, Carlos tried to ask questions that would indirectly reveal Paz and Jorge's entire relationship. He gathered they were more "business partners" than lovers, but while Paz slicked all of her fingers with food, Jorge often touched her arm or patted her bottom with a free hand.

She wiped her mouth and hands with the kerchief, staining the cloth orange with grease. She stepped close to Carlos and took a swallow from his cup; she'd drained hers and left it on the sidewalk. His heart raced as she remained beside him. Paz said, "I'll see you tomorrow, Jorge."

Jorge cleaned his hands on his own kerchief and pushed them into his pockets. Carlos was surprised the man still had room for them. Then he noticed the telltale bulges of stolen items extended halfway down both trouser legs. The thief had pockets as deep as the Navidad stockings Mamá had been hired to sew for Anglo children. "No," he said. "We have things to do. You'll see Carlos again—when's the next *fiesta?*"

"Saturday." The food churned in Carlos' stomach while he contemplated being alone with Paz, who'd chosen him. "But if she doesn't want to go yet, I'll walk her home."

"Go play with your horn, my friend. Paz—let's go."

Paz smiled as she looked from Carlos to Jorge and back. She slid two fingers between ebony studs that held Carlos' ribbed shirtfront closed and traced a circle over his heart before withdrawing her hand. "Would you like me to go with Jorge? Hmm, my friend?"

Carlos recalled how easily he'd overpowered his father, a much brawnier man than Jorge, to whom he said, "I don't want to fight you, but if I have to, you'll get hurt." Even as he said it, he wondered what the hell he was doing. Wheels squealed as the *enchilada* vendor pushed his cart around the corner and trotted away.

"Thanks for the warning, my—" He glanced at Paz and shut his mouth. From his pocket, he drew a slender piece of metal. A five-inch blade hissed out.

Carlos' only weapon perched bell-first at his feet. He knelt to grab his trumpet as Jorge sprang forward. The thief thrust his knife as Carlos raised his left arm to protect his face. The blade jabbed through the tuxedo sleeve but bounced off a cufflink, reemerging through another puncture like a shark fin in black water. Carlos swung his trumpet upward against Jorge's arm. The thief grunted and released the knife, which held fast in his jacket.

Another swing and the trumpet bell slammed against Jorge's hipbone, yielding a second gasp from the man. Carlos stood and raised the horn overhead. A dozen men and a few women shouted encouragement, demanding a prolonged fight. As Jorge held up his hands to block the club, Carlos reared back and kicked the man's knee with the hard toe of his patent leather shoe. The thief lurched as Donati had. Carlos brought the horn down on the back of Jorge's head, knocking him flat.

Blood stained the trumpet's dented bell from a gash that matted Jorge's hair. Carlos felt reverberations in his arm and leg from the blows he'd delivered, pulsing with the pounding of his heart. The knife slipped from its holes in his jacket and clinked against the pavement. He looked inside his shirtsleeve for blood, but he'd gotten lucky. Most of the audience cheered though some yelled for the man lying on his face to keep fighting.

Paz had not moved. With the grease-stained handkerchief still in hand, she took Carlos' trumpet from his loosened grip and wiped blood from the brass circle now concave in spots. He indicated Jorge, who'd begun to groan a little and twitch his legs. "Do we just leave him here?"

"Sure, but leave his knife, too. You don't need it." She tucked her arm in the crook of his elbow and led him down the street. "Where did you learn to fight like that?"

"I saw a priest kick a man earlier tonight, strange as that sounds. The rest was just bashing, like swinging a railroad hammer. I've bashed things all my life."

Carlos glanced behind him. A few *tejanos* stayed near Jorge, recreating the fight for others who'd missed it. A man dropped to one knee as another pretended to lunge. The whole drama played out again, with a second man falling— this time in play—to the pavement. Carlos hadn't realized he did that much; he'd just acted on instinct. Someone pocketed the knife as Jorge gently probed his bleeding head, his cheek still pressed against the street.

Carlos asked, "Will I have to watch my back now?"

"No. He respects getting beaten—it doesn't happen often. He won't misjudge you again." She dropped his kerchief in a barrel-fire. The cloth ignited and writhed in the flames, charring until the updraft spewed blackened fragments into the air.

"It'll be bad for you though," he said.

"No—Jorge needs me."

"Why do you need him?"

She shrugged, but her arm tightened in his. "Reminder of home. His jealous streak shows sometimes, but he knows I do what I want." When Carlos asked what she wanted to do, she said, "You ever been on a train?"

*

Paz took Carlos through a switchyard where hundreds of boxcars loomed, and past an enormous roundhouse where locomotives awaiting repair jutted out like the splayed fingers of a glove. Along the way, she picked up a discarded tarp and canvas drawstring bag lying in the gravel and handed them to him. A shrill whistle sounded; Paz pointed to a long train depot. White smoke gushed from the stack atop a locomotive engine and steam shot from its sides as the train eased forward. Paz took off her shoes, tossed them to Carlos, and dashed toward the train without a word.

As he ran, Carlos dropped her shoes in the sack along with his trumpet and slung it on his shoulder. The cloth tarp hung around his neck. He kept pace beside her, hopping over rails and dodging equipment. She reached the train—a few passenger coaches near the engine and a score of boxcars behind them—grabbed the iron bar that formed a ladder step, and began climbing a boxcar. Carlos gripped the lower rungs, his feet aloft. The train began rolling fast enough for the breeze to cool his face. He called over the grinding of the wheels, "Why are we doing this?"

With no ground lights nearby, Paz was a vague silhouette above him. She stopped, took a hand from the rung above her, and lifted one leg and then the other. She opened her hand and Carlos reached out as the air carried the falling object away from him. His fingers closed around red *bragas* trimmed with lace. She resumed climbing and he followed, setting any other questions aside.

He slid her underwear into the sack and stood beside her atop the boxcar, facing into the wind while holding Paz's hand. The southern neighborhoods twinkled with electric lights as *los suburbios* slid past a half-mile away on both sides, the shrill whistle keening at each crossroad. His hair blew back, and air got trapped in his jacket, puffing the sleeves and inflating the tail. Paz lifted her arms skyward, and rocked back on her heels as the air pushed at her. Black hair swirled behind and the short skirt rippled high on her thighs. A corona remained around the waxing moon. In its light, he could see her body outlined as the wind pasted the dress against her. She looked at him and, with a knowing smile, let herself fall backward.

Carlos dropped to his knee for the second time that night. He got one arm behind Paz and the other underneath, her bare behind resting against his sleeve. Staring into her hazel eyes, he considered what he was about to do: lay with a common thief, someone who took advantage of the poorest and most defenseless. He knew he should wait to find *la doncella*, but the wind funneled between her thighs and she gasped and wriggled against him.

He lowered his mouth to hers. The air had dried out his lips, but her tongue moistened them as she tasted and then penetrated him, their first kiss repeated. She then let him do the same, sucking his tongue as he eased the tip into her mouth. Paz opened her legs farther. Carlos finally broke their kiss; the wind snapped a thread of saliva that had connected them. He asked, "Here?"

Paz dragged her knuckle against the roof of the boxcar. "Too rusty. Let's move forward." She kissed him again, hard and fast, and seized his shoulders to lever herself upright above him. For a moment, she held his head in place. Her fingers raked his hair as her skirt pushed against his face, folds of cloth over warm, musky contours. She pulled the sack from his shoulder and sprang onto the next car. He followed—hawk-like with the wind rippling the wings of his jacket sleeves each time he went airborne—until the rooftops felt smoother beneath his shoes. White smoke, smelling of chimneys, tasting of ash, blew over and around them. The stack was a few rooftops ahead, beyond the tender. As Houston disappeared behind them, the whistle cried goodbye. The engine's headlight illuminated prairie grass that bent away as the train passed, leaving dark waves in its wake.

He took her hand again and put his lips to her ear. "How do we get back home?"

"You may not want to go back." She sounded far away over the train's clatter.

Before Carlos could speak again, Paz put her hand against his mouth. She pulled the tarp from around his neck and, gripping one edge, tossed it up into the roiling cloud from the smokestack. The cloth unfurled like a flag, snapping in the wind. She told him to sit on top of it when she brought it down. When he did so, she kneeled, securing her end.

He had to raise his voice to be sure she heard. "Come here."

Paz dragged the tote with her. She knelt between his shoes and untied his laces. The wind quickly cooled his feet before the tarp's edge blew over them. She called for his jacket, folded it, and stuffed it into the sack. Paz pushed down his knees and straddled his hips, knocking him back on his elbows. Her fingernails nimbly unfastened the cufflinks and studs. She pushed inside his shirt. Strong fingers kneaded the muscles of his chest and shoulders. Paz reached behind him and yanked the shirttail from his trousers and helped him out of the billowing sleeves. After securing the tote between the cars by its drawstring, she crawled back to him. Without a word, she climbed on top.

*

The train slowed as it approached a crossing; its shrill whistle screamed in their ears. Carlos dressed again as best he could, though his fingers still trembled with the aftershocks of what Paz had done to him.

They kept their shoes off, figuring they'd land safer on bare feet. Paz preceded him down the closest ladder, the tarp slung around her neck. She turned on the bottom step and jumped away, the cloth flashing as she tumbled in the grass.

He descended, but stopped when he saw the windows of the passenger car atop which they'd made love. Moonlight splashed through the opposite windows, and he could see the people jostling side-to-side as the coach rocked. They slept or looked straight ahead. No one saw him staring at their dark eyes and familiar complexions, the resignation carved in their faces, the clothes of workers who were much too poor to afford train fare.

His people—those Pedro and his fellow *vigilantes* were trying to save—were being forcibly shipped back to Mexico. He felt ashamed over romping with Paz just above their heads, but felt nearly as guilty about his reckless freedom: sinful adventuring in the country he called home while others who behaved morally were punished. Still, out there on the prairie, Paz waited in the moonlight. Carlos clambered down the ladder, tossed the sack ahead of him, and leaped into the night.

CHAPTER 14

The tarp lay upon the prairie, a pale square in the endless sea of grass, and Paz sat naked atop its center. Carlos drew closer, the recovered sack swinging from his shoulder and straws of grass splintering beneath his feet. He wanted to explain what he'd seen inside the train, talk about that looming danger: his chance of getting caught in the broad net cast by *la migra* was even greater than stepping into Donati's trap. But the moonlight made crescent shadows below Paz's breasts and a black oval of her navel like a cat's eye. The darkness between her crossed legs was the mouth of a cave. She held out her arms to him.

He glanced at the stars—just points of light, he told himself—and said, "We've got lots of walking to do." His voice sounded too loud, now merely competing with insects.

"We have all night. Why are you shouting?"

He lowered the sack with his trumpet inside and knelt before her. "Would you like me to play something for you?"

"Oh yes, but now I want to show you how to get music from me."

*

Carlos dragged up to the group waiting outside the warehouse doors just as Mr. Glickman made his final selections.

The foreman hesitated before picking him last. Dressed in his rumpled tuxedo jacket and slacks, with two studs missing from the wrinkled shirt whose bib-pleats folded over or stuck up as randomly as his hair, Carlos received stares from everyone, just as he had since trudging into town.

His muscles ached with fatigue. Paz had insisted on many stops along the way. His virtue had become so easy to surmount that, as dawn showed details of her body the moonlight could not, she merely had to halt, point at the ground, and say, "*Aquí.*"

One of her lessons even took place in the practice spot introduced to him by Oscar, another fact that shamed him. Except he didn't crave absolution. Only being with Paz again that night—meeting under an agreed-upon bridge that crossed the Buffalo Bayou—would satisfy him. Sleep would have to wait. His tired jaws yawned. He rubbed his stained, unshaven face and went to work.

*

Carlos told himself he was having a love affair with Paz, that the feelings she stirred went beyond physical desire and satisfying his curiosity about a woman's body as well as his own. But he didn't feel affection for a sweetheart, only need. They seldom talked the way he'd imagined chatting with a *novia*. Her interests seemed limited to money—how to get it and how to spend it—and sex. At least that was all she'd reveal to him. He'd soon stopped asking her opinions about la migra, Donati, and tejanos they knew. She viewed everyone as a mark who she ranked from easy to hard (none impossible); a player, from gangsters to priests, who all competed for the same pot of money (none more accomplished than she); or an obstacle to be overcome (none insurmountable). Paz had limitless self-confidence and depthless cynicism. She drained him of optimism as well as energy.

She also maintained a relationship with Jorge Flores. Carlos saw them laughing together during the Saturday *fiestas,* their bodies touching with the casual intimacy he'd once seen in his parents. Jorge avoided him and Paz never talked about her partner, but she sometimes failed to meet Carlos on prearranged nights or on the Sundays when he rented a room so they could spend the day together. The original hotel she'd selected, like many of her favorite hangouts, was in the worst *barrio* slums, dubbed *El Alacrán* for the scorpions who Paz called "players." Later, he'd spent plenty to get a nice room with a brass bed and clean sheets in a better part of *El Segundo Barrio,* but Paz wouldn't always keep her promise to show up and never offered excuses.

By October, the pattern for their encounters had been set. They met at the nicer hotel or some secluded spot outdoors. He had changed boardinghouses, taking a full room for himself, but women weren't allowed inside, and Paz wouldn't tell him where she—and most likely Jorge—lived. Carlos always arrived first at their designated place. As he waited, he would chide himself for his weakness and speculate about whether he really wanted to see her again. If she didn't show up, he'd walk home feeling sorry for himself and vulnerable, afraid Ranger Donati lurked around each corner. If Paz did arrive, he'd forget his fears as they'd screw and then lie together in relative silence for as much time as they had; if they did talk, he remembered little of what they said. He'd stopped offering to play trumpet for her because she always said, "Later."

He thought back to the Five of Coins—the pitiful men struggling beneath circular stained glass, ignoring the implicit warmth inside the church—as he sat naked but alone in his hotel room on a Sunday morning in late October. The brass bed creaked beneath him, a sharp sound full of reproach. The pocket watch Paz had talked him into buying read *el diez.* He still sent a few dollars to his father, but lately spent the rest of his earnings on satisfying Paz's acquisitiveness or dressing himself according to her instructions.

Carlos got dressed again, pulling on the new pinstripe suit Paz had said he should own. He left the room key with the clerk and walked west. Mass at *Misión Católica* wouldn't start for another hour; he had time to make his confessions before the service. He passed the City Market, its empty stalls looking as lonely as the room he'd vacated. After turning south, he walked six blocks to the squat brick building without adornment.

In between Pedro's reappearance two months earlier and Paz's seduction, Carlos had gone twice weekly to Mass at the mission where his friend had duties. Oscar had said he didn't mind that Carlos went there instead of his Guadalupe Church; the bandleader expressed his pleasure that Carlos was attending services anywhere.

Since the *Diez y Seis fiesta*, however, Oscar's displeasure in the time Carlos spent with Paz—and their obvious activities—was made equally clear in private lectures and firm, public criticisms when *El Mariachi Santa Cruz* practiced. Playing trumpet, the bell of which still needed to be repaired, gave Carlos as much joy as ever, but he'd stopped growing as a musician. He'd also stopped attending church. Oscar referenced his own chaste courtship of Marguerite, carried on without interrupting his worship, vocal exercises, song arrangements, and work with each band member. He'd even promised to get Carlos a good-paying job on his locomotive repair crew if Carlos would resume his progress with the trumpet. That meant limiting his time with Paz. Or abandoning her altogether. As Carlos opened the tall wooden door of the mission, he finally felt ready to accept Oscar's offer, and whatever penance Pedro had in store.

Candlelight from wrought iron sconces flickered on the exposed bricks and thick beams of the vestibule. The wood floor had been worn smooth by the faithful. He touched the suit lapels and hand-painted tie cloaking his heart and wondered how his life would've been different if he'd maintained such a path. Through a doorway, the nave glowed from a number of flickering *cirios.* Votives brightened the altar and the cross that stood in the back, which was as tall as a sheltering tree.

Near the front of the nave, three old women, draped with black *mantillas* like the wings of crows, knelt and prayed. Two more sat in wooden pews near the confessionals. Wrought iron candelabras with seven thick candles apiece stood at intervals against the side walls, perfuming the air with hot wax and smoke.

The pews were smooth and hard, like the benches on his only bus ride. He took a seat behind the women waiting to confess. Their bony fingers touched and rotated wooden beads as they murmured in voices as fragile as the wax stalactites suspended from the candelabras. Finally, his turn came and he prayed Pedro would be his confessor.

Carlos shut the door of the booth behind him and knelt before the latticed grille. The close air smelled of the camphor in the old women's clothes and the smoke and tallow from a few votives perched on a narrow shelf nailed below the screen. One of them guttered, its flame flickering and hissing. The other side of the grille had no light, but Pedro sat close enough that the votives cast tiny diamonds of light on his face and curling gray hair. The skin bracketing his cocoa eyes crinkled as he smiled at Carlos, who asked for Father Rodríguez's blessing. "It's been six weeks since my last confession."

"Much time for contemplation and reflection, if put to good use. What sins will you confess about that time?"

"Lying with a *sirena,* Father, a thief who steals from our own. Also, I beat her partner senseless; he is another pickpocket."

"Fornication, battery, and abetting criminals—these are serious indeed, Carlos. And if the thieves victimized Anglos instead of *tejanos,* their wrongs wouldn't be diminished. How else have you sinned?"

"I turned my back on God and you and the faith you were giving me. I coveted and I spent my money foolishly. The money I could've given to my father or the Church I spent on her. Or to hide my skin with silver." He loosened his tie and unbuttoned his jacket in the stifling booth. The watch felt heavy in his pocket. He imagined he could hear its ticking; his heart had sped up to keep pace.

"You remembered my grandfather's proverb—thank you for honoring him. You'll also remember that, for penance, the confessor usually assigns a number of prayers. In your case, I'd serve you better by turning your focus toward learning something new. You have a keen memory and strong musical ability, perfect for the verses and refrains of *el mexicano rosario*." Pedro said a blessing of absolution and opened the door of his booth. "Step out. There's no one else waiting."

The priest took a seat in the last pew, and Carlos perched beside him, twisting a black button on his new suit jacket. From the pocket of his cassock, Pedro withdrew a wooden rosary, a circle of fifty-four beads, four of them larger than the others, connected to a tarnished medal. Below the stamped copper disk hung a pendant with another large bead and then four more small spheres from which a plain cross dangled. Pedro explained each large bead should remind Carlos to recite the "Our Father" prayer he'd learned and the ten small beads in between—*la década*—each stood for a "Hail Mary," with additional prayers to be recited between the tenth "Hail Mary" bead and the next "Our Father."

"The small beads between the cross and the 'Our Father' bead are used for optional prayers. The Anglo priests teach that you begin the devotional with the cross and end when you return to the medal," Pedro said. "Our customs say otherwise. The *mexicano* devotional begins and ends with the cross. What'll keep your musical interest is that we mix in hymns, psalms, and litanies borrowed from the Bible and the liturgy of the Mass, invocations that blend as seamlessly as one of your *jarabes*. I'm sure it's all written down somewhere, but I'll teach you by ear, the way it's always been passed along."

The worn rosary felt light and smooth in Carlos' hand, the wooden balls turning easily on their cord, spinning all the way around unlike the ebony buttons on his jacket with which he continued to fidget. He said, "I've heard men call these worry-beads."

"I'd call your suit buttons the same. Your girlfriend told you to buy these clothes?"

"And my shoes and this." He lifted out the pocket watch, heavy as lead compared to the rosary in his other hand. The links of the watch fob glinted as the chain swayed. Carlos handed it to Pedro. "I'd like to donate this, Father. I need to make room for your gift."

Pedro set the timepiece beside him. "You can give away reminders of her, but what will you do when she's standing before you?"

"I handled her thieving partner the same way you took care of Donati. I never thanked you for risking yourself to save me."

Pedro told him about seeing through the ranger's disguise and sensing this was the man hunting Carlos. He said, "The only sacrifice was that I can't return to your *fiestas* and hear your music anymore. But this mission isn't well-known, so I doubt Donati will find me."

"You could cut your hair and change back—"

"No, that would be a bad surprise to the faithful who still come here. No one needs to see my scars again. But you changed the subject. What will you do when this woman reappears? She knows she can tempt you with more than a drink of water."

Carlos looked down at the rosary he caressed. "I'd forgiven her so quickly for taking the money you gave me. Now I have to forgive her for leading me down the wrong path, and tell her to leave me alone."

"The *rosario* will help you find your way back. And I will."

"Can I help you with your other work?"

"Of course. We work at night, since *la migra* conducts their raids during the day. We try to move as many as we can from one *barrio* to another or even pay for bus fare or a truck to take them to another town." He lifted the watch. "This will get many *tejanos* to a new home."

"I'll sell my suits and shoes and give you that money also." Carlos thought of the families on the train, those too late to help. "Is there anything else I can do?"

"Next time we hear about their plans for a raid, you can help lead the fortunate ones back here."

"You just get everyone running down the street?"

"Too many would be hurt in the stampede. We move them through the city unseen—thanks to the sewers."

*

During that week, Carlos left his boardinghouse after supper each day, but only to practice his trumpet. He'd paid to have the bell unbent, another expense related to Paz. His rough treatment hadn't damaged the horn's tone. Rather, he could hear his neglect in the low-flying crescendos and phrases that failed to express the power—the emotion—the trumpet would readily grant if only he'd nourished his skills. He practiced for hours in the spot where he and Oscar had started together and he and Paz had desecrated. He hoped that rededicating himself to music would again sanctify that ground.

El Mariachi Santa Cruz met on their street corner to practice a few nights before the *Día de los Muertos* festivities. This time, Oscar had only compliments for Carlos. The bandleader made no mention of Paz or the previous six weeks of uninspired trumpeting. He promised to get Carlos work in his engine crew, which required strength the other musicians—all small, slight men—didn't possess.

Hector poked Carlos with an elbow and said, "Now that you're Oscar's favorite again, maybe you can relax on Saturday nights. You've been as jittery as a jumping bean. Was it the girl who kept you stirred up?"

"No," Carlos said. "Someone else." He told them the story of Donati and the Klansmen and added a description of Pedro's heroics while disabling the ranger on the evening Paz reappeared. "Every night we're out here, really every time I'm on the street, I half-expect Donati to find me." He turned his back to the road as a sedan rolled past.

Félix Herrera, one of the violinists, said, "What if we find him first?"

"What do you mean?"

"We can mislead him, tell him you went to Dallas or Austin. Hell, Santa Fe."

Oscar agreed. "We'll protect you. You've re-devoted yourself to the music. Let us show our commitment to you. We'll all need to memorize a story. First, tell us what this Donati looks like."

*

On Friday, November 1, Carlos went with Oscar to Our Lady of Guadalupe to commemorate the first Day of the Dead: All Saints' Day and the Vigil for the Little Angels. The church stood much taller and grander than Pedro's mission, and the pews were full. Those few men who attended kept their hats in their laps, while nearly all the women covered their heads in colorful scarves, some made of silk, many hand-painted. The woman in front of Carlos held an infant whose pomegranate-sized head rested against her shoulder. Moist, unblinking eyes regarded him from pudgy folds the color of brown sugar. As the priest on his distant altar conducted Mass in unintelligible Latin, Carlos prayed for the soul of the last baby boy his mother and father had tried to bring into their lives and the other angelitos they'd lost.

Rather than attend the service at Pedro's *Misión Católica*, Carlos had gone to Guadalupe so he could accompany Oscar to the rail yard where he now worked in the bandleader's crew. He'd wanted to explain to the warehouse foreman that he'd taken a job paying him two dollars more each day, but ultimately decided on his parents' approach—simply to disappear one day—since it involved no confrontation. If Mr. Glickman had gotten angry, Carlos was afraid he would've agreed to stay to appease him.

Oscar had a crew of ten, including Carlos, working in the three-story high roundhouse where they serviced and repaired locomotives. Deep bays over which the engines were parked allowed access to the undersides: massive axles, wheel bearings, and cranks. Oscar had taught Carlos how to lubricate the oiling points and described which parts saw the most wear and tended to fail. He described the valves and other features of the crew cabin and the tender coupled to the engine and told Carlos how the boiler, firebox, water tank, and other parts worked together to produce the steam that drove the train. Also, Oscar explained the differences between each engine they worked on, as individual as musical instruments: how to drive them and how to brake using steam and reverse-gears.

Carlos' sensitive, musical hearing was handy in distinguishing problems inside the boiler, as well as driving the train from the roundhouse. Since he wasn't able to see the closing distance between the engine and a car in need of coupling, he had to learn to park a train by ear.

His strength proved useful in disassembling and putting together massive iron and steel components. By each day's end, his legs would tremble as he braced his body under another ten-foot long shaft of solid, oily metal. Then his shoulders and biceps would take the weight, levering the linkages off their fittings and staggering across the greasy concrete floor to a worktable. His back tightened and he'd squat and set down the metal with care so it didn't injure the men waiting to hammer it true again. He was surprised his hamstrings and gluteus muscles ached most of all from the lifting and lowering, but Oscar had joked that he'd quickly feel like the engine being repaired: he'd have a tender behind.

*

On the evening of November 1, Carlos' legs cramped as he trotted past an oncoming trolley on his way home to supper. He felt a hitch in his stride he couldn't seem to stretch out, and he rolled his shoulders to keep his torso from feeling as tight. Whereas he had taken rest breaks in the warehouse by staying ahead of the other workers, in the roundhouse Oscar had assigned him a good many tasks to speed his learning. As Carlos walked, he quizzed himself on the component names and gauges in the locomotive. He mentally noted some questions for Oscar and then resumed reciting the passages of the mexicano rosario Pedro had taught him so far, including Angelus and the Litany of the Blessed Virgin Mary.

He glanced up from his rosary periodically as he walked the final blocks toward his new boardinghouse. With the shorter days, he usually arrived home just before twilight, soft yellow candle-glow behind some windows and pale kerosene lamplight in others. Even in the dimness of the street, he could see Paz standing on the sidewalk in front of the converted, now ramshackle, *casa grande*. She wore an outfit he'd bought: a short, fawn-colored skirt and an off-the-shoulders cream blouse with a plunging neckline. One of her butter-yellow shoes tapped the rapid rhythm of his heartbeat as he tried to remember the words he'd rehearsed. Somehow, Oscar and Pedro's lessons were much clearer in his mind.

She crossed her arms beneath her breasts, pushing the tops of them farther out of the blouse. Her weight shifted to one leg. He knew how tight the sinew in that length of thigh and calf would feel in his hands, against his lips; the other calf would be loose, the skin and muscle below her knee deceptively soft, yielding to his fingers and mouth. He knew how that stance would tip her pelvis, inviting some access— front and back—while denying other approaches. He knew all about her body, but her smile mystified him, as did the look in her eyes. She waited until he'd reached the street corner, two doors from his home, before speaking. "Your landlady wouldn't let me stand under the portico."

Carlos slid the rosary into his pocket. "She doesn't like women around her door."

"I don't like them around my man. Who is she?"

"Señora Gómez—the landlady?" He closed the distance between them, thinking about where he'd wanted to steer the conversation and how off-course he was already.

"The one you're laying now. You meet her at church?"

"I'm not courting anybody—"

She draped a demure hand over her cleavage. "Is that what we're doing, *señor*?"

"We're not doing anything now."

"I know. I was just thinking today how much I miss your—"

"Stop." Carlos glanced at a curtain being held aside near the doorway.

She snorted. "You're embarrassed by what we did, by what I taught you."

"I'm ashamed to have been with a thief, one of the scorpions in Schrimpf Alley. If you worked for a living instead of stole—"

Paz laughed and shook a finger at him. "You don't think that's work? Try it sometime."

"Then maybe it would be easier to make money at an honest job."

"And be penned in somewhere with a boss telling me what to do? No thank you. You told me about that Anglo down south who wouldn't rat on you, how he offered you work on a plantation. Work like that, or your warehouse job, would be no better than death to me. I don't know how you can stand having others—whites no less—decide your fate."

"How can you stand robbing others, especially our own?"

"You'd rather the Church get it so they can build even bigger monuments to a dead god? How about a money-order to Mexico so their poor uncles and cousins can afford to drink and whore? Someone will take that cash from them—why not me?"

"You and Jorge, you mean. You're still with him."

"We work together."

Carlos glanced around to make sure the man wasn't in sight. He muttered, "You sleep together, even now."

"I do what I want. Just because you shot your seed into me doesn't give you any more claim than he has. And he's been doing it a lot longer."

"Why? Why do you let him?"

"I owe him my life." Paz raked jittery fingers over her scalp and through long, straight hair. For the first time Carlos could remember, she looked vulnerable. Or at least she acted that way. She stared at her shoes and said, "When I was six, my mother abandoned me in the apartment we shared with other families. Some older boys—twelve, fourteen years old—lived there. When it was clear Mami wasn't coming home, they tried to touch me. Jorge heard my screams and ran into the building."

"He was only eight?"

"That's right, but he had a baseball bat he used to carry around. Jorge hit those boys so hard he broke his bat. I think he killed one of them."

"And you stayed with him and he protected you and one day he touched you."

"No, I started it. Jorge once had a little sister who died in a house-fire that killed his whole family—my scream reminded him of her. He looked after me, taught me how to steal until I was much better than him. He didn't ever want me for a lover, but when I was fifteen, I took him one night after I got him drunk." She finally looked at Carlos again. "With the window finally broken, he stopped guarding the house. I could have him whenever I wanted. He's been with as many other women as I've had men since then, but you always have a special place inside for the first one. Who was your first, Carlos?"

It was his turn to look away. The evening star glimmered above, lonely in an indigo sky. He recited what he'd meant to say at the start: "I want you to stay away from me."

"I've marked you with my body. Stained you all over. Whoever you take up with, you'll think of me. When you thrust into a nice, respectable girl, you'll compare her jagged dryness with my embrace. When she just lies there whimpering, you'll remember how I rode you and cried out your name. When you want to do the things you crave— thanks to me—she'll look at you with disgust." Paz creased her face into a sneer of revulsion. "She'll call you *un pervertido* and make you feel dirty. And you'll remember that you have been everywhere inside me." She dragged her fingers from her lips down between her breasts. "And I happily smeared you all over my skin."

He willed himself not to picture them together, the wild abandon she'd shown and encouraged in him. Thinking instead of the Ten of Cups, he couldn't picture Paz beside him under that rainbow, the ultimate prize of love. He said, "I can't forget you, but I can't be with you again. You're not someone I'd ever want to marry and have kids with."

"But what if I'm carrying your baby?"

She left him standing there beneath the darkening sky.

CHAPTER 15

O n the morning of November 2, All Souls' Day, Carlos
went to *Misión Católica* instead of joining Oscar at
Our Lady of Guadalupe. He'd spent a sleepless night
despairing over Paz's news. He finally understood how Papá
could've objected to a baby he hadn't wanted. Worse than the
unwanted baby, though, Carlos hated the idea of having to
marry Paz.

A few members of the congregation had arrived early and
sat near the altar, but the mission was largely vacant. Carlos
sat in a pew near the sacristy and caught the eye of Father
Perez, the bespectacled priest who'd helped Pedro carry
Donati away. The priest finished donning his pure white
vestment, pulling the gown flush against his black cassock,
and called to Pedro.

"Father Rodríguez," Carlos said when Pedro walked into
the nave, his cassock not yet covered. "I need your guidance."

"The rosary hasn't helped?"

Carlos withdrew it from his pocket, his thumb and index
finger automatically touching the large "Our Father" bead on
which he'd stopped. "It's kept me from pulling the buttons off
my clothes. Now I understand the worry-bead jokes."

Pedro sat beside him, hands hidden in his pockets. He
looked at the altar. "This has to do with the woman?"

"She waited for me outside my rooming house. Paz says she's pregnant."

The priest hung his head for a moment before staring at Carlos. "Paz…she's bringing you anything but peace I'd say, looking at your tired face."

Carlos rubbed his burning, irritated eyes with his palms. "I know what I need to do, but I don't want to do it."

"You were trying to end your dealings with her. Now we're talking about a new beginning together."

"You'll perform the ceremony?"

"Certainly. So this is the Tower you'd told me about. The crisis that brings change."

The edges of the rosary cross pressed into Carlos' hand as he squeezed. "No change I want."

"But your mother—and father—raised you right: *la cortesía mexicana.*"

"How soon could you marry us?"

"Talk to your lady—we'll do it after Mass one day. Would you like a distraction tonight after the *fiesta?*" Carlos nodded, and Pedro continued, "We heard this morning that there'll be another roundup, this time in the Magnolia Park *barrio* near the Ship Channel."

"I've wandered around there, back when I was first looking for Paz." He swallowed hard. "I know it well."

"*La migra* wants to net a hundred at least. Father Perez will meet you at *Teatro Juárez* at midnight—without his vestments—and he'll lead you from there. Wear dark clothes." He patted Carlos' shoulder and said, "About Paz: this is God's will."

"Father, maybe it's just a taste of hell."

*

Oscar gathered the band in his rented room before sunset to prepare for the festival. He reminded the musicians of the play-list as they dressed in their peasant outfits, looping the drawstring belts into tight bows, white camisas dropping like ghosts over upraised arms and bare brown torsos. Carlos wore a tight black shirt and dark slacks under his costume.

The musicians helped each other apply ghoulish makeup, and their laughter was infectious as they swabbed white and black paint over each other's faces. Carlos flinched, squeezing his eyelids tight, before Oscar dabbed the brush against them and swirled black paint around the sockets. "Wait a minute for it to dry," he said, and outlined Carlos' nose and mouth in black as well. The sharp odor of the paint overwhelmed the stink of mildew from the walls of Oscar's room.

The thick white undercoat had already dried smooth over Carlos' face. He blinked rapidly, his lids feeling thick as they compressed above his eyeballs. Turning his face about, he examined the makeup in a hand mirror Hector's wife had loaned to them. "Well, I sure look like I'm dead."

"Just don't play that way, birthday boy," Hector said. "Twenty-one and making up for lost time!" He dropped a wide *sombrero* atop Carlos' head and another on his own. "Now, Oscar, remember to sing like you have some meat on your ribs."

Oscar finished unbuttoning his work shirt, chuckling. He painted thick bones over his broad cinnamon chest and the outside of his arms. The bandleader stood still, a massive skeleton with arms outstretched, waiting to dry. Then, he tapped the straw fedora on his head and led his band out of the boardinghouse and over to their street corner.

The decorations looked much the same as the year before: the paper cutouts of skeletons linked hand-in-hand fluttered from lampposts and fabric ghouls hung in shop windows. However, the crowds painted in black and white were smaller and fewer vendors called out their specialties—skull-shaped marzipan candies, *pan de muerto, atole,* and dark, yeasty *anima*s—from the sidewalks where pots of marigolds and cockscomb were scattered in less abundance. The roundups by *la migra* were taking their toll.

Men lit torches in the twilight, the flames rippling with the sound of sails catching the wind. They pushed their fire-tipped poles into the prepared trash barrels and set them ablaze as the crowds cheered, their skull-faces grinning. Carlos raised his trumpet and confirmed the *embouchure*. As his tongue tapped the interior of the cone, he recalled exploring Paz's body. He took a deep breath to steady himself. The last barrel was lit. Loose papers became fireballs as they twirled from the barrel in the updraft and fell to the street, charred. The bands began to play, and the *fiesta* commenced.

He kept his eyes focused on the painted revelers stamping a *zapateado* in front of the band and singing along with Oscar. Children dashed among them dragging their cloth skeletons. Carlos watched for Paz, but also for Donati. Despite his disguise, he still felt exposed at the front of the band; he had no one in the audience to protect him that night.

At the crowd's edge, he recognized Jorge Flores. The rail-thin man hardly needed the skeletal makeup. Stark white and black paint merely accentuated the tautness of his flesh between bony forehead and pointed chin. Jorge's black lips pulled back in a pantomime of a smile, and he waved.

Hector, on Carlos' right, misplayed a rare chord on his *vihuela*. Carlos turned his head that way, still trumpeting. Paz stood three feet from him in her multicolored dress from the year before. Her face gleamed with white paint; black highlights to her eyes, nose, and mouth completed the mask. She looked at him without expression and pointed as she'd done in September, her index finger descending. Except this time she stuck her hand in the bell of his trumpet, gagging the sound, as if she'd shoved her finger down his throat.

Carlos stepped back—jostling Oscar who'd just finished the refrain—and came in late on the next bar. Facing forward again, he slurred two measures to catch up. He could no longer see Jorge on the street. Some dancers shouted at Paz, calling for her to leave the musicians alone. Others yelled names at her: *fulana, mujerzuela*. While infuriated at her, fingers slamming the valves and breath spitting from his mouth, Carlos felt equally upset at those who called his future wife a tramp.

She moved slowly into his view—unstoppable, undeniable—arms held high, fingers close together and arched like snake heads. Sensuous twists of her body and the shaking of her breasts against the tight dress made the bands of orange, purple, green, and gold look alive as Paz undulated and stomped. Her face rocked back and rolled from one shoulder to the other. The copper curve of her throat caught the firelight and she swallowed, her muscles and tendons rippling.

He closed his eyes a moment to put himself back into the music, get that sensation of flight again, but his anger and a nagging lust weighed him down like an anchor. He glanced at Oscar, but the bandleader faced the crowd of dancing couples who stamped close together, noses nearly touching. The hulking skeleton serenaded them about love that brings death and the deadliness of life without love.

When the song ended, Paz stepped forward, but Oscar blocked her, nearly treading on Carlos' sandals to get to him first. Oscar asked him, "Can you focus, please?"

"Of course—I'm sorry."

"It's okay, but you're going to have to do something before she makes you crazy."

Paz appeared again at Carlos' side as he told Oscar, "I plan to do something—I'm going to marry her." Her cheeks hollowed as her mouth opened soundlessly. He said to Paz, "For the baby."

Her voice was as quiet as a final breath. "There is no baby, you fool."

Oscar grasped her elbow. "You need to stay away from the band, *señorita*. You're interrupting us." As the crowd called for the next song and other bands played on farther down the street, Oscar escorted Paz to a sidewalk.

Carlos rubbed the sweat from his upper lip. Swaths of black and white paint smeared across his hand. Paz stared at him; she folded her legs and sat on the curb, hugging her sides. His anger at her lie cancelled his earlier fury as he realized he was free.

Oscar clapped his shoulder. "Remember how you used to dream of escaping with the hawks? Time to take wing, Carlos." He raised his voice, calling for the next song, "*La noche y tú.*"

As dance partners joined hands, they spread into a wide arc around the band. Soon, they hid Paz from Carlos' view amid swirling skirts and jaunty legs. He closed his eyes again and heard his tone slowly ascend.

*

The band paused between sets and accepted refreshments offered by a social club hostess. Carlos guzzled the lukewarm water. Paz approached as he lowered his cup. She'd washed off the skull makeup, soaking the bodice of her dress, the colored bands now dark over her breasts. Smudges of white streaked her jaw and black paint traced the age-lines beside her mouth and eyes. She said, "Was that drink as good as what I gave you?"

"No, but it'll do. Why did you lie to me?"

"Did you really think, with my experience, I would accidentally get pregnant? I just wanted to say something as cruel as what you said. But you'd lied first—you really would marry me."

"Only because it would've been the right thing to do. What I said wasn't a lie at the time. If there's no baby, then we're through. We're not meant for each other." When he saw her about to argue some more, he had a sudden inspiration. "If someone besides me tells you this, will you leave me alone?"

"Who?"

"A woman named María. She's a tiny woman, a dwarf, who tells fortunes."

"I've heard of her. If this charlatan tells you to stay with me, you will?"

He waved to Oscar, who'd called an end to the break. "Do you really mean marriage?"

Paz snorted. "I mean what we were doing before you left me for the Church. Carlos, you're going to taste me all over tonight." She raked her red-painted nails across his arm and stepped back into the crowd.

After *El Mariachi Santa Cruz* played a final encore, Carlos asked Oscar what time it was. Two hours remained before he had to meet Father Perez on the southeast side of town. He accepted the band's compliments and the slaps against his back and shoulders from the crowd as he reached Paz. "I only have a short while, so let's go."

She entwined her fingers with his. "I plan to win our bet, so we'll need longer than 'a short while.'"

He told her to hurry and weaved through the loud, milling audience, pulling her along. Shouting over his shoulder, he asked, "What happened to Jorge? Lots of easy marks on the street tonight." Including me, he almost added. He sent up a prayer that his fate and Paz's wouldn't be linked like their fingers.

"I haven't seen him." She squeezed his hand and said, "As a special treat, I'll take you to my place when you lose."

He led her a few blocks north of the business district to the brightly painted row house. Without knocking, Paz pushed open the blood-red door and stepped inside the candlelit room. He stayed in the doorway. As before, he smelled roasting pecans and cinnamon.

Paz called, "Hey, come out here. Our fortunes need telling."

María emerged from the back room and sat again at the round table, candles already pushed aside. She wore the same satin robe of golden eyes rimmed in heavy-lidded scarlet. A deck of cards shuffled like the rustle of leaves through her deformed fingers. "*Hola,* Carlos. And Paz Flores?"

Sweat chilled Carlos' ribs. "Paz—"

"You're wrong," she said. "Jorge and I never married."

"The drunk you both stood before was a real preacher."

"That was just for fun—we were kids. Tell me my real name. I heard if you couldn't, then the fortunetelling was free."

"Paz Zaragoza, then." She smiled, revealing the four gold canines. "Did you really think I would get the preacher right, but miss your family name? I cannot afford such charity. Please sit and we will get started—Carlos has an appointment."

Paz took the seat across from María, and he sat on the fortuneteller's left again. He put a folded dollar bill beside María's scrawny, hair-dappled arm and said, "I'm trying to avoid that Tower you told me about, but Paz—"

"I want us to stay as lovers."

"Ah, The Lovers." María's extra-jointed thumb nudged against the stack of cards, pushing the top third off-center. With the yellowed fingernails, she pulled a card from the deck and flipped it over. A man and woman, explicitly nude, stood in a garden, a different kind of tree behind each of them. An angel on broad wings hovered overhead, his arms outstretched to encompass the pair. A mountain peak loomed in the distance between the man and woman, and a stream separated them in the garden.

Paz tapped Carlos' hand. "Look at you staring. It's like you've never seen a naked woman before."

He blushed. "She looks like the one on a card I'd picked, the *doncella* under the Star."

"If that's a maiden then she isn't me. And that miniscule man sure can't be you."

María said, "Notice that the man stares at the woman, just as you said, but she is looking at the angel above. The Lovers are not in harmony. To achieve that, they must climb the mountain together. Only then can the branches of the Tree of Life behind the man and the Tree of Knowledge behind the woman be united. Paz, do you wish to see whether you and Carlos will make that journey together?"

"Could we just stay in the garden and make a bed on the ground?" Paz focused on the card's location as María slid the Lovers back into the deck.

"A stream divides you there. You can join him only atop the mountain. To be true Lovers, your commitment must be stronger than lust." She slid the deck toward Paz, instructed her to ask her question, and told her how to prepare the cards for selection.

"Will we—me and Carlos—still be lovers?" Paz scraped a fingernail down the stack of cards, making a sound like stitches tearing. She cut the deck into three piles and carefully stacked them again, leaving one card jutting out. She fanned the oversized cards across the table before her and nudged her chosen card slightly above the others.

María said, "Please select the six cards that call to you. The first pick is your self, who you are at this time." She left her chair and stood beside Paz, her dark, hairy face on level with Paz's frown of concentration. María placed Paz's first card on the table above the long row of choices. "The second card will give you perspective on your question of love—how you have handled its challenges to this point and how you will likely do so in the future."

Paz snatched up the card on which she'd remained focused, and María put it to the lower right of the first card. Paz picked three more cards quickly. Her bare foot rubbed down Carlos' calf, starting from the back of his knee. She winked at him. María called the final card a prophecy about her question, and Paz said, "Wait. I want the Lovers there—what I picked as my second card."

"No, the Lovers is still in the row in front of you. Pick the one that feels right."

"I kept my eye on that card. You're a liar and a fraud." Paz's spittle flecked the hair on María's cheek. "I've hustled card games since I was ten."

"Then you know I did not cheat—you would have seen that. Pick your last card."

Paz pushed up the cards on either side of the one she'd pre-selected. She said to Carlos, "You choose. Neither one feels right to me."

"They don't call to me either." Carlos reluctantly tapped the edge of a card farther down the row. "That one is strong."

Paz nodded and handed that card to María, who put it into the upper right position. "The first," she reminded, "is the self." She turned over the center card and said, "The Moon." A blue moon, its sleeping face in profile, sent rays down on a dog and a wolf that howled back at it. In the foreground, a blue crayfish crawled out of a pool. "Mistress of the night, when deception and danger reign. Emotions are volatile and uncertain. The crayfish represents fears that keep surfacing, memories of unpleasant times."

Paz glanced from the picture to Carlos. "Stop looking at me like that," she said. Her index finger stabbed at the face of the Moon. "What's good about this card? Tell me something nice."

"She rules the realm of intuition and dreams. Fantasy. In your sleep you find the answers to your problems. The second card says how you have managed the challenges of this love affair and will continue to. Let us see what you felt so strongly about." She flipped the second card.

"*¡Qué diablos!*" Paz touched the back of her head.

The pictured man lay facedown on a desolate marshland. Ten swords pierced his head and his back. Beyond a lake, the horizon barely lightened with the dawn. "The Ten of Swords means the end of a relationship, perhaps killed before it really began. But there's the promise of—"

Paz pushed out of her chair, overturning it. Candlelight reflected off the tears in her eyes. She loomed over María, who looked back without expression. "Shut up! Stop it! This is a trick." Paz grabbed the card Carlos had chosen, looked at it, and sailed it into the nest of candles.

As the oversized card rested atop the burning wicks, flames pushed through the paper, augmenting the illustrated fires burning in the Tower. Carlos snatched the card away and dropped it on the table. He slapped his hand down and the Tower disappeared under his palm as the candles jumped and rocked. The fire singed him before he killed it. As he watched, blisters formed on his paint-streaked hand. The white and black smears blossomed with welts.

Paz ran outside and slammed the door behind her, causing a thunderclap and a gust of air that blew out three of the candles. Carlos looked from the Moon and the slaughtered man under the ten swords to his injured right hand. The burns throbbed and his fingers stung from the slap against the hardwood. With his left hand, he turned over the cards Paz had pushed up, but about which neither of them had felt anything. One was the Lovers, the other the Ten of Cups. He dropped them over the charred Tower and said, "Am I past it now?"

María gathered the cards, including Paz's three choices that had remained facedown. "The Tower answered your question about the next few years—change will rule your life during that time."

His swollen palm ached; a new blister had formed on his middle fingertip. He lifted up his trumpet and rested his fingers on the valves. It would be painful to play for a while. "Please tell me again. Do you see violent change—ruin?"

"If everyone behaves as they always have, you might face that."

He pulled out from the pile one of Paz's other picks. "This was her enemy." He turned it over and revealed the King of Swords, whose dark eyes stared out at him.

"No, Carlos. That was in the upper left position—he is Paz's ally."

*

Carlos closed María's door. For the first time he felt scared of Paz, who paced on the nearby street corner. He still had to walk five miles to reach Magnolia Park and meet Father Perez. In addition, he had to wash off the white face-paint and stow his peasant garb. There was no time for another confrontation.

Her voice sounded raw. "Come home with me, Carlos."

"No, this can't work. If you didn't already believe that, you wouldn't have gotten so upset. It's over, Paz—*adiós*." He headed east on the deserted sidewalk. His way was dimly lit by the past-full moon glowing through a haze of clouds.

Her voice echoed off the row house frontages. "I can be your *doncella*."

"That's just the moon talking, spinning another fantasy."

Her heels jabbed the sidewalk as she ran, the thud and slap of each step drawing closer. Paz grabbed his arm, nearly causing him to drop his trumpet. "Don't you walk away from me. Those pictures—"

He shoved her, but then reached out as she fell into the street. She landed on her hip and a forearm. Her face showed nothing at first as she looked at him. An instant after he called an apology and held out his hands, Paz began to sob and massage her wrist. A door opened across the street and a man called out, asking what was happening.

Carlos straightened as she wailed louder. "Stop it, Paz. You're not hurt. I wonder if you feel anything." He resumed walking.

"Come home with me," she called, her voice under control again.

What was so important about going to Paz's home? He thought of the other thief. He hadn't seen Jorge since the *fiesta* started when the man had grinned and waved. Carlos' steps stuttered as he decided between checking the savings he kept hidden in his room and reaching the priest on time. He reminded himself to follow through on his commitment, but, as Paz shouted his name, he dashed north through a trash-strewn alley. Staggering over discarded rubbish, he ran toward the boardinghouse.

After sprinting six blocks, the trumpet flashing in his hand as his arms pumped, he leaped up the stairs. The front door opened. Carlos stopped his momentum under the portico, his burned palm slapping the crumbling brick façade beside the doorframe.

The landlady stood in her tattered housecoat, a moth-eaten *rebozo* covering her shoulders. "Sr. Moreno, I was just about to go up to your room and complain about the noise."

Sweat pricked at his scalp. Carlos preceded Señora Gómez inside. She slammed the door and followed him up the sagging stairs, her candle providing scant light. He stormed down the dark halls, recalling how he'd defeated Jorge before. His palm was gritty with brick dust and slick from the pus of torn blisters. He wiped his hand on his pants, leaving wet stains, and hefted the horn like a club. At the end of the hallway, wood slid and banged against other boards from behind his closed door.

Sra. Gómez said, "Sr. Moreno, you know my rule against having a guest in your room."

"This is no guest. Better stay back, you might not be safe." Carlos softened his stride as he approached. He pulled the door open—his bed blocked the entrance. The mattress was gutted, cotton stuffing tossed everywhere. Jorge stood at the far corner of the room, surrounded by scattered planks studded with bent nails and a floor honeycombed with dark holes. Skull-paint still concealed his face. Beside him sat a flickering candle and a dirty drawstring sack filled with Carlos' savings.

Carlos thumped his trumpet against the mattress with the sound of a body-blow and raised his weapon again. "Leave the money and I'll let you go."

"Your arm is big, my friend." Jorge lifted a three-foot board with nails poking through like snaggleteeth. "But this time mine's longer."

Sra. Gómez shouted for help as Carlos climbed over the bed and raced forward. Jorge thrust the board toward his ankles, making him swerve and misstep. His left leg fell into a hole and cracked through the ceiling below. He toppled as he swung the trumpet. The thief swatted his arm with the plank, yanked the horn away, and dropped it on his bag.

"That's everything I have," Carlos shouted as he struggled to pull himself up. The boarders who lived in the room below thumped his leg with a broom and cursed him.

"Then that's all I'll take." Jorge gripped the board with both hands and slammed it edge-on against Carlos' face, knocking him backwards. The thief grabbed his sack and the trumpet and vaulted the bed. His footsteps echoed in the dank hallways, as the landlady screamed louder.

Carlos groped at the bloody mess of his face. Nails had just missed ripping his skin, but his nose and chin were wet and numb. His lips felt like they'd been torn in half. Blood ran down his throat from biting his tongue with teeth that wobbled in his ringing head.

*

Several men pressed rags to Carlos' wounds, nearly suffocating him, while another boarder fetched a doctor from the Mexican Clinic. His neighbors pulled him onto the bed they'd hastily re-stuffed and placed it in the corner, trapping him on two sides. Carlos focused on the pain. Hurt was the only thing he had left.

The *tejano* doctor used alcohol to scrub paint from the wounds, setting them on fire. As he stitched and swaddled Carlos' face, the tenants reassembled the floor, a jigsaw puzzle that included the bloody plank they tried to wipe clean. The doctor reset his nose with cold, pinching fingers. The bone and tissue crackled as he reshaped Carlos' profile.

After the doctor had gone, Sra. Gómez finished the job of washing the remaining paint from his face. The landlady showed a gentle touch as her cloth stroked the skin around his closed eyes, pressing lightly against his eyelids. The alcohol fumes raised fresh tears. Holding back his hair, she scrubbed his brow, easing her pressure when she touched the old indentation left by the Klansman's boot.

As she made a final pass over his upper face, this time with a cloth dampened with hot water, Carlos had the sensation of being prepared for a vigil prior to his funeral, as the neighbors in La Marque had done with Mamá. Sra. Gómez stripped away the false mask of death so the real one could be seen.

With a start, he remembered where he was supposed to be: Father Perez was waiting, a hundred or more desperate people needed him. He tried to rise. His head pounded and the ringing in his ears increased an octave. She pushed him back down, murmuring about rest. He considered eternal rest, an escape from pain and guilt. The condolences from mourners would be undeserved. Father Perez and Pedro needed his apologies for failing them.

The landlady departed, closing his door. In the moonlight, the walls and floor still seemed to pitch and roll as he clutched the edges of the ruined cot, lumps of batting like fists under his back. He closed his eyes, wishing for the blackness that had seemed so easy to slip into while the doctor had worked on his face. Carlos tasted the inside of his raw, salty mouth, wincing as he grazed the deep cuts through his lips. They parted just enough for him to breathe. Stitches felt like coarse scars. Too-tight bandages, the swelling, and multiple bruises all called for his attention.

His burned right hand had been treated and wrapped. He still felt the brass curves being pulled from his grip by the thief. Jorge could've been through in a few minutes. The money had been stacked under just a couple of boards. If the man wasn't so greedy or Carlos had followed his instincts and kept his appointment, he might be sleeping now, broke but uninjured, his wealth gone but not his music.

Paz was right, he thought, everything tonight was a trick. He wondered if Jorge would give her a share of the $127, payment for keeping him away from home. Both of them may as well have been the ranger's allies in his ruin. His fists clenched and blood pulsed in his face, aggravating the wounds.

Thoughts of the Star's maiden failed to calm him. He tried to envision the Ten of Cups and the promise of a happy family, but couldn't summon a trace of hope. Carlos said a bedtime prayer, much different from the one he'd learned from Mamá: he prayed for Donati to find him.

CHAPTER 16

❦

Jack leaned across the leather seat of his Cadillac Phaeton
Murphy, midnight blue with a black cloth top and white-
wall tires, fenders, and running boards nearly as wide as
his foot was long, headlights the span of his hand, and a silver
hood ornament of a woman with swept-back, winged arms.
A beauty of a car bought with "gifts" from his father. Just in
time since Hanson's wealth had been wiped out in the stock
market crash—now what good was the old man? Jack grasped
a smooth enamel knob and cranked down the passenger
window; his breath and cigarette smoke had fogged the interi-
or glass, obscuring his view of the darkened street.

Navigation Boulevard was the main thoroughfare for
tejanos in Magnolia Park, now the largest Mexican enclave.
The crowds had gone, but one man in black clothing loitered
in front of the theatre, staying in the shadows. Banners of
linked skeletons, *papel picado,* swayed from the marquee
above his head and yellow, orange, and purple flowers littered
the sidewalks like toys abandoned by a fleeing child.

Since September, a half-dozen of Lebrun's raids had
yielded no, or few, deportees. Entire tent cities had been
vacated before the Immigration trucks arrived. Whole
tenements had been swept clean, as if the agent's team had
already rounded up everyone and then forgot they'd done so.
Lebrun had blamed Jack and every other lawman in Houston

for not being able to stop leaks from their departments and had sent damning reports to the Labor Department as well as officials in Justice.

Jack had parked at a cross-street a block from the slums, planning to prevent another embarrassment. His jug of tepid coffee sat on the floorboards beside the lidded bucket he'd use as his toilet. His whore Linda's place was only a quarter-mile away. He glanced into the spacious backseat but then dismissed a wistful thought.

His knee had returned to its former low-grade throb. A day after the *Diez y Seis* street fair, the deep bruise on his kneecap had told him his leg hadn't just collapsed as had happened once before. Jack had visited the Guadalupe Church in town and the Immaculate Heart of Mary in the Magnolia *barrio* several times, but none of the priests had even remotely resembled the bearded one. Not surprisingly, no one fingered a priest matching that description. He wondered if the bespectacled *tejano* in front of *Teatro Juárez* could be the other one who'd carried him to the clinic.

Some anarchists, masquerading as clergy when it suited them, were operating a kind of Underground Railroad. What Jack couldn't figure out was why they took him to a doctor instead of killing him and dumping his body. He drew his revolver and placed it on the seat.

The loitering man returned a watch to his pocket, glancing up the street again. A truck turned a corner and roared past Jack's position, making enough noise for him to switch on the engine without being obvious. The truck's headlights glinted off the man's glasses. He seemed to look directly at Jack. Then he ran in front of the truck.

Brakes squealing, the driver swerved. His truck careened across the median and slammed into the storefront of a dress shop. Glass shattered and bricks tumbled onto the hood. Tumbling from the cab, the Anglo driver was a bloody mess. The fleeing man's body was not on the street—he was probably mashed across the truck's grill.

Jack parked at the curb in front of the shop. He banged the walnut steering wheel, cursing as a cool breeze blew across him. The man must've noticed the car window had been lowered, no longer reflecting the streetlights, and knew he was being watched.

The driver moaned on the sidewalk, and Jack gave him a handkerchief to mop the blood from his forehead. He switched off the truck engine before kicking some glass aside and easing past the warm hood. Standing in the display case, Jack thought he spotted the black-clad *tejano* in the carnage of mannequins, but it was only *Día de los Muertos* fashions.

More bricks collapsed from the front wall, so he hopped into the store, landing, as always, on his good leg. He kicked at the wooden bodies as the proprietor and his wife ran down from their home above, robes and dressing gowns flapping. They shouted at Jack in rapid Spanish; speaking much more reasonably, he answered in their native tongue.

Jack left them mourning over the wreckage. He limped across the street, estimating how far an average-size man could be knocked by a fast-moving truck. Forty feet? Eighty? He started out in a wide arc and drew closer to the likely spot of impact as people left their apartments above the shops to gawk. *Tejanos* surrounded the truck and moved in and out of the ruined store, some in their bedclothes and others fully dressed, men pulling suspenders over shoulders with their thumbs and women straightening their skirts as they surveyed their neighbor's misfortune. One fellow kneeled beside the truck driver and offered him a smoke, the cigarette poking out of his pack like a bony fingertip.

Either the fleeing man was knocked onto a rooftop, or he didn't get hit at all. Jack walked to the theatre and glanced at the street. As with his rolled-down window, a black gap loomed where there should've been something solid. The manhole cover was gone.

*

When Carlos tottered out of the boardinghouse dressed in his Sunday suit, a cool wind pulled at his bandages. Sra. Gómez had fixed his tie, protesting all the while that the doctor said he should stay in bed. But the doctor hadn't failed his friends and a hundred or more other people in need. Carlos had to make his apologies and seek forgiveness.

His head still throbbed in a dozen places and the ear-ringing persisted. The muscles in his neck had seized up, forcing him to turn entirely in order to see left or right. Pain raced through his whole body. Walking jarred everything, so he stepped gingerly on the balls of his feet, avoiding some men still passed out on the sidewalk, reminding him of how Paz had left him the year before.

The worst pain remained in his face. That he could barely speak well enough for his apologies to be understood was just another thing to be overcome, penance for selfishness.

Guadalupe Church services had ended, but a number of parishioners stood in small groups and talked, mostly older women and mothers who kept their children close by as they chatted. Oscar stood at the vestibule entrance talking with the priest. His *novia* Marguerite and her mother had joined a circle of other women. Carlos looked away from their stares and hobbled up the church steps to greet his friend.

"What happened to you?" Oscar touched his own mouth.

"Jorge Flores happened to me."

Oscar and the priest held his elbows and led him into the nave, seating him in the last row of pews. Carlos recounted Saturday night's events with short sentences. His words sounded thick as his swollen, bisected lips collided prematurely and refused to separate entirely. He concluded with, "He took your trumpet, too. It's my fault."

"Don't worry. We'll get you another horn."

"Can't play again. Mouth ruined." He felt the stitches in his lips pull and tear the skin. Blood began to seep from the wounds again, salty on his tongue.

"You'll heal. Playing is as natural to you as flying is to your hawks. You'll always have a home with *El Mariachi Santa Cruz.*"

Carlos closed his eyes and touched Oscar's jacket sleeve with his bandaged hand. "Thank you, my friend." Though it was Jorge's favorite phrase, Carlos refused to let the thief take his words, too. "I need to see Pedro—Father Rodríguez." He grasped the back of the pew in front of him to stand, but Oscar put his arm across Carlos' chest.

"I'll get us a taxi."

"Save your money. I can walk."

"Nonsense." Oscar patted his pocket. "This one's a gift from the band."

In the back of the taxi—Carlos' first-ever ride in a car—Oscar pushed folded dollar bills against his unharmed hand. "You'd forgotten your tips from last night. How much money do you have?"

"Six dollars plus this." He pushed the cash into his pocket without counting it. The taxi bounced on its springs, stabbing his neck and back. Neighborhoods scrolled past the windows and, despite the pain, he twisted from his waist so he wouldn't miss the views. A trio of sparrows flew alongside the taxi, flapping and then dipping and rising on the air streams with wings folded. The taxi bobbed with them—Carlos didn't need to be a hawk to fly.

Oscar said, "Don't worry about your job with the railroad. Until you're able to lift again, I'll put you on the lighter duties, driving the trains around the yard. You'll love it. Do you want to room with me to save money?"

The sparrows scattered as a line of trucks passed in the opposite direction. One of the birds might not have gotten clear; he couldn't turn around far enough to check. "Need to be on my own." He feared Jorge ransacking Oscar's place. Moreover, if God answered his prayer, he wanted to be alone when Donati found him.

*

As Carlos repeated his story, Pedro insisted there was no reason to apologize. Father Perez joined them and related his escape into the sewers—his instincts had warned him about a lawman nearby.

Carlos said, "Fighting Jorge or running from police: my choices last night."

Oscar leaned over the back of a pew to face him. "Maybe your night could've ended worse. If you were there on time, you both would've fallen into a trap."

"A hundred taken in?"

Pedro said, "Probably. Father Soto went there right after Mass to see. They're onto us now—our work will only get harder." A gentle smile crinkled the skin around his eyes. "Of course, for you, things will be easier. You've survived the worst of it."

*

Carlos had the last of his stitches removed the day before the railroad laid him off, in January 1930. He was furloughed along with another fifty workers with low seniority, victims of the worsening economy. Oscar fought for him but lost; Carlos suspected his friend nearly lost his own job in the process.

Oscar again offered to share his room, but he refused. He went back to the warehouse, but the foreman told him they'd cut back as well. None of his former Sunday jobs were available either.

He tried to find work in *barrio* shops, but many were closing as their customers lost jobs. With each request he made, the shopkeeper's horrified stare followed by a rapid look away reminded him of the damage Jorge had done. Deep scars cleaved his lips and chin. The tip of his nose was scarred as well and the cartilage in its bridge had reset like the craggy

Sierra Madre. With thumb and forefinger, he could squeeze the ridges and make them crackle.

Throughout the neighborhoods he saw others looking for work, going door to door. Members of clubs and *mutualistas* stood on street corners calling for money, clothes, and food donations, with nearly empty baskets at their feet. Needy families crowded sidewalks in front of churches and soup-kitchens. Charity was still available to Carlos, but many were swallowing their pride: he knew those options would disappear soon enough.

The factories, breweries, and mills were not hiring either. He searched for weeks, skipping meals. Supper was included in the rent he paid; he'd saved enough to live there another month if he only ate that one time each day. No longer did he stay in crowds and remain wary of his surroundings—if Donati still hunted him, he was in the open.

He only hid himself when helping Pedro and the other *Misión Católica* priests. Janitors and other workers who traveled through City Hall and police precincts still relayed occasional tips about upcoming raids. Carlos sometimes acted as a lookout to spot the police who inevitably lurked within a car parked near the targeted slum. Fogged windows or a thin line of cigarette smoke would tell on them, or he'd see an officer with a full bladder scramble into an alley. He learned the sewers well enough—traveling the city underground and, occasionally, underwater—so he could lead families to the Mission. Terrorized parents clutched their half-asleep children as Carlos would hold his kerosene lantern high, his knuckles scraping the low ceilings, and yell instructions and warnings over the constant, stinking rush of water and sewage.

After a few hours of sleep, he'd awake to cold air and the putrid smell and dripping of the dungarees he'd draped over the sill of his room's open window, and return to his search for work. He walked many of the same streets looking for a job as he had searching for Paz—he'd seen neither she nor

Jorge since that second night in November. Pedro had spoken to him about forgiveness, but his muscles still tightened at the memory of Jorge's board slamming across his face; his jaws still clenched at the thought that he'd slept with that man's wife. He felt far dirtier recalling his lust for Paz than he ever did while wading in the sewers. Excrement could be washed away, but memories abided.

Carlos dreaded looking for work in the Anglo wards west of downtown, but he thought it was his last chance. He crossed the Buffalo Bayou and tried the Sixth Ward, where some *tejano* landmarks existed—a row of shops and the Mexican Presbyterian Church—among the Anglo buildings and rail yards that weren't hiring. He entered what appeared to be a shoe factory. Before he could ask about a job, a white man shouted at him to leave and seized his arm, though Carlos stood nearly a foot taller. Spit flecked the man's lips as he yelled, "Didn't you see the sign?" The man pulled him back onto the sidewalk and pointed to a large placard near the door. "'No Mexicans, Negroes, or dogs,'" he recited. "I don't care if you're just one or all three. Stay the hell out of my place or I'll call the cops!" He shoved Carlos' arm away and slammed the door behind him.

Many other businessmen in the Anglo wards also made the dividing line very clear. He did find a couple of openings, but they paid Mexicans just five cents an hour. He overheard a restaurant manager tell a white applicant the evening dishwasher job paid twenty cents; Carlos was hired for the nickel rate. He also got a day job sweeping streets in the Sixth Ward. Combined, he'd earn eighty cents working sixteen hours each day and have less than two dollars left after paying the rent at week's end. Although he'd miss supper at the boardinghouse, he was allowed to scrape anything left by the restaurant diners into a bowl he had to bring with him, using his own fork to eat.

Oscar had told him that, according to the newspapers, conditions were worse in other parts of the country—

Houstonians weren't suffering by comparison. Of course, those probably were English language newspapers talking about Anglos. If not for helping Pedro and the other priests resist *la migra*, Carlos thought he'd try another city or even return to Casson where Sr. Webster long ago had invited him and Pedro to work on the nearby plantation.

He ate supper and walked to *El Mariachi Santa Cruz's* corner to hear them practice for the upcoming *Día de los Santos Reyes fiesta*, celebrating the visit of the Three Kings from the Orient. Oscar had hired a new trumpet player from Beaumont named Alfredo Paredes. Carlos had tried hard not to criticize the man's technique; he'd even befriended the short, thick-set musician and offered helpful advice. But the pain of not being able to stand in the center of the band's *serape* of sounds and play Oscar's music was sometimes greater than the pleasure of being with his friends. That night—with two jobs lined up that still wouldn't yield any money to tithe or send to his father, his dreams again jangled by Paz, and Alfredo misplaying "*La noche y tú*"—his desire to move was strong.

While Oscar called for a break and instructed Alfredo along with Félix Herrera and his brothers, Hector joined Carlos against a brick storefront. Carlos shared his news about the nickel-rate jobs. He said, "When my family landed in bad times, we'd just head to the next town or *colonia*. Taking to the road was like taking another step toward the good life."

"But you never found it, did you?"

"Mostly it was just the same." He touched the boot mark in his forehead and said, "Sometimes worse. But I'd always get excited about trying a new place." He decided to say what he'd been mulling, to hear a reaction. "Maybe it's time again."

Hector frowned and fiddled with the tuning keys on his *vihuela*. "You're young—it's easy to run away from things. When you get older like me, the world gets smaller and the new towns seem like places you've already been. Then, it's easier to stay put and struggle with your problems until you solve them." He shrugged. "Or until they kill you."

"But what if I could be running toward something better?"

Hector smiled, the creases in his leathery face deepening. "Ah, yes, that's what it feels like to be young." Oscar called to him and he left Carlos, returning to his place in the band.

CHAPTER 17

꙳

Jack parked near Market Square. On the Cadillac's hand-stitched leather seat, his current sketchpad lay atop the wrinkled drawings of the Morenos. A small envelope stuck out from behind the pad's cardboard cover. Through his rolled-down window, he watched the activities of the merchants and early evening shoppers in the City Market and searched their faces as always. A spring breeze carried the smells of smoke and engine exhaust, but also *turcos* fried crisp with ground pork, raisins, and nuts inside, *pan dulce* and other sweet, yeasty breads, and the fresh custard and caramel scent of *flan*. *Tejano* food vendors shouted about deep discounts, but had few takers. Sign of the times, Jack thought: poor people holding onto their money.

Anglos eyed the Phaeton and then him as they passed. Most *tejanos* and Negroes seemed to know who he was and never looked his way. That was a problem he'd had trying to get information about Gerardo and Carlos. Even when dressed as a worker, they still saw a ranger. Linda had explained that he had the eyes—the judgmental stare—of a cop. Many of the colored had learned to spot that warning sign as children. As a kid, he too could always spot a lawman: it was a survival instinct.

Jack pulled out the envelope. His name and address had been written in careful, evenly spaced letters all the same size. The proud penmanship of one who hadn't been doing it forever. Photographs flexed inside the envelope. He tore off the short edge bearing a stamp canceled in Brownsville and shook the snapshots into his hand.

Three small, white-bordered monochrome pictures, three grades of exposure: all of them demonstrated that the thousand dollars sent to Jack's Mob acquaintances in Brownsville had been well-spent. The first, dim shot depicted a close-up of his penniless father lying in a bed. Hands crossed over his chest didn't conceal the dark stains on his nightshirt. Jack estimated three revolver rounds, probably .45 calibers. Blood splattered J. Bainbridge Hanson's neck and jaw from the bullet impacts. The next picture, overexposed, showed the foreclosed mansion in flames at night. The fire had burned so hot that windows blew out. The photographer managed to catch such an explosion on the second floor: the casement sailed into the sky, a thick trail of flame and smoke behind the streaking fireball. Comet Donati over Paris couldn't have been more spectacular. The third and clearest exposure showed the smoking rubble that remained the next day. Parts of two charred walls still stood, joined at a corner, the outline of a couple of windows like the eye sockets of a skull.

Final payment of Hanson's debt to the woman he'd destroyed. Jack had balanced the accounts as best as he could. The photographs slid easily into his breast pocket behind the steel post of the badge.

He thought back to the window blowing outward. With the pad propped against the steering wheel, he flipped through pages, looking for the next clean sheet. He'd almost filled his latest sketchbook. An increasing number of desperate people had made the last few months busy. One man for one riot: the ranger's creed. The Anglo officers he'd trained with used to joke about him, "One half-breed, one laugh-riot." Now they asked him for help with their unsolved crimes. Jack hadn't daydreamed about killing them in years.

A crude, early sketch, folded many times, slid into his lap. It was a picture of his mother he tried to correct once in a while: her eyes too far apart, the sweep of her hair all wrong, chin too pronounced, skin shaded too dark. Much too dark. Jack's hands were almost brown in the sunset, his coloring absent of the Anglo who'd raped her, who'd made him. He balled up the page and threw it into the street, toward a storm drain. Startled by his action, Jack commanded his fingers to close and open, restoring control.

The ball of paper sailed back through the window frame and bounced off his arm. A *tejano* stood near the sewer grate, blue shirt and denim trousers, a porkpie hat. He made a quick gesture with his head and started walking.

Jack followed in his car. He studied the man, his walk, his profile. Delicate cheekbones, a mustache that didn't make him look older than his twenty-five or so years. Over the purr of the Caddy, Jack heard someone call out, "¡Eh, Félix! ¿Cómo estás?"

The man turned, caught himself, and plowed ahead. He stopped in front of a *teatro* that imported talkie picture shows from Mexico and played Hollywood titles, some dubbed into Spanish. Jack parked at the curb among rusting flivvers and ramshackle jalopies. He brought his sketches of the Morenos.

The man named Félix said in English, "You look for some man?"

"Yes, and his son." Jack held out the drawings.

Félix looked up and down the street. He nodded toward the entrance and replied in Spanish, "Inside. I don't want to be seen talking to you." He pushed the door open and approached the woman selling tickets from her desk in the small lobby. "Two, please. My friend is buying."

Jack passed over twenty cents to the woman eyeing his badge, and followed the man through a swinging door. They entered a large, dark room where two dozen people, in scattered groups, sat in rows of wooden folding chairs.

The audience faced a smooth, pale wall that held the images of an Anglo man driving a woman through some town, all in shades of white and gray; the man's voice didn't match the movement of his mouth. A bulky projector and sound machine sat at the back of the room, clicking and blowing and producing garbled Spanish translations. Cigarette smoke drifted up through the funnel of projected light.

Jack sat beside Félix, who took the first seat on the back row, closest to the exit. The man leaned close and glanced at the sketches. "Moreno, right?"

"Where are they?" Jack held up a five-dollar bill.

"They? I only know one."

"His name?"

"Gerardo." Félix took the money with long, graceful fingers, like a musician's. When he'd lifted his elbow, fresh sweat showed in the armpit of his shirt and down the side, the stain as dark as blood in the projector's reflected light.

Jack draped his arm over the back of Félix's chair and murmured, "Not his son?"

"No. He said his son left for New Mexico—Santa Fe—six months ago. Gerardo headed that way by bus the other day."

"Which day?" Jack clamped his hand around the back of the man's neck.

On the wall, the scenery behind the couple changed abruptly to the countryside, and they talked of their love for each other. Félix tried to pull free of Jack's grip. He said loudly, "Tuesday or Wednesday, I forget."

"How did Carlos get out there?"

Félix raised his voice even more. "Gerardo didn't say, just showed me a letter—"

A stout man seated beside his wife and three children whispered, "*Silencio.*"

Félix shouted, "You be quiet." Jack squeezed harder and felt him sway.

The man stood as his family turned in their seats and frowned. He pointed his finger at Félix. "Shut up!" A number of others, including the projectionist, yelled for silence as the couple on the screen mooned over each other.

Félix kicked the chair in front of him and sent it crashing into some others. Everyone shouted. Félix stood as Jack clawed at his neck and grabbed the man's collar. The back of the shirt tore all the way down. He let it go as he got up.

The angry patron shoved chairs out of the way, clearing a path toward him and Félix, and swung his fist, but Félix dodged. Jack staggered as he caught the blow on his shoulder and flicked his blackjack against the stout man's temple. The fellow toppled backward. Félix escaped through the swinging door, torn shirt flapping, as several other men charged Jack.

A single word from Jack stopped them: *"Rinche."* Even the man holding his head stopped writhing on the floor and now covered his face as if to hide. Jack dashed through the exit and yelled in Spanish at the woman taking tickets, "Which way?"

She looked not at his eyes but again at the encircled star on his shirt. She pointed right. He ran through the front doorway and, on instinct, went left. Ahead, in the wake Félix had carved through the pedestrians, he saw a blue shirttail and dark skin turning a corner. The porkpie hat lay on the sidewalk.

Jack pushed the blackjack into his pocket, drew his revolver, and ran through the diminishing gap in the crowd. Fire as white-hot as the destroyer of the Hanson mansion seared his left knee as he followed Félix. From experience he knew he couldn't run hard for more than a minute before his leg would give out. Still, the pain was worth it. Interrogating Félix would lead him to one or both Morenos. And then the final pursuit of the man who'd crippled him. And peace. Jack ran faster and people spun out of his way.

He turned the corner onto a street with only a few pedestrians. Félix was in clear view a block away, arms pumping fast, blue shreds of fabric flapping like pennants behind him. Jack shouted, "Halt." He slowed, braced himself in a shooter's stance, and fired once. The man fell, blood seeping from a hole in the back of his right leg. Everyone else on the sidewalk ran or took shelter in doorways. Félix pushed himself to his feet and faced Jack, breathing hard through his mouth. They were alone on the block in the dying light.

Félix feinted toward the street and hobbled through the open doorway beside him, entering a four-story apartment building. Jack ran hard again. Entering the foyer, an echo of breath like a high-pitched sigh greeted him. He followed Félix up the central staircase. The man's right shoe dragged against each wooden step and thumped the edge of the next one.

Jack's boots made a steadier racket as he climbed the dark stairs, but his left leg began to hesitate. Faint light illuminated the top floor. Jack called in echoing Spanish, "If you're running, Félix, you have something to hide. If you're hiding something, I'll get it out of you." Doors opened and shut, for a moment brightening different parts of the stairwell with the faint glow from kerosene lamps or pale candlelight. He sighted upward and listened. More doors opened. He glimpsed the man starting up the next flight and fired. Even with the reverberation of the gunshot, he heard a gasp and stumbling and rapid breaths. Then he heard Félix begin to climb again, slowly now. No more doors opened.

Tired of the chase, Jack moved faster. He felt wetness on a handrail and thought he could see spots on the stairs as his eyes adjusted to the dimness. Probably winged him. Footsteps faltered above him, and the panicked breathing sounded louder. The stairwell lightened as Jack caught up. From the third floor, he shot the man's other arm, knocking him down on the top landing.

Félix began wailing as Jack mounted the flight of steps separating them. The door to the roof was open. The man crawled up through rays of orange sunset. On the landing sat a young, tan-skinned boy in dirty shirtsleeves and tattered trousers smoking a cigarette. The boy looked up at Félix, then down at Jack, and said in Spanish, "Will you kill him?"

"Go home."

"This is my home. He's bleeding on it." The boy blew a trail of smoke into the light. Its comet tail broke apart, forming a swirl of complex patterns that rose and disappeared.

Félix kept moving on his elbows and knees, dark stains spreading on his clothes. His cries filled the narrow space until he pulled himself outside.

The boy said, "He won't tell you anything."

"I know. It's too late though." Jack took the cigarette from the boy and inhaled deeply, making the ash glow like the sinking fireball in the west. He handed it back. The boy's fingers felt cool against his. Round burns pocked the child's arms.

Félix crawled across the roof, his hands and knees crunching the loose gravel. Forty feet up, Jack had expected the air to be cleaner, but thick brown smoke wafted over him. He said, "Damn you, stop!" and shot the man once more. Félix kept crawling toward the edge, dragging his bleeding legs. The fresh wound through his shoulder barely slowed him.

Jack ran as fast as he could. His left leg crumpled as he drew near. The revolver fell onto the gravel as he grabbed Félix's ankles. The man had nearly hurled himself off the rooftop. Jack rolled him over. Félix's face was slick with sweat; his eyes, mouth, and nostrils were open wide, as if the man took in as much of the world as he could. His head and torso cantilevered over the ledge, suspended, bending away. Félix's arms hung behind him, fists clenched, blood dripping off his wrists. A crowd had gathered and many of them pointed upward. They glowed, lit by the headlights of cars stopped in the street.

Jack shouted, "How do you know the Morenos?" When Félix only keened through his open mouth, Jack shook the man's legs and demanded, "Where are they?" He began to pull his prisoner toward him.

Félix's arm came forward and fingers sprang open. Jack lifted his hands to his face, a reflex. Gravel bounced off his palms and fingers and the man's shoes grazed him as Félix toppled from the roof. The onlookers screamed, but Félix was finally silent. Jack kept his hands over his eyes as the body slammed into the sidewalk.

Witnesses' cries drifted up as Jack holstered his gun, limped to the stairs, and descended. He looked for the boy on the landing but only saw smears of Félix's blood and an old, stubbed-out cigarette. Clamped between his finger and thumb, the tip was ice cold.

CHAPTER 18

ꝑ

Pushing a broom along the streets of the Sixth Ward in April was the easiest job Carlos had ever done. The weather had not yet turned hot and humid, and the air occasionally smelled of flowers and pine trees. However, being confined outside during the longer spring days made him jumpy. He'd forgotten his death-wish, so Oscar's news had brought back his fear of the ranger.

The story about Donati's brutal murder of Félix Herrera—shooting him to pieces and then throwing the poor musician off a rooftop—had been told to Oscar by one of Félix's brothers, another violinist in *El Mariachi Santa Cruz.* Yonis Herrera had assumed Félix spotted the ranger and fed him the tale the band had fabricated to lead Donati away from Carlos. But Félix had also known where Carlos really lived and worked.

Oscar had insisted that the ranger would've seized Carlos that same night if Félix had told him anything. Despite his friend's logic, Carlos felt vulnerable as he cleaned the concrete walks and streets.

To keep his mind busy on something other than Donati's renewed threat, he concentrated on the *mexicano rosario.* He swept the sidewalk opposite a small, well-tended park, trying to contemplate the sacred heart, but his romantic one kept interrupting. Instead of a focus on the liturgy of the Mass, Carlos considered three unmarried young women he'd seen in the Communion line on a recent Sunday. To his disappointment, no single face stuck in his memory; they blurred into one pretty picture.

He glanced across the street where a lovely *tejana* mother had turned the corner and walked alongside the park, pushing a pram. He'd seen her earlier that week and once the week before, always with her baby, always staring down at two or three pages of handwriting. The woman stood only a few inches above five-feet, and her figure looked petite within her white-collared, black cotton dress. Nevertheless, her light-tan complexion caught his eye, as did the wavy black hair that bounced on her shoulders with her athletic strides.

The woman kept her face lowered as she read another letter, glancing ahead periodically and adjusting the course of the carriage. Her mouth turned downward as she stifled a yawn.

Carlos cursed himself, having forgotten which decade of the rosary he'd begun while eyeing some other man's wife. A rich man's wife at that: rings glinted on several fingers and earrings swayed beside her face. Something displeased the woman in her reading—she crumpled the sheets together and looked up the sidewalk and behind her, but no trash cans had been set out. She tossed the paper ball toward the street, but met Carlos' gaze as she did so. The woman lunged to catch her litter, but the paper rolled into the road.

He pushed his broom onto the pavement, earning three squawks from the horn of a passing car. The baby began to cry and the woman bent down to comfort her child. Carlos checked for more traffic and swept up the balled pages, moving it across the street and onto the sidewalk a few yards behind her.

The woman straightened and smiled. Carlos smiled back, but quickly closed his mouth after he saw her notice the deep scars on his lips and chin. He stammered a hello.

"*Buenos días*," she replied in a pleasant, high timbre. "Sorry I didn't see you over there. I could've thrown my trash across the street to you." Her Spanish sounded educated, sophisticated.

"I have to do this side anyway—to make room for the trash I'll sweep tomorrow."

She laughed, a musical sound like shells tumbling in the surf, and Carlos tried to keep her laughing. He danced a little *zapateado* behind the broom, his sandals making satisfying stomps as he slid the horsehair bristles across the concrete. He captured wrappers and cigarette butts, and eased the trash to one side.

The woman applauded softly as he finished his dance. "I didn't know the city was hiring dancing street sweepers now. You're like something from a picture show."

Oscar had taken him to some of the *El Teatro Azteca* moving pictures, an odd mix of chorus lines, cartoons, and yodeling cowboys. "Oh, yes. In these hard times, they want everyone to dance and sing our troubles away." He polkaed a little closer and glanced into the carriage. The baby's blue eyes regarded Carlos, and a pudgy pink fist emerged from the nest of soft blankets. Carlos blinked and looked at the woman.

"No," she said and laughed again, covering her mouth. "Not mine, but Morris is so precious I wish he were. I'm his nanny."

"Any beautiful babies of your own?" He cradled the broom handle and dipped it like a dance partner.

"No babies and no husband, dancing or otherwise."

"All alone then?"

"*Santa María*, no! So many men smother me up close and through their letters that I can hardly breathe." She gestured with her black pump at the balled paper among his trash. "That's one nice thing about getting a love letter. Too bad I can't do that with some of the men."

Carlos nudged the crumpled letter with his sandal. "Poor fellow. He showed his heart to you, open to the slightest pinprick." He pounded his fist against his chest. "And you stab him with a knife."

The woman smiled again, but shook her head. "No, the only thing he revealed was a lack of imagination and an over-reliance on the word 'love.' He uses it like my mother uses chilies: when in doubt, throw in a handful."

"Ay." Carlos leaned on his broom, gazing at her. "He does sound tedious."

The woman blushed. She busied herself with the baby's blankets. Glancing up, she said, "He did show an eye for detail."

"Oh?"

"Yes, his descriptions were very thorough."

"Hmm."

The woman straightened again and grimaced, letting him off the hook. "He described every inch of me in lurid detail, all of which he loves, of course. I didn't realize I was being so immodest. I need a *mantilla* and a few more layers of clothing."

"Maybe he has a good imagination." He shrugged. "You're dressed very properly."

"Perhaps you didn't look as hard as he did."

"Oh, no, I did." He nearly bit his tongue trying to shut his mouth ahead of the words. He touched his forehead in salute as she grinned at him, and pushed his broom past her toward some loose newspapers. "Sorry to have bothered you," he said over his shoulder. "Please have a nice walk."

He shook his head and, looking up and down the road, moved the trash across the street. *¡Idiota!* He watched the suitor's letter roll ahead of him and knew his chance with her or anyone she knew was in the same heap. Cursing himself again, he crossed the street again and resumed sweeping the other sidewalk, thinking back to his place on the rosary. He risked another look and saw that she kept pace, not watching him but taking her time.

He returned to what had worked well at the start, clowning and dancing behind the broom periodically, his sandals providing rhythmic syncopation on the concrete. He pushed the trash into a larger heap at the corner where a wagon would come by later and pick up what he'd collected.

She dallied at the opposite corner. He shuffled his steps— the *huapango*—as he paused to let a car go through the intersection. The driver flipped a cigarette onto pavement. Carlos pushed the smoldering butt and other, flattened ones to her corner.

"I don't smoke, thanks," she said, "but I'm glad you came back for this." She dropped a folded envelope onto the ground.

Carlos saw the writing on the front, probably her name and address. He swept it up casually, hoping the cigarette wouldn't char it.

"Forgive my rudeness," she said, "but what happened to your mouth?"

"Danced too close to my last broom. Those splinters are deadly."

"Maybe it was a jealous boyfriend?"

"Nothing so romantic."

She leaned on the carriage handle and asked again.

"A man hit me with the floor of my apartment."

The woman put her hands to her mouth. Looking at her eyes, he thought she winced, but then he could hear her swallowing a laugh. She said, "I'm so sorry. It's not funny. It's just the way you said it."

"I got tired of explaining how a thief whacked me with a board." Carlos pushed the broom forward, and they resumed walking. The envelope skittered ahead. He continued, "It hurt, regardless of how I tell it, but what hurt worse was losing my music. I'd played in a *mariachi* band in *El Segundo Barrio*. The thief took my trumpet, too."

"You're a musician, and you can dance. You're a good talker with a sense of humor. Why are you pushing a broom?"

"That's what people pay for, Anglos anyway. It's hard to find work; I'm lucky to have this and my night job. I've worked in their warehouses, picked the food they eat, and laid railroad tracks and fixed their trains. You're well-educated, but take care of a white family's baby and probably keep their house clean." He shrugged. "It's what they pay for."

"At least they pay for that. Would it be better for you in Mexico? I hear lots of people are going back."

There was no point in telling her many of those going back were doing so at gunpoint. He simply said, "No—America's my home."

"Well, that's the way it is in your home. I do a good job taking care of their baby and, you're right, their house. But it's a beautiful house, and I get to live in it. They give me bonuses and treat me well. Better than a lot of maids and nannies. You sound like you resent the people who pay you."

Her lips still curled upward in a smile, but he couldn't tell if she was challenging him or just bantering. He lost his nerve and said quietly, "I feel trapped by it sometimes. I don't want to argue. I shouldn't be wasting your time."

"Don't be ridiculous. I like talking to you. It's so nice to have a conversation with a man who only does a little *macho* strutting." She flashed her white teeth again. "If you're looking for a job with more variety, my employers need someone to do all the outdoor work: cutting tree limbs, keeping up the yard, and also some furniture-moving inside I can't manage. It's still rough labor, but might pay better than this. Are you interested?"

"Yes, if they don't mind someone who'll dance with a tree branch."

"They wouldn't notice if you danced with the whole tree. When we stay in our proper places, we're invisible, right?"

Carlos nodded, relieved he hadn't offended her. He said, "Please let me know. I'll be here this time tomorrow and every day except Sunday." He reached down and picked up the envelope. Waving it, he announced, "So long as careless people keep littering our streets and sidewalks."

She rolled her dark chocolate eyes. "See you tomorrow, then." The woman wheeled the buggy to the next corner and did a few heel-stomps of her own. When he laughed, she looked back, catching him as he wiped the envelope on his sleeve.

*

Pedro looked at the envelope and whistled, prompting Carlos to wonder if he'd spent his day mooning over someone unattainable.

The priest pointed at the address. "Poplar Street's in the First Ward, a very nice neighborhood in the western suburbs. We've received some charity items from that part of town."

"The writing is hard to make out. I smudged the ink. How do you think she'd pronounce her name?"

"Domenica."

"Her first name, I meant."

"You mean you didn't even introduce yourself?"

"At first I thought we'd say just a few words. Then I thought she wouldn't want to ever talk to me again. At the end, we already acted like friends. I figured I could get it from the envelope, but I'm afraid I got it pretty dirty."

"It looks like 'Daniela Domenica.' Lovely name for a lovely woman, right?"

"It is and she is. You'd mentioned trying to find someone from our congregation for me. I hope you're not disappointed."

"My Lord, no, Carlos. You were much more successful on your own than I was going to be." He stroked his beard and smiled broader. "Still, I was starting to enjoy the notion of matchmaking. It's another way to be an instrument of God." Pedro handed the envelope back to him and said, "If you get this other job, maybe the next fellow who sweeps the Sixth Ward will meet the love of his life, too."

"So long as it's not Daniela—I've got enough competition already."

CHAPTER 19

C arlos checked the sun in the perfect bluebonnet sky to confirm he was on time. He chewed on cedar shavings, which Oscar had recommended for sweetening the breath. With no oncoming traffic, he used his broom to scrape away the flattened dung from the horse that pulled the trash wagon. On Tuesdays, more scat than other garbage lay in the street.

Daniela rounded the corner with the pram and gave him a little wave. He left the dung curbside and collected cigarette butts with the broom as he crossed the street, calling, "Any letters to add today?"

"Mercifully, no. It was a calm night. Little Morris cried during most of it, but I like that much better than the racket of sonnets and speeches. Give me a screaming baby every time. Between this one's colicky fits, I did ask about the job for you."

"Should I get ready to cry, too?"

"I hope you'll laugh. They trust my recommendation and want you to come to work at their house tomorrow morning. The job pays two-fifty a day plus dinner at noon. It's not much money for all the work, I'm afraid."

Carlos stomped his heels a few times and dipped his broom handle. "It's a lot more than I make with two jobs. Thank you for asking for me."

"I have a confession, though. Here's where I hope you'll laugh," Daniela said. She gripped the handlebar.

"What is it?"

"You didn't tell me your name yesterday, and they asked, so I had to give you one. I couldn't say I recommend you but don't know your name. Now you're Felipe Villalobos."

"Felipe Villalobos?" He laughed out loud.

She shook her head, smiling. "I'm very sorry. They asked and I said the first name that came into my head. He was a boy who lived next door when I was growing up. Will that be all right?"

"My real name is Carlos Moreno, Daniela Domenica. But you can call me Felipe anytime." He bowed.

She curtsied. "I'm glad you kept that envelope. I brought you some directions to Poplar Street." She removed a folded piece of paper from her purse. The stationery smelled of her lilac scent.

"You perfumed your note." He held it to his nose and smiled.

She blushed. "I must've had it on my hands when I touched the paper."

"It's very nice," he said, and unfolded the page to look at it.

"Sometimes you can't see the street signs, or they're not where you expect them, so I put down landmarks too, stores, big houses you can't miss. You'll find it."

"Who will I be working for? It'd be good to know in case the police stop me."

She handed him a small card.

He blinked at the long name. "How do you say it?"

"With great difficulty. It's Mikhail Strugatsky. The 'Esquire' after his name means he's an attorney-at-law."

They recited the name together a few times. Carlos repeated it once more to make sure he had it right. He dared not demonstrate his ignorance by asking what an "attorney-at-law" did, but the "law" part scared him—he hoped the man wasn't part of the police force.

Daniela said, "I'm glad you'll do this. It'll be nice to have a friend around. It's a big house, like I said, and often there's just me and Morris and the cook. Sra. Strugatsky spends most of her time at social engagements. She'll be there tomorrow morning, though, to tell you what needs to be done first."

"I'll miss meeting you on this walk."

"I do like to get away, out among a few of our own people. I'll still have to take Morris every day," she said, "but you'll be much busier than you seem to be here."

Carlos hung his head. "I'm not a lazy man, I promise." He paused, not daring to say more, and then thought: what the hell. He told her, "I'm very productive except when a beautiful woman is near. Then I prance and chatter like a mockingbird."

"Well, thank you," Daniela said. "Coming from your mouth, the compliment sounds sincere."

"My mouth?" He covered the scars.

"Don't misunderstand me. I'm saying you're more… genuine…than other men I know."

"I don't know how to be anyone else. Except for Felipe Villalobos, of course. When should I be there?"

"Nine. There's a big clock, one of the landmarks, so you can see whether you're on time. *Hasta luego.*"

He watched her move over the sidewalk and around the corner. He slowly covered the same ground with his broom, imagining he could feel the warmth of her footprints on the concrete.

*

Oscar studied the map and the business card in his dank, candlelit room. From his past railroad jobs, the bandleader knew the west side of Houston. "Including the suburbs, where I shouldn't have wandered." He added more pictures to the map and explained the route, ever the teacher.

Carlos thanked his friend and said, "I guess I'm scared about being late. I want to make a good impression with Daniela."

"She sounds like someone your parents would love. I'm glad you put the business with Paz and Jorge behind you. Get those scars healed and come back to play with us. Alfredo's getting better, but he doesn't have your style."

"I'll let you know how this works out."

"Do that. I'll tell the band what you're up to. Working for a lawyer on the west side—" Oscar whistled and shook his hand as if to cool it.

*

Carlos warned Sra. Gómez he would be up early. He went upstairs with a pitcher of stove-heated water, a cake of Octagon soap, and some extra towels. Keeping a single room, especially with his savings gone, had seemed crazy. Now he appreciated the privacy. He wanted to be alone with his feelings, the butterflies in his stomach, the tingling in his fingertips. His heart raced when he thought of Daniela.

By candlelight he bathed himself all over, enjoying the thrill of standing naked in his private room. He ran a washcloth over the long, thick muscles of his arms and chest, reddish-brown skin that shined with beads of water. Warm rivulets followed the waterfall of short hairs that flowed from his navel and down over the trunks of his thighs.

He scrubbed his back, stretching the broad muscles over his dense bones. All good and necessary for the work he'd done in the past and would do until he was stooped and crippled. He tried to imagine himself at double his age, remembering his father's deformed hands and battered shoulders, the spine that could never straighten, and the face that would no longer smile.

Carlos toweled himself and wiped the water from the floor. His body creaked and popped as he bent to blow out the candle. He knew he could tolerate that same life if he could share it with someone who had Daniela's humor and straightforwardness. Someone his parents would have loved. Climbing between the cool sheets, he thought about the woman who'd believed enough in him already to risk her reputation with her employers. He said his prayers, including the fervent wish that he would not disappoint this *doncella*.

CHAPTER 20

༝

C arlos walked through the Anglos' downtown business
district, smelling Daniela's lilac perfume on the map as
he referred to its landmarks. Streetcars clattered past in
the opposite direction, but this time his destination was where
some of the passengers had started. He crossed the Buffalo and
passed the streets he'd swept for a few months, moving deeper
into the Anglo wards. At least the police and *la migra* were
more likely to be in the *barrios* than on these streets.

The morning light flashed gold at him from a storefront
up ahead. He noticed the three balls above the doorway, a
building Oscar had noted on the map. The nervous excitement
of seeing Daniela gave way to shock. A trumpet stood on its
bell behind the display window. Carlos pressed his hands to
the glass and admired its bold lines and sensuous curves. Then
he noted the dents in the bell—it was his; Jorge had hocked
it. If he saved his money and stayed lucky, he could get back
some of what the thief had taken away. When he stepped
away from the window, his damp, grasping handprints slowly
faded before his eyes.

Pedestrians stared at him as he continued westward. He
probably was the only *tejano* on their streets at the moment.
A few blacks walked toward the suburbs as well, dressed in
servant uniforms. The cluster of offices and shops eventually
gave way to broad, shady boulevards with large brick houses

on multi-acre estates. He found Poplar and counted the homes on his left as he passed them, stopping in front of the eighth one. Daniela opened the front door of the manor and waved. He walked up the long drive, noting the trees that needed pruning, the grass he would cut, the immense flowerbeds that his mother would've loved to tend. There did seem to be enough to keep him busy.

Daniela met him at the top of the drive, in front of a wide carport that sheltered a black automobile. Oil drips on the concrete indicated another driver already had left. She asked if he had any trouble.

"Not at all, thanks to you."

"I'm glad. You're actually a little early. Have you eaten breakfast?"

He shook his head. "I didn't want to be late."

"Well, come in. There're always leftovers."

"Who's the cook?"

She said, "Mrs. Gretzenbach, another hard name. The Strugatskys brought her with them when they came from Europe. She keeps to herself. When she does talk, she tells me how much she misses her home."

"We have that much in common. I've known homesickness, too."

"She probably won't say much. She doesn't like 'Mexicans,' as she calls all of us, even though I was born here. But I'm light-skinned enough for her to at least mumble a few words." Daniela gave him a nervous smile and said, "I'm just warning you. You'll look very... foreign to her."

He brushed the scars on his mouth and chin. "I'll try not to scare her."

"I'd warn you even if you were perfect. Come inside. It'll be fine."

Carlos followed her around back. Her slender body swayed within the black uniform, each leg revealing itself in turn, her calves shiny in their stockings. His body began to react—the last thing Sra. Gretzenbach needed to see—so he shifted his focus to the shrubs and flowerbeds in need of care.

"Who worked out here before me?"

"A fellow named Rigo," she said, glancing over her shoulder. "He stopped coming over a week ago. Maybe he decided to go back to Jalisco. I heard the government is giving free rides or something." She shrugged, her shoulders moving in unison.

Carlos pictured this Rigo: tending the landscape each day, lulled by the expensive surroundings, and then suddenly getting snatched off the street by *la migra* and finding himself in a crowded train headed to Laredo and then south of the border. He shuddered.

She pointed out a large wooden outbuilding set deep in the backyard: his tool shed. At the back door, Daniela said. "This is where you'll report each morning. Sometimes Sra. Strugatsky will tell you what to do and sometimes she'll pass instructions through me."

Daniela led him into the dim kitchen. In unaccented English, she said, "Mrs. Gretzenbach? This is Mr. Villalobos. He's our new groundskeeper."

The woman at the stove took a long pull on a cigarette as she looked Carlos over. Blue-gray smoke hazed her features. He couldn't guess her age or even the color of her eyes. He smiled, and she exhaled smoke through her nose and mouth and jabbed the cigarette into a delicate teacup. A gray wisp climbed up from the china to connect with the cloud around her head.

Daniela indicated the table against the kitchen wall where some dishes with leftover eggs, sausages, and toast awaited washing. She got a clean plate and flatware and made a place at the table for him.

"Thank you, I can help myself," he said in English for the cook's benefit, while knowing his accent only emphasized his foreignness. "You have things to do. I don't want to make you late with your chores."

She looked at Mrs. Gretzenbach, then back at Carlos, and left the kitchen.

"Thank you for breakfast, madam," he said. "I know this will be good."

The cook lit another cigarette with the snap of her thumb against a match. She turned back to the pan she'd been scrubbing.

He ate quickly, thanked her again, and went back outside. He took a deep breath that Oscar would have applauded and blew through his nose and then his mouth to clear them of acrid smoke. The door opened behind him, and he turned. "Mrs. Strugatsky?"

A graceful woman, perhaps thirty years old, appraised him from the step. She wore tailored clothing and careful makeup against her very fair skin. Carlos quickly lowered his gaze to her stocking-covered ankles and high-heeled black shoes.

In gruffly accented English, she asked, "What do you call yourself?

"Felipe Villalobos, madam." He was grateful Daniela had introduced him to the cook; he'd needed to be reminded of his new name.

"Ah, yes, Felipe. Where do you come from?"

"I've lived my whole life in Texas, traveling with my parents."

"Are your parents here?"

"No, madam. They're both dead." It was easier and shorter to explain that way, he reasoned. He quickly traced a cross over his heart and kept his gaze on her still, small feet.

"Do you have any other family?"

"No, madam."

"How do I know you'll stay, when there's no one here for you?"

He met her eyes for a moment and spoke in his most careful English. "Mrs. Strugatsky, you pay a good wage. The job will be very enjoyable—the land is beautiful." He nodded at the greenery and flower beds. "Who would not want to work here?"

"My husband spends six days every week in an ugly office in town, so there are such people." She waved her hand at the tall grass near her shoes. "Our last groundskeeper abandoned us, so you can see there's much work to be done." She listed his tasks for the week and then said, "Do you have any questions?"

"No, madam."

"I have one other. What on earth happened to your face?"

Carlos drew in his lips and touched the groove in his chin. "I surprised a thief in my room, and then he surprised me."

"Good Lord. Please don't bring any surprises to our door."

"No, madam."

"Good day, Felipe," she said, turning back to the kitchen.

"Good day, Mrs. Stru—"The door shut before he finished. Carlos went to the shed and rolled out the mechanical grass cutter. He felt along the dull blades and retrieved a file he found lying under a pile of tools. After sharpening the mower, he went to work. The cross at the end of his rosary swung from the handlebars as he recited while keeping the mower in line with the previous swath he'd cut in the acres of pillow-like grass.

During the balmy morning, Daniela took Morris for a long buggy ride, calling to him on her way down the drive. In the afternoon, he raked the clippings around the house and watched the windows as she dusted, swept, and polished inside. He admired her ease within the electrified mansion. She casually turned lights on and off via switches on the walls, ran a cleaning machine over the carpets, and listened to the radio as she did her chores. Her hips swayed to the jazz music with strong trumpet parts.

As the sun descended behind the pine trees, Carlos sat on his haunches and cleaned and re-sharpened the mower. He found a whetstone and sharpened the long shears and hand clippers and used the file on the shovel and the spades so all would be ready for him.

He went to the kitchen door and knocked. The cook stood at the bank of windows, regarding him. He called, "Good evening, madam. See you tomorrow." She made no reply other than to cloud the glass with smoke.

*

Carlos approached the landscape as he had done with his music, always striving to make it better, never satisfied. He also challenged himself to court Daniela, and do it so carefully she might not even realize it—as she probably wasn't aware of her body's reaction to the trumpets playing for her on the radio. If he could give her that kind of pleasure, he'd avoid being lumped in with the men who smothered her.

After a quick meal at noon in the hazy kitchen, they would sit on the back steps and tell each other their stories. Daniela talked about growing up with two older sisters who made her laugh when they weren't teasing and pummeling her. They'd given her incentive to learn how to fight with her fists and feet to defend herself; a handy skill around aggressive—now former—suitors. Both her sisters had moved to Corpus Christi after they got married, but her parents still lived in Houston; Daniela had spent her whole life in the Bayou City. She'd been taught by the nuns at Our Lady of Guadalupe School. Instead of bragging about her education, though, she told funny stories about the nuns, pantomiming their expressions and movements within the confines of their habits.

Carlos told her about the joy he'd felt playing trumpet with el Mariachi Santa Cruz and helping Pedro at the mission. For her safety, he didn't discuss his resistance work, only the charity. He told her his favorite stories but realized he had few humorous episodes in his life. Looking back, there was very little to laugh about, so he told her of the bad times: his mother's death, the Klansmen and Ranger Donati, and Félix's murder. He told her about Jorge. When Daniela described her tiresome, well-heeled suitors, Carlos confessed about the wrong path he'd taken with Paz.

Her first love had been the real Felipe Villalobos, a beautiful boy with long eyelashes and a shy smile. One day he began to stare back at all the other girls who'd watched him for years while he and Daniela chatted in the cool, dark stairwell beside her parents' shop. He'd broken her heart with the casual cruelty of many adolescents. "I'd loved him since we were six," she said. "For years we'd talked about getting married and making all those serious adult plans children do. His pledges—and my trust in boys—didn't last very long after our first kiss."

Once during their noontime chats, she took Carlos' large right hand in both of hers and studied the scars and creases, witnesses to *peón* labor etched across his palm and fingers. "It's like holding a history book," she said. "Everything you've ever done is written here. Your fingertips are tough from picking crops; calluses show me how you held railroad tools and mattocks. Cuts, burns, and splinters from your work in the city."

He said, "Let's see yours." He slid his hand beneath hers, feeling them tense a little. "Ink stains and calluses on your left fingers—"

"From letter writing."

"Faint scars on your fingertips. The cotton fields? Picking okra?"

She laughed. "Paper cuts. Safety pins."

"But the top of your palm shows me how you grip the handle of Morris' *cochecito* and these marks are from mops and brooms."

She shook her head. "The hands of a working woman."

"I've never known any other kind. They're honest hands, and you have the fingers of a scholar."

Daniela hid them in the folds of her skirt. "The man I dated last night said I'll need to wear gloves with my wedding gown to cover them up."

"You're getting married?"

"Not to him," she said with a shake of her head. "Not to anyone."

CHAPTER 21

"Good morning, madam," Carlos said to the silent cook on the first Monday in May. "And good morning, miss," he added as Daniela came in. "*Feliz Cinco de Mayo.*"

"Hello and happy holiday," she replied in English. "I still can't believe April's gone already. Mrs. Strugatsky said she wanted the flowerbeds replaced today. Summer's coming on strong."

"But lots of the spring colors still look good."

"It's the perfect day to put in something more seasonal. Before dinner at noon, we'll take a wide cart to the nursery and fill it up."

He retrieved his spade after breakfast and went to work digging up the spent blooms in the dozen large flowerbeds on the grounds. He only took out the ones that were dead or dying, unwilling to remove the flowers that still thrived.

They left for the nursery before the day grew too hot, with Carlos pushing the enormous, flat-topped wheelbarrow in front of him as Daniela walked alongside. They quadrupled the weight he had to push back to the house with flats of marigolds, coneflowers, foxglove, vinca, snapdragons, cosmos, and zinnias. He'd lost himself in a fantasy that they were shopping for flowers to grace their own home. Hefting a rainbow of blooms, he followed her back toward Poplar

Street. "What should I do with the good flowers still in the beds?"

"The garbage truck will come through in a few days. Heap everything on the cart so they can get it."

"It's a waste to throw out something that's still blooming. In the fields, you pick the crops when they're ready, sometimes going back over the plants many times to get everything at its peak. With flowers, I guess there's no 'ready.' You just take them out when the seasons change."

She glanced back at him. "You don't like change?"

"I've been told to get used to it. But why take something pretty out of your life?"

"Because you're replacing them with brighter and fresher blooms."

He set the back end down a moment and rolled his shoulders. "But the older flowers are still beautiful. They're staying hardy in the hotter weather. I'd keep them as long as I could."

The challenging smile reappeared as Daniela looked at him. She folded her arms like one of the teachers she'd mimicked. "So let's say your wife has given you lots of children and survived illness and hardship—a long, difficult winter and spring. It shows in her face and her body. You won't look for a fresher, brighter one to look pretty for you all summer and fall? Someone to make you feel young and *macho* in all those sweaty months before the frost?"

"She'll still bloom for me. I'll make her happy and keep her smiling and she'll bloom." He tried to understand the sudden seriousness of her mood.

"But when she's spent, and her seeds have all dropped? When the last petals are gone, and she's just tired limbs and tattered leaves? What then?"

He nodded at the cart, thinking about the varieties of flowers they'd considered. "Those snapdragons will be very tempting, sure, but I'll care for the seeds and ease the flower out of the garden. Don't forget that I may be on my way out too—none of us are perennials."

"You'll help them grow and prosper like their mother?" Her voice was a whisper, and he had to read her lips.

"Yes," he said gently, "I'll do that." He brought the volume of his voice back up. "How are your romances?"

Her smile looked brittle as her voice broke. "None of them as romantic as a gardener tending to a dying flower—while new blooms wait to take its place."

Carlos lifted the cart and moved forward again, wondering what to say if she began to cry. He couldn't believe that this beautiful woman imagined the same grim end as he did for himself. "You're twenty-one, like me, but already picturing yourself as old someday."

"It'll happen." She glided her hand over the flats, making the flower heads dance and sway in response. "Even to the brightest flower."

They stopped at an intersection. One expensive car cruised down the boulevard behind another, shiny metal and paint and glass, as unreal and unattainable to him as unicorns. Was Daniela as unreachable? He took a breath and risked his heart again. "I would care for that flower. I would tend to its seeds."

"I'm sure you would." She looked straight ahead as she crossed the street. He could see the glint of her moist eye and the tension in her neck.

As they rounded a corner onto Poplar Street, he said, "I've wandered my whole life. When I could make my own choices, I left my father—trying to get the ranger to follow me, leading the evil away. Instead of only looking over my shoulder, though, I was moving ahead, toward something better. I took a wrong turn, but now I feel like I'm there."

"Being the Strugatskys' gardener? Don't cheapen your dreams."

"Being with you. There's nothing cheap about that dream."

She glared at him, mouth turned down. "You haven't known me long enough to say that."

"A tree knows when it's in the right soil, the right place to grow strong, as soon as its roots touch the ground. It knows whether it'll struggle or prosper in that spot. Reaching deeper and farther out only tells it what it knows already."

Daniela closed her eyes and swayed a little. A mockingbird called and then called again, imitating different birdsongs, trying to get a response. Black waves of hair tumbled against her temples as she shook her head. She stepped back and looked at him from under slender, arched brows. "Words. They're just pretty words. Put them in writing, Carlos, and they can join the others in my stack."

"I mean what I say."

"Just like all the others. They all claim to mean exactly what they say." She started forward again, doubling her pace. He had to trot behind the cart to stay beside her, but she soon slowed down to a stroll again. "Sorry, but I'm disappointed. You paint beautiful pictures—play enticing melodies—but it's just romantic fluff, milkweeds that blow away with the slightest upset in the air. Thank you, at least, for not saying, 'I love you.'" Her voice took on a harsher tone. "But I think you want what they all want."

"What's that? Please say it so I can tell you if you're right."

She stopped and held his gaze. "To win me and lock me away, to take me out when the mood strikes you, safe from other men but a prisoner, too." Her hands clenched into fists. "I can't count the boyfriends who've said they never should've let me 'get away.'"

Carlos set down the cart with a thump. "I'm not like them. I want someone who'll work along with me, who wants to share my risks. I want someone who's not afraid to sacrifice and suffer to make a better life for our children."

"Good words again, fine words." She clapped her hands. "¡Viva! They make me feel challenged, like I should throw my hat into your ring. Very good, Sr. Moreno, but they're just words." Daniela touched the flowers again and her voice softened. "I've caught so many in lies and contradictions. I'm tired of men trying to trick me into saying 'yes.' It's a word I never use."

"I'm sorry you have to be so careful," he said. "I'm sorry an honest man is viewed with *sospecha*."

"And I'm sorry to doubt you. I'd hate to see those pretty words fade and die on their innocent stems."

Carlos nodded, lifted the cart, and walked beside her in silence. The mockingbird continued its different calls, trying to draw a response. Daniela looked sad and tired as she left him in the backyard.

He rolled the cart from bed to bed, setting out the fresh flats of blooms in groups of colors and patterns she had suggested at the nursery, layouts that flowed from one complimentary shade to another with small changes in height. Using Daniela's ideas as a foundation, he conceived some designs of his own, inspired by Oscar's *mariachi* tunes: full of contrasts that still blended into a pleasing overall pattern. Their conversation—all of the places where it had gone wrong—looped through his mind without end.

At each bed, he took up those flowers he had left alone in the morning. Before he planted the new flats, he dug a fresh bed behind the shed, where the gentler morning sun would shine, and used topsoil from the established gardens to mix in with the native clay. He made sure the shed concealed the new flowerbed. Satisfied that his secret garden couldn't be observed from the house, he replanted the past season's flowers and watered and mulched them. A diverse mix of hardy, tenacious pansies, petunias, nicotiana, calendulas, and dianthus was hidden from view. Carlos knelt before his creation and tore the envelope with Daniela's name and address into small pieces. He pushed the scraps into the soil beside each survivor.

Replanting the dozen show beds took the rest of that afternoon and all of the following day. He'd seen Daniela just twice, during quick and quiet dinners. He knew he'd ruined their friendship.

When he questioned his urgency, two pictures flashed in his mind: his mother lying dead in a lake of blood and his father standing in a crippled hunch at the cemetery, neither one even forty years old. As he watered the last of the beds, he wondered if he'd lived half of his life already. He was running out of time.

CHAPTER 22

🐝

Caravans of sorrow—caravanas de dolor—*carry our* compatriotas *back to Mexico.*

There is no room on the payrolls of employers: jobless gringos *have decided they can do the work they shunned before and will accept poverty wages.*

There is no room on the welfare rolls of states: Anglos come first.

There is no room on the muster rolls of poor houses, hospitals, asylums, and government-aid camps: whites only.

There is only space on the trains and trucks bound for la madre patria: *always room for one more.*

They roll down from Los Angeles and across the Southwest, from Chicago and across the Northeast. The United States will ship two million souls to Mexico, half of them American-born or legal residents.

Wealthy undocumented Mexicans stay, but poor American citizens are thrown out. Hundreds die on the airless trucks and trains. Families get split on one side of the border or the other.

Mexican officials welcome los repatriados *back to the motherland. They assign the arrivals to resettlement centers, many at the southern end of the country, a thousand miles away. There is work to do, but the indigenous farmers resent "los americanos" with their foreign ways and corrupted* español *and do not cooperate.*

Most of the resettled head north again. However, America is as far away as a star, a place they might only reach again in their dreams.

CHAPTER 23

❧

No one at the bus stations in Houston or Santa Fe had recognized the men in Jack's drawings. U.S. Government postal workers in both cities had denied delivering correspondence between Gerardo and Carlos Moreno. Félix's story obviously had been a diversion and there was just one reason for that: one or both of the Morenos had to be close. Jack rubbed his aching knee as he drove Immigration Agent Guy Lebrun through town.

"This sure is a swell car, Jack. Tell me again how a ranger affords a Caddy?" His breath, smelling of tobacco and peppermints, permeated the air despite the lowered windows.

"A gift from my father, like I said."

"If Pops is so well-heeled, why aren't you a stockbroker or a lawyer?"

Jack glanced over. "Because I always want to be on the right side of the law."

Lebrun put his hands up, willing to surrender only when bantering. "Want to change your bet about who's on the wrong side?"

"I still vote for the janitor. Someone skulking around late at night, reading the stuff in our desks and file cabinets, pawing through the trash. I should've thought of it before."

"Janitors that can read? Nah—it's the messenger boy. He's handling notes all day."

Jack had planted copies of a false memo about an upcoming raid in the files and wastebaskets, while Lebrun had the courier deliver a different red herring that gave a separate location. If anyone tried to move the Mexicans from either spot, the leak would be uncovered and maybe the people initiating the evacuations could be caught as well. If nothing happened, they'd come up with other possible sources and try again, as they had for months.

Lebrun shot the cuffs of his olive-drab shirt. "I know your old man can spring for ten bucks, but let's raise the stakes of our bet. I've been taking in the local color—paid for a fine little *chica* named Linda last night. Maybe you know her." He crossed his legs, scuffing the shiny walnut-burl dashboard with the toe of his shoe, and smirked at Jack. "Whoever loses pays for the next go-round."

*

Carlos went straight to his flowerbed on Saturday morning with water he'd drawn from a hand pump near the back door. His plantings did well, despite the rising heat and humidity. He watered them all and appraised each one's health. A few plants put forth new leaves and buds, and one vinca even boasted a fresh white bloom.

"Car...Felipe?" Daniela called from the back door.

He came around to the back of the house and wished her a good morning.

She invited him inside, not meeting his eyes. Breakfast was a feast of leftovers from the Strugatsky table: meats, breads, and cereal. Daniela made small talk about Morris' progress, speaking with pride about his latest accomplishments. Mrs. Gretzenbach said nothing, but smoked and ate with equal enthusiasm. Dinner was a similar scene, after which Daniela did not join him on the back steps; he figured that ritual was finished.

At the day's end, he stood before his secret garden plot, making sure all was well before departing. Since he wouldn't be there on Sunday, he gave his flowers an extra drink. Daniela stood at the back door when he walked from behind the shed with the dripping watering cans. He set them down and said, "Lots of work to do here, like you promised. On Monday, the grass will have to be cut again."

"I'll need your help inside too, moving some furniture." She handed him three five-dollar bills, his wages for the week.

"Certainly. Thanks for this." He pocketed the money. "Do you have plans for Sunday?"

"Mass at Guadalupe with my parents in the morning. Tonight I have to sort through my offers so I can cast suspicion on some other young man tomorrow." Her smile looked apologetic. "I know I've been cold this week. I just wish you hadn't pushed things, that I didn't see your hat in the same ring with the others. I miss my friend."

He patted his hair. "Does it help that your friend has no *sombrero* for your ring?"

"It's good that you don't take yourself so seriously or act like you have big plans to get rich. For a man from a… modest background, you never pretend you can offer more than yourself. Lots of men try to put up a false front."

"I found out a while ago that everything—and not just money—can be taken away in a flash. All I can pledge is myself. I just have to hope that's good enough."

She looked at him for a long moment, her mouth bending down, fingers twisting her rings, and then said goodnight.

*

Carlos found Paz sitting on his bed on Sunday afternoon. An emerald dress—another of his purchases—hugged her body, which was clearly naked underneath. She wore her hair piled high, with loose tendrils caressing her neck, and looked as bright as her new shoes. Hands rested primly over a paper sack on her lap.

He closed the door and kept his voice low. "Why couldn't you stay away?"

"*Hola*, Carlos. ¿*Cómo estás?*" Her voice sounded as airy as a greeting after Communion.

"How did you get in here?"

"I'm very well, thank you," she continued, a polite smile fixed on her glossy lips.

"Paz! Tell me."

She sighed, her tone falling to its familiar timbre. "One of your neighbors snuck me inside for a dollar. He was glad to do it; he said you're not having any fun lately."

"I'm doing fine without you. Is Jorge worried I'll come after him?"

"Revenge isn't in your nature. You beat him the first time, but if you were really dangerous, he wouldn't have come here that night."

"So why are you here now? There's nothing more to take."

"I want to give you back the money I lifted during our first dance and what Jorge shared from his theft. It's fifty-five in all." Paz set the bag on the bed and returned her hands to their delicate fold over her short skirt.

"If you think we're even, then you don't understand me. You can't have me again. Ever. If you want my forgiveness, it's yours, but everything between us is dead."

"I felt so bad about your injuries. I spied on your progress as the bandages came off and then the stitches. You didn't curl up and pity yourself—you kept going. Seeing that changed my life. I found honest work, sewing in a factory. No thieving, no marks."

"I'm glad. Wouldn't you say it's easier than your old life?"

She shook her head. "I have no control, no say in what I do or when and how to do it. I miss that a lot. But now I'm like respectable people." She re-crossed her bare legs slowly, flashing him.

"A respectable woman doesn't bribe her way into a man's room. A decent woman wears underclothes." Sweat dampened his upper lip. He looked at the floor so he wouldn't see her.

She stood, making the bedsprings squeak. "I'm sorry for everything that happened. Please hold me."

Carlos pressed against the door. "I can't. Keep the money, Paz. It's what you need."

"No. I need you."

"Sorry. I love someone else, a woman I'd marry if she'd take me."

Her voice became hard-edged. "Who is she?"

"She's educated, classy. Maybe I'm just howling at the moon again."

"You're just saying this to hurt me, like before. I was confused about what I wanted—I'll never be with anyone again but you."

"But that's not your nature." Carlos opened the door and stepped back into the hall where the air felt cooler. He breathed more easily.

"I'll show you I've changed." Paz walked out to him, her steps slow and sure.

He seized her wrists and wrenched them upward. Before her fingers closed into fists he saw the familiar calluses, but, as he'd suspected, no new wounds. "Where are the needle pricks, Paz? The punctures? When my mother started sewing piecework she'd said she bled every day." He pushed her away from him. "You're still a villain."

Paz laughed through her nose. "Carlos, you have no idea how bad I can be."

She looped a black tendril of hair behind her ear and walked down the hall. Her heels echoed like hammer blows.

*

A letter lay in Carlos' secret flowerbed on Monday morning. He crouched and stared at it a moment. The beige envelope reclined on brown earth, surrounded by bright green foliage and a few blooms. The leaves and petals still held on to the dew, but the paper felt smooth when he slid his fingers across it, as if the letter had been set out just before he'd arrived.

Nothing was written on the face, and the back was sealed. He touched it to his nose, smelling lilac perfume, and then to his mouth, where Daniela must have licked the gummed edge to close it. He wriggled his little finger into the corner of the envelope and tore upward with care. Inside, he found a note on matching stationery, one brief line in beautiful script. He walked around the shed.

Daniela watched him from the kitchen window. He went inside, holding the paper out to her. "¿De tú?" he asked.

She glanced at Mrs. Gretzenbach, who eyed them from the corner, a column of ash burning near her lips. "Let's go outside a moment," she replied in English. "Show me something." Daniela touched his sleeve and led him back to his garden. In her melodic Spanish, she said, "This is new and old at the same time, new bed, old flowers." She looked at him, fingers spread on her hips like the morning rays of sunlight. The corners of her mouth curled into the familiar dare. "A little like you: young man, old values."

Carlos shrugged. "Some of them weren't ready to go on the trash heap."

"Just like you said."

"Of course. Look how well they're still doing." He crouched and pointed. "Many have new green. See how bright those tiny leaves are? New leaves on old flowers." He squinted as the sun blazed behind her head. A yellow corona made the black waves shine like the maiden's under the Star. He could no longer read her expression in the brilliance.

"How long will you keep them?"

"As long as they live. They'll die sometime." He stood, keeping a respectable distance from her, and put the letter and envelope in his breast pocket. "After the last one goes, there may be ones from the new crop who'll need a home back here."

No mockingbird sang that day. He could hear Daniela breathe. The air seemed to catch inside her, and she looked away from him, toward his promise kept. Her voice sounded as soft as her hand had felt on his sleeve as she asked, "How was your Sunday?"

"Fine. Father Rodríguez had a small attendance, but he took me on his visits to the very old members and the sick ones who couldn't come to Mass. They're good, faithful people. Their lives have been very hard, but they're hopeful—it's always inspiring." He looked at the flowerbed instead of her and asked, "You're still saying no to everyone?"

"Of course," she said, imitating him. "Sunday's date wasn't nearly as inspirational as your *ángelos*, though one little affirmation from me would've been like heaven to my caller. He's the best of them, the one I should choose." She pulled at her fingers, for once not wearing her rings. "But, he has even more competition," she continued. "A fellow my father recommended to me. I've said Father owns a business. His partner's son, Rubén, is just finishing a college degree, first one in that family. Naturally, they're very proud. My father is too—he thinks I'll make the perfect graduation present."

"His words?"

"Mine. I'm sounding bitter again." She sighed. "Everyone wants me to make a choice and to pick him or his man. No one will be happy until I choose and then only one or two will be happy with my selection."

"At least two, right? Including you?"

"You know I won't. Don't tease me. No, just the man, and any sponsor he had, will celebrate. Then he'll stop pursuing, stop trying. When the prize is in hand, why break your neck? Off I go into his cage, though a well-appointed one to be sure." She traced the edge of the flowerbed with the toe of her shoe. "On Sunday evening, my date parked out front and walked me up the drive. All night he'd fed me lines from his love letters. He knew them all by heart. I checked later to confirm my suspicion; he got them perfect, word for word. As if there was nothing else to say but what he'd written already. It was like listening to the same song on the radio, over and over."

Carlos stayed silent, not daring to hope.

"I realized how phony he was, just playing a game. Figure out how to say all the right things—the right way—and then keep saying them until the prize is won." Daniela grimaced. "Sorry, I'm as repetitious as they are."

"What did you do?"

"I sent him home. He acted hurt and confused, because he thought he'd done everything right. I was angry and ready to punch him in the nose and join *La Madre Benita* and the Sisters of the Divine Providence at Guadalupe. So I stomped around a while out here in the dark and literally tripped over your flowerbed."

"I noticed the viola on the corner looked a little squashed."

"Sorry, that was me." Her voice caught again, and she cleared her throat. "You repeated your words too, but with actions. This was something you hid, that you did for yourself, because you meant what you said. You didn't want me or anyone else to see it."

He straightened the viola and resettled the dirt around its stem. "I was afraid I'd be told to rip them out and put a new crop back here, too. Mrs. Strugatsky doesn't seem to be as sentimental as you." He stood beside her, closer this time.

"I won't tell anyone. I wrote that note to let you know how happy you made me. It was so dark last night, dark in my heart too, and then I stumbled on a shining truth you had kept secret." Daniela touched his sleeve, this time pressing against his skin. "Is your hat in the ring?"

"No," Carlos said, "not that one." He toed a circle in the bare patch where she had laid the letter. "There's our ring." He pantomimed tossing a hat from his bare head into it.

"A private ring and an invisible hat in a secret garden." Her fingers remained on his arm. "If I pick it up, it might show. Will we try to keep it quiet?"

"Why should we?"

"So the rest of the world can stay the same. That one little 'yes' will throw everything into the air."

"I don't want a secret *novia*, and I don't want to be a secret *enamorado*, hidden away and taken out when no one's looking."

"My own words used against me." Her left hand touched his other arm.

"I have feelings about this, too."

"Yes, naturally."

Carlos looked into her dark chocolate eyes. "'Yes?'"

"Yes." She held his gaze.

"You said you never use that word."

She smiled. "I like the way it feels in my mouth when I say it to you."

"Then I hope you say it often to me."

"Yes, I will. Yes, yes." She laughed. "Yes."

He looked around them. "Is everything up in the air?"

"It's still our secret."

"So should we go eat breakfast or roll around in my flowerbed?"

"Yes."

"Which?"

"Let's eat. I'm starved." Daniela stretched upward and kissed him.

Carlos drew back, afraid of how his lips felt to her. She moved her hands to either side of his face and pulled his mouth down to hers. His hands on her shoulder blades descended slowly.

Daniela pressed herself to him as they continued to kiss. Her hands explored the muscles of his back as her breath warmed his skin. He imagined he could feel her heart slamming against his chest. His heart responded in kind, in harmony.

He broke off the kiss, tilting his chin back and gulping air. "I've forgotten Oscar's breathing lessons. He said they'd be useful for this."

She laughed and kissed his throat and the cleft of his chin made deeper by the scar. The scent of her hair and the soap she'd used on her skin made him wish he'd bathed since Saturday night. She held her face to his shirt and inhaled. "You smell so good."

"Sra. Gómez washed it for me."

"No, it's you. Your body smells as good as it looks." She kissed the placket above his heart.

"I'm not too…dark?"

"Are you serious? I love the color of your skin. It's the first thing I noticed about you, how handsome you look in the sunlight." She squeezed his arms hard, bunching his sleeves in her fists, and whispered, "Like rawhide I want to wrap tight around me."

His face became serious. "But my scars—"

"You're dashing—how many times do you need to hear these things? Your kiss felt like two mouths on me. I think I enjoyed it, but with all this talking I need a reminder." Daniela stretched up and kissed him again for long minutes. Her lips brushed his as she said, "I made you miss your breakfast."

"Mrs. Gretzenbach mustn't see me like this."

"She wouldn't notice a thing. She doesn't really see us."

"But I see her. That smoke dribbling out of her nose and mouth, those sad eyes. I couldn't look at her after being ravished by you."

"Is that what I did?"

"You did," he said, smiling against her lips. "You took advantage of me."

"I like kissing you, Carlos." She lowered her heels to the ground, still staring into his eyes.

"You know I'm poor. I can't dress you in fine clothes or jewelry. We won't even have a cage I could lock you in."

She held up her naked fingers. "I won't miss any of it. When do we stop hiding?"

"When we risk getting into trouble every time we see each other," he said.

"I'll tell those other men I've decided to become a bride of Christ. Some of my best friends joined the nunnery. It's a believable lie." She leaned into him again.

He struggled to keep his hands on her sleeves. Daniela's comment about the rawhide made him want to strap his arms around her. "I don't want the *señora* to yell at you for starting your chores late."

"When can we risk this again?"

"Soon. I'll see you at dinner." Carlos pushed his hands into his pockets to keep from touching her. He walked around to the front of the shed, glancing at the window. No one was there.

Daniela sauntered back to the house, her hips taunting him. Smiling, she looked over her shoulder, mouthed, "Yes," and walked inside.

He went into the tool barn and rolled out the lawn mower. He tried to lose himself in the precision of cutting straight, parallel swaths, and the fifteen mysteries commemorated in the rosary, but his mind kept replaying their kisses, the touch of her body, and the passion of her words. He felt much closer to winning the Ten of Cups than having to face another Tower. Carlos prayed he would not mess up. He set the beads on the handlebar, the cross swinging at the end of its pendant, to continue with the Glorious chaplet, feeling reborn himself.

CHAPTER 24

✤

At dinner, Mrs. Gretzenbach spoke to him for the first time. "Felipe, look at this." She removed a small photograph from her apron pocket, holding it by the corner with tobacco-flecked fingernails. Her harsh accent sounded similar to Mrs. Strugatsky's. "I see you two. You are falling in love, no? I miss my love, my Karl. He was so good to me."

Carlos took the sepia picture, careful to touch only the edges. "When was this?"

"In 1914, just before the war that took him from me."

In the photograph, she sat under a tree beside a young man with a picnic spread around them. Karl had light-colored hair, worn long behind his ears, and handsome, serious features. Her heart-shaped face was pretty, her hair dark and curly under a sunbonnet; she'd smiled wide for the camera.

He looked up at the cook to spot any resemblance to that woman.

She nodded at the picture. "You're not supposed to smile, right? Everyone is supposed to look serious. Like Karl there. I couldn't help it. He made me so happy, I smiled all the time." She grinned in a hideous pantomime of the picture, teeth yellow like her nails, fingers of smoke caressing her cheeks and hair.

He passed the photograph to Daniela and said, "He was killed in a war?"

"Yes, in France. It was our war, our country started it. The same bullet finished my life when it ended Karl's. So it's nice to see young people in love—you two make me look at my picture often."

Daniela leaned forward. "Please don't say anything to the Strugatskys. It'll look bad for me, like I was trying to get Felipe hired for the wrong reasons."

"Don't worry. I just wanted you to know how happy I am to see you finally take a chance, Daniela. When Karl and I had that picture made, we'd thought we still had a lifetime together, that there would be thousands of photographs to come. This is the only one I have, taken a day after we got married. Karl carried our only wedding picture to his grave at Verdun."

*

Carlos sat in the shed, sharpening and cleaning the mower in the waning daylight when Daniela's shadow fell over him. He pushed the mower aside and stood up, wiping his hands on a rag. She reached behind her and closed the doors; the only light came from the dim glow underneath them. They bumped into tools and laughed as they banged toward each other.

She walked into his outstretched hand and pressed her breast against his palm. He apologized and slid his hand, now tingling, under her arm and around back, drawing her to him. They kissed hard. Carlos tried to hold still so they wouldn't collide with the sharp and heavy tools arrayed about them. Without the sight of Daniela for distraction, he recalled how Paz kissed, the way her body felt. Daniela's mouth was smaller, her tongue demure; she was far more petite—small and slender in his arms rather than *voluptuosa*. He had to stop kissing her to cease the comparisons. Paz had been right about her curse.

Daniela hugged him, breathing hard. She said, "Please don't make me wait much longer. Let me talk to my parents."

"No—they'll never agree to it. How will you describe me? A *bracero*? A brute with a scarred mouth and a broken nose?"

"Hush." She put her warm fingers on his lips. "I love your mouth. Kiss me with it." She touched the back of his head and rubbed his spine, her fingers not as sure as Paz's.

"I wish I could see you," he whispered.

"That's the problem with living in secret. No one can see us, but we're blind, too. Kiss me again in the sunlight soon." She leaned away and touched his face again. "Sra. Gretzenbach's story made me grateful you told me your feelings as soon as you did."

"None of us has much time."

"That won't be our story, I promise you. Wherever you go, I'll go, too. Even to war." Daniela gave him another long kiss. "I love you, Carlos Moreno."

"Daniela Moreno. How does that sound to you?"

"Like music. Much better than 'Sra. Villalobos.' I have some money saved. I want you to get another trumpet and serenade me."

"Thanks, but I'm not as poor as last week. I'll have to start over again and practice a long time before I'm ready to play for you."

"You can give a performance to announce the birth of our first child—how's that?"

"How much time will that give me?"

"If I get my way it'll be less than a year, so hurry." She opened the door and waved to the back window.

Carlos could see the cook give a small wave back. "Our secret place is no more."

"She won't talk, don't worry. I have a visitor tonight: Rubén, my father's choice. I'll tell him of my departure for the cloister."

"You'll make a lovely bride."

"*Gracias—buenas noches.*"

"I love you." He had to restrain himself from reaching for her again. "I'll be tending my garden again in the morning."

"I'll find you."

*

On Tuesday, Carlos walked past the pawnshop on his way to the Strugatskys but didn't see his trumpet in the window. In his pocket he carried the fifty-five dollars from Paz and his other savings to make sure he'd have enough. He peered through the window to see if the horn had been moved, but couldn't spot it among the shelves of goods. Fists clenched, he cursed whoever had beaten him to the purchase the evening before.

Daniela apparently saw something different in his expression when she met him behind the shed. She said, "What is it?"

He held her face and kissed her. "Nothing. It's silly. I told you about that thief pawning the trumpet my friend Oscar gave to me?"

"Yes?"

"Well, I was hoping to buy it back, but someone got it yesterday."

"We can find another one. I told you I have money saved."

"That one was special." He shook his head. "I said it was silly."

"I could tell you're distracted. You haven't even checked our garden. We're still getting some new growth."

He glanced at the flowerbed. In the center of the bed, a lump of brown vegetation with four limp stems had sprouted within the ring he'd drawn. Carlos frowned and knelt. He touched the leathery strands and rubbed his fingers over the coarse base: rawhide strings and burlap. He looked up at Daniela's wide smile before digging all around the sack, feeling familiar, tubular contours within it. He unearthed the gift, his breath ragged as tears rolled down his cheeks. Carlos moaned softly as he withdrew the polished trumpet. The brass felt warm and alive in his hands, as if nature just had given birth to it.

He hugged Daniela tight against him, crying unselfconsciously. He kissed the top of her head and all over her face. "Thank you for this. I've never received a better present." He remembered his earlier ranting as he stood outside the pawn shop and fought to control his tears.

"What is it? You don't sound happy."

"I cursed whoever bought the trumpet for having the luck to get to it before me. I cursed you."

"It's all right. I would've done the same thing, except maybe I'd have thrown a rock through the window, too." She shook her head. "You would've thought *La Madre Benita* and the nuns had taught me better than that."

He choked out a laugh as his tears subsided. "You learned a few things outside of school. Show me again." He bent down and pressed his salty mouth to hers. The *embouchure* felt perfect.

She rested her face against his chest and kissed his heart. She held him for a while, looking up at his face. "You're killing me. I can't wait any longer—let me take you to meet my parents tonight. They live above their store on Commerce Street. It's on your way home. The Strugatskys are planning an evening with Morris so I won't be missed."

"Are you sure your parents will approve of me?"

"When they see how in love we are, how happy you make me, how could they not?"

"Don't you want to give them some warning, a day or two?"

"No, then there'll be endless questions and speculation. Better to do it this way. We need to decide whether to marry in your *misión* or Guadalupe. Your friend, the priest, sounds very nice. Ours is conservative. He might want to see us courting under my mother's nose for a year before he consents to marry us."

"You don't feel like we're rushing into this?"

"I don't feel like we're going fast enough." She laughed. "I don't know what's gotten into me. The kind of thoughts I'm having about you should wait until I'm your wife." The color rose in her cheeks but she continued to hold his gaze.

He felt his body respond to Daniela's attention and his own thoughts. His only regret was that he'd ever given in to Paz— it still was impossible not to make comparisons. The sooner he could bury those memories, he decided, the better. "All right, we'll do it tonight."

CHAPTER 25

☙

As the sun set, Daniela stepped outside wearing a lemon-yellow blouse with short sleeves and a demure neckline and a long ocher skirt with matching shoes. "It's time to become a future son-in-law. Are you ready?"

"Let's go." Carlos held her hand and his trumpet as they set out, not caring who saw them or what anyone thought.

The air felt perfect, the warmth tempered by a pleasant breeze, probably the last mild day before summer humidity and heat would suffocate the city. He tried to talk of inconsequential things as they walked. Daniela seemed to share his nervousness; she laughed too much at his little jokes and held his hand too tight. He wanted to know if she had doubts about this visit. Maybe she'd want to keep to the secret a little longer. He'd quickly agree to that if she said as much. At the same time, though, he wanted them to run headlong toward the new life he desired with her, so he didn't ask.

They speculated about the possible reasons for the huge mixed-race crowd on Congress Street as they approached from the west. Every face looked away from them, toward the business district of *El Segundo Barrio*. Men and women craned their necks and tried to push closer to the object of their attention. Blended in with their voices was another sound. Carlos could swear it was music.

He tapped the shoulder of a *tejano* vendor selling fruit juices and other refreshments and asked what was happening.

"*La migra*—they killed a priest an hour ago."

Several others joined the conversation. Apparently, Immigration agents, assisted by local police and rangers, had ambushed a priest and shot him in the back when he tried to run. The man was rumored to be one of those helping *repatriados* escape. Crowds had gathered to protest the violence, shaking fists and throwing garbage as the patrol cars roared through the *barrio* with the body. The lawmen had left a wide puddle of the man's blood on the street.

Fear and rage paralyzed Carlos as he pictured Pedro or one of his other friends shot dead, or, worse, being tortured for information before a jail-cell execution.

Daniela said to the vendor, "What's up ahead?"

"Our people, dozens of them. They've barricaded Congress and the surrounding streets—it's beautiful."

She asked if she and Carlos could get through.

"They don't want people hurt. It's just them against the law. They're daring the police and *la migra* to come for them."

Daniela pulled on Carlos' arm. "My parents—I need to make sure they're all right."

"I've got to go to the mission and find out who was shot."

Another man pointed at Carlos' trumpet. "They did let some of the bands in to play for them."

Over the crowd noise was the faint crescendo of a horn leading a heroic *mariachi* ballad. It was just like Oscar to stir things up by supporting this romantic lost cause.

"Come on," Daniela said, tugging his arm again. She didn't wait for his reply, but pushed northward up to Commerce Street, taking him with her. The scene looked identical on that thoroughfare, a massive crowd watching the barriers. Distant sirens redirected some attention to the west. Daniela maneuvered through the onlookers, elbowing and shoving.

Carlos yelled, "Let me." He moved in front of her and cleared a wide path, reaching the obstruction of mattresses, wagons, boxes, and wood and metal scraps that cordoned the street. Sharpened stakes faced outward toward him and jutted from the top of the six-foot-high palisade. Looking through the many gaps in the fortress, he could see *tejanos* standing guard with axes, *machetes*, and railroad hammers. He could hear a few bands more clearly, including Oscar's. He called to one of the guards, "We need to get in. We're musicians." He held up the trumpet.

"No, don't you hear the police? We'll have a war any minute."

"They have guns," Daniela shouted. "You'll all be killed."

"Maybe, but we'll take some of them to hell with us. That's the only way we'll leave our home."

Carlos looked up at the second stories of the buildings behind the wall. Faces peered down from nearly every window. He pointed them out to Daniela. "Lots of shopkeepers and their families still inside. Your parents are probably all right."

"I have to know. Please!" She searched his face.

"I'll get you in," he said and pulled her away from the barricade. "But you might get a little dirty."

*

When the sewer water rose above Daniela's shoe tops, Carlos offered to carry her. He rolled up his pant legs and lifted her with ease. He tried to tell her why he was able to navigate underground, but the sluice and echoes made conversation difficult. She nestled against him, cradling his trumpet, as he carried her through the tunnels. When the stench appeared to overwhelm Daniela, she pressed her face against his shirt, hot breath over his heart.

He hurtled troughs of effluent and heaps of waste illuminated by waning light through the storm drains. Mindful of rats, Carlos stayed away from the slime-covered walls and putrid corners. She'd estimated her parents' store was a few hundred yards from the palisade, so he counted his strides and set her down near a ladder. "We'll come up in an alley south of Commerce," he said in her ear. "The shop shouldn't be too far away. Let me go first in case there's trouble." He took the trumpet so she wouldn't have to climb with that burden. As he grasped the rungs, he leaned close to her again. "Don't stand under me. God alone knows what'll be dripping off my sandals."

"Memorable last words." Daniela hugged him and kissed his mouth. "You're so romantic. Bring me back down here on all of our anniversaries."

Carlos ascended, the coarse metal tubing wet and cold in his hand. He tucked the trumpet under his arm and secured his grip. At the top, he pushed upward with his palm, moving aside the heavy manhole cover. The sky looked dark blue as the daylight faded, and he spotted the North Star. He'd brought them up in an undefended path between the major streets. Across the road to the north and two blocks south, he saw men pacing in alleys beside their barriers that helped to isolate Commerce and Congress from the rest of Houston. He could hear Oscar's band south of him, on Congress. If not for Jorge, he'd probably be with them…and know nothing of Daniela. The sirens sounded close and seemed to come from all around, echoing off the buildings and pavement strewn with trash, overwhelming the sounds of the crowds beyond the makeshift walls and competing with the *mariachi* bands on the two main thoroughfares.

He rose to street level, called down to Daniela that it was safe, and soon helped her to her feet. He left the manhole uncovered in case they needed to escape. She took the lead and scampered to the street corner. Some of the armed *tejanos* in the barricaded alley north of Commerce shouted at them to get back inside. Looking west, Carlos could see the palisade they'd gone under. Another barrier sat a quarter-mile to the east, with *El Mariachi De León de Veracruz* playing for the men guarding that end of the street. Rebels paced beside their flimsy forts, awaiting the professionals coming with guns and—for the survivors—deportation trucks.

Daniela led him one block east and stared through the plate-glass window of a dry goods shop. "I expected their place to be ransacked. The barrels and tables are gone and the tools look picked over, but—" She quieted when the sirens ceased and were replaced by megaphone-amplified threats bellowed by the police. The bands played louder and the men at the barricades jeered.

She opened a door next to the store, revealing a narrow stairwell in utter darkness. "Come inside, you'll be safer in here. I won't be too long."

He closed the door behind them and listened to her climb the stairs, her footsteps echoing in the cool black space. The rebels countered the lawmen with profane shouts. Carlos was relieved she didn't want to introduce him under such circumstances.

She knocked at the door on the landing and said, "Father? It's Daniela." She unlocked the door and went in, leaving it ajar and brightening the upper stairs. Her voice drifted down into the confine of wood and brick. "You're both all right?"

A man said, "We're fine. The young men requested politely and didn't take more than they asked for." His accent sounded similar to Daniela's but he didn't speak as precisely.

"But they stole hundreds of dollars from you."

"We gave them what they wanted, a good business decision. If they survive the police, maybe they won't loot and burn our place, killing us or costing us thousands."

A woman's voice, as melodic as Daniela's, asked, "How did you get through?"

"They let me pass, Mother."

Her father said, "What's that smell? Daughter, what are you tracking into the house?"

Daniela's voice changed, becoming as defensive as a scolded teenager. She said, "It's nothing. I must have stepped in—"

"Your shoes, my God, your feet…did you come through the sewers, child?"

The volume of threats and curses and music increased outside.

"I had to make sure you were all right. I was so worried about you."

"How did you manage it?"

"There was some daylight still, Father. It was easy really. I—"

"Nonsense. What's going on?"

Carlos left the trumpet on the bottom stair and trotted up, his intentionally heavy footfalls halting the interrogation above him. He rolled down the cuffs of his pants, though his feet and sandals looked more disgusting than his calves. Rapping on the wood frame, he stepped into the light and filled the doorway.

Daniela's voice quavered as she said, "This is Carlos Moreno. A friend."

"Good evening, Sr. Domenica." Carlos then nodded to Daniela's mother and said, "Good evening, señora."

Her father folded his wiry tan arms against his starched dress shirt and neat tie. He appraised Carlos through silver-framed glasses, his lips sneering. The electric lights from several fringed lamps gleamed off his head, which was almost bald.

Daniela's mother wore her hair in a tight bun, the black going to silver in strands like shooting stars. She concealed her figure behind a heavy apron and blousy smock dress and pulled at her fingers as her gaze swiveled from Carlos to her husband and daughter.

Carlos glanced down at his feet. "For fear of tracking in more of the same, I'll just stand here."

"No," Daniela said, kicking off her shoes. "I'll get some towels." She crossed into the adjoining kitchen and began to open drawers.

Her mother followed, saying, "There's a rag pile under the sink."

After cleaning his feet and ankles and washing his hands, he crossed the small sitting room barefoot to greet her father. "Sr. Domenica, I'm sorry for the mess and for this surprise." Her father considered his proffered hand a moment before grasping it. Carlos let his fingers get squeezed tight. He looked the man in the eye, seeing his dark reflection in the glasses, the scars darker still.

Her father crossed his arms again. "Surprise?"

"Yes, *señor*. With the barricades and the police, this is not the best time to meet—"

"How do you know my daughter?"

Two open windows faced Commerce. Carlos glanced at the gentle billowing of the curtains as Spanish curses, chants of defiance, the steady rap of metal on metal, and *mariachi baladas* overwhelmed the hostile warnings of the lawmen.

He said, "We met while she was walking the baby she cares for, at a park near the Mexican Presbyterian Church. Excuse me, please." He took two steps toward Daniela's mother and gently extended his fingers. "It's very nice to meet you, Sra. Domenica. Again, I'm sorry for the bother." She touched him with a thumb and forefinger, like a pincer, and slid her hands into her apron pockets. Carlos returned to stand in front of the master of the house.

Sr. Domenica said, "You were loitering in the park on a workday?"

"I was working for the city, doing maintenance."

"'*Mantenimiento.*'" He mimicked Carlos' accent. "Is that how you come to know the sewers?"

"Yes, *señor*." Explaining his rescue work, he decided, was more problematic than lying.

"Is that what you still do?"

"Your daughter was kind enough to get me a position with her employer." He smiled at Daniela.

She swayed slightly, watching her father and pulling on her fingers. She cleared her throat and said, "Let's all sit. Can I get anyone water or tea?"

Her father said, "There's no need to be a maid in your own home. He sat in a straight-back chair and called to his wife, "Camelia, bring us something to drink."

Daniela led Carlos to the loveseat on the opposite side of a low table. Her mother brought a serving tray with cups of lukewarm tea. She seated herself in the other hardwood chair, flanking the loveseat.

Carlos sipped from his teacup and set it in the saucer with a fragile clink. Metal pounded on metal outside and the volume of chants rose above the music.

"Tell us about yourself, Carlos," Daniela's father said.

"I was born south of Ciudad Juárez in 1908—"

"A child of our revolution." He nodded toward the windows. "That one was a little more ambitious than tonight's uprising."

"We moved to El Paso del Norte in 1911 during *la Tormenta* and headed east. My father and mother worked very hard on farms and for the railroads. She died in childbirth."

"I'm sorry to hear that. Is your father living here?"

"No, *señor*. He was leaving for Galveston when I last saw him."

"Brothers or sisters?"

"None survived very long. My youngest brother didn't live through that final childbirth either." He nodded as Camelia made sympathetic sounds.

"A hard life. A life of poverty and want."

"Yes, but they taught me to work hard, too."

"I'm sure you have. You don't get muscles like that doing accounting or running a store. You've also lived hard. Did you get those scars in a brawl or from the cops?"

Daniela stood up, shouting, "Father, please!" The chants and rhythmic pounding continued, as did the bullhorn invectives.

"Sit down, daughter. Listen and be quiet. Go on, Carlos, tell us."

"A thief broke into my room and did this."

"Uh huh. What are your prospects?"

"*Señor?*"

"You didn't just happen to be on hand to help my daughter through the sewer—you were traveling as a couple. You ran up the stairs to save her from her ridiculous lie. You have feelings for her."

"*Sí*—"

"It's clear what this 'surprise' visit was meant to be: Daniela wants my, our, approval for a marriage. I want to know how you'll earn enough to support a family."

"I'm saving money and have more than enough to pay the rent every month."

"And if you lose this job?" He held up his hand. "I know you're a hard worker, but times are hard, too, and sometimes things happen."

"I have a good friend with a railroad. He got me an earlier job. I assist at *Misión Católica*. The priests there could help me find work."

"Doing '*mantenimiento*'?"

"Yes, *señor*, probably."

The older man stood up and lifted a newspaper from a stack on his end table. He held it out to Carlos. Sr. Domenica raised his voice to be heard over the racket outside. "Please read the Houston *Chronicle* headline to me."

"Headline?"

Daniela reached for the newspaper, but her father held it away. Her flushed face began to perspire. She said, "Please don't!"

"The big type on the paper, Carlos. Please read it to us. Tell us the most important news of the day." He draped the paper over Carlos' leg. The tempo and intensity of the rhythmic pounding outside increased.

Carlos stared down at the newspaper as if it had become a coral snake. He could tell it was upside down, but nothing more. "I cannot, *señor*, I'm sorry."

"Well, don't feel bad—many cannot read English. My daughter was fortunate enough to go to Our Lady of Guadalupe School, but you've had a life on the run." He picked up the other two papers. "How about *El Tecolote?*" He tossed the paper into Carlos' lap. "Or *Gaceta Mexicana?*" The final paper thumped hard above Carlos' groin as Daniela shouted for her father to stop.

On Commerce, the taunting sounded maniacal, as if the *tejanos* were beating down their own walls in fury. Still, Carlos could hear Daniela crying beside him. "I'm sorry," he whispered. "No."

"Did the thief leave you blind, Carlos Moreno?" He stretched his name broadly.

"Stop this!" Daniela stood up again, face scarlet, her fist slapping into her palm.

"Well, Carlos?"

"I can't read." He slid his hands under the papers and laid them on the table that separated him from Sr. Domenica. He glanced up at Daniela and watched her tears as she squeezed her eyes shut.

"I guessed you cannot, Carlos," her father said, almost yelling to be heard. "I just wanted you to say it in front of my good-hearted daughter. You seem like a nice enough fellow. I'm sure you work hard. But, you aren't for her." He lifted the newspapers. "I was past thirty before *Gaceta Mexicana* made sense to me. I was forty, an old man, before I could read the English paper front to back. Illiteracy kept me down, kept my family down. Daniela and her future family deserve better— she has many educated Spaniards to choose from."

Carlos flinched at the Spaniard remark. Even if he could read, he was too dark to be accepted. "Yes, *señor,* I understand." He moved unsteadily to the door. He held the jamb to keep his balance and called, "Daniela, I'll wait downstairs to get you home safely."

She started toward him, but her father grasped her wrist. He said, "I'll do that, thank you. *Buenas noches.*"

Carlos nodded to her parents. He slid into his filthy sandals and walked down the stairs, putting his hands on the brick walls to steady himself. He heard Daniela crying and shouting and her father's tone, loud but deadly calm.

Their voices ceased when the first police car rammed the barricade on Commerce where Daniela and Carlos had stood. The crashing and screaming was quickly duplicated at other barriers. Carlos peeked through the doorway. The sedan had backed up and now slammed through the palisade, the headlamps shattering and windshield cracking. Gun smoke poured from the side windows and *tejanos* with raised axes and clubs toppled backward. Police officers emerged from all four car doors, still shooting. The other young men fell beside the breach.

Over the gunshots and cries at the other barricades, he heard Daniela shout, "You can't make him go out there."

Carlos weighed the risk of the unfolding mayhem against another confrontation with her father. He watched the police drag bodies to the sidewalk and begin to dismantle the palisade. They threw scrap lumber and mattresses beside the stacked-up corpses. Thinking of Oscar and the other musicians, he said a prayer for their safety.

Daniela screamed again. Her pleading sounded hysterical. Not waiting to see what her father had in mind for him, Carlos swung the door wide and bolted for the alley. Too late, he remembered his trumpet when he reached the street corner, but it was the sound of another Spanish voice begging and crying that made him pause.

In the alley to the north, that barrier remained intact. Two *tejanos* had a laborer in ragged denims facedown on the street. For some reason, they hacked and clubbed the pleading man with a crowbar and hammer.

Carlos ran back across Commerce and up the barricaded alley. He yelled, "Police coming up the street!"

The men paused in their butchering. One bellowed, "This one's a filthy spy."

Carlos said, "I'll finish him for you." He yanked the crowbar from the man and knocked the hammer from the other's hand. With the bloody iron tip pointed toward their startled faces, he shouted, "Hurry now—run!" He helped push them over the barricade.

When he turned the wounded man over, his first thought was that he should've run as well. The long tan face was streaked with blood but still unmistakable. Dark eyes from the King of Swords stared at him. Donati.

"Moreno." The ranger spastically clawed under his work shirt, groping at his hip. He said in Spanish, "Of course you're one of them...of course." The pale whites showed as his eyelids slid shut and his hand went limp.

Carlos hefted *el rinche* and felt the man's blood soak his hands and clothes as he carried him to Commerce. So long as Donati bled, Carlos knew he was alive. He shouted in English, "This ranger's hurt."

An officer up the street dropped plywood onto the pile on the sidewalk. He drew his gun and shouted to his partners, "It's a trap—they're Mexicans. You there! Stop!" He fired.

The ranger's left leg jerked and both legs swung on Carlos' arm.

Daniela screamed his name from the second floor window as he dashed across Commerce, drawing fire from both ends of the street. A policeman yelled, "Goddammit, Pete, you're shooting at us!"

Carlos lowered the ranger into the manhole. He had to let Donati drop the last few feet and then mounted the ladder. He pulled the metal cover over his head as bullets ricocheted on the pavement above him.

Carrying Daniela through the sewers at dusk had been romantic in an earthy way. Running with Donati slung over his shoulder was terrifying in the scant light from the grates and the sounds of the police splashing after him. He kept thinking he should leave the ranger somewhere, but he knew the police would kill Donati before getting close enough to identify him. He didn't want his own soul damned by enabling the man's murder.

Carlos outpaced the weak flashlight beams and furious curses as he carted the lawman north, under the remnants of the barricades, and then east. He apologized whenever the ranger's leg struck a corner or they went under a fall of wastewater. His progress slowed as he worked his way along by memory and moonlight. If Donati survived he would owe his life to Pedro and the other mission priests who had taught Carlos the routes beneath the city. One of those priests might have been executed by Donati earlier that night.

At another ladder, he propped the wounded man against a lichen-covered wall, climbed up, and pushed aside the heavy lid. The Mexican Clinic was just down the street. Sirens wailed from several blocks south. He expected to see some survivors from the fall of the barricades, but the street was empty of people. He descended again to get *el rinche*.

*

By the time Carlos left the clinic, the first of the looters had emerged. With all the police occupied to the south with the rebels, men with a different goal dashed from side streets. They spread out, armed like their revolution-minded peers with hammers and hatchets. The thieves were utterly silent until they began to smash windows, pound through doors, and raid shops up and down the sidewalks. They stayed in each store only a minute or two and ran from target to target, their sacks expanding steadily.

Jorge Flores vaulted from a shattered jewelry store window, a cloth bag swinging from one hand. Carlos was relieved he didn't see Paz among the looters and then felt shame that he'd thought of her, still hoping for her reform. He shouted Jorge's name.

Swinging around, the thief gaped. "Your timing is always bad, my friend," he yelled back before sprinting down the street, looking for other unspoiled opportunities.

The jeweler ran outside, wearing a dressing gown and pointing a revolver. He fired again and again as the looters fled. The fourth shot caused Jorge to stagger. The sixth shot pitched the thief onto his face. The sack flew from his hand. Bracelets, rings, and loose gems clattered on the street, bouncing toward a storm drain. Jorge lay still as the jeweler kicked him and retrieved the merchandise that had not been lost within the city's bowels.

Jorge's fellow looters vanished as they'd come, without a sound. Carlos returned his gaze to Jorge and blamed himself for the thief being killed—the second man shot that night because of him. The jeweler rapped Jorge's head with his toe and spit on him. Carlos trotted back inside the Mexican Clinic to call for a doctor, knowing he was too late. He felt like the angel of death.

*

He soon took to the sewers again. Even with the possibility of police down below, the streets seemed far more dangerous. When the ranger regained consciousness, he would redouble his manhunt. Carlos could only hope that Donati's recovery was slow.

The constant rush of water and the unrelieved stink overwhelmed his other senses as he shuffled west, toward the Anglo neighborhoods, where few would guess to look for him. He braced for the touch of flashlight beams or echoed gunshots. In some places the maze became a confusion of construction where an apparent pedestrian tunnel system was forcing the sewer to be dug deeper.

His memory continually replayed the shameful encounter with Daniela's parents. He experienced it just as he had hours before, with panic-sweat and racing heart. Daniela had regarded him with such an expression of pain and shame; then she couldn't bear to look at him at all, no doubt feeling betrayed.

He finally ascended a ladder and then didn't stop running until his feet touched the cool grass of the Strugatskys' backyard. The shed doors opened at his touch and shut without a sound on the hinges he'd oiled. As he lay on the swept concrete, he imagined a final, tearful goodbye with Daniela. Another lost love, another Tower after all. He'd have to start over yet again. When he said a quick prayer, though, it was for Daniela to make a wise choice among her legitimate suitors. For her to find the lasting happiness, the promise of the Ten of Cups, that had just eluded him, maybe forever. Carlos curled on his side and willed himself to sleep.

CHAPTER 26

Daniela walked out the back door, a sleepless night showing under her eyes, as Carlos dried his face and hands beside the spigot. Faded blood had soaked into his shirt and slacks in huge spatters; he had rubbed a towel hard against his skin to dislodge crusty red smears. She looked him over as if not believing he was there. "No," he lied, "I'm not hurt."

She cried out and ran to him, hugging his damp neck and kissing him. "I was afraid you weren't coming back. Seeing the police shoot at you scared me to death, worse than—"

"It's all right." He stepped back, afraid of Donati's blood touching her.

"No, it's not. I'm so sorry about what Father did. Please forgive me. I didn't know. I didn't understand."

"You did nothing wrong." Carlos kept her at arm's length, the hourglass of her ribs and waist and hips against his hands. He took in her scent, her voice, memorizing all of her. "Your father's right. You deserve an educated man who'll make a good life for you and your children. I'm sure Rubén and the other Spaniards will welcome you back from the convent."

"Stop talking like that." Daniela put her hand on his mouth.

He kissed her warm fingertips. "I'm just stalling, so I don't have to say goodbye."

"Don't ever use that word with me. I want you—and I'll have you—no matter what they say."

"Do you mean—"

"Yes."

Tears sprang to Carlos' eyes as he embraced her, forgetting the rose-colored stains on his clothes. Her mouth warmed his until their smiles broadened too much to kiss.

She said, "It's not even eight o'clock. When did you get here?"

"I spent the night in the shed, afraid to go home. The man I saved, he's the Texas Ranger I told you about."

Her fist closed over the front of his shirt. "Why did you save Donati? He wants to kill you."

"It all happened so fast. I saw two rebels hacking an unarmed man to death, and I had to stop them."

"I hope you left him in the sewers."

"I took him to the clinic. After I'd started, I couldn't stop saving him. That would've been a mortal sin."

Daniela gave his shirtfront a little shake before letting go. "You're a much better person than I am. Won't he still come after you?"

"He'll look for me as soon as he can. In his condition, he might send others—I need to leave town."

"You're not leaving without me. Do I have time to pack anything?"

"I don't know. They could be here in a minute or never figure it out. But—"

"Give me just half of that minute." Daniela dashed into the house.

He tapped his fingers against his slacks with nervous excitement but also fear, for her safety now as well as his. He needed advice about many things. Hopefully Pedro or one of the others would be alive at the mission, and not with a squad of policemen keeping them company.

Sra. Gretzenbach opened the back door. "You're coming in for breakfast, Felipe?"

"No, thank you."

"What happened to your clothes? You look like you've been to war."

"I still am. How long did your country fight?"

"About five years. We lost."

Daniela wriggled past the cook. She'd changed into a short-skirted summer dress of green and white with red and gold piping. His trumpet gleamed in her hand.

He said, "I hope we have that long at least. *Adiós.*"

Carlos took off at a trot, holding Daniela's hand and clutching his trumpet. He returned his gaze to her repeatedly as they ran up the street, her graceful collarbones, the hint of cleavage. Compared with her usual prim outfits, she was almost naked beside him.

As they approached the end of Poplar, he pulled up short. Someone had tracked him to his hideout. He muttered her name aloud, "Paz."

She'd dressed very conservatively: high-necked gray blouse, a concealing camisole beneath, and an ankle-length skirt that almost hid the dove-colored shoes with high heels. With black hair piled expertly and makeup applied with equal care, she was a vision. Each time Carlos saw her, she looked even more beautiful and less desirable.

As Paz approached them, he whispered to Daniela, "She's the big mistake I told you about."

"She's gorgeous. I hope you think you're making as big a mistake with me."

Carlos called, "I didn't know I was missing my shadow until you showed up."

"You're missing a lot. I trailed you here on Monday morning to see if this was where you had your *novia.*" Paz stopped a few feet from them and glanced at Carlos' gore-stained clothes. She then turned her full attention to Daniela and looked her over. "So this is the one I lost to."

"It wasn't a race," he said.

"Life is a race, whether you want to be the first to get something—someone—or need to outrun a bullet. You two look like you're racing somewhere."

"I'm sorry about Jorge. I saw him die." He said to Daniela, "Looting near the clinic last night. He'd robbed a jewelry store. The owner shot him in the back."

Paz said, "His friends told me. Life is a race—you see?" She stared at Daniela, hands on hips. "I claimed him first."

He said, "There's no time for this. The police might be on the way. You don't want to be seen with me."

"I've been dodging the police all my life; they're predictable. Should I be scared of you, Carlos? Your nature is clear, too. What danger am I in?"

Daniela pulled back her fist and punched Paz in the mouth. The woman fell hard, head bouncing on the pavement, gray sleeves outstretched, dazed as a bird that had flown into a window. Daniela squeezed her knuckles and groaned, "*¡Santa María!* That always hurts."

He looked down at Paz, the thief dressed as a lady, lying on the oil-spotted road with blood on her lips, and then at Daniela, the Catholic school graduate in the saucy outfit rubbing her swollen hand. He said, "Why did you do that?"

"She's lucky I didn't club her with your trumpet. Let's go, before she comes to." She grabbed his hand and sprinted a few blocks to the business district where she pulled him into the pristine alley behind a row of boutiques. Daniela kissed him hard and pressed herself against him. "You feel how fast my heart's beating?"

"You keep surprising me. I forgot about the fistfights with your sisters."

"Yes—I like to show you new parts of me." She grinned and put her left hand, pink and puffy, against her chest. "Not the usual picture of the blushing bride, is it?" She laughed and then tried to compose her face. "Sorry I'm so giddy. Last night I thought I'd lost you forever. Now I'm running away with you, fleeing the law, and having fistfights with the *demimonde*."

"The what?"

"It's French—a loose woman, *una sucia*." She looked him over. "We need to go back into the sewers. If any Anglos see you like this, they'll think you butchered a rich family." She pointed at a manhole cover near her feet and said, "After you, *señor*."

*

Carlos brought them back up in a trash-strewn alley, wet filth smeared on their legs and shoes. He led Daniela through the quiet backstreets to the block behind the mission where a hand-pump perched in the bare clay soil. She took off her shoes and pulled down tan stockings, grimacing as slime separated from the porous barrier over her tan skin. He crouched and rocked the pump handle and tried not to stare at her lithe, bare legs. She held his trumpet as she stuck one calf under the stream and drew in her breath as cold water sluiced over her leg. Carlos washed her smooth, muscular calves and small feet, delicately boned and rough-soled. He scrubbed her shoes and began to rise.

"Do the first one again," she said. "You might've missed some." Her head rolled back as he massaged her instep. "And the right one again, just to be sure." Finally, she tapped his thigh with her wet toes. "Your turn, my love." Her skirt rode well above her knees as she squatted beside the pump, grinning up at him.

"Oh," she said, "the cold water feels good on my hand." She flexed her swollen fingers under the flow, then cleaned his sandals and took his suspended foot between her hands and scrubbed away clots of sewage. The water ran off and formed a number of small streams. Not quite the picture of *la doncella* under the Star, but close. As she cleaned his other foot, the back door opened.

"Excuse me," Pedro intoned, "but the Primitive Baptists conduct their foot washings in the Fifth Ward." He walked toward them, his broad smile lifting his beard. "*Señorita*, you are not authorized by the Mother Church to perform baptisms, so please explain what you're doing with this man's leg."

She set Carlos' foot onto his sopping sandal. "Sorry, Father, I'm just helping Sr. Moreno clean off after a long journey."

Pedro shook her wet hand and traded introductions. "It's a pleasure to meet you, Daniela Domenica. Please come in. I'll get some towels."

They followed the priest into a musty room of exposed brick and wiped their shoes on a dingy mat. Two walls were cluttered with cans of paint, loose boards, electrical wires, and other building supplies. A dim light bulb swung overhead; the back door was left ajar to let in the sunshine and fresh air. Pedro handed over some thin towels and turned away while Daniela rubbed her bare legs.

Carlos explained the bloodstains on his clothes, leaving out the humiliation that preceded his rescue of Donati. He said, "Father, the riot that started it all—who was shot?"

"Father Perez. He's dead." He crossed himself, head hung low.

Carlos made a cross as well. "I'm sorry. He'd escaped from danger before."

"Not a chance this time—they were waiting in ambush. A lawman must've recognized him—maybe the one Perez ran from on the night of your injuries."

Daniela rested a hand on his arm. "You were there when it happened?"

Pedro quickly swiped a finger across his eye. "He drew them away from my position and some of the deputies fired. The places the bullets hit him...I've seen men die. I know the look of it. He's a martyr." He withdrew his rosary and clutched the cross. "So is the man we had inside the police department, a janitor named Hidalgo. He took his own life yesterday, damned his immortal soul to keep the secret."

Carlos said, "I'm afraid I sacrificed myself too, when I saved Donati. Since he knows I'm here, I have to leave."

"Where will you go?"

"Remember Sr. Webster in Casson gave us a note if we ever wanted jobs?"

"I think I've still got it. *Un momento*." He left through a door in the opposite wall.

Daniela rubbed Carlos' back. "I'm sorry about the men you worked with. I didn't know you were such a hero."

"Just an apprentice." He tugged at his shirt. "This blood is from the one who helped to murder the real heroes. He's the only one I know I saved."

They held each other until Pedro returned with the stationery. The priest said, "All it says is, 'OK—Tom.'"

He passed it to Carlos, who glanced at the message he couldn't read and handed the note to Daniela, saying, "I'll hate doing farm work again, but I don't know of a better place to go."

"My sisters in Corpus Christi," Daniela said. "They'll set us up. I've got train fare."

Pedro shook his head. "They might be watching the bus terminals and train depots, even if not many *tejanos* can afford tickets. The usual ones riding trains these days are *los pobres* we failed to save."

Carlos said, "You're in danger, too. Come with us to Casson. Maybe they can use a priest at the workers' *colonia*."

"Being cast into the wilderness is a respectable biblical punishment—and preferable to stoning—but Father Soto and I will see how we can carry on here."

Carlos said to Daniela, "Are you sure you want to go into the wilderness with me?"

"Not as an unmarried woman. I won't scandalize Father Rodríguez."

The priest smiled. "We need a wedding to cheer things up. Normally, of course, I'd hold the ceremony during Mass tonight, but your circumstances are...special. Let's just do the service in here."

Carlos felt the hot sun on his back from the open backdoor. He looked down at the side-by-side shadows he and Daniela made on the floor as Pedro left the room again. He asked, "You're absolutely sure?"

"Only about you." She hugged him hard.

Their shadows now overlapped entirely, forming something new. He closed his eyes and rocked her against him. "Isn't it proper that I ask you to marry me?"

"So ask me." Her arms cinched tighter around him.

"Daniela, will you choose me for your husband?"

"Yes, Carlos. But only if you'll have me as your wife."

"All right, you two," Pedro said, with Father Soto in tow. "Let's do this before you get into trouble. Well, deeper trouble." He introduced Daniela to the other priest, opened a book, and flipped through a few sections. "Now, stand beside each other again and face me." He recited, "Carlos Moreno and Daniela Domenica, you have come together in this church so that the Lord may seal and strengthen your love in the presence of the Church's minister and this community," he said, indicating Father Soto. "Carlos, have you come freely and without reservation to give yourself to Daniela and will you lovingly accept children from God if this be God's plan?"

"I have and I will."

"Daniela—"

"Yes!"

The priest chuckled as he repositioned them, facing one another. "Since it is your intention to enter into marriage, join your right hands and declare your consent before God and His Church. Carlos, do you promise to have and to hold Daniela, from this day forward, for better, for worse, for richer, for poorer, in sickness and in health, until death do you part?"

"I do." Carlos stared into Daniela's eyes.

"Daniela, do you promise to have and to hold Carlos—"

"I do, from this day forward."

"God's blessing is bestowed on your decision. What God has joined, men and women must not divide." He closed his book. "Carlos, you may kiss your bride."

Carlos drew Daniela toward him, released her hand, and wrapped his arms around her. He touched his mouth to hers with the tenderness that he prayed would mark all of their moments together. He kissed her cheeks and prayed, too, that their lives would be free of the chaos that had marred the past twelve hours. He tasted saltwater and drew back.

Daniela cried as she laughed. "You've made me so happy," she whispered.

The priests left the room, blinking back tears. Carlos and Daniela sat on the floor, legs outstretched, fingers interlaced, their heads resting against one another, saying nothing. Pedro returned with two apples and cups of water. "Sorry I can't offer a better reception."

Carlos said, "After giving us God's blessing and your sanctuary, Father, this is more than generous. *Gracias.*"

"I hope it doesn't seem too biblical, what with your impending exile."

Daniela bit deeply into the apple and wiped a trail of juice from her chin. "Should we get started or spend the night somewhere in Houston?"

"The *misión* may be the safest place for you. I'm sorry you can't share the same room, but it's only for the night. Some lessons from the Tree of Knowledge will have to wait until you're in the wilderness."

"It'll do for tonight—thanks again," Carlos said. He finished his apple, its tartness reminding him how thirsty he was. The water eased down his parched throat.

Pedro said, "Good. I'll prepare the rooms and get you a clean outfit."

She said, "Any idea how I can get my clothes and things from the Strugatskys?"

"If the police traced Carlos to Poplar Street, we don't want to lead them here. Same with Carlos' place. I have a friend who works as a handyman a few blocks from Poplar. He can watch the house and send anything they might throw out, but that's about all."

Carlos said, "I'd like to get word to Sra. Gómez that I'm sorry if the police cause her any trouble and that I appreciate her kindness."

Pedro handed over some folded sheets of paper and a battered fountain pen from his pocket. Carlos shook his head with a sheepish smile, and said, "For the second time in two days, I have to admit my ignorance. Sorry, Father, I can't read or write."

"My gracious, I'm the one who should apologize. I didn't mean to embarrass you. When you brought Daniela's envelope to me, complaining about the legibility, I thought you just needed glasses."

"I'm sorry for the deception."

She said, "When I gave you those directions, how did you find your way?"

"I fooled Oscar. He knew I wasn't familiar with the First Ward and went over the details and drew extra pictures." He grimaced and said, "I'm very good at getting people to read for me, and I can memorize quickly. It's all a game. A lie."

Daniela touched his arm. "And who read the note I left in your secret garden?"

"No one," he replied, withdrawing it from his shirt pocket. "Until now." He handed it to her. The envelope was marked with rosy blotches that had bled through the cloth.

She lifted the water-stained page from the envelope, but didn't glance at it. Instead, she looked at him and recited, "Carlos, I will never doubt you again." She held the paper out to him and pointed at the first word. Her voice sounded raw. "That's how your name looks." Daniela pulled back her hand and wiped away fresh tears.

He studied his name and repeated the sentence as he touched each word.

Pedro squatted beside him. "You've got an excellent teacher. You'll learn in no time. Meanwhile, I'll get word to Sra. Gómez for you." He stood and walked to the door behind the altar. "Get comfortable in here; it'll be a while before the church is unoccupied. But no hanky panky. This looks like a mud room, but it's still part of God's House." He winked and closed the door behind him.

Carlos took Daniela's hands again. He kissed her softly. "I'm sorry about your wedding night. Nothing about this has been romantic."

"We're holding and having, that's the important part. I can still remember your hands rubbing my legs and feet and the feel of bathing you—that was very romantic." She lifted his dark hand to her mouth and met his eyes while she kissed it wetly. After a few moments, she said, "Why didn't anyone ever teach you to read and write?"

"I'm not sure if my parents could. Papá taught me some math so I wouldn't get cheated, but that was all. He's never written to me though I've sent lots of money. When I was growing up everyone figured I couldn't read and explained everything to me. After I got here, everyone thought I could and I played my tricks to keep them thinking that way."

She said, "I hope talking about it doesn't embarrass you."

"I just don't want to keep you or our children down."

"Learning to read will be quick and easy. Please don't keep anything else from me. You're a smart man—I want you to show me everything you know."

Heat rose in his face and he glanced away. "I've learned a lot of wicked things."

"Take the next hundred years and show me all of it."

"Is that how long we'll have together?"

"Yes, Carlos." Daniela smiled. "Yes."

*

He changed into the denims Pedro gave him, making Daniela face away as he stripped and dressed again. He should've sent her outside, but couldn't resist the thrill of standing naked behind her for a moment, hoping she'd turn. Her hands clenched and her muscles appeared to vibrate with the tension of keeping still. When he told her the last button was in place, she slumped beside him against the wall and napped.

Following the evening Mass, Pedro appeared with the Eucharistic bread and wine. Carlos stood in the dark behind the mission to give Daniela privacy as she confessed. His lusty behavior had been another sin that required the priest's absolution after he and Daniela traded places. When they knelt together to receive Communion, the holy symbols of flesh and blood gave him relief; he had shed all physical reminders of Donati.

Pedro said, "I'm sorry the day has to end with you going to separate cells, uh, chambers. You need to get an early start, so let's get you settled." Carlos retrieved his trumpet, and they followed Pedro into the empty nave. The candles had been extinguished and large electric lamps glowed overhead. The priest said, "We did have a visitor asking for you, a well-dressed woman with a busted lip. I sent her away, of course, and have confessed my lie to Father Soto."

Carlos thanked him and took Daniela's bruised hand in his.

Adjacent rooms beside the confessional booths were lit and tidy: the bed along one wall and, against another, a desk upon which sat a filled wash basin beside a soap bar and towel. "Now then," Pedro said, "my room's on the other side of the nave and Father Soto's is too, so don't even think about consummating anything but a good night's sleep." They nodded solemnly as he wagged an ink-stained finger. He dropped his hand and grinned. "Of course, there's nothing wrong with kissing the bride again. Sleep well and dream of better days to come."

When Pedro shut the door to his office and living quarters, Carlos took Daniela in his arms and kissed her, stopping before he had a new obscenity to confess. He got lost for a moment in her gaze before wishing her a good night. They went into their rooms and closed the doors. He stood his trumpet beside the basin and undressed to shake out his borrowed clothes, which were gritty from the mud room.

A light bulb dangled from the ceiling. Clad only in dingy boxers, he examined himself in the brightness, guilty but excited again to be nearly naked in the holy place with Daniela so close. Her humming sounded louder through the plaster than it should have.

He put his ear to the wall and moved along as she splashed water and sang to herself. Her voice seemed loudest when he drew close to a narrow painting of angels in ascension. Removing it revealed a wooden grille two-thirds of the way down the wall, with the back of another picture on the other side. The grille probably had been put there to give the church another confessional if attendance grew. He crouched and whispered Daniela's name.

"Where are you? You sound so near."

"Take the picture off your wall."

The backing lifted up and then Daniela's dress descended until her scrubbed, grinning face was inches from his. "Let me get a chair," she said, "and you can confess all."

He got his chair as well, the wooden seat cool under his cotton-clad bottom. He put his hand against the grille, and she did the same. Fingertips pressed together through the flimsy lattice.

She made her voice deep and sober. "What is your confession, my son?"

He looked down; the old, thin boxers did little to hide him. "Lust. Unrepentant lust."

"And you feel this even now?"

"I'm afraid I do."

"And do you have evidence of this sin, so I may judge its seriousness?"

Carlos slid his fingers from the grille and stood up, moving the chair aside. He turned to present his profile.

Her voice lost its depth and sobriety. "*¡Dios mío!*"

Carlos looked down at himself again and whispered, "Will you absolve me?"

"I will, but please sit again. Please. Your un-repentance is, uh, disturbing your confessor." Daniela put her fingers to the grille again so he could touch them.

"Do you also have unrepentant lust to confess?"

Her eyes widened and her fingers pushed against his. "I do."

"Show me." When she blushed and protested, he said, "It's only fair."

She stood and backed away. Her fingers trembled as she undid the buttons down the front of her dress. She let it fall to the floor and quickly pushed off her slip and garter belt as well. A one-piece foundation garment of creamy lace and cotton lifted her bosom, cinched her waist, and gripped her upper thighs. "I'm afraid," she whispered.

"You have nothing to fear from me. Confess all."

"This is God's House. He sees everything."

Carlos said, "He sees everything everywhere, not just in His House."

"That doesn't make this right." She began to pull on her fingers.

"Okay but come closer. Closer still. Touch the wall with your hands and your heart." He heard her fast, shallow breaths as she stood above him in her underwear. Carlos imagined her cheek, palms, and breasts pressed against the cool wall. Now the grille obscured too much, and he muttered and flexed it with his fingers, almost punching through it.

Daniela laughed quietly and sat down. A flush had spread from the top of her bosom to her face, and her pupils were wide. "Oh, we've sinned *mucho*, Carlos. Better try to sleep."

"*Buenas noches.*" Carlos walked under the bulb and extinguished it with a downward pull of the chain. Yellow light from Daniela's room angled through the grille onto his floor like individual rays of sunshine, and he stepped into them. The slim golden shafts slid up his legs as he moved toward her. Finally, he stood in place and felt her gaze on him.

She exhaled, her breath sighing through the grille as she leaned forward and blocked the light. "You couldn't resist, could you?"

"No. It's part of my wickedness."

She whispered, "*Te quiero,* Carlos."

"*Te quiero mucho,* Daniela." He touched her fingers through the grille again.

"Last night I couldn't sleep. Tonight, I don't want to."

"You will though," he said, "and you'll dream of us with no walls in between."

Daniela stood and moved toward the dangling light bulb, rocking her bottom at him. She looked over her shoulder for a long moment and then pulled the chain, casting both rooms into darkness.

CHAPTER 27

Lebrun's humid breath stank of peppermint and cigarettes when he leaned in close to Jack. "Tough luck, *amigo*—you win the bet and then can't collect on the hooker."

Jack's nostrils twitched. He peered up at the bright-pink face with its bulbous forehead and the sharp nose inches away from him. Sound played a trick: the man's voice seemed to come from the bottom of a well. Unless, Jack thought, he himself was the one *subterráneo*. Or underwater. His mind felt too fuzzy to work out the logic, but he did realize he was thinking *en español* for the first time in years. He sensed deep pains in his head and back and that damned left leg, but nothing on the surface. He moved his lips but couldn't be sure what he said, which language, or whether any sound came out.

"Cat's got your tongue, ranger? You're one lucky sonofabitch. Some Mexican lunatic dragged you through the sewer and resurfaced with you near that little clinic they got. The guy dropped you like a hot potato before he could go through your pockets—must've heard some sirens. He even left your gun. At least the doc there had the sense to call a real hospital. I hear you smelled bad enough to finally pass for one of them."

Jack noticed Lebrun almost never blinked. He tried to focus on the sentences, but managed only to hold onto random words: lucky lunatic sewer pockets, gun real bad. Even these he found too slippery to grasp for long. He attempted to raise his hand and push the florid face away, but the sheet held him down like lead.

"Tell me, Jack, was it just the one greaser that mashed you, or did you get KO'd by a more respectable number?" Lebrun laughed a cloud of sweet stink. "Whatever happened to that one man-one riot shit you rangers are famous for?"

CHAPTER 28

Carlos sensed it was dawn when Pedro rapped on the door. "I'm awake, Father. I'll be with you in a moment." He stretched and yawned.

He could hear the priest knock on Daniela's door and heard her reply through the grille. When he clicked on his light, she walked to her chair, revealing a blur of tan skin and the contours of her underwear and then her face. His body responded instantly to her tousled hair and sleepy eyes. "Good morning, wife."

"You're right, I slept." A blush added heat to her smile. "But none of my dreams could compare with last night." She glanced at her door as Pedro called good morning to Father Soto in the nave. "We better hurry. Be sure to move your chair back."

Carlos saw another blur of skin and cotton as she replaced the painting. He returned his room to its ordered state and dressed. Daniela took his hand after he closed his door and they greeted the two priests.

Pedro indicated a satchel, *sombreros,* and two skins of water lying on a pew. "You have a very long and boring walk ahead of you." He presented two large corn muffins for breakfast and packed the trumpet in the knapsack.

Carlos finished his meager breakfast and said goodbye to Father Soto. "You'll find a lot of willing helpers."

"Maybe, but none as able. We'll send for you when it's safe to return." He congratulated them on their marriage and departed through the vestibule.

Carlos turned to his friend. "We'll give you sanctuary at the plantation if it gets too dangerous here, Father Rodríguez."

The priest grasped Carlos' arms, his moist eyes blinking. "Call me Pedro. You have too long a trip ahead of you to waste your breath on '*padre.*'" He laughed with Carlos and said, "You'll only be a day's walk away—I might surprise you some evening. Of all the surprises in the last eighteen months, your marriage is the most miraculous. You found your missing half in Daniela; your mother and father would be proud. We're counting on receiving letters. I put our address in the satchel beside Sr. Webster's note."

"I'll write as soon as I can," Carlos said. "Daniela will put down my words until then. Thank you for everything." He hugged Pedro and the priest's powerful arms tightened around his shoulders. Carlos slung the gear over his shoulders while Daniela kissed Pedro's cheek and said goodbye. The priest blessed them, and they exited through the back door.

*

Carlos and Daniela headed due south and finally passed the Anglo neighborhoods at the city limits. They endured, as Pedro had predicted, a tedious hike on a hot and humid summer day. The sun glared through a milky white sky. Grassy prairie extended to the hazy horizons all around them, with only a few heat-warped trees to break the monotony.

They agreed Donati could have lawmen patrolling the highways, so they kept away from the roads and nearby train tracks, tromping through the endless prairie. Daniela wanted to make plans: choose children's names, decide where they'd settle down, pick the kinds of work they ultimately wanted to do. Carlos convinced her to save her breath for the long walk. He held her sweaty hand in companionable silence and shortened his strides to match hers.

Though they often paused to rest in the flat, unvarying countryside, sitting together or lying side by side, only once did he think about Paz seducing him on the tarp with the grasslands all around. He quickly willed the tawdry images away.

Early in the afternoon, Daniela declared a *siesta* as they neared a thicket of scrub and slender trees that cast a few shadows. They collapsed in the modest oasis. He fretted over her. With a pocketknife Pedro had included in the satchel, he cut vents in her shoes to relieve her blistered feet. He soaked a kerchief for her and tied it around her neck, kissing her dry lips. Like himself, she looked like she could wring a bucket of sweat from her clothes. He had offered her his shirt to protect her arms, but she'd declined. Now, she dabbed precious water on the sunburns that splotched her fairer skin.

Daniela ate another red apple and spit the seeds into the grass. She leaned beside him against a tree. "I'm eating a lot of apples, husband, but not getting the knowledge I'd hoped for."

He patted her hand. "I'm guessing we still have more than fifteen miles to go. It's hard to judge, though, since we've strayed so far from the railroad and highway. Pedro's right; there's something almost biblical about this journey." He soaked a kerchief for himself. Lukewarm droplets ran down his neck and into his shirt, cooling his skin. The *sombrero* rested on his knee; the crown's interior was sweat-soaked and a wavy band of salt ringed its outside. He swished a little water inside his mouth and let it slowly trickle down his arid throat. "Tonight, I'll make it up to you." He took both of her hands, mindful of the bruised knuckles on one and the patches of sunburned flesh. "It'll only get better."

"In what ways?"

"All ways." He gently kissed her chapped lips.

An hour into their continued trek, as the heat continued to rise, she began gasping and panting. He taught her some of Oscar's breathing techniques. By the late afternoon, with the sun still blazing overhead and the air sticky, she continued to breathe as he'd shown her, but each step seemed to be a struggle. He held her upright and managed to keep them moving.

As the sun descended behind them, they approached Casson. A large railroad depot sprawled on one end of the main street. A steam locomotive pulling a long line of passenger and freight cars moved out from the station and headed south. The engineer blew his whistle as the train passed behind the nearby buildings, across the street from the Webster general store where Carlos and Pedro had visited less than two years before. Trucks with wood-sided beds and black-painted cars parked diagonally in front of the shops. Anglo men on the plank sidewalks tipped their fedoras and Stetsons to passing ladies who nodded in reply. One woman twirled a parasol resting on her shoulder. Carlos recalled Sr. Webster's warning that others in town might be more sympathetic to Donati. He and Daniela skirted the main street and continued hiking through the prairie.

Five miles south of Casson, they crossed the railroad tracks and highway and headed due east in the twilight. A sunken dirt road led them past vast cotton fields and hundreds of acres of vegetables: broccoli, squash, tomatoes, and other summer staples.

Ahead of them, scores of farmworkers emptied harvest baskets into a line of large trucks along the road and received their wages from the Anglo foreman. The *tejanos* stacked the baskets, piled up cutting tools, and walked away from the fields in groups and pairs. Single men and mothers leading their children went into a cinder-block store beside the fields to exchange their money for supper ingredients they carried away in their arms. The women left the store still deflecting high-pitched pleadings for treats. Their husbands had gone ahead of them, smoking and murmuring, heads down, backs bent.

Farther along, a two-story plantation house loomed. Twelve columns supported a deep wrap-around porch. Four chimneys crowned its gray roof, and scores of windows graced all sides of the mansion. Electric light blazed from every pane. The radiance shone on the sheds behind the house and the barns to the right, as well as the detached kitchen connected to the back of the *casa grande* by a covered walkway. The glow also brightened the dirt road, but the workers turned before crossing that swath of gold. They followed a worn path to a colony of fifty wood shacks on the other side of the lane where the light did not reach.

Carlos and Daniela mounted the mansion's porch steps. He removed his hat and withdrew the Webster stationery from the satchel. Daniela swayed beside him, the porch lamps illuminating ringlets of her sodden hair and sunburned skin. They had agreed that, since Daniela's English was much better, she would make the introductions. Shortly after she knocked on the black-enameled front door, a tall, slender Negro woman in a black uniform opened it.

Daniela said, "I'm Daniela Domenica, uh, Moreno. Mr. Webster invited my husband to work here a few years ago." She introduced Carlos and handed the note to the maid.

"Mr. Webster doesn't give out many of these. We have some room for y'all, sure. I'm Beatrice Riley. Everyone calls me Bibi. Me and Olivia Brightharp—she does the cooking— live in the first house on the end there." She pointed across the lane at the worker's colony. "Two doors down there's an empty one. Rent is ten dollars a month. Come on in for a minute."

Carlos followed Daniela inside where the maid left them, striding up a long flight of polished wood stairs. The expansive foyer had a fifteen-foot ceiling bordered with white crown molding and supporting a two-tiered electric chandelier. The floors were heart-pine and waxed to such a finish he could see Daniela's reflected legs and skirt. Wings of the house spread in both directions, bright rooms of gleaming woods and leather, massive fireplaces, and ornate wallpaper. The Strugatskys place had been as big, but not nearly as grand.

Daniela glanced sidelong at a large hall tree that was backed by an eight-foot tall mirror. She turned to face it and gasped, "*¡Cabra!*" Her fingers raked through wild hair, pulling out bits of grass and trying to push it into a fluffier shape as he reassured her that she looked gorgeous. The sunburned flesh on her face and body glowed scarlet under the bright lights. She sniffed for a moment and quickly lowered her arms within the sweat-stained dress. Close to tears, she said, "You married a smelly, filthy *vagabunda.*"

"I married someone who was strong enough to walk thirty miles, and so courageous she left every comfort behind to be with the man she loves." He held her reddened cheeks and kissed her. "A man who smells worse, looks worse, and isn't fit to sleep beside."

"Bless your heart," Bibi called, a little breathless as she clomped down the stairs with an armload of linens. "I'm glad I was getting together the makings of a bridal suite." She thrust the white sheets and pillows into Carlos' arms. "I figured you for newlyweds. There's a well near our place and a stove to heat the water if you want to scrub off." She inhaled deeply a few times and said, "Those stairs would like to kill me. You wouldn't be wanting a maid's job, would you, Daniela?"

"I've done it before." She brushed sunburned fingers over her blistered arm. "It might be better than working outside."

"Come back in the morning when Mrs. Webster will be here. Maybe we can fix you up. Mister, you look like you know all about farm work. They're out in the fields from dark-thirty to dark-thirty. Mr. Reynolds, the foreman, will point you in the right direction."

"I'll be there," Carlos said. He thanked her for the linens and passed over ten one-dollar bills for the monthly rent.

Bibi fanned the money like a *flamenco* dancer. "We're happy to have y'all. Enjoy your honeymoon."

*

Daniela took some of the sheets from Carlos' arms as they followed the dim path that had been taken by the laborers. "This is a nice place you found," she said. "Bibi's so friendly and that house is—"

They stopped and looked upon two rows of twenty-five flat-roofed shacks. Each two-room structure had a shallow porch. Two small windows gapped in both the front room and the back, each bracketed by hinged shutters. A foot-high crawlspace under every home provided additional ventilation. Stovepipes jutted through the roofs, but some also had fire pits near their porches. Shallow privy trenches reeked behind all of the houses.

A dirt street separated the two rows. Some people ate on their porches, but most *obreros* had staggered into their homes and not come out again. In the twilight, cooking fires shone from open windows and doors, and smoke from the stove pipes carried the smells of frying grease, *tortillas*, beans, and chilies.

At the end of the street, Carlos gave the thin pillows to Daniela so he could lower a bucket into the wood-framed well and draw it up. Taking a gourd ladle from the well's edge, he dipped some water, made sure no mosquito larvae floated in it, and presented it to her.

She squinted at his offering. "Does everyone drink from that?" When he responded that they probably did, she made a face and said, "You first."

He sipped the water. "It's cold, only a little bitter. Have some."

She tasted it and then drank and dipped more until she'd emptied the bucket. Rivulets of water moistened her reddened face and the flushed skin above her breasts.

He took Daniela's hand and said, "Let's move into our new home."

They walked along the row on their left. Bibi and Olivia's house was dark. A quilt hung on the back of a chair on the porch. The door and shutters were painted in the same black as the plantation house's trim. Orange-yellow firelight illuminated the next house's front windows and open door. A woman at the stove wrapped a rag around the iron handle of her frying pan and flipped well-browned cornbread onto a wooden plate. Four small kids played with stick dolls out front and greeted Carlos and Daniela when they said hello.

Daniela stepped up onto the porch of the third house and shouted. She dropped her hat and the linens and retreated to the street where she brushed spider silk from her face and hair and then arms and hands. The children laughed and imitated her panic for each other until their mother called them inside to eat. Daniela walked forward again, waving her arms before her, and went through the open doorway. Carlos got caught in the rest of the web that had been above her head. He scraped the strands from his face and hair and left his gear beside hers. His struck match tickled his nose with sulfur before he handed the flame to Daniela along with the matchbox Pedro had packed.

Planks creaked beneath their shoes as they walked through the small, musty front room. A low cot with a narrow mattress angled across the floor, the only furnishing besides a tin two-burner stove balanced on crumbly bricks in the back corner. A wall with an open doorway separated the rooms. She waved out the match and then extended her arms to catch more webs. Another lit match revealed a second cot, but nothing more. Daniela crouched, felt the mattress, and then smelled it. Her nose wrinkled and she sneezed, dropping her flame onto the dry wood floor. She stamped out the fire and sat on the edge of the creaking bed, sniffling in the dark.

Carlos found the box in her hands and lit a fresh matchstick. Her nose ran and tears spilled from her eyes as she looked away. He waved his match out and held her. "They're all like this, some with more webs than others."

She inhaled, making a wet sound, and tried to laugh. "I feel guilty for not saying goodbye to anyone, for not explaining. I miss Morris' sweet little fists. I miss my things."

He rubbed her back, feeling damp skin beneath the summer dress and the contours of her underwear. "I'm sorry. I know it's awful, walking all that way in the sun just to come to this." He stroked her hair; the sweat and skin oil made his fingers slick. "I'll help you get used to it. Tomorrow's Friday, so we'll make some money this week. Even better, no more worries about Donati." He kissed her and, when he spoke again, his lips caressed hers. "And, best, we're together."

"I know I'll grow accustomed to it. Your whole life has been like this—I'm such a *nene* to be crying, but when we went inside that house and I saw the luxury, I thought…" He lit a match while she pinched the mattress between her thumb and forefinger. "I don't blame you for having to leave Houston. It's just bad luck." She untied the sweat-crusted kerchief from her neck and wiped her face.

"Your father would say this is what comes from marrying a *peón*, a man with no prospects."

Daniela blew out the flame above his fingertips and kissed him. "We're living our vows. This is the 'worse' part."

"How can I take you to 'better'?"

"I'm desperate for a bath. Let's take care of that, and we'll move on to other things."

CHAPTER 29

The colony was awash in moonlight and the flickering glow from stoves and fire pits. Carlos had found a tin pail beside their stove; he taught Daniela how to use the windlass to draw from the well. He returned to their home to figure out the stove so he could heat some bathwater. Once the fire was lit, he arranged their "bridal suite," as Bibi had called it.

When he went back to the well, Daniela was using a bucket of water as a wavy mirror, still grooming her hair. He said, "You look beautiful. I love you." He clenched her against him and kissed her wet lips until her mouth felt warm against his. Carlos wished he didn't feel better by the minute in the familiar surroundings of a plantation, hidden from danger. Their house looked much nicer than he'd expected. He'd never had privacy, let alone a porch and a stove, in the camps where his family had lived, and they'd always had to provide their own bedding. He wished he hated their situation as much as she obviously did. Still, he said, "If you want to, we'll move on."

She rubbed her face against his shirt. "Let's see what happens here. I'm tougher than I look. I'd like to get a few things for us and the house, though. I can't stand being this dirty and having nothing clean to put on. How much money did you bring?"

"I have sixty-three dollars and twenty-six cents. Remember, I planned to buy back the trumpet on Tuesday when you surprised me with it. I had all my savings with me, just in case. Then that night…Anyway, I never got home to hide my money again."

She said, "When I went upstairs to change out of my uniform, I took all my savings, too. I guess I have about three hundred dollars in my pockets, maybe more." She laughed and nodded at his incredulous look.

"So, we're in the middle of nowhere with a fortune?"

"Yes, here we are in the wilderness, alone under the stars." She cinched her arms around his waist. "We've both eaten the apple, husband. Now what?"

"Let me show you what I know."

Carlos led Daniela inside where the pail full of water steamed atop the stove. He shuttered the windows and closed the door, bathing the room in the oven's orange glow. The water had heated enough to scald his finger—it would cool to the perfect temperature by the time they were ready for it. He closed off the burners and killed the fire, but the embers still yielded enough soft light to see her smile. "It's going to stay very hot in here from the stove, so you might sweat even as I bathe you."

"If you're going to be the one to bathe me, I'll sweat anyway. Where's the bed that was in here?"

"We've got a double now in the other room." He unfastened the buttons on the front of her dress and whispered, "If you're too tired or sore from the sun—"

"You're not trying to back out, are you?"

"Never. I just want this to be nice and romantic for you."

Her hands gripped the back of his waistband. "You're being very romantic, but you need to understand something."

"What's that?"

She said, "Don't be too nice."

CHAPTER 30

La labor—fieldwork, farming. It is the fate of many campesinos *to tend another's fields. Their hands rest only when the sun does.*

They have knowledge in their hands—a brilliance of touch. The feel of things becomes second-nature: wood handles and hafts, rawhide and hemp. Shapes press and burn into their palms and fingers and remain even when they set things down. Beyond the man-made, though, they know the feel of the earth and her bounty. They know the green snap of vegetables wrested from stems and the brown sigh of land giving up its produce as they pull like midwives.

The sun feels brutal but the rain can be worse. They wring their hands during the storms that keep them from the fields and steal money from their pockets. Downpours overflow privy trenches. Disease worms into their open sores and the poison is swallowed by their unwary children.

They turn then to the healing touch of the curanderas. *And as they stare at their walls and pray for their bodies to recover faster, their hands itch with the missing feel of tools and plants and soil. Finally, they mend and return to the fields that have not missed them.*

Every day, with the coming dawn, they curse the end of night and the need to toil over another's harvest. Every day they wake before sunup but need not work—or cannot—they curse the chance they have lost.

Then they dream again of going to the city.

CHAPTER 31

Carlos made his way to the plantation on shaky legs. He couldn't start every day the way he and Daniela had just done if he intended to work hard until dark. She had surprised him by waking first and coaxing him from sleep. Her inhibitions were fading fast, helping him to bury his guilty memories of Paz. He'd left Daniela dappled in sweat upon a tangle of sheets; she'd allowed him to go only after he'd promised to reveal more secrets that night. Each memory he created with Daniela helped to shroud the origin of that guilty knowledge.

The fields sparkled with dew in the faint morning light. Early risers lifted up baskets and tools and chose their rows. The earth gave just a little under Carlos' feet, like pie crust above a dense filling, as he crouched to cut stalks of broccoli.

His body found another rhythm and his mind drifted now in somber directions. He knew they couldn't hide on the plantation forever; he and Daniela could only amass savings if they returned to city jobs. Other than Houston, the nearest big cities were hundreds of miles away. How far could Donati reach? In what town would they be safe buying a train or bus ticket? Carlos imagined the bleeding ranger in his arms again as he carried to the scales a harvest basket heaped with broccoli crowns. A dying King of Swords in horrible pain: Donati's end would've been so easy to achieve in the sewers, so quick and merciful. And there wouldn't have been a need to run anymore. Then at his own death, Carlos thought, his soul would go to Hell forever, but at least he wouldn't have damned Daniela and their children to miserable lives.

He rolled his shoulders and flexed his back, sore from yesterday's long hike and sleeping on the decrepit bed. With a grimace, he reminded himself he'd felt relieved to be there. How long would it take to get used to a farm schedule again, racing nature every day and often losing? Grueling labor had stolen his childhood and ruined the health of his parents and all of the other adults he'd stooped beside. Images flashed behind his eyes: mangled *peón* fingers, twisted spines, knees that popped and cracked like dry kindling, and a landscape of scars that covered every *campesino* he ever knew. Good people trapped by poverty and a lack of prospects, to use Sr. Domenica's word. He needed a plan to get them to a home where they could prosper.

*

He left the fields at dusk and stood in line with the others to get paid by the Anglo foreman. With six quarters added to the savings in his grimy pockets, Carlos crossed the sunken road and stopped at the well to wash. He scrubbed his skin and called goodnight to the new friends he'd made. Daniela propped a broom on their porch and approached him with a white towel. Through a glaze of water, he saw she wore a new white dress. He dried himself and grimaced at the dirt he left on the fluffy cloth. "Thank you. I missed you today," he said. He kissed her and noted how clean she smelled. "You're very beautiful. I'm sorry I'm such a mess."

"Go in and sit down. There's some cold water on the table."

"Table?" Carlos looked at her broad smile for a moment and then glanced at the luxurious towel. He walked onto the swept porch and stepped inside.

She had a kerosene lamp lit on a circular oak table that was surrounded by four matching chairs with hand-carved backs and legs. Beside the lamp sat four glasses and a tall pitcher, flatware, and two plates covered with cloth napkins. Flies crawled over the napkin folds and hummed their frustration. Through the open doorway he could make out a wardrobe in one corner of their bedroom and a tall wicker hamper.

Carlos sat and sipped the water. When his mouth and throat felt wet, he took a long swallow and refilled his glass. She sat beside him, and he took her hand. He asked, "How much has our fortune shrunk already?" The nervous quaver in his voice shamed him, as did the blood rising in his face.

"The furniture's on loan from Sra. Webster. She runs the *hacienda* as well as the general store with her husband Tom, the man who gave you the note. You'll like her. She hired me immediately, but instead of putting me to work upstairs, she took me into town and gave me a store discount on some things. She showed me some other shops, too. I spent about thirty dollars of my...our...money. Olivia Brightharp, the cook, sent me home with supper so we saved a little there." She lifted a napkin to reveal fried pork chops, mashed potatoes, and green beans, and then covered the plate again to thwart the flies.

"Why didn't she sell you the furniture, too? Then she could've taken even more of our money."

Her eyes widened at his sharp tone. "I told her we won't be here very long, maybe six months. She was kind to do this. Sure she made a profit by selling me things from their store, just like she pays us and then has the grocery right there to take the money back. That's just smart business. Why are you angry?"

"Thirty dollars is what I'll earn in a month! The other people here—they'll know how much better we're living. They'll resent us, coming here from the big city and setting up house with fancy things."

Daniela stood, fists on hips. "About half of what I spent was to buy gifts for the other families—fresh linens, new bowls and cookware, toys for their children." Her voice continued to get louder. "I'm not going lie and pretend to be poor. I'm not going to hide the fact that we have some money. So I thought I'd make it clear I'm willing to share some of it."

He held up his hands. In a tone as soft and calm as he could manage, he said, "It's just that I spent the day thinking about how to get to the 'better' part of our vows. We need to save as much as we can."

"For me, 'better' means having a toothbrush and soap and clean clothes. I needed everything to set up a home. While we're here, we can't live like—"

"Like I usually live." Carlos scraped at the dirt caked under his nails.

"Yes, if that's how you want to put it." She dropped into her chair and tapped her fingers against the tabletop, a rippling rhythm like a storm of hailstones. Finally, she said, "That's the first time I haven't liked saying 'yes' to you."

His stomach tightened. "Sorry. You're going to have to teach me how to enjoy money. My father treated every cent as precious, something to be hoarded."

"And your mother?"

"He handled all of it. Whatever we made we gave to him and he decided how to spend it. Rarely, he'd treat us to a meal in a diner; most times we ate Mamá's simple cooking. Once, though, Papá paid for bus fare and we moved a long way."

"Where did you go?"

"La Marque, where my mother died. That was the farthest I'd traveled in one trip—it must have cost a lot. You'd said you always lived in Houston?"

"I got to travel some. When the store started making money, Father took us on a vacation each year. Nothing grand. Usually a beach or Corpus Christi to visit my sisters."

"I don't understand that word '*vacacion.*' What's it mean?"

Daniela held his face in her warm hands. "We have a lot to teach each other. Let me show you how to start enjoying your money." She carried the lamp into the bedroom. The adjoined beds had been made, fresh linens as smooth as ice. She opened the wicker hamper to reveal her traveling dress and other laundry, including the well-used sheets. She dropped in the towel he'd dirtied and closed the lid. "I got you some more clothes, too. I'll do the wash every Monday. Sra. Webster lets me use the lavatory in the house, but I'll get a tub delivered so you can bathe when you want."

"If you'll scrub my back, I'll bathe every night."

She rubbed her hands together, saying, "That's a deal!"

In the carved oak wardrobe hung a week's worth of black dress uniforms and casual clothes she'd bought in town, in addition to work shirts and dungarees for him. A pile of towels sat on a low shelf. She unlocked a drawer to show where she'd stored her savings, the dollars neatly stacked. Carlos added his money, and Daniela locked it again and handed him the key.

"Thank you for your trust," he said.

"You're welcome." She took a duplicate key from her dress pocket and grinned.

He opened another drawer filled with lingerie, but she covered his hand before he could explore the satin and straps. "No, I control this treasure box. You have your surprises, I have mine." She pointed out a basin with shaving gear and some bristled utensils beside the towels. "We have tooth powder, too. Now we can clean our teeth after supper."

He ran his tongue around the inside of his mouth. "I'm sorry, but you'll have to show me how to do that, too."

"You've never brushed your teeth?"

"I scrape them with a flattened twig. Lots of times I'll chew on cedar shavings or other wood to get a good taste in my mouth."

"That explains your sweet breath, but it's amazing you still have all your teeth."

He shrugged. "A couple of them hurt whenever I eat something sweet, and the ones in the front still feel loose, but that's it. Maybe I'll have to do a lot of brushing before they're better."

"Sra. Webster's paying me three dollars a day—twice what you made—so we can afford plenty."

He whistled two notes at once. "Does she need more help inside?"

"Only if you can get into the uniform. I'll warm our supper and you tell me what plan you came up with to make our lives better."

He followed her into the front room saying, "Two ideas: walk east into Louisiana and hope that Texas Rangers can't follow us there or steal a train and take it wherever we want."

"Why not a bus or a car?"

"I can't drive either of them."

"I can't either. Keep planning—I'll fix supper."

*

On Saturday night, the workers lingered outside after sunset to socialize. The foreman had reminded everyone to return to the harvest on Sunday after worship, where a lay volunteer, a rezadora, would lead the workers in prayers. Campfires flickered in front of many of the houses, sending long shadows of the farmhands across the dusty ground and up the wooden walls of their homes. As he and Daniela greeted their neighbors—single men and families resting after their long week—Carlos wished *El Mariachi Santa Cruz* was there to reward everyone with music. He needed to invent a new embouchure so he could play again; maybe he'd form *El Mariachi Moreno de América*.

Dirt stained the men's clothes, but damp collars and cuffs showed where they'd washed before they ate. The men maintained the courtly manners of past generations, *la cortesía mexicana*, welcoming Carlos and Daniela and listening with fascination to details of city life, but slumping shoulders and concealed yawns revealed their exhaustion. Those in their twenties already showed signs of the wear that deformed the workers in their forties.

Even the youngest women had at least one child and usually two or more, including a newborn. These mothers' bodies still looked youthful and their voices and occasional giggles almost sounded girlish. In every case, though, their slenderness came from poverty rather than good health. Their faces sagged with the same exhaustion that plagued the older mothers—who repeatedly called after children running everywhere through the colony and meted out discipline for misbehaving kids and husbands alike. As Carlos had seen with countless families, the women wore the pants.

One young woman who literally wore the pants was the only Anglo in camp. Jacinda Webster was a slender eighteen year old, tall and deeply tanned with sun-bleached hair. She wore a denim, snap-button shirt, with the sleeves rolled back over taut brown forearms, and blue jeans tucked into black cowboy boots.

Daniela shook her hand. In English, she said, "Jacie, you look just like your mother, especially your eyes. They're striking—very beautiful."

Jacie playfully fluttered the lids over her glowing green irises. "Thanks. The cat's eyes usually skip a generation, but I got lucky, I guess." She appraised Carlos for a moment before extending her hand. She said in Spanish, "I know you."

The comment made Carlos pause: he certainly didn't recognize her. Her palm and fingertips felt coarse, the hands of a laborer, not a teenaged *gringa*. He replied in Spanish, "You saw the *mariachis* in Houston?"

"I do like the music, everything *mexicano* really, but that's not it. *El rinche*—I remember him, and I was in my parents' store when you came through with the scarred man."

Carlos relaxed as he recalled the girl with green eyes who'd given him a thumbs-up. He said, "I have a few more scars of my own. How did you remember me?"

"Everything about that day stuck in my mind—I was scared for you and so proud of my dad." She stared openly at him.

Daniela took hold of Carlos' arm. "How do you come to speak Spanish so well?"

"I spend most of my time here in the camp, fixing the houses, teaching English and beginning arithmetic to the little ones who don't have to spend all day in the fields. Sometimes I school the older kids at night. They're all teaching me, too. I'm also learning some country medicine. Let me introduce you to their healer and her husband, César."

César Baptista was a fifteen-year veteran of the Webster *hacienda*, compact and densely muscled, with shaggy black hair and a ready smile that displayed a gold tooth in place of one of his incisors. He led the way to a house at the end of the row, closest to the prairie. Pots, jars, braziers, and stacks of leafy branches and twisted roots littered the porch and frontage of the Baptista home. Herbs hung upside down from the porch ceiling like bats in a cave. César's wife, Letty, stood by two low-burning fires wafting smoke that turned blue in the moonlight.

Letty looked to be thirty or so. She stood six inches taller than Daniela, and her figure was much fuller beneath her short-sleeve tunic and simple skirt, though Carlos tried not to notice. She wore her loose black hair down to her waist, with thick braids of grass holding most of it away from her face. In the light from her fire pits, her skin glowed bronze and her pewter eyes shimmered.

Carlos said, "Jacie told us you're the camp's *curandera*."

Letty slid her arm around César's waist, her hip nestling against his. "Yes, and a midwife and sometimes the camp cook." Her voice sounded like a purr emanating from deep within her chest. "Some have called me a *bruja*, but César's the only one I've ever put a spell on." She smiled, showing white, even teeth. "I take care of most of the needs of our people and the lay preacher sees to the rest. You're newly married?"

Daniela assented. She put an arm around Carlos, mirroring Letty.

"Then you'll be seeing a lot of me in the coming months." She nodded at a satchel she'd set at her feet and said, "Of course, I do have some things to help stop pregnancies and births. Lots of babies soon after marriage can spoil the fun."

Daniela's grip on Carlos tightened. "No, thank you. We're good Catholics."

Letty shrugged and said, "Good Catholics need good midwives. This is where you'll find me. Congratulations on your marriage—I predict lots of beautiful children." She lifted the satchel onto her shoulder. "Please excuse me, but I need to collect some herbs that are best harvested under the rising moon. Come and see me soon, Daniela. I have lots of useful advice for new brides." She kissed César with an open mouth before striding into the dark countryside.

*

Carlos lit the kerosene lamp and followed Daniela into the bedroom. He said, "No wonder César's smiling all the time."

"I'm not going to let you go out at night, with Letty and Jacie prowling around."

"Even to use the privy?"

She snorted. "Especially if you put yourself on display."

"Why are you so jealous? Every time we met a woman tonight, even mothers, you grabbed me like they might snatch me away."

"They made me feel ugly." She scratched at a patch of loose skin on her arm. "My sunburns are peeling and—"

"If it'll help, I'll say you're *bella* every other minute, but you might stop hearing me. Besides, it's not the other women you're jealous about." He dropped his shirt in the hamper. A mosquito landed on his bare chest and he slapped it. "It's me."

Daniela said she didn't understand.

He crossed his arms; the biceps rose against his palms as he flexed. "You're not telling them that I'm yours; you're reminding me that I'm taken."

She sat on the bed and lowered the zipper on the back of her dress. The unfastened seams bent away from her shoulders like wings. "Maybe I'm still thinking about Paz. You're sure you prefer me?"

"I didn't choose between you two. I rejected her and then God brought you and me together." He knelt beside her, his trouser knees crunching the dirt that was impossible to keep out of their home. "If I met you first, I never would've known her."

"But you did know her, in every way."

"I shouldn't have given in. I wish I'd stayed pure for you." Carlos wrapped his arms around Daniela and held her against him. He pushed up her camisole, unclasped the brassiere, and stroked her bare, damp back. "I'll always love you and I will never leave you. You'll never have a reason to doubt me." Her muscles relaxed against his hands and she sighed over his shoulder. He drew back, sitting on his heels.

A sly smile curled her lips. "I guess there are advantages to one of us knowing what we're doing."

"I'm glad you do," he said and kissed her for a long moment. "Because I'm learning as I go."

*

In the lamplight, Carlos felt his heartbeats slow. He caught his breath and asked, "You're not still thinking about Paz, are you?"

Daniela squinted up at him and growled, wriggling beneath him. She bumped the tip of his nose. "You did too good of a job of distracting me. But I hope you weren't—"

He kissed her, tasting the sweat above her lips. "No, I've forgotten all about her."

"Right afterwards, though, you bring up her name. I don't want to talk about that *sucia* ever again. Let me enjoy the afterglow." He asked what that was, and she replied, "It's the light in the sky after the sun sets. But it's also the warm, cuddly feeling I get after we make love, when we're still coupled like this. I feel so close to you." She kissed him. "I feel our souls interlocking."

"We fit perfectly, in every way."

"*Sí.*" Daniela stroked his back and moved her hands upward as she hummed the love song he'd taught her, "*La noche y tú.*" Her fingertips brushed his face, his hair, and then descended past his shoulders again. She sang softly to him:

Still so far away in the countryside
Where star shine glimmers like your eyes
Outracing falcons, the moon as my light
I'm captivated by the night and you.

Carlos recovered quickly as she sang to him. He rose up on his elbows and looked down between them.

She laughed and pressed him tight against her. "Mmm. Now, was there something you wanted to talk about?"

"I forgot." Carlos slid his arms behind her and felt her warmth along his palms and fingers. "I hope this won't spoil your afterglow."

"Always more where that came from."

CHAPTER 32

Jack blinked awake when a young Texas Ranger named Miller dropped his bulk onto the old wood chair beside the hospital bed. Despite a cracking noise, the seat managed to support the lawman. Jack looked at him from the corner of his eye, since he couldn't move his head.

Bandages encased him, holding his ribs together and swaddling his skull. Thick pads protected his back and kept his neck straight. He couldn't feel his left arm, couldn't make his fingers move. His gun hand—his picture-drawing hand—was useless, maybe forever. Jack's good leg rubbed against the plaster of Paris around his left calf where the cop's bullet had fractured his tibia. A tall white curtain bisected the small room, just like the boardinghouses he'd seen in the *barrios*. From the other side, a man groaned almost nonstop and called on absent doctors and nurses to save him.

The corners of Miller's mustache curled upward with his smile. He asked, "How you doing, sir?"

Jack thought of a few terse responses, but Miller was his man outside for a couple months and needed to be encouraged. He said, "OK. That morphine packs a wallop. What do you have?"

"The night you got socked, we counted sixteen rioters who survived the arrests. I had this guy—one of them musicians inside the walls—who you need to know about."

"Had?"

Miller slashed his thumb across his throat. "Couldn't hack the questioning, just gave out. Before that, we had him naming names: greasers involved in that mess." He put his boot against the side of the bed. "Said he played trumpet in a band where he replaced that guy you've been looking for."

Jack recalled the fresh pain all through his body as the dark face hovered above him. "Carlos Moreno."

"Yeah, said that Moreno has a job as a groundskeeper on the cushy west side, working for some swell who's a lawyer."

"Any names?"

"He didn't know. Believe me, we made sure."

Jack said he believed him.

"But here's the funny thing, sir. A Mex family reported a missing girl, probably a kidnapping. Who cares, right? Well, we only noticed because the daughter who pulled a Houdini had brought over a boy on the night of the riot—your guy. She wanted to marry him. The parents are right around the corner from that alley where you got…Anyway, the girl worked as this rich lawyer's maid on Poplar Street."

"Let me guess." Jack knew by Miller's deliberate pacing that Moreno had escaped again. He waited for the story to end while ordering his body to heal faster.

"Right—we checked, and their groundskeeper had gone AWOL with her the next morning. He went by some other name, but the description you gave matched, right down to the new scars on his kisser."

"You have the girl's name?"

"I sure do. Even better though, her mother gave the local boys a picture." Miller pulled a snapshot from his breast pocket, behind the encircled star.

The close-up picture showed a young *tejana,* maybe twenty years old, at the beach. Fingers fanned along the sides of her face to hold dark hair back as the wind swept over her. The short sleeves of her summer dress rippled against her raised arms; the bodice pressed tight against her chest.

Prettiest smile Jack had ever seen. *Una ángela,* he decided. On the back, a Houston police officer had written his rank and name, an address, the date of receipt, and "Subject: Daniela Domenica."

CHAPTER 33

🐦

The June sun supplied more than a dozen hours of light and heat. Carlos worked from when he could barely see the crops at dawn until he could no longer see them in the evening, stopping only to eat a small lunch he bought from the onsite store. In the gloaming, he stepped onto the porch of his home and stretched his back again. Well-water dripped from his scrubbed face and hands, but cooled only a little of his skin.

His stomach growled and he sniffed the air to guess what supper Daniela had prepared, but he could smell nothing but his sweat and the dirt embedded in his clothes. Perhaps he had time for a cold bath. He imagined the painful, delicious chill over his body and managed to raise goose bumps on his arms. He enjoyed daily baths now, especially because of Daniela's eagerness to help. One time, they had overturned the metal tub and a gray tidal wave washed through the front room and into the back before draining through the planks. They were engrossed in each other, though, and hadn't noticed the puddles until the next morning.

Carlos wiped his face on his sleeve. He glanced toward the western sky, still pale blue above the dark landscape. Afterglow, he thought with a smile, and opened the door.

He expected to feel a blast of heat from the stove, but no fire burned in it. Daniela hadn't set the table. Dim light shone

264 | THE FIVE DESTINIES OF CARLOS MORENO

in their bedroom, a ring of silver flickering high on the walls, cast by the kerosene lamp that hung from a bent nail he'd put in the ceiling. A scorched odor tickled his nose. He shut the door and called, "Dani, don't you want to eat?"

"Supper's in here," she responded.

Carlos thought back to their last meal in bed. He trotted to the bedroom but stopped in the doorway.

Daniela sprawled across the bare mattresses, propped up on her elbows. Small designs, brown and wet, tattooed her naked body. Her fingertips were stained dark and rested below her breasts, both of which had patterns drawn over them. She grinned, her mouth and chin smeared brown. "I mean dessert's in here. I've had an awful sweet-craving lately."

"What is this?" He walked to the foot of the double-bed and stared.

"This is the alphabet in chocolate. All you need to know to read and write is on my body. Every word we say can be spelled out with these letters, and some letters can have several different sounds. After you repeat what I say, you may eat the letters. From A," she wiggled her right foot, moving the stepladder-like character back and forth, "to Z." She shook the lightning bolt atop her left foot.

He imagined her painting herself from the chocolate-streaked pan that sat on the floor beside the bed. As he scanned from her forehead to her feet, he counted thirty designs. He said, "Will I learn to read *inglés* the same way?"

"It'll be easier and harder—the Anglos don't have as many letters, but their letters can make more sounds."

He removed his shirt and tossed it in the hamper. "This wouldn't have worked if you were teaching me the trumpet."

She laughed, making the letters dance. "I'd have found another way. You just use your fingers and mouth, right?" She pointed toward A and told him the sound it made. "Like in 'Carlos.'"

He knelt at the foot of the bed and repeated the sound. Beneath and around the sweetness, her skin was warm and smooth and tasted a little spicy, as if she'd pressed cinnamon into her flesh. He took his time, to make sure he got each letter perfect and to cleanse her skin. In an hour, he'd recited the entire alphabet and replaced the dark brown streaks with a flush that spread over her face and body.

"I hope you never lose your sweet tooth," he said and sucked her fingers until they looked golden again. A few of his molars ached from the sugar, but he lowered his mouth to Daniela's and removed the chocolate that ringed her lips.

After their kiss, she tilted her head back, exposing her slender neck. She exhaled hard and asked, "Do you want to try spelling my name?"

"I was just thinking about how to do that." Carlos moved down her body. He licked the shape of a D on her right thigh and said the letter. He moved down to that foot to trace an A. He continued with N on her left bicep, I on her forehead, and E on the right side of her abdomen, tickling her as he licked three parallel strokes. He moved to her left breast for the L and finished at her right foot. "Daniela," he said and re-pronounced each of the letters. "I had no problem memorizing thirty parts of you. Give me another one."

"Remember how I wrote your name in that note?"

"C-A-R-L-O-S," he recited. He licked a C on her right knee, made the A, and then an R on the back of her left hand. He licked down and across her nipple and formed his mouth into an O and kissed her breastbone. She squirmed and giggled as he finished by tracing a serpent to the left of her navel.

She sat up and kissed him hard. "Time for a test—show me what you've learned." She lay back, and Carlos showed her everything.

*

While working in the fields, his thoughts of Daniela had once inspired music and musings. After the chocolate lesson, he dwelled on letters and sounds and her thirty parts. He devoted hours to spelling in his head as his body performed the relentless toil. Whenever he thought of a word he wasn't sure how to spell, he added to a memorized list. Since she hadn't drawn letters on her back, he pretended to cover those smooth tan contours with likely misspellings.

Every evening he recalled his questions so Daniela could review her thirty parts with him. Then, she would quiz him with new words. Before she challenged him with sentences, she decorated her body with chocolate again, and he learned to punctuate.

She corresponded with Pedro weekly. Carlos would now try to read her notes aloud before she mailed them, and read Pedro's replies, sent in care of the Webster plantation. Pedro had confirmed Donati was recovering in the hospital and the forced repatriation of *tejanos* continued unabated; he and Father Soto could do little to stop *las caravanas de dolor*. Pedro had advised them to stay at the plantation, since the Websters were looking out for them.

Carlos wanted to send their next letter, so Daniela bought a stack of paper, a cigar box full of pencils, and a sharpener she clamped onto the side of the table. He learned to write the capitalized block letters she had tattooed in chocolate. After practicing, she gave him the chance to print his name on some forms the Websters had obtained for her, pages filled with typed words and blank lines. First, she read them to him: a Declaration of Intent, Petition for Naturalization, and an Oath of Allegiance to the United States. "Are you sure you want to renounce your 'allegiance and fidelity to Mexico'?"

"My fidelity is to you," he said. "I'll always live where you live."

"So you don't care where you call home?"

"No, I love the country that helped to make you who you are." He printed his name on each of the Labor Department documents.

As his confidence grew, he began to compose love letters to her before he went to the fields each morning. His first one read, "DANIELA, I LOVE YOU. THANK YOU FOR YOUR FAITH IN ME. I WILL KEEP TRYING HARD."

He found her reply on his pillow that night, written in her flowing hand, with loops and curls like petals, and read: "Carlos, my pride in you is only exceeded by my love. You could not make me happier." This he regarded as a challenge.

CHAPTER 34

A month later, Daniela greeted Carlos' return from the fields with another surprise. She sat on their porch, her chair leaning back against the front wall. As he approached, swiping well-water from his face, she lifted his trumpet and blew into the mouthpiece. A squeal peeped from the bell.

"In *mariachi*," he called, "no one sits."

She tipped forward and the chair's front legs thudded onto the porch. "In my condition, I'm going to be doing a lot of sitting." Daniela stood and waggled the trumpet at him. "You better start practicing now, Papá. Letty says you have seven months. I didn't want to tell you until I was sure."

Carlos dashed the rest of the way to reach her. "Do you feel all right? Can I get you anything?"

"I've been a little queasy, so Letty gave be some herbs to chew. The only thing I need is for you to hold me."

He lifted her off the porch in a fierce embrace. "Instead of sitting, why don't you just let me carry you around?"

"I only hope you'll be able to still get your arms around me next year."

Carlos set her down, gave her a soft, slow kiss, and said, "It's settled then. Since you can't make the long walk to Louisiana, I'll have to steal a train for you."

She handed him the trumpet. "Our baby isn't going to have a wanted man as a father."

"I'm already that. Say it again, Dani."

She seemed to know just what he wanted to hear: "Our baby. Our baby!"

*

Carlos dressed in the dark, lifted his trumpet, and crept out of their house to practice. A waxing moon provided dim light on the prairie as he walked a few miles east of the camp, the mugginess of the mid-July night washing over him. Grass crackled under each stride as crickets and cicadas sang all around him. He looked at the twinkling bowl of stars and hummed *La noche y tú* with three fingers tapping the trumpet notes against the valves. He remembered how hard he'd pushed himself to learn to play the first time, and hoped he could do it again.

He planted his feet, facing away from the *colonia*, and raised the horn. The division in his lips no longer felt deep, but the scars were coarse and his jaws and cheeks seemed less flexible. The proper *embouchure* eluded him as he breathed and blew. Sounds emerged like the wailing of new widows, the lament of doves. In every note he heard loss, as air keened through the channels of his scars.

Finally—maybe inevitably, he thought—a sex practice he had perfected on Daniela unlocked the secret of his new *embouchure*. Instead of locking his lips hard against the metal cone, Carlos relaxed his mouth. He made it soft, malleable, and formed a seal around the metal as smoothly all-encompassing as jam around a spoon. Her sensual technique became a means of salvation for his music. In no time he was aloft and, only weeks later, he soared again beneath the stars.

*

"Supper was delicious, your best yet." Carlos set the cloth napkin beside his plate smeared with a ghost of the paella she'd made along with tiny specs of panochitas that had tasted as good as his mother's cookies. He'd left nothing for the flies.

"I want you to know how much I appreciate you." Daniela's foot stroked the inside of his thigh. She pointed at him and announced, "*Jacarandosa.*"

"J-A-C-A-R-A-N-D-O-S-A. A good word—you're very lively tonight. What are you thinking about?"

"A trip. You said you've never had a vacation. Jacie plans to pick up a big load of goods from Houston tomorrow for her parents' store and then drive back on Saturday. She said we can go with her." She rubbed her abdomen and said, "I want to visit my parents and share our happy news. You don't have to see them with me if that would upset you. Wouldn't it be nice just to lie around a hotel room—something you've never done?"

He recalled the last time he was idle in a hotel room, looking at the pocket watch he would donate to the Church, the suit of clothes Paz had picked out draped over a chair. "I'd love to," he said, "but I won't be safe there. Remember Pedro writing that he still doesn't go out except at night, even with Donati in the hospital? The ranger might have friends hunting in the *barrios* who'll recognize me as well."

Her face fell. "Fearfully peeking through the hotel blinds won't be a fun time for either of us. It's just that I see how hard you work and I want to give you something special."

"Our baby is the most special gift you could give me. You're teaching me to read and write, still giving me spelling quizzes." He nipped her finger. "Still satisfying your sweet tooth and mine. You work hard for the Websters—how about a *vacacion* for yourself?"

"We've never been apart before. You'll work even harder: nothing but harvesting and trumpeting and only two hours of sleep without me to wrestle you down."

He thought for a minute and said, "I'll take a separate trip: to find Papá in Galveston and tell him he'll be a granddaddy. If I leave tomorrow, I can be back by Saturday night."

Daniela set the dishes in a basin for washing. "Suddenly this whole thing seems like a bad idea. I'll be riding around in the Websters' truck and enjoying city life again, while you'll be tromping for days in the sun with no guarantee your father will still be there."

"It'll be a reminder of what you gave up for me and what I gained. Hopefully you'll miss me enough to come back." He went into the bedroom and returned with his trumpet.

"That's not fun—" She lifted her chin and peered at him through half-closed eyes. "All right, let's do this. You'll get your treat yet."

Carlos said, "It's my turn to do something special for you. Let's take a little walk."

He carried a chair and she walked alongside with his trumpet. Stars filled the night sky and a bright moon spread blue-white light over the prairie. A breeze stirred the grass into waves. His practice spot was an island of flattened straw in an ocean of silver and shadow. After settling her, he paced off seven long steps and turned. Butterflies quivered in his stomach and his hands sweated. He was more nervous than he'd felt before any *fiesta*. The grass rustled against his waist as he lifted the trumpet to his relaxed mouth.

Daniela gripped the chair seat while he played, as if rocking on a boat, a maiden under the stars who listened to the songs of the sea around her. She cried as he serenaded her. Tear streaks turned glassy in the moonlight. The still-new voice his trumpet carried out to her sounded plaintive in his ears when once it had been brash. Melancholy *tragedías* became heartbreaking and his *corridos* turned heroic. He watched her sway and tremble.

Oscar's love songs were his favorites, and he saved them for last. Sweat dripped from his face and darkened his shirt as he began his finale. Carlos sang in his quavering brass voice of tenderness and passion—a brittle sound, as if, at any moment, all could be lost.

He finished with a triumphant serenade. Daniela held her sides and swooned. Her body rose, as if she was about to levitate above the seat to catch the notes while the pitch of his horn traveled higher. He concluded on a soft refrain, his purest, most gentle note, like the final "I love you" he often breathed into her skin before sleep.

Carlos felt the circular compression that remained on his cool mouth, and tasted a metallic tinge and salty sweat on his upper lip after lowering the trumpet. Daniela leaned forward, eyes closed and mouth slightly open. His kiss eased her back against the chair.

"*Te quiero*," she whispered.

"I love you more."

"Not possible. Thank you for my gift. You worked so hard to give this to me."

He touched the mouthpiece to her abdomen. "Bless you, child." He slid the neck of the trumpet up between her breasts and said, "Let's go to bed."

"Let's stay here."

He laughed. "You'll be too tired to walk home."

"We'll see who gives out first." She held his face and stared into his eyes. "Don't you think I deserve an encore? Besides, we've never made love under the stars."

He set the trumpet on the ground and exorcised another demon from his past.

CHAPTER 35

❦

A *tejana* cleaning woman emptied the wastebasket beside Jack's hospital bed. His neck brace and many of the bandages had been removed, allowing him to turn his head as he tracked her, trying to determine what was out of place. Though darker and a little older than he preferred, she was beautiful in a brassy way, black hair piled up with fetching wisps dangling against her neck, smock blouse and skirt purposely tight to show her impressive figure. Probably too attractive to be a janitor, but that wasn't it: there were only so many jobs a Mexican woman could do after all. She pushed the cloth divider aside and her heels clicked against the floor as she crossed into the other half-room with her trash bag. He had it: her black pumps were far too classy and impractical for the job she was doing.

"Nice shoes," he said in Spanish.

She returned to his room a few moments later and stopped near his feet, where his chart hung from the metal bedstead. The woman said in a husky Spanish whisper, "Staring at women isn't going to help you find the man you seek."

Jack's heart slammed against his chest as she nodded at the obvious question on his face. The woman glanced at the bedside table where there was a scattering of exercise tools he'd had Ranger Miller deliver to strengthen his weak left hand: a rubber ball for squeezing, a new sketch pad and pencils, soft wood blocks, and a small whittling knife. The crude head and forelegs of a galloping horse were emerging from one block of wood. He also kept Daniela's photograph propped up against his wallet. The woman smirked. "Find her and you find Carlos, is that the idea?"

"You seem to know all about him…but what can you tell me about her?"

The woman touched her mouth. "She throws a hard left for a *chica*."

"Daniela's no girl. Carlos found himself an angel."

"Maybe, but he had me first, ranger." She introduced herself as Paz Zaragoza.

"What's the price for what you know, *señorita*?"

"A thousand dollars—"

"That's a lot of money."

"I'm not through. I also want Carlos when you're done with him."

"There won't be much left."

She walked around, slow and sure, to stand beside Jack's left side. Her trash bag dropped to the floor, making a heavier sound than Jack expected. He glanced over the edge of the mattress. Wallets, money clips, key rings, and watches lay among the blood-spotted gauze and tissues.

He wondered if she'd grab the whittling knife, but, no, she'd brought her own—the woman flicked out a blade and thrust it at his face. He flinched, eyelids slamming shut, but the metal didn't touch him. When he looked again, the lashes of his left eye brushed the knifepoint. Her hand held steady as she said, "Carlos told me the story of why you're after him, Ranger Donati. He knows nothing, but that won't stop you. How much easier would his life be with his *ángela* if I pushed this into your brain?"

Jack feared breathing, let alone responding. He pressed as deep into his pillow as the high-backed metal bedstead would allow. The knife followed, but he refused to close his eye again. The blade was so close it almost disappeared from view; he mostly saw her fist.

She said, "I can't handle him at full strength. Do whatever you want with the angel, but only make Carlos docile enough that I won't have to fight him."

"Permanently crippled?"

"If you'd like, but if you unman him I'll do worse to you. You have the *dinero?*"

"I can have it for you in a few days." Tears formed as he kept his eyes open.

"No—you'll have your ranger and police friends with you then." With her free hand she scooped his wallet and keys from the bedside table, knocking the picture facedown. "I'll take whatever I can find at your place. But not a penny more, I promise."

Jack hadn't trusted banks even before their collapse; a professional thief would easily find the accumulated cash payments from his father. He knew she wouldn't stop at a thousand dollars.

She said, "Now then, Carlos told me another story, about a sympathetic Anglo who shielded him from you."

It made sense. The Morenos couldn't have eluded him without a lot of help. "Who?"

"Down the hall there's an office with a phone where I'll give you something better: proof. First, you need to know that I learned about your Linda—even followed her around one day. If something very bad happens to Carlos, she'll also get worse. You'd miss having her around—in case the *ángela* doesn't put out."

She pulled the knife from beside his eye. As he blinked away the strain and tears, she looked at the back of the snapshot and read Daniela's name, her full lips moving. "Come on," she told him, "let's go."

Jack leaned on a hickory cane as he limped beside her to the office. Bandages kept his back warm but the barely closed gown chilled his rear and legs. The ward was quiet late at night: no orderlies or nurses bustled among rooms, no doctors glided in to look at a chart and then depart without a word. Just a few groans from patients in pain echoed in the hall.

Paz opened the lit, unlocked office, dropped her trash bag by the door, and sat at the cluttered desk while he took a chair on the other side. She lifted the receiver from the black Bakelite phone and asked in accented English for the Casson exchange. Even before the operator connected her, Jack knew who'd lied to him about not ever seeing the Morenos.

"Can you please connect me with the Webster place?" the woman asked. She listened a moment and said, "The plantation number, please." She waited again, idly opening drawers and peering inside. "Good evening, sorry for calling so late. I have a friend I'm looking for named Daniela. She's not there? Oh, she doesn't work at night. I understand." She winked at Jack. "I'll try again during the daytime. Thank you."

Jack gestured for the receiver. Clutching it, he announced, "This is Texas Ranger Jack Donati."

A woman's high-pitched voice said, "This is Darla Webster, ranger. What is this about?"

"You're harboring two fugitives, madam. Daniela Domenica and a man named Carlos Moreno. I'll be coming down in the morning."

"To arrest them?"

"I need to talk with them. Maybe we can make this easy. I'll be staying at your place as a guest." When she started to protest, he talked over her: "You and your husband will be brought up on charges if you warn them. But it'll be worse for you than that." He thought of the photographs of his father's death and the flaming mansion. "When I get there I'll show you some proof—" he winked back at Paz "—of what'll happen if you don't cooperate." Darla didn't reply, so he wished her a good night and hung up.

The woman had her knife out again as the receiver came to rest. She gripped the cord connecting the handset and its base, forming a loop above her hand, and sliced through the wires. Before he could react, she snatched his cane and her bag of stolen valuables and dashed from the office, leaving him with no way to call anyone and a long struggle back to his room.

CHAPTER 36

ϙ

The following morning, Carlos held Daniela's hand as they talked to Letty on their porch. He said, "We're taking a trip for a few days, that's all."

"You're leaving. This is *adiós*."

Daniela, dressed in her black uniform for a half-day of work, said, "Just *hasta luego* for three days. We're even heading in opposite directions, so you know we'll be back."

"Is it *el rinche*?"

"No," he said. He'd told Letty and César about Ranger Donati looking for him. "It's the baby." He touched Daniela's abdomen. "She just wants to see her parents and share the good news. I'll try to find my father and do the same."

Letty told her, "It's very early but I'm guessing you'll have a girl."

"You never guess," Daniela said with a laugh. To Carlos, she cried, "A daughter!"

Letty said, "If you're lying to me and never come back, I'll put a witch's curse on her and both of you." She flashed her bright smile. "For a short trip, though, I wish all of you good health." She pecked Daniela on the cheek before lifting her satchel and hiking back down the lane toward the eastern countryside.

Carlos hugged Daniela from behind. "You think she'll find our favorite spot?"

"Probably, but she'll be proud of me. It was one of the things she'd recommended as part of her advice to new brides: 'Make use of nature.' Are you sure you're ready for that long walk?"

"Why wouldn't I be?"

"Remind me who gave out first on the prairie."

He squeezed her and pushed his face into her warm, sweet-smelling hair. He murmured, "That's not fair. You got to sit on the chair most of the time."

When he released her to shoulder his knapsack and canteen and put on his *sombrero*, she said, "You have enough to drink and eat?"

"Thanks to you. I see you packed corn muffins and apples."

"For old times' sake. Jacie's supposed to pick me up in the afternoon," she reminded him. "We'll be in Houston in less than an hour. I wish you'd come with us."

"I wish I didn't have any reason to stay away."

"See you on Saturday night. I hope to have another surprise awaiting you."

"Better than the other surprises?"

"You'll have to come back to find out." She kissed him goodbye.

Carlos turned around once at the well and waved to her. He knew if he turned again and saw the brave smile that failed to mask her worry, there would be no way he could continue. He followed the path to the sunken road. An unoccupied black car sat in front of the plantation house.

He passed the fields where his friends waved their short-handled tools and joked with him about losing money by going for a walk. Carlos turned south, staying a mile from the road and train tracks, as the sun heated his body and insects hummed around him. He thought back to the time he'd moved northward on that highway with Pedro, who was now a wanted man himself because of his assault on *el rinche* and his help with the underground. Daniela, too, had become an exile. Everyone he cared about had picked up the curse that pursued him.

Carlos recalled Papá's final lesson—"Never backtrack, son"—as he did precisely that. He prayed he would not bring the curse with him.

*

Jack sat at the head of the Websters' dining table, which had room for twelve. The skin beneath the remaining bandages around the top of his head and torso itched. He would have to get the town doctor to remove the patchwork of stitches—the nightshift nurses had refused to do so before he'd left the hospital with Ranger Miller's help.

Early morning sunlight streamed through a row of windows along one wall and birds sang from bushes and fields. Miller, thick arms crossed over his bulk, leaned against the rococo wallpaper nearby rather than directly behind Jack, who recognized his training of the young lawman: always have a clear field of fire. At the other end of the table sat the Websters, robes covering their bedclothes: Tom with his red-tinged gray eyes and Kraut-gassed voice, his wife Darla, and their daughter Jacinda, strongly resembling the mother whose hand she clutched. Darla was the only Webster whose gaze looked clear. Jack knew she was his main opponent as she leveled her green-eyed stare at him the way he'd often sighted down rifle barrels.

He repeated his right to commandeer the Webster house for the purpose of surveillance and possible detainment and arrest of Daniela and Carlos. At Jack's request, Miller reiterated that any interference would mean the Websters' arrest as well. "And," the junior ranger added, "if your peons get in our way, we'll put them all on Mex Ex." Miller sounded pleased with his rhyme. When Darla asked what that was, he said, "An express train for Old Mexico. Plenty of white folks will do their work now; we'd be doing our country a favor."

"Thanks, ranger," Jack said. He addressed the Websters again, primarily Darla. "I think we understand each other. You'll need a story to tell the maids, the cook, anyone who asks. I'll be Darla's distant cousin from south Texas, say Laredo, named Juan Diego. Easy name to remember—no one will be surprised you people have some greasers in the branches of your family tree. I'm recovering from a car wreck that took the lives of my wife and two babies."

Tom said in his damaged voice, "And how long will you be staying with us, Cousin Diego?"

"A few days, maybe less, depending on how cooperative everyone is." He dismissed Miller, who asked Jack to telephone if he needed him. Miller made a slow journey through the room, breathing loud as he stared at the Websters. He stomped across the foyer and slammed the front door behind him. A few moments later, his black Model A Ford drove off. It had been Jack's car before he'd bought the Cadillac Phaeton. Paz Zaragoza had helped herself to the Caddy, however, and plenty more. The cost was worth it now that he was here. So close to the man he sought and the woman he longed to meet.

Darla said, "You know my brother, Buck, works for Governor Sterling. He could take away your job in a blink and maybe put you in jail."

From his breast pocket, behind the badge, Jack took the three Brownsville photographs, smaller than the one of Daniela that rested closest to his chest. He stood, using his legs alone, pushing his body to serve him again. His left leg had its old throb plus the new pain of his mended calf, like an icy fire when he put weight on it. He limped to the teenager Jacinda who leaned away, toward her mother. He set the snapshots in front of the girl as gently as he could, as if sharing last year's Christmas memories.

*

Jack settled into the Websters' guest bedroom and waited for the maids to report to work. The room had been Buck's; photographs of Darla's brother shaking hands with Governor Sterling, President Hoover, and other politicians and celebrities hung in black frames along the four walls. The Websters had each bathed in the lavatory next to his room and scurried past his open door, not looking as they retreated to their domiciles. They'd reassembled downstairs, and Jack heard Darla repeating his story to the cook, asking the woman to make an additional breakfast.

He'd changed into powder-blue pajamas and piled a mound of pillows against the headboard of Buck's bed. Hobbling across the floor to the armoire beside the door, he used his weak left hand to open the wardrobe and lift his gun belt from a hook. The encircled star flashed on the holster, stickpin burrowed in the leather. His arm strained as he carried the rig back to bed.

Jack drew his revolver left-handed. The leather seemed to sigh as the barrel scraped free. The six cylinders gaped: Miller had followed his order to unload it. Jack aimed at the lit hall chandelier and cocked, his arm drooping under the weight. His teeth gritted as he forced his hand to rise. He squeezed the trigger and the hammer slammed against a hollow cylinder. Jack cocked and fired again, strengthening his hand as he shot imaginary bullets at the delicate crystals and hand-blown light bulbs. He fantasized about taking Daniela and finishing his enemies, from Moreno to the man with the axe handle, the one who Paz Zaragoza had said Carlos didn't know. Soon enough he would discover if the thief had spoken the truth. His left knee throbbed in time with the impotent clicking of the revolver.

Jack lowered the gun as he panted. He knew he would've missed most of the glass targets he'd chosen. Not nearly good enough, he thought: when you've waited for years, you want the first bullet to strike home. The shots that followed would be gravy. Noise and smoke and blood to exorcise any lingering ghosts.

The front door opened downstairs and two women entered, chatting. One of them sounded like a country Negro, while the other spoke in almost accent-less English. The latter woman said, "—just through Saturday." She laughed, a bright and happy sound. "You'll hardly know I'm gone."

Jack had known only Mexican women to express such sudden gaiety between ordinary sentences, like gifts they gave to themselves and their listeners. He holstered the gun and shoved the rig under the lone-star quilt before wiping his face on the sheet.

Below him, Darla greeted the women and explained a guest would be staying for a while. Her voice sounded tight as she conveyed his story. The Mexican woman said, "I planned to go to Houston today with Jacie—would you like me to stay?"

"No, no, please go ahead. Please. That'll be fine—she'll enjoy the company. He's resting now, best not to disturb him."

How like his recent luck, Jack thought: the woman he wanted to see was returning for a few days to the place from which he'd come. Perhaps Carlos would stay here, at least, afraid to run into him or another lawman in Houston.

The maids went about their downstairs chores, and whenever one approached the steps, Darla distracted her with another task. Meddlesome bitch. Keeping his left hand under the covers to mute the noise, Jack worked the action of the revolver over and over until sweat stung his eyes and soaked his pajama jacket. Finally, the women had to come up to continue with their labors.

As the fall and echo of footsteps overlapped in the stairwell, Jack leaned back against his pillows, covers up to his chest and hands folded atop the quilt. He shivered as the sweat that had soaked his pajamas chilled his skin. Dark patches of blue cotton stuck to his breastbone and beneath his armpits.

Darla peered into the room first, her mouth as thin and straight as Paz Zaragoza's knife. "Juan?" she said, her pitch traveling up. "I have two ladies here who'll help you with anything you need." She first introduced a skinny black woman named Beatrice who promised to go check on his breakfast and clopped back downstairs.

Daniela stepped into her place in the open doorway, a simple black dress showing off her petite figure, as Darla announced her as "Daniela Moreno." Moreno, not Domenica. Somehow, the fact that she now was married to Carlos made him hate the man all the more. Daniela's hair had grown out a little since the picture had been taken, tumbling over her shoulders in black whorls, making her even more stunning. She curtsied a short ways, a quick dip from her knees. After greeting him in Spanish, she continued in English, "I'm sorry about—Oh, you must have a fever!"

She rushed to him, a look of concern on her angelic face. Her warm wrist rested against his brow and the bandages just above as she judged his temperature. He inhaled the smells of soap and talcum powder. His gaze began to drift over her as she stood close, but he willed himself to close his eyes before his staring became too obvious.

Jack decided to reply in Spanish and shut out Darla from the conversation since the woman still loomed in the doorway. "I'm sure it's nothing, thanks. I was just thinking about my wife and babies—all dead now—when I heard your laughter downstairs. You brought back good memories, something I haven't been able to do on my own for a while. And I dreamed and forgot....then I touched the bandages on my head." He shivered again.

She removed her wrist, but placed her hand on his left arm, soft as a second sleeve. She glanced at Darla and said in English, "Please don't relive it. Mrs. Webster told me everything. Can I get you fresh clothes? Some water?" She warmed him with her smile.

He stayed with Spanish. "To sit and talk would be the greatest kindness."

"I'm only here a short time today," she replied in English again. "So I need to get some things done for Mrs. Webster. I'll check on you soon."

"*Es muy amable de su parte.*"

She pressed a bit firmer, a gentle squeeze. "Anything to help."

Daniela left the room and walked around the banister to a linen closet, but Darla lingered, eyes narrowed. Jack pointed his left forefinger at her, thumb cocked. He shot her.

The knuckles standing out on Darla's suntanned fists grew whiter. She turned for the stairs; he had to admit she had a nice figure for a woman near his age. Too bad her kind would never thaw.

Daniela smiled as she passed his room with arms full of pure white linens. He smiled sadly in reply. Her face peeked back around the doorjamb and she said, this time in Spanish, "You sure there's nothing you need?"

"I don't want to interrupt your work."

She returned in a few minutes with a glass of water for him and pulled a chair to his bedside. On his end-table lay the block of wood from which the horse was taking shape. Beneath the wood and knife was his sketchbook with the photograph of her tucked inside, along with an enlargement he was drawing. She said, "How long does it take to do a carving?"

"I used to make toys in a matter of hours for my children. With this hand of mine…" He held his left palm open beside her knee. "Maybe it'll be days now."

"Doing this will help you to remember the good times much more than my laughter. You don't need me braying like a horse to remind you."

Jack grinned and had to deaden his expression before he forgot himself. Maybe he'd linger here for weeks or months, getting to know her and turning her sympathy into love. He could have Carlos interrogated in secret and his body hidden, and then comfort Daniela, who'd believe that her husband had abandoned her. "You said you're going away?"

"I'll be back at work on Monday."

"A family trip?" He brushed the bandages over his scalp, trying to stay in character. He had not been so giddily nervous around a woman in decades.

"Not really. My husband's going one way and I'm going the other."

As he sipped the cool water she'd brought, he made a mental note to have Miller send some cars down the local highways and alert deputies in the towns, probably as far south as Galveston. "I hope there are no...troubles between you."

"Heavens no. Just parents who live in opposite directions."

"I wish you both a safe journey, Sra. Moreno. The roads can be deadly."

*

On Friday morning, Carlos pulled up the weeds that grew over Mamá's grave and, in the separate section for los angelitos, his unnamed brother's resting place. Dew slicked his palms and fingers. He wet his kerchief with water from his canteen and rubbed the accumulated grit from their burial crosses. The wind had pitted the white paint in spots and blasted it from the wood altogether on the west-facing edges. As he cleaned, he told Mamá his happy news, though he'd spoken to her in his prayers many times before.

He walked to the strip of sand fronting the bay, opened his knapsack, and took out the last corn muffin. As with the other three, Daniela had wrapped it in a note—now grease-stained—written in Spanish and then English so he could practice. He read: "I was adrift in a sea of sharks and shoals. You rescued me with sail and rudder. You taught me to navigate by the stars and steer according to my heart's desire.

Now, as we follow our calm-sea course, you serenade me and fill me with wonder, and I love you."

Carlos reread both versions several times. As he recited from memory, he put the paper beside the others in his pack. Daniela's words embraced him while he hiked along the lonely coastline, far from the roads. At the handyman's ramshackle shed, he removed his hat and knocked at the open doorway. "Mr. Shapiro?"

Isaac Shapiro looked up from his project, sanding another burial cross. He removed the pipe from his mouth.

"I'm Carlos Moreno, sir."

"My God, it's been a while. You look taller." The old carpenter came around the bench, shook his hand, and peered at his face. "You have some kind of accident?"

Carlos touched his mouth and chin. "It looks worse than it is. Have you seen my father in Galveston, sir?"

"He's probably on the fishing pier. I've seen him there a lot."

Carlos asked how Papá looked.

"Like he's had a better few years than you, if you don't mind me saying so. He married a widow and got a ready-made family in the bargain: a couple of boys near-about your age who fish with him, plus a girl or two, and I think a couple of grandkids. He's done nicely for himself, meaning no disrespect to your mother."

Carlos fought the urge to turn and head back to the Websters' *hacienda*. He didn't want to meet a bunch of strangers. He just wanted to see Papá and swap stories and maybe play a tune for him. He took a breath and quieted his thoughts. "Could you take me over there, please?" He reached into his pocket. "Is it still six bits?"

"Times are tough, so I lowered it to four."

He handed over fifty cents. "When can we go?"

Sr. Shapiro led the way down to his rickety dock with the rowboat tied to a lichen- and dropping-covered piling. As they approached, seagulls cried and flew over the bay.

George Weinstein | 291

"I can row, sir, if it would be easier."

"Well let's just call this a rental and I'll go back inside. Have the boat back by five."

"What time is it, please?"

"It's half-past ten."

"I'll have it back well before then. Here's another dollar, so you won't lose money because of me." Carlos passed over a wrinkled bill, dropped his knapsack into the bow, and held the piling as he stepped into the ancient craft, adjusting his balance to keep it from capsizing. He sat and lifted the oars while Sr. Shapiro untied the line. Using one of the old wood paddles, Carlos pushed away from the dock and called goodbye as the carpenter waved.

Carlos rowed into Galveston Bay, found a comfortable stroke, and enjoyed the feel of slipping over the gentle waves. At times he could convince himself that when he pushed the oars against the water, he stood still but pulled Galveston closer to him.

He checked over his shoulder and adjusted his course toward the northern tip of the island, mindful of the shipping lanes. Large tankers and freighters skirted the Galveston wharfs as they headed northwest toward the Houston Ship Channel. Some ships were docked at the island, but fishermen far outnumbered the longshoremen.

Broad piers were filled with anglers who nearly stood shoulder-to-shoulder. Anglos largely fished with one another, but *tejanos* and blacks mixed freely as they cast into the green-gray water. Carlos rowed parallel to the docks, far enough out to observe them without feeling inspected himself, but close enough to stay clear of fishing trawlers and the big boats. He searched for Papá's familiar hunched posture among the colored men and boys wiggling their cane poles and chatting. Just as he had started to lose hope, there—with young *tejanos* who looked like brothers on either side of him—stood his father.

Carlos rowed closer and turned the boat so he could face the pier. He shouted, "I backtracked, Papá. Look where it got me."

His father lifted a tall, broad-brimmed hat as his rod dipped toward the water. "At least no one followed you!" His voice sounded cheery, and he appeared to be smiling. "I'll meet you at the dock there with the other skiffs." Papá pointed with his hat and gestured at his stepsons to pull in their lines and follow him. He handed his pole to one of them and walked quickly in his knock-kneed gait toward the dock.

Carlos pretended to race, but then drifted the last fifty feet so Papá could win. The rowboat bumped among the tied-off skiffs. He tossed the line to his father, who waited, panting, at the edge of the dock and let Papá pull him onto the slick wood decking.

He hugged his father for a long moment and then stared at the details of the familiar—yet new—face he regarded. Papá had shaved off his thick gray mustache. The dark pads under his eyes had faded, and his hairline was neatly trimmed below his new hat. Carlos looked him over, noting the ironed work clothes and barely creased cowhide boots.

His father reached up with his damaged fingers and touched Carlos' cheek, near the corner of his mouth. Papá's eyes brimmed with tears. "What did they do to my son?"

Carlos smiled, feeling the blunt ends of the fingers slide against his skin. "It's not as bad as it looks, Papá. Just a thief I surprised. You've been through worse."

"True." His father withdrew his fingers and brushed under his eyes. He turned as the brothers approached with their fishing gear. "Boys, meet my son, Carlos."

One young man introduced himself as Emilio. He said, "We've heard so much about you."

"Yes," the one named Arnoldo said in response to Carlos' raised eyebrows. "*Padrastro* compares everything we do to the way you did it and finds fault with us." He smiled but shared a look with his brother.

Emilio patted Carlos' shoulder and said, "Your father talks about you a lot: 'Carlos could do this. Carlos could do that.' He's very proud of you."

Papá chuckled and said, "Now I'm proud of you boys, too. Don't forget I raised this one, so I've known him much longer." He turned to Carlos. "Did you come for a visit or to stay?"

"Just a visit, Papá. I have lots of news, and I want to hear about your family." He pointed at Sr. Shapiro's skiff. "Let me take you out into the bay, and we can talk."

His father nodded. "All right, boys, you'll have to catch dinner and supper on your own. Better double your usual haul—my son used to eat half his weight at every meal."

Emilio and Arnoldo walked back to their spot on the pier, talking and looking over their shoulders. Carlos said, "Do you need some help getting into the boat? It's a little wobbly."

"I can do it." Papá dangled his legs above the skiff while grasping the edge of the pier. He dropped onto the bench seat, almost overturning the craft.

Carlos stepped down, untied the line, and lowered himself onto the other bench. He rowed back into the bay and turned south, to stay in the channel between Galveston and the mainland. Papá draped his arms along the gunwales and grinned at him. Carlos predicted that when he thought back to this day, he'd most remember that look of honest joy.

CHAPTER 37

❧

"You first, Papá," Carlos said. "When did you get married again?"

"Two years ago. Matilda is from Puerto Rico. She'd moved around and finally settled on Galveston because she missed being on an island." His index finger thrust into the air, looking straighter than before. "You see? Some people take comfort from being surrounded by water."

Carlos let out a slow, calming breath. "How did you meet?"

"She works in a fishery. I brought in my catches to sell, and we talked. Her husband died of pneumonia about the time of your mother's death, so there was a lot to talk about."

"Do you ever visit Mamá's grave?"

"This is the first time I've left the island since Sr. Shapiro brought me over."

"I could take you there now."

"No, I remember what it looks like. That's enough." He rubbed his bare upper lip and looked away toward Galveston. His three blunted fingers tapped against the edge of the boat. "You've been safe, other than the robbery?"

"*El rinche* never found me," he lied. "Even better, I got married a few months ago."

"*¡Muy bien!* What's her name?"

"Daniela Domenica. You'll like her. She's educated and beautiful and very caring. She taught me to read and write."

"You have a need for that?"

"Maybe one day. She made it fun to learn. We leave each other notes: love letters and jokes."

His father said, "Very romantic. Your mother and I started out that way, too. Not writing, of course, but we were close."

"Daniela's carrying our first child, probably a girl. Mamá had always wanted a girl."

"You'll do well raising a female. You understand them better than I can." He rubbed his upper lip again. "The money you sent had come in handy. With a baby on the way, I now understand why you stopped."

"I couldn't send more only because we moved to a place with no post office." Another lie, but he didn't want his father to worry about Daniela and him in hiding and the lingering danger of Donati discovering where he or Papá had gone. Carlos drew them even with the colored cemetery on the mainland and halted the skiff. He passed over thirty dollars from his pocket and used the oars to maintain his position as water tried to nudge the small craft toward the beach. He said, "You look so different without your mustache."

Papá counted the money and pushed the cash into his pocket. "I feel different. I am different. Mustaches and beards are good for hiding behind, but hiding's not living. Now, I live."

"You mean you were hiding the whole time I was growing up?"

Papá kept looking at Galveston Island in the distance. His voice took on the hard edge from the time before Mamá died. "I certainly hid during those last few years."

"I could tell something was strained between you and Mamá at the end."

"You weren't paying attention—it was there for a long while."

"Back when we were in Port Lavaca and Mamá told me about the baby?"

"Carlos, I don't want to talk about this."

He tried again. "Since the Klansman cut you?"

"Cut me?" His father raised his voice. "You've always put it that way, 'I'm sorry he cut you, Papá.' I'm sorry he kicked you, son. What he did to me was saw off my balls and put them in my hand while you and that ranger watched. I can still feel the wet lumps burning here!" He thrust out his left hand. "He would've sliced off my *pene*, but he got distracted by my big, strong son crying on the ground. So, thank you anyway for letting me still pee like a man."

Tears stung Carlos' eyes as if he'd been slapped. "I'm sorry, Papá, I didn't know. No one would talk about it." He thought again about failing Papá by not putting up a fight. His ears burned with the cries and laughter of years ago when the Klansmen held Papá down and the ranger stood by. The memory of Donati made Carlos ask, "Did you see the man who made them stop, the one called Rafael Bernal?"

"He made no noise, just swooped in and clubbed those bastards—I heard bones snapping. Sr. Bernal shoved a kerchief on my groin and put you over his shoulder. He picked me up and carried us home."

"Did he say anything?"

"I still held my balls in my hand, son. I could feel my life draining through the seat of my pants—you think we had a conversation?" He looked back toward Galveston and shrugged. "Maybe I fainted. Anyway, next thing I knew, I was in bed." His left hand squeezed into a fist. "My hand was clean and empty. Elisa had thrown them away."

Carlos winced. "Did you want to keep them?"

"Of course not, but there was something reassuring about holding them, like they were still a part of me."

Then a chill ran through Carlos. "'Miracle baby,'" he whispered. Stronger waves carried the skiff toward the beach and the cemetery, forcing him to paddle again.

"That's right! Two years later your loving mother died trying to give me someone else's son." Papá finally looked toward the graveyard—he spit into the bay.

Carlos let go of an oar and crossed his forehead. He asked who the father was.

"She wouldn't say. She kept insisting it was ours, that it was a miracle. I think she welcomed a parade of lovers after throwing my balls in the street."

"We moved from Port Lavaca to La Marque—"

"When she couldn't hide the truth from me any longer. She baked *panochitas* to tell you her good news. I had to get us away from that stable of Don Juans. She disgraced me."

"After the funerals, you told me God only punishes the wicked. You were talking about her."

"And those sons of bitches she laid. God will revenge me on them too—it's all I've ever prayed for."

"Why didn't you explain to me what was happening?"

"What was the point? Would you have spent the last seven months of her life wondering what we'd done to deserve her betrayal?" He glared at Carlos. "Would you have hated the mother you'd loved before?"

"I don't...No. Nothing would've been different. Except I'd have understood more."

Papá said, "I've never figured out her hold on you. There you were laughing together, feeling that damned baby move under her belly, and finishing each other's sentences. I hated both of you sometimes."

"You didn't—"

"I wanted to yell out what she'd done. So someone would've been on my side."

"I was on your side too, Papá. You never talked to me like this before."

"None of it matters. You'd forgive that woman anything."

"Is it better to forgive her nothing?"

"You see?" His voice rose to a shout again, "Already, you're trying to wipe the dirt off that image you have of her, like some droppings on a statue of *La Virgen de Guadalupe*. You ignore that the slime is dripping out of her, not on her. The filth is inside; it's part of her."

Papá continued in a taunting voice, "What if you found out your Daniela had done this to you? What if that baby girl isn't yours?"

"She'd never do that."

"Wouldn't you have sworn the same thing about your mother? If Daniela did, wouldn't you want to know why and how could she? Wouldn't you feel betrayed? Angry?"

"Yes. Yes to all that." Carlos jabbed his thumb against his chest and said, "But, I'd also want to know what I'd done to make her unhappy, what I could do differently. Maybe it couldn't ever be the same again, but I wouldn't hate her."

"Then I raised a better man than I am."

"No, sir...Mamá did." He wanted desperately to tear down the man in front of him, but clenched his teeth instead. What was the point of a longer argument? Why hurt his father who still hurt so much? He turned the skiff around and rowed hard back toward the dock. Each time the paddles lifted from the water, droplets pattered onto the surface like rapidly fleeing footsteps.

He focused so much on yanking Galveston closer he barely heard his father's soft question: "Do you hate me?"

The oars crashed against the water over and over as he pulled the island to him and tried to silence the footsteps he heard between the strokes. He plunged across the shipping lanes, heedless of the oncoming freighters and tankers. When the rowboat reached shallower water, Carlos glanced at his father's downcast face. "No, Papá," he said.

"It's almost noon. Come home and have dinner with my family. We'll talk about other things."

"No, Papá."

"You're not hungry? You used to eat half your weight—"

"No, Papá." Carlos used the boat's speed to knock the other skiffs aside. The stern thumped against a piling, sending a jarring shock through him.

His father grasped the pier and stood on quavering legs as the boat rocked. Arnoldo and Emilio arrived and helped

Papá onto the slippery decking. He turned and held out his hands. "Throw me the rope."

For this parting, Carlos couldn't think of some brave sacrifice he could make, some *diablo* to lure away. He wanted only to flee from his father's anger and his own grief. He jabbed the oars into the water and pushed the dock away from him. "No, Papá," he called. "I'm going home. *Adiós.*"

*

Carlos told Sr. Shapiro to keep the extra money and started walking toward Casson. The trumpet pressed against his back through the knapsack, reminding him of all that had gone wrong with his reunion plans. He didn't really notice the waving prairie grass around him, didn't feel the burn of sunlight, or the choking humidity. Instead, he saw Mamá's melancholy smile when he'd asked if she was happy and heard her voice on the hot wind: "No, but I'm in love. I don't think about happiness anymore." She'd told him of the affair, in her way. And revealed her suffering because of what she'd done.

Oscar had once said: "Things are just as they should be." If Mamá had never taken a lover or if she'd survived the birth… maybe he would not have gone to Houston and now would not be returning to Daniela, who was carrying their baby.

Life was a house of cards, he decided: replace just one that was wrong and the whole *casa* would come down, all of the good parts lost along with the destiny he changed.

CHAPTER 38

❦

On Saturday evening an afterglow of pale light hovered over the western prairie and a train roared southward in the distance, leaving faint, familiar music on the wind like Carlos' first night in Houston.

He lengthened his strides as he neared the workers' shacks beside the Webster plantation. Campfires flickered in the breeze, and he could see a steady, purposeful movement of people in the lane between the shacks. When he trotted closer, he could tell they were waltzing. They danced to *"La noche y tú,"* sung in Oscar's rich bass and played by *El Mariachi Santa Cruz*. Except no trumpet led them.

Carlos sprinted toward the camp, pulling his knapsack off his shoulder and digging out the horn. The grass crashed beneath him as he ran. He stopped behind the row of houses, took a few deep breaths beside the reeking privies, and set the trumpet to his mouth. He waited for the final verse.

His brass voice stopped Oscar's song. He walked around the side of the shack, trying to play without smiling at the bandleader's incredulous stare. The crowd cheered and resumed dancing with even more energy. The musicians picked up the last two lines and performed in concert with Carlos as he took his place beside Oscar:

With your love no more will I crave darkness
I'm ready to face the dawn beside you!

Nearly two hundred men, women, and children erupted with shouts of "¡*Viva!*" and riotous applause. Oscar and Carlos hugged and Hector and the other musicians patted Carlos' back. The pressing crowd parted for Daniela and closed again behind her.

Carlos kissed and embraced her. "How?" he asked.

Daniela had to yell in his ear as others massed around them to welcome Carlos home and cheer the band. "I warned you that you'd get a surprise! Jacie helped me scour the *barrios*. A musician told us where Oscar was hiding. Up in the Fifth Ward, working for Oriental Textile."

Oscar said on Carlos' other side, "So this crazy *gringa* Jacinda has the foreman pull me out of the warehouse this morning. Said she was a *Chronicle* reporter and had a story about me being a witness to a murder she was writing about. Daniela's with her as 'the grieving widow.' They invited me to come down here and we rounded up the rest of the band."

Daniela's expression turned serious. "A lot's happened since you left. There are still other surprises, not all of them good."

"You're all right? Our baby?"

"We're both fine." She hugged him hard and patted his back. "You and Oscar catch up first. I'll see you at home."

"I love you!" he said.

"I love you, *guapo*. Talk to your friends."

Carlos drew Oscar toward the well, acknowledging more welcomes and compliments along the way. "What's this all about?"

"It's not my place to say. I told you that you'd always have a home with our band; your wonderful wife's brought the band to your home."

"Where was home for you after the barricades were overrun?"

"We all left town, except Hector, who gave me some speech about facing your problems instead of running away. All the jobs are drying up outside Houston, so the rest of us came back anyway. Even in the city it's hard to find steady work. I think the police stopped looking for us, but we ruined the Saturday concerts. None of the bands have dared to perform. I couldn't even go to Guadalupe to pray."

Carlos hadn't seen Oscar's girlfriend in the crowd. "I'm sorry you had to leave Marguerite behind."

"No, she did that to me. She married a man her parents approved of and moved to San Antonio."

"That's terrible! But still—why return to farm work?"

"Like I said, Daniela wanted to surround you with friends."

"What's your second reason?"

Oscar laughed. "You don't forget a thing. We were too afraid of the police to even practice anymore. It was like spending my life with one eye closed and an arm tied behind my back. I was going crazy." His face turned serious, grimmer than Carlos had ever seen. "Crazy with guilt too— our trumpet player ran the wrong way when the barricades fell. People told us the police took Alfredo away. My stirring things up might've gotten him murdered or shipped south with other *repatriados*. It was pointless to risk everyone like that. My guilt kept me in Pedro's mission for many days after I returned to Houston."

"I know that guilt very well. How is Pedro?"

"Go ask him yourself." Oscar pointed toward Carlos' house and propelled him that way with a firm hand behind his back.

Daniela and Jacie stood on the porch, talking with a priest who faced away from the dirt lane. A black cassock stretched across his broad shoulders; his gray hair was close-cropped. Carlos called Pedro's name and trotted the rest of the way, dropping his hat and gear beside the porch.

Pedro turned. Like Papá, he, too, had removed his disguise. The scars in his scalp and clean-shaven cheeks, as well as the gash around his neck, showed vividly in the firelight. He embraced Carlos in the street, gripping him hard for a moment. Pedro said, "It's wonderful to be able to hear you play again. God's resurrected your music."

"Have you left Houston for good? Your beard—"

"When Daniela and Jacie told me, I knew I had to stop hiding." As Oscar approached, Pedro said, "We've all come to help you."

Daniela called from the porch, "Father, I haven't told him yet."

Pedro steered Carlos to his home, saying, "Then it's time you knew." He addressed Jacie and Oscar: "If you please, I ask for a few minutes of privacy. For confessions." Carlos and Daniela entered the house and Pedro followed, closing the door behind him.

*

Daniela lit a kerosene lamp that cast just enough light to emphasize the furrows in Pedro's face and neck as he sat at the table. Beside the lamp lay a slim book and two envelopes, one letter-sized and a larger, overstuffed one. Carlos took his seat across from his friend, facing the door through which trouble would surely come. Unless he went out to meet it. He said, "Donati's here?"

"He arrived at the Websters' the morning you left for Galveston," Daniela said, "and masqueraded as an injured relative. The pretending was for me, mostly, and I fell for it. The ranger had already told the Websters exactly who he was and what'll happen if they try to interfere. It's as terrible for them as it is for us. If we run, they'll probably die."

"Everyone who's tried to help me has been hurt by this curse following me."

Pedro said, "But look at how many have rallied around you, have risked themselves despite the danger. Sra. Webster sent Jacie and Daniela to Houston with a note for me, telling about Donati and asking me to do whatever I could for you."

"She's treated us very well," Carlos said, patting the table that belonged to her.

Daniela said, "She's still giving us gifts." She lifted the envelope thick with paper. "I told you when you married an American citizen you'd gain certain rights…"

Carlos took the envelope and pulled out the sheaf of papers. The first page was a small piece of stationery he recognized as one of the forms Daniela had brought home. His English had improved, so he could read, "Oath of Allegiance," at the top, followed by a declaration renouncing fidelity to "Pascual Ortiz Rubio, President of Mexico"—handwritten on a blank line—below which the oath continued with the support and defense of the Constitution and laws of the United States of America, an obligation taken without reservation. "SO HELP ME GOD" was printed in capital letters at the end, below which he had signed in similar block letters. A date, "this 16 day of July, A.D. 1930," had been filled in under his name, followed by the cursive signatures of a clerk and a deputy clerk. The final completed line contained a series of "Line", "List", and "Certificate" issue numbers preceded by the words "Petition granted."

The two pages after the Oath were the other completed forms, a Declaration of Intent and a Petition for Naturalization with "United States of America" printed in large letters at the top. A copy of the Constitution made up the remaining pages, too many words to read as his vision blurred with tears.

"It's official," Pedro said. "I'd planned to make a special trip to get it to you. And here I am."

Daniela laid her hand over Carlos'. "It usually takes years to be granted this, but Sra. Webster had her brother work some magic and turn years into months."

"So I can't be repatriated to Mexico?"

Pedro said, "If they support and defend their own laws— as you've sworn to do—but we all know they do what they want." He lifted the smaller envelope. "I've prepared a letter of introduction for some priests in Corpus Christi, where Daniela's sisters can help you. I'm sure we can get you two down there somehow without harming the Websters or anyone else."

"Why don't I just go to Donati and tell him what I know?"

"You don't know anything that would satisfy him." Daniela's moist eyes gleamed. "He'll torture you and there's nothing you could say that would be good enough. He'll kill you."

"But until I confront him, everyone is in danger because of me."

Pedro said, "We're all here because of you, Carlos—because of our love for you. But the real reason you're all in danger is because of me." He tapped the book with his envelope. "Take some time to read this."

"What is it?" Carlos flipped open the slender volume and glanced at the handwriting, a mix of bold slashes and elegant loops.

"A journal I started after Daniela and Jacie came to see me. These are some stories you both might like to know."

Carlos moved his chair closer to Daniela and set the book between them. The dim lamplight shone on the pages as he read in Spanish:

> I was twenty-five when I became a revolutionary during our war for democracy in 1910. I'd considered myself a man of peace until President Díaz's troops looted my home, raped my wife Carmen, and murdered her and our three children. I heard their screams and came running in from the fields just as their throats were being cut.
>
> I attacked the four Federals with a pitchfork, my only weapon. Their first shot almost split my head in two. There were other

bullets, fired through my side and shoulder. They meant to kill me, but their laughter hurt their aim. They dragged me inside and forced me to kneel beside Carmen. The one who'd cut her throat sliced open both my cheeks. A rifle butt broke my nose. They brought in some cheap rope from their saddlebags to tie my hands. A crude noose was tossed over the rafter beam. They stood me on a chair with the rope around my neck and secured the other end to the front door. Then they all took turns trying to shoot off the chair legs.

After the second leg went skittering away, I lost my balance and hung, twisting and writhing. Their rope and knots were poor, and my neck was thick. I strangled as they mounted their horses. That's how they left me, dangling a few feet above my slaughtered family. But, one of them had also left his gun belt, forgotten in the excitement.

My lovely wife Carmen should've been dead, should've received that mercy of peace, but she'd always been a wonderfully stubborn woman. She pulled the soldier's revolver from beneath her and pointed it up at me as I swung. Carmen ended my misery, though not as I'd desired. She shot through the rope, a miraculous feat. Death would've been so easy to give me, but she granted me life before she closed her eyes and joined the angels.

I buried my family that evening. With the gun and the ammunition in the belt, I taught myself to shoot straight, though my best shot never matched Carmen's only one. I joined the Revolution and sent many

Federals to Hell. But no amount of revenge satisfied me, for I only stole life. My Carmen, she'd cheated Death.

During the first night of the Battle of Ciudad Juárez, May 1911, I saw her twin in body and spirit—a refugee with a small boy—hiding in one of the houses we occupied as we fought our way to the city garrison. The beautiful woman's name was Elisa Moreno and her son was Carlos, but she didn't tell me that at the time; she only had thoughts of her husband Gerardo. He'd been trapped outside when the shooting started. She asked me to find him. I told her I would, but discovered I couldn't move from where I'd crouched beside her. I felt as if a witch had put a spell on me. My best friend Rafael reminded me that we had a city to capture and steered me away.

I tried to forget the married woman whose name I didn't know. Forgetting her should've been easy when the Federals counterattacked the next night—they killed Rafael and a few other comrades in an old church before losing heart and retreating—but I wanted to find her to talk through my grief. Forgetting should've been easy on the third day when General Navarro put out the white flag and we revolutionaries claimed the city, but I wanted to waltz in the streets with her.

I didn't find Gerardo Moreno until after the battle. He and Elisa stood outside the house they'd occupied, shouldering makeshift packs. I remember how carefully Elisa shielded her boy from the hot sun as she and her husband skirted the revelers. I followed them past the Anglo photographers selling souvenir tintypes of the battle. Along with many others, we crossed the dry backbone of the Río Bravo, what Americans call the Grande, and stepped onto U.S. soil. I trailed them through the well-dressed crowds of Americans throwing sweets and silver dollars to my compatriots on the other side. We entered El Paso del Norte and I began a new life.

But I couldn't forget Elisa. I'd rekindled feelings of love, or what I thought was love. Really it was sinful obsession: coveting another man's wife. I followed the Morenos and others as we traveled the old U.S. Army trails through Texas. Often, I worked on different plantations than the Morenos, trying to thwart my desires, but I always gave in and snuck away to steal glimpses of Elisa in the fields. I tried to content myself with that. In the process, I watched Carlos grow up.

Sometimes Elisa spotted me, but she never said anything. Not hello or even, "Go to hell!" Little Carlos spied me once. He was probably eight. I remember watching him and Elisa plant onions together on the same row. Carlos kept looking up at the hawks that circled overhead, imitating their caws. Elisa joined him and they both laughed so hard and made it look like such fun I forgot myself. I cawed, too. Elisa didn't notice, or pretended not to, but Carlos smiled and waved at me. For that brief moment, it felt like the three of us were a family. That feeling kept my spirits up, but also worsened my longing.

Ten years after that, the Morenos went to work on a huge ranch north of Victoria. It was so big I allowed myself to work there, too. I saw Carlos and Gerardo walking off the property one night, leaving later than most of the others. I remember going back to get an axe handle from the scrap bin. I wanted something to crack open the nuts from a tree near my boardinghouse. On the path to town, I heard Donati's friends attack. I heard their curses and the blows. And then came the screams.

I ran, but I was too late. Three Klansmen laughed while Texas Ranger Donati stood by idly, staring up at the sky. In my mind, I saw the Federals again as they gloated over my desecrated, slaughtered family. I felt invincible, kicking the ranger's gun away and breaking his kneecap, feeling the skulls soften within those absurd white hoods, hearing the disabling cracks of their limbs.

The injured ruffians lay in the dirt making pitiful sounds. I wanted to finish them, to kill my memories. But then I remembered their victims, and I thought of Carmen. I chose instead to cheat Death. I rescued Elisa's beaten son and her castrated husband.

Elisa and I stitched the wounds before Gerardo bled to death. When she had stopped crying, we talked for the first time in nearly sixteen years. I made the mistake of admitting that I hadn't killed her family's attackers and then had to restrain her from running outside with a knife to do what I would not. That was the first time I held her, the flat of the knife blade against my back as she let herself be dissuaded. To protect my identity from the ranger and the Klansmen, we concocted a new rescuer of her family: a hulking man with a dangling mustache named Rafael Bernal, in honor of my dead friend.

Carlos hired a wagon to carry the family to Port Lavaca, the nearest large town, where he and his father could heal, find new jobs, and avoid the men who'd attacked them. Elisa whispered this to me behind the rooming house as her son loaded the buckboard out front. I promised to find them again, to watch over them, and I did.

I've always had a knack for repairing things. I lived above the auto garage I bought in Port Lavaca after briefly returning to Mexico to say a final goodbye to the graves of Carmen and my children and sell my family's farm. Elisa would bring over her latest sewing project and talk during my afternoon siestas. I played the role of her friend and confidant and tried not to let my feelings show. Being so near to Elisa, but not able to touch her, felt like a dream I'd once had about Carmen: swimming toward my wife, ever closer, but always out of reach.

During one visit, Elisa told me how gruffly Gerardo now treated her and Carlos. Her husband never smiled or joked anymore. He wasn't tender or kind to them. She missed the marriage she used to have. I asked if she could be in love with another man. At first she said she didn't want to be. When I asked if she was, Elisa said, "I can't."

I maintained my patience. I didn't take advantage when she cried, but merely reassured her. After a year, when Elisa said she'd fallen in love with me, I counseled her. When she told me she'd scream if I didn't hold her, I soothed her with words and sent her away. But, later, when Elisa held me down and kissed me, I let her.

We became reckless. After a few months, our carelessness showed in the changes to her body. She told me she often cried: for us, for her shame, for her fear of another stillbirth or waking one morning to discover another breathless baby. Elisa cried because she'd begun to initiate relations with Gerardo as soon as she'd guessed she was pregnant. She cried the hardest in my arms after she'd refused Gerardo's order to go to an abortionist and Gerardo spent that money instead on bus tickets. He told Elisa he was taking her away from all of her lovers.

I sold my garage and pursued her again, farther up the coast to La Marque. Seven agonizing months of tears and guilt—as Elisa told me of pretending for her sweet son and disbelieving husband—and brief moments of tenderness, so touching. That all came to a bloody end on the floor of the Morenos' rented room. I could do nothing but escort home the stricken midwife and help to dig my lover's grave and the resting place for our son.

There was one thing more: I'd made a covenant with Elisa to watch over Carlos, always. When my landlord mentioned overhearing the conversation about Ranger Donati searching for the Morenos, I had to warn them. I knew the ranger really wanted me, but I was unwilling to give up my life. Instead, I tried to protect theirs.

As Carlos and I dug the graves for Elisa and the child, the thought haunted me that I was burying the second woman I'd ever loved. I decided I needed to devote myself to something greater than my base desires. I remembered meeting the priest from Galveston, Father Vignaud, the man who spoke for God, who talked to God and received answers. An idea began to form.

From my grandfather's eager Latin lessons, I'd understood much of the funeral rites. If I could master the language, perhaps God would explain what had happened since Carmen's death, when I had been possessed by one kind of demon and then another. I focused on Vignaud's armory and uniform—Bible, rosary, crucifix, cassock, and collar—weapons and shields to battle and defend against the Devil, to signify purity, to gain access to His attention.

I shoveled the earth over Elisa's shroud and filled the grave of my son, the last of my little angels. Tamping the dirt with the back of the shovel, my idea solidified as well. I would persuade Carlos to go with me to Houston, and then I'd enroll in the seminary where they would teach me to understand God's responses to my prayers and others'. For the first time in two decades, I had no obsession—merely a plan.

God spoke to me after the funerals. He did so through Elisa and Gerardo's son. Though not yet twenty, Carlos showed me the courage that I, at more than twice his age, had always lacked. He offered to risk his own life to save his father. Carlos journeyed to Houston as a decoy, luring Donati while traveling with the man whom the ranger really sought to destroy.

At the seminary, my instructors helped me to absolve the sinner Pedro Rodríguez had become, and gave me a chance to be a Father to the young man I would be honored to call son. But they could not transform the coward into a hero. I eagerly agreed to help thwart the illegal, immoral repatriations, but knew I was only deferring the sacrifice God required of me.

I chose not to heed Him until now; my soul is damned because of that. I am sorry so many have suffered. My sacrifice comes much too late, but I am committed fully to it. At last.

CHAPTER 39

The Hanged Man asked, "Can you ever forgive me?"
Carlos closed the book and pressed the heel of his
hands against his eyes. "You exaggerated my sacrifice
while ignoring your heroism. God won't judge you as harshly
as you've done."

"Your mother is dead because of me. All of you are in this
position because I tried to hide my sins."

Daniela clutched Pedro's hand and Carlos' and held them
up. "Carlos and I are joined together because of you. You
instilled faith in him, taught him forgiveness and hope. If
you love who Carlos is, then love yourself as well."

While Pedro hung his head, Carlos opened the front
door and invited Jacie and Oscar inside. He explained that
Donati was after him only to get to Pedro. "We need a plan
to protect our friend."

Oscar sat beside the priest and said, "What if we try to
get everyone out of here tonight? Jacie and her parents, the
workers and their families?"

Daniela said, "I'm sure Donati is ready for anything. It
would be a massacre."

Carlos sat Jacie in his chair and leaned against the door.
"Oscar, you told me earlier how pointless it was to risk the
band, but now you're talking about risking everybody."

"It was pointless supporting the barricades because now I see that it could've only ended the way it did: death for the unlucky and repatriation for the survivors. No one would've gained any freedom from it. Donati's one man with only so many bullets. I might die, but someone will get to him and then everyone will be free."

Pedro said, "No, then everyone will be running from Donati's comrades. It has to end here with me."

Jacie had pulled Carlos' naturalization papers from their envelope and glanced through them. "Carlos, why do you want to be the citizen of a country that would do such terrible things to you and your people?"

"Because the same country offers me the best chance to make a comfortable life for my wife and family. If America will just let us alone to do that, I'll keep working hard to make everyone richer."

He took a breath and continued, "Here's my plan. I'll go to Donati—alone—and tell him all about Rafael Bernal and how he said he was going to…California."

Pedro shook his head. "And he'll say, 'OK, you're coming along with me and if he isn't there, I'll kill you.'"

"It'll give us time to come up with something better."

Daniela stood. "I love you, but strategy is not where you do your best improvising. There's something about me that Donati likes. He was very friendly the morning he got here and, *Santa María*, I was as sweet as *flan* to him. Maybe I can lead him away from here."

"Dani, that's a fate worse than death. What kind of strategy is—"

Jacie slapped the table. "Stop it! Why do we have to decide anything tonight? We're not harvesting, so everyone's off tomorrow. The ranger doesn't expect to see Daniela until Monday. Since he hasn't made a move, why should we?"

Oscar tapped her hand. "Pretty smart for a kid."

She smirked at him. "I didn't provide us with an answer—just gave us more time to argue tomorrow. If Donati lets us go to church, I'll sound out my parents." Jacie left the table. Carlos opened the door for her and she patted his arm. "Congratulations, citizen. *Buenas noches.*"

Carlos wished Jacie a good night and closed the door behind her. He said, "Pedro's being very quiet, Oscar. Would you spend the night in here and make sure he doesn't leave?"

"Of course." The bandleader took Carlos' place at the door, sitting and blocking it.

Pedro rested his forehead against steepled hands and began to pray.

*

Jack raised his binoculars again and peered through the panel of windows in the upstairs foyer that looked down on the workers' village. Darla and Tom Webster had gone to bed and the house was dark. He watched the Webster teenager striding away from Carlos and Daniela's shack, heading home. Some tejanos still wandered around the camp as the fires died. A group of children pretended to play mariachi instruments near the well. They took turns running from between two houses, holding an imaginary trumpet to their lips and joining the band. Jack had seen—and heard—the crowd's response to Moreno's arrival. Carlos had an army of defenders who would tear any lawman apart.

His plan had begun to unravel. Getting Carlos away without Daniela's knowledge, having the Brownsville crew wring from him the identity and location of the mystery man, and hiding Carlos' body afterward looked impossible against a horde that was determined to protect one of their own. The night of the barricades was a reminder of just how dangerous cornered animals could become.

He grasped the banister in his left hand, a stronger grip than yesterday, as he descended the stairs one at a time: his left knee seemed to be weakening as the rest of him healed. He patted the back of his head, now free of bandages and stitches; the shaved-off hair was growing back in patches of short spikes among the gouges and scars.

Jack hobbled into the study off the main entrance and sat in the dark, trying to massage the fire out of his leg. The Webster girl closed the front door behind her and glided upstairs, catlike in her stealth. After she'd retired to her bedroom, he lifted the telephone receiver and called Immigration Agent Lebrun.

*

Carlos whispered into Daniela's ear, "How were your parents?"

She lay on her side, spooning against him in the dark. Their reunion had been chaste because of Pedro and Oscar's presence in the other room. "Mother was happy for me after she got over the shock, though she's worried about our future. Father predicted disaster, even after I told him you're a citizen now and learning to read and write in two languages. They'd been scared by my disappearance."

"Maybe we should've written to them."

"No," Daniela said. "My parents reported me kidnapped. Mother even gave the cops a picture of me. Father would've given them any postmarked letter from us."

"So the police somehow connected you with me... Alfredo—the trumpet player Oscar hired after me—he might've told the police where I was working."

"But how did the ranger know to find us here, of all the places we could've run to? No one knew about Sr. Webster's job offer except us and Pedro, right?"

The name felt like a spiked ball gouging his windpipe and tearing his mouth: "Paz."

CHAPTER 40

For the first time in months, Carlos listened to Pedro perform Mass. Daniela sat beside Carlos, holding his hand against the blue skirt of her dress. The priest used their porch as his pulpit. The congregation, which included Oscar, a few other men, and over one hundred women and children, sat in curving, colorful rows, a rainbow spread around Pedro.

Carlos had spent a sleepless night agonizing about yet another mistake he'd made with Paz, and her threat to be a worse villain than he could imagine. María had been right: she must've allied herself with Donati. Daniela's forgiveness had been immediate, too quick for Carlos to believe she wasn't upset at him about this looming threat. The ranger now knew her and "liked" her, in Daniela's words, because of his own indiscretions. Even if he sacrificed himself, she'd still be menaced by Donati. As with Pedro, the lawman would trade one obsession for another.

Sleep had been impossible too because of his friend now speaking for God and bestowing His blessings. After Jacie left the night before, the priest had not uttered another word except to bless everyone and wish them a goodnight. As Pedro now recited the liturgy, his downcast eyes concealed his thoughts, his soul, from Carlos' view. Still, he knew his friend—the Hanged Man literally and figuratively—planned to die that day.

Pedro had packed wisely again, this time bringing the Eucharistic bread and wine. Daniela had volunteered the front room for confessions and had invited him to use the house as his church if anyone wanted to speak with him after Communion. Jacie had stopped by before she and her parents went to the Methodist church in town, offering to help him teach Bible stories when she returned.

As scores of *tejanos* lined up to receive the sacraments, a long rumble sounded from the north. A train had pulled into Casson at the start of the Mass, much earlier than usual on a Sunday. Now, the growl of diesel engines grew louder until Pedro called out to everyone, "*¡La migra!* Go to your homes. Make sure your children are at hand. Leave no one on the street!"

Women broke from the line, holding their babies and calling to their oldest to herd their brothers and sisters toward home. Their high-pitched cries could not compete with the shriek of brakes as trucks turned onto the sunken road. The massive vehicles rolled toward the colony.

Sobs turned to screams as the trucks crushed the washboard ribs of the dirt road and then the path leading to the village. Olivia and Beatrice had emerged from the first house and joined Daniela in pushing gawking *tejanos* back to their homes. Oscar and the other musicians grabbed children who'd wandered or run from their houses. César hoisted a fleeing child to his shoulder, setting the boy higher than anyone else in camp, likely giving him the first view of the olive-drab uniformed men behind the trucks' windshields. The boy clutched his clothes with tiny fists and mewled above César's head.

Carlos yelled, "Where's Letty?"

César's gold tooth flashed. "Off on one of her fieldtrips."

"People are going to get hurt—we need her."

"She'll come running when she hears all of this." César took the crying child to a woman shouting her son's name in the street.

The first truck leveled the wooden housing built around the well, crushing the windlass and sending the bucket flying, its long chain trailing behind. Carlos stood in the center of the camp as the tin pail tumbled toward him; the rusty links thrashed around it like a snake and narrowly missed lashing *tejanos* as they leaped aside. He stuck out his foot to stop its journey, but the chain wrapped tight around his calves, seizing him. The shock of the impact knocked Carlos over as the lead truck thundered toward him.

Pedro knelt and unwound the chain. His fingers moved fast as he said a low prayer that sounded to Carlos like the Last Rites. The truck's brakes moaned and the dust raised by its tires overtook them as the vehicle slowed and stopped a few yards away.

Nine other trucks halted behind the lead. Cab doors sprung open and backdoors swung wide as Immigration agents and deputies piled from the trucks. A florid-faced man in olive-drab, the uniform tailored to accentuate his deep chest and narrow hips, stepped from the lead truck's passenger side. He hitched up his waistband, which bore the weight of a gun belt, as Pedro helped Carlos to his feet. The uniformed man tossed his cigarette aside and said, "Father, I'm Immigration Agent Lebrun. The workers here are in violation of US immigration law and will be repatriated to their country of origin."

"Agent, these are American citizens." Pedro patted Carlos' shoulder. "This man, for instance. I'll show you his naturalization papers." He took Carlos by the arm and walked to his house, Lebrun stalking behind. The lawmen were opening doors to the other shacks, firearms holstered and clipboards in hand: ready to tally their catches.

Daniela stood on the porch, pulling her fingers. Tears wet her face and blouse. The tunic had un-tucked from her skirt and rippled against her waist as the wind blew clouds of dust. She preceded Carlos and Pedro inside. Agent Lebrun stood in the doorway.

The priest reached for the envelope, but Carlos grasped it first. He admired how Pedro had always shown pride and dignity around Anglos but was determined to speak for himself. He said, "My papers, sir," and withdrew the Department of Labor forms. "I am a United States citizen."

The agent glanced at the Oath of Allegiance. "And not a moment too soon, *señor*. How about her?" Lebrun pointed the documents at Daniela. "How about you, sweetie? Eh-citizen? You eh-speak the English?"

"There's no need for that," Pedro shouted.

Carlos snatched the papers away. "I am a citizen because my wife was born here."

"Let's see her birth certificate, then, some kind of proof."

Daniela exhaled slowly and said, "There's nothing. My parents in Houston have all my records. Did I communicate in the English vernacular with sufficient clarity, sir?"

"Huh. You talk real pretty, toots. I'm sure you'll wow them in Oaxaca. Come with me." He stepped into the house.

Carlos blocked Lebrun's path. "You have no right."

"I have all the rights. You've got a lot to learn about this place. Step aside."

"Get out of my house!"

Daniela screamed as Lebrun drew his revolver and fired. The bullet spit flames through Carlos' abdomen and seared his back as it exited. Breath left his body. He fell backward into his blood that had sprayed the floor.

As Pedro lunged toward Lebrun, the agent put the end of the gun barrel against the priest's forehead, cocking the hammer again. "Give me a reason, *padre*. Any one will do."

Carlos tasted wet iron that came up his gullet, and he coughed and vomited blood. His insides seemed to be melting. He braced for more gunshots, waited for Lebrun to kill him. Over the quickening rhythm of his pulse, he heard heartbreaking screams. He prayed Daniela's cries wouldn't be the last sounds he heard from her before he died.

Pedro backed away, his hands up, fingers curling like wilted petals. The Immigration agent stepped over Carlos and pulled Daniela into view, her feet stutter-stepping as he tugged her across the floor. Carlos thought he could summon just enough energy to trip Lebrun. Instead, his weak fingers grazed the back of Daniela's leg. She looked over her shoulder at him before Lebrun dragged her away, so many emotions in her face Carlos couldn't read her expression. And then Pedro hovered over him, his face also changing by the moment. And then Carlos saw nothing at all.

*

Jack hobbled toward the lead truck, sidestepping and pushing through long queues of tejanos—adults with many children in between—and their uniformed escorts. A sudden wind nearly tore off the fedora he wore to cover the angry, crescent-shaped scabs on the back of his head. He intercepted Lebrun as the agent pulled Daniela behind him. "I'll take this one."

"You think I'm rounding up girlfriends for you, Jack? She's an illegal and she's going home." He handed her off to another Immigration officer with a clipboard.

Daniela murmured answers to questions as she wept, looking down, away from Jack. Tears made overlapping circles on the dirt at her feet. He said, "She's wanted in Houston—" He thought of the Zaragoza woman's comment about a punch. "For assault and battery."

"This honey? She couldn't batter a cake. Anyway, we'd rather deport them than have the taxpayers pick up a jail tab. You want to arrest somebody, take her husband in for interfering with a federal agent. Though he's probably dead now."

Daniela's face dipped lower and her skin reddened as she cried without restraint. Jack opened his mouth and closed it again. He'd have to start over again and find Gerardo Moreno. Unless Daniela knew. Jack's hat blew off his head and covered the tear-stained dirt near her shoes. He bent to pick it up and heard her sharp gasp.

Lebrun said, "Jesus H., Jack."

Jack imagined her gaze taking in the crosshatched stitch marks bordering the seams of deep gashes and ugly red scars that cratered his head and neck. Jack straightened, returning the felt hat to his head. She finally looked at his face, and he said, "You see how I've suffered?"

Her voice was scraped raw, as if she'd swallowed glass. "You'd be dead if Carlos hadn't saved you."

Jack grabbed her upper arm and led her beyond the front of the truck where a crushed bucket and long, rusty chain lay. The diesel engine idled, creating a racket. She wrenched out of his grip and swung at him with a swift left hand. He caught her fist in his palm and closed his fingers around it. "A woman in Houston warned me about that." He pulled her nearer so he wouldn't have to shout. "Lying in the hospital, I'd wished Carlos had let me die, Daniela. Now I can't do anything for him, but maybe I can protect you." He felt her warm breath, her mouth almost close enough to kiss.

"Why would you?" She looked into his eyes and then tried to back away. "Are you crazy? You think I have one good feeling about you?" As she yelled, her spittle sprayed his face.

"Just now you felt sympathy for me. I heard it in your voice. It's a start."

"That was disgust, ranger." Daniela wrenched her hand away. "Don't ever touch me again."

Jack wiped the dampness from his face as agents led Daniela to the back of the truck and ushered her inside. Lebrun applauded. "You know, Jack, maybe I'll take her as my own joy-toy. I didn't think you went in for women with spunk."

"I misread her. Misread everything. Come on and show me this man you killed."

As Jack passed the empty shacks, he wondered if the Websters would bring in Anglos to do the farming. What would they make of *los altarcitos*; the greasy smells of *tortillas* and beans trapped in the walls; brightly colored *serapes* and dark *mantillas* scattered across the floorboards as pallets for the children? Some would find hex signs carved in the wood. Anglo children who liked to dig might uncover clay figurines or *amuletos* buried beside the porches. The women had prayed to *La Virgen* for eternal salvation and entreated their ancestors' gods and spirits for daily protection. The whites wouldn't understand; Jack wondered if he did.

The Websters' Ford Victoria skidded off the highway and tore down the sunken road. Lebrun told his men to get ready to roll out. He tossed a peppermint into his mouth and crunched it. Jack let him deal with the Websters, who stormed into the camp yelling at everyone in a uniform. From Carlos' porch, a familiar figure summoned Jack with a wave of his hand.

The black clothes and bright Roman collar above the cassock confused Jack for a moment, but he recognized the face: the blurred, fractured memory in the moonlight coalesced as he saw the scars and broken nose in the daytime. Jack had to smile at the man's bravado as he realized that the same one who'd broken his knee had re-injured him in Houston.

The priest extended his arms and grasped the post on either side of him, blocking the closed door. He said in accented English, "Leave Carlos alone, Donati. I'm the one you want."

"I guess no one tipped you off about today's raid, priest. If you really are a man of the cloth."

"I am. My name is Father Pedro Rodríguez. Your leg is still bothering you, ranger. Or is it your conscience?"

Jack drew his revolver and cocked the hammer. "You were in disguise that night in Victoria."

"Indeed. This is the real me."

"But you wore a mask in Houston, too: long hair and a beard. You were hiding from me."

"No, from the truth."

"The truth is you're a dead man." He had trouble keeping his aim steady and wondered if he should switch to the lighter Remington derringer in his pocket.

The priest said, "That applies to all of us." He closed his eyes and prayed aloud.

Jack recognized a few words in Latin, something a priest had recited as he'd watched his mother die in the TB ward. Why couldn't he shoot? He wanted to yell at Rodríguez to hurry so he could kill him. He would've laughed at the absurdity of it, but he couldn't breathe.

Rodríguez said, "Thank you for letting me finish the Sacrament."

"Last Rites weren't necessary." He exhaled and shot Rodríguez through the left knee. The man staggered but held himself upright, his hands still grasping the poles on either side of him. His gaze remained steady as Jack told him, "We're even."

Lebrun ran over, freed from the Websters as Tom pulled his raging wife and daughter back to their car. The agent looked from Jack to the priest, arms outstretched, both feet planted. A dark stain seeped through Rodríguez's legging.

Jack said, "This is the one who crippled me in '26."

"You're a piece of work, Jack. Women outwrestling you and priests whipping you. I wanted to cap this bastard earlier, but hell, there's no point in torturing the guy." Lebrun pointed his gun at Rodríguez. "You know the penalty for attacking a lawman?"

The priest didn't reply. He peered into Jack's eyes and nodded once. Lebrun's bullet snapped Rodríguez's head back.

Jack stared at the dead man, waiting for him to collapse, but his body held firm.

"Never saw that before," Lebrun said, holstering his revolver. "Wonder if that's my second kill today." He walked behind Rodríguez, lifted one foot, and shoved against the priest's back. Fingernails scraped the posts, and the body toppled to the ground.

Lebrun pushed the door open and daylight streamed inside, enabling Jack to see two black women, the maid and the cook, kneeling beside a narrow bed. Carlos lay on his side, shirtless, his face to the wall. Torn sheets looped around his torso; crimson blood leaked through the makeshift bandages in front and behind.

The agent shrugged. "Okay, so I'm only one for two. Babe Ruth doesn't hit for that kind of average." He stepped over Rodríguez, facedown in the dirt. "You should've simply executed him, Jack; you let this get too personal. You look like you're gonna cry—I thought Texas Rangers were tough guys."

Jack holstered his revolver. He said to himself, "Yeah, me too."

Lebrun walked down the lane and climbed aboard the lead truck. Diesels bellowed as the caravan rolled through the colony and mounted the sunken road in front of the Webster's plantation house. They roared past the fields and returned to the highway, thundering north toward the Casson train depot. Jack had requested a nonstop express to Laredo for the repatriates, who now included Daniela.

He sat on the ground beside Rodríguez. He'd expected his leg to feel better, as if delivered from a curse, but the pain was excruciating.

Lebrun's men had missed one. A buxom *tejana* with long black hair she kept out of her face with thick braids of grass stepped from the back room and checked on Carlos. She changed the bandages and swabbed ointment where his skin had been rejoined and stitched together. The woman carried a white sheet outside and covered Rodríguez. She leaned close to Jack, saying in Spanish, "You're responsible for all this? Pedro's death, my husband and everyone else being taken away?"

"I am. How did they miss you?"

"I slipped in from the prairie after Carlos was shot." She peered at him, her eyes as bright as nickel plating. "There's a long line of people who would kill you. Is there anyone who would heal you?"

Jack stopped massaging his leg. "It doesn't matter anymore."

"Even a dying man wants relief."

"I need to talk to Carlos before I can rest." Jack accepted her hand and she pulled him upright with surprising ease. He walked inside the house and the two Negroes left without him having to ask. Jack shut the door behind them.

*

When Carlos awoke, he first thought he was back at the barricade but he and Donati had somehow switched places. He felt the molten pains consuming his body, the blood staining his skin, while the King of Swords knelt above him unharmed, dark eyes staring down. Donati even said in his deep, soft voice, "Moreno."

Carlos swallowed a few times, wetting his mouth and throat. "Is Daniela safe?"

El rinche smirked. "Her only concern was for you, too. I don't know why I thought she could be mine." He removed his fedora and covered his left knee with the crown. "Lebrun, the one who shot you, took her away."

"She's an American. Those children are Americans. Many of the workers, too."

"By rights you should be on that train."

Carlos flexed his empty fingers. The documents were no longer in his hand. He pointed at the table and waited until the ranger picked up and read the Oath of Allegiance. "You uphold the law. Why are you breaking it?"

Donati's hand dropped to his holster, but stopped. His face had dampened with sweat. He yelled, "How dare you call me to account! What do you want from me?"

"Not mercy, Ranger Donati. Only justice."

A car stopped nearby. The ranger stood and murmured, "My name is Diego." A smile tilted his mouth and a faint glimmer brightened his eyes before he crossed the room and opened the door. The liveliness in his face had gone again when he stepped aside, revealing Paz dressed in her dove-gray outfit. She pointed a small revolver at the ranger.

Diego turned to him and said, "You want justice? Then it's time for me to pay up on a deal I made."

CHAPTER 41

Paz aimed her small gun and the revolver she took from the ranger at Letty and Diego as they half-led, half-carried Carlos to a dented blue car. Olivia and Bibi had helped him into a fresh shirt, now stained with blood as his wounds continued to weep.

"When you stole my Cadillac," Diego said to Paz while he opened the paint-stripped passenger door, "you couldn't drive, could you?" He settled Carlos against the leather seat and lifted his legs onto the carpeted floorboard. *El rinche* began to speak to him but then looked away and shut him inside.

Paz replied, "I learn as I go." She gestured with a gun at Pedro's body under the sheet. "I guess you got what you wanted. You don't feel cheated, do you?"

"Yeah—in every way."

Paz slammed her door shut as she slid beneath the wooden steering wheel. She dropped the small gun in her lap and the larger one on the floorboard beneath her feet.

"I hope you don't bleed on these nice seats." She brushed the hair off his forehead, as she'd often done after sex, and said, "He didn't hurt you too badly, did he?"

Carlos remembered the changing looks on Pedro's face and Daniela's, the love and concern shown for him, all wasted. They, too, should feel cheated in every way. He said,

"Everything that happened today is your fault," though he applied that to himself as well.

She turned the wheel hard and then had to bank again to avoid the open well, now just a deep hole in the ground. The rear end fishtailed on the dirt as she drove too fast. The winged arms of the silver hood ornament glinted in the sun like devil horns. "Nonsense—I just got here. I was in a dank rooming house in town waiting for a sign. Those trucks headed for the train depot told me it was time to rescue my love. Remember our train ride?"

The car bounced onto the sunken road, making Carlos groan. They passed the driveway where Jacie sat in the Websters' sedan. The girl held his gaze as he went by.

Paz drove to the highway intersection. "Which way, lover?"

"Go to hell."

"South it is." She turned left and sped up.

He knew how Paz would act. She'd pretend nothing was wrong between them, and she'd never stop trying to seduce him. He'd refuse and resist and even fight sleep, until he had to fight her. She might shoot him or he might get away, but Daniela and their baby would be long gone by then. Freedom would only be meaningful if he had it now.

Paz looked over her shoulder and laughed. "You have an admirer, dear. A blond-haired *gringa* is following us." She rubbed his thigh, close to his groin. "I thought you preferred older women."

"Daniela's my age." He glanced behind at the car trailing them.

Her voice was suddenly cold. "Daniela didn't save you just now—I did. When I put my mark on you, I made you mine."

Carlos played with the crank beside his leg and discovered how to lower the window. The air whipping in made it harder to hear her, easier not to listen. His body pressed into the seat as Paz drove faster, aggravating the exit wound in his back.

The prairie blurred on either side. The line of concrete on the horizon looked like the edge of a cliff.

He shouted, "You're a very good driver." When Paz flashed a bright smile at him, the wind swirling her hair, he asked, "Can you go any faster?"

"Of course. Say goodbye to that girl." She mashed the accelerator and looked over her shoulder again.

He grabbed the steering wheel and spun it out of her grip. For an instant he felt the stomach-dropping vertigo of real flight as the back end whipped around and the Cadillac became airborne. Then it turned over and smashed against the highway and tumbled endlessly. Carlos flew through the open window, thrown clear of the disintegrating machine. He blacked out as he bounced and rolled across the prairie.

His body seemed to wake up before his mind. He came to while crawling through the grass on bruised elbows and knees. Finally, he comprehended that he was making his way back to the smoking wreckage that had settled on the road. He wiped blood from his eyes and tried to decide if the Cadillac was right-side up. Nothing looked familiar. The tires and cloth roof were gone as was the silver hood ornament of the winged woman. The fenders had shredded, and the glass had been pounded into shards and dust. A dull gray undercoat showed where the blue paint had been scraped away as if by gigantic talons.

The demolished chassis singed his hands as he pulled himself upright against it, fighting dizziness and nausea and the protest of every muscle. Stitches in his abdomen and back had torn open; blood poured freely again. The car seemed only half as tall as it had been. He realized he stared not at the top but the blackened underside, reminding him of the trains he'd repaired: skeletal steel without the grace of skin.

At his feet, the collapsed roof lay on the road like a pool of black blood. He lifted the coarse fabric and bent support brackets, revealing a broad puddle of crimson that nearly submerged Paz's snub-nosed revolver. There was no sign of the thief. The stolen Cadillac entombed her.

He dropped to his torn knees and levered the driver's door open a few inches. Blood flowed through the floodgate and carried Paz's hand into the gap he'd made. Her arm was vertical: she was upside down. Clothes and flesh hung in loose red flaps, nearly indistinguishable. Her wrist was slick, still warm, but he could find no pulse. His thumb slid against the blood on his gashed forehead as he traced a cross.

Diego's revolver lay farther north on the highway. Carlos saw it as he staggered toward Jacie, who had pulled up in the Webster's car and was running to catch him.

*

In the afternoon, a half-hour before the train was due to depart, Jack followed the folk healer from the colony into the exposed-brick-and-beam railroad station, passing two guards Lebrun had posted. The woman carted on her shoulder a bulging satchel that included her medicines. Jack's knee felt a little better. Though he was reluctant to credit plants and roots, Letty's medicine seemed to have worked.

Nearly thirty Immigration officers and deputies leaned against the station walls with holstered revolvers and long-barreled shotguns on display. One end of the depot opened onto a loading platform. The steam locomotive sent from Houston hissed alongside the wide concrete apron. Four commuter cars and a caboose sat behind the black barrel-shaped engine and adjoining coal-tender. Condensation trickled down the steel plates of the train and beaded on the windows and fist-sized rivets.

The crowd of men, women, and children who sat or lay in clusters, spread over the terminal's scarred wood floor, shouted greetings to the *curandera*. Daniela and a man with a gold tooth ran to her. Jack intercepted Moreno's wife as she tried to move around him. "Carlos is alive."

"Where is he?" Daniela looked past him, as if her husband lingered at the station entrance. Her renewed hope tore through his heart like a bullet.

"Safe with the Websters. I couldn't bring him since he has his papers in order." He pressed into her hand the carved galloping horse he'd finished the night before. He was proud of the subtle musculature he'd coaxed from the wood, the ecstatic face of a beast in mid-romp. It was the only art he'd ever created that wasn't a copy.

She touched the braided black mane and tail he'd threaded through the wood. Her free hand flew up to her hair and the look of horror—disgust—returned to her face. He'd plucked the strands from her brush and comb set and somehow she knew.

Jack said in his gentlest voice, "You'll be running free in no time." He walked toward the railroad office beside the platform, still feeling the tension that had seized her hand, all tendons and bone. No softness for him. He only paused a moment when he heard the wooden figurine bounce on the floor.

The office door opened, and Lebrun emerged with the railroad operator. Clicks from the telegrapher's Morse code trailed them. Lebrun said, "No stops, right?"

The operator adjusted a band on his sleeve and made it level. "That's right, we cleared the line. Straight through to Laredo."

Jack said, "I brought in one more."

"Glad you finally joined us, Jack. Thanks for helping out. We brought in a hundred and eighty-one." Lebrun stared down some of the *tejanos* looking at him. "Let's get them loaded up, boys," he shouted. "It's starting to stink in here."

Lawmen slid open the passenger doors on the four cars. Others prodded, coaxed, and kicked the *peóns* to their feet, grunting orders in English and pointing with their guns. Babies mewled and children cried. The adults said nothing nor showed any emotion as they gathered their families and shuffled aboard the day-coaches.

Daniela followed the folk healer and others onto the last commuter car. Jack willed her to turn around, to at least look at him a final time, but she did not. He scanned the station, now empty except for milling lawmen, but didn't see his gift on the floorboards.

The Southern Pacific engineer leaned out of his cabin. Lebrun directed six of his men to the caboose. After the guards boarded, Lebrun pointed southward. The engineer ducked inside and began to open the valves.

As the locomotive rolled out of the station, the engineer blew his whistle and the cry of escaping steam echoed in the depot. Two Immigration agents leaned on the back railing of the caboose's observation platform; one of them lifted his hat and waved it as the train accelerated along the track. Jack looked at his watch and said to Lebrun, "Going to wait around to make sure they get there?"

"What's the matter, Jack? Got a bad feeling in your leg?"

"I just want to make sure nothing goes wrong. Texas can surprise you."

Lebrun checked his own pocket watch. "They'll connect with the main line at El Campo. We'll have the stationmaster call us when they go through. El Campo. Hell of a name for a town—at least 'Houston' sounds American."

"*El campo* means 'the countryside,'" Jack said, looking at the swaying prairie grass beyond the tracks, losing himself in the waist-high stalks. "A peaceful place."

"What we call the Sticks." Lebrun pivoted and started back to the office, but skidded on something. "Goddamn! I nearly broke my neck." He lifted a small carved horse in mid-gallop. "Some kid's toy. Waste not, want not." The Immigration agent side-armed the figurine into the prairie grass, which swallowed it up.

*

Carlos told Jacie she was watching the train more than the narrow, pot-holed road that paralleled the tracks. The Webster's Ford Victoria sedan bounced and his head struck the ceiling, aggravating the ache in his neck. With all the windows down, he doubted she could hear him. He rubbed his scalp—yet another bruise—and looked through the windshield for other craters.

A cloth cap hid Jacie's hair and dark sunglasses disguised her unmistakable eyes. Both she and Carlos wore bandanas around their necks that would soon cover the lower halves of their faces and his most distinguishing scars.

Twenty miles east of El Campo, smoke and steam jetted from the side of the engine and sparks leaped from the locomotive's wheels as the brakes were engaged. Screeching of metal-on-metal reached Carlos' ears. The elder Websters had blockaded the tracks.

Jacie sped off the road. She plowed through grass and over flat, dusty earth, her fingers crossed as she gripped the steering wheel. Carlos prayed no one would die as the result of his plan. The kerchief smelled of sweat when he pulled it up. As they approached the slowing locomotive, his slick hands shifted on Diego's heavy revolver.

The train came to a full stop. When Jacie halted behind the caboose, two agents stepped onto the observation platform. Carlos swung open his door and crouched behind it, wincing as the fresh stitches tugged at his through-and-through gunshot wound. Pointing the gun at the men, he ordered them to put their hands up and then remembered to cock the hammer. Jacie aimed a sawed-off shotgun, looking much more at ease.

As the men descended the steps, hands held above their Stetsons, another four agents joined them. César and Oscar followed them onto the rear platform, pointing two of Sr. Webster's revolvers that Letty had smuggled in her satchel. The *curandera* straddled the end doors between the fourth day-coach and the caboose; she waved a gun overhead, and called something inside the passenger car.

Oscar, César, and a dozen other *tejanos* dismounted and disarmed the agents, removing their gun belts and checking their pockets. One of the lawmen crouched and started to pull a diminutive gun from his boot. Carlos squeezed the trigger as Diego had taught him earlier in the day. He was now accustomed to the strong kick of the ranger's revolver. Dirt exploded beside the lawman's foot and his empty hands flew upward.

"Check their boots," Carlos yelled and swung his aim toward the heads of the other agents. The lawmen sat and pulled off their footwear, yielding another gun and two knives.

César told the barefooted agents to walk south. "We'll shoot you if you look back." The three-man train crew marched on a course to meet the lawmen. The engineer glanced behind him and a shotgun boomed from the front of the train, a warning shot. The lawmen and crew hunched their shoulders and kept walking.

The other coaches emptied as men, women, and children celebrated on the prairie, hugging and dancing in circles. Those who stayed inside held each other across the seats. Carlos could see their smiles through the windows.

Daniela shouted his name as she stepped from the train. Disheveled and dirty from a night on the floor of the train depot, she'd never looked more beautiful. He caught her in his arms and staggered, not quite able to conceal a groan as she aggravated his injuries. She ran her hands over his stitched forehead and pulled down his bandana to kiss him and fuss over the abrasions and cuts on his cheeks and chin. Letty had also patched an ear, a shoulder, and both knees, all damaged in his flight from the Cadillac. He held Daniela and told her about Paz, his return to the colony, and Diego's agreement to help with his plan.

She said, "I'm glad you don't sound guilty about what you did to get free of Paz."

"I'm getting beat up plenty without doing it to myself." Her warmth in his arms, the intensity of her loving stare, drove his heart into a gallop. "I can't undo my mistakes, Dani, but I can learn from them and count my blessings."

"How many have you counted?"

He kissed her again and said, "As many blessings as there are stars."

Jacie suggested the captured weapons get passed around, earning compliments from Oscar. She sent some men ahead to gather the supplies in the truck her parents had used to block the tracks. Carlos called to her, "Remember the signal we'd agreed on with Diego."

She walked back to the car, removing her disguise as she went, and retrieved a large American flag. Daniela mounted the caboose and helped her secure the forty-eight stars and thirteen stripes over the rear railing of the observation platform. Jacie got a few men to help her move steamer trunks on board from the car she'd driven, along with the large bundle she had helped Carlos gather. His trumpet lay on top. When the men returned, Carlos supervised the transfer of Pedro Rodríguez's body, wrapped in a winding sheet, from the backseat to the caboose. As his friend was resettled, he told Daniela the story of Pedro's death as Diego had told it to him. He tucked the shroud around the Hanged Man's broad shoulders and took Daniela's hand as they walked down the rear stairs.

Oscar hugged them both and offered to take over the engineer's duties.

"*Gracias, no,*" Carlos said, holding his wounded side. "Feel free to shovel some coal, though. I'm going to teach Dani how to drive one of these. In case we ever have to steal another train."

At the front of the locomotive, Jacie's parents were removing their disguises: canister gas masks and wide-brimmed helmets, souvenirs of war. Sr. Webster had backed the truck off the tracks. Dust and captured insects dulled the black paint, still tacky where they had covered up the Webster General Store advertisement. *Tejanos* took boxes of canned and bottled goods from the rear of the truck and loaded them on board the day-coaches and caboose. The Websters had also packed as many items as they could from each house in the colony. Sra. Webster called out the names on each bundle and handed them over.

Carlos offered his hand to Jacie's father. "You saved my life and now my wife's and so many others'."

"Maybe I've finally paid that debt from the Great War." He hugged his daughter's shoulders and said to her, "Hop in the Victoria, and we'll follow you home."

"I'm going with them, Dad. Time for me to leave the nest." She told her parents she'd packed for the trip, grinning at their stunned expressions. "What better way for me to see the world than on a stolen train with almost two hundred fugitives?"

Sra. Webster argued with her but finally relented: "Do what you want—you always have. I knew you'd never get married and have a family like a normal girl."

"I might do those things after a while, Mom—"

"But there won't be anything normal about it," her father finished for her.

"And I can't even nag you about not having enough food, money, or clothing." She cried as she hugged and kissed her daughter.

Jacie held her father a moment and then trotted back to the train to help get everyone on board. Carlos and Daniela said goodbye to the Websters and promised to write. They walked alongside the barrel-shaped engine that continued to huff and sigh. Carlos said, "The K-Class Pacific's a beauty. If I was going to steal a train, this would've been my pick." For luck, he patted the circular emblem on the engineer's cabin, the Southern Pacific Lines trademark of railroad tracks converging toward the rising sun. He quoted to Daniela from Oscar's song, "I'm ready to face the dawn beside you."

She held him gently around the waist and said, "It does feel like a new day."

"And you're my morning star." He handed her into the cabin where Oscar was busy shoveling coal into the furnace. The bandleader showed her how to toot the whistle. Carlos donned the striped hat left behind by the engineer and mock-frowned at Daniela. "Strategy is not where I do my best improvising, huh?"

"I'll never doubt you again." She held his face and kissed him.

He watched the boiler's pressure rise as Oscar worked to feed it. When they were ready to go, Carlos looked down both sides of the train. Though Jacie and others had ushered everyone inside, he called, "All aboard," for the pleasure of it. He asked Daniela, "What are your orders, boss?"

"Let's go!"

They waved to the Websters as the train eased forward and then picked up speed, carrying them away.

*

Lebrun checked his watch. "Ring up El Campo again. They're now an hour late." He looked at Jack and said, "Goddamn Texas."

The phone rang as the operator reached for it. Jack heard the voice on the other end say, "This is El Campo. Your train just passed by."

"But everything looked okay?"

"No problems. Had a good head of steam."

The operator said, "Good. You think they had to clear something from the tracks?"

"Lots of ranches around here and no fences."

"Yeah, there're so many blasted cows you can't plow through them all."

Jack asked, "Can I have that for a second?" He took the receiver and cradled it between his shoulder and neck. He said, "This is Texas Ranger Dieg...Donati. You're sure nothing looked peculiar?" He removed his badge and toyed with the stickpin on the back.

The El Campo stationmaster said, "Nothing at all. 'Course it was going like a bat out of hell when it came through, so I couldn't see much."

"But you could see the caboose as it was heading away from you."

"Sure. No one on the platform, but Old Glory was flapping in the breeze."

The stickpin broke off in Jack's grip. "Just what I was hoping to hear." He hung up and said to Lebrun, "Two of your guys were taking in the view from the platform."

"You see, Texas Ranger 'Dieg'? My men have it well in hand. When you think at all, you think too much." He squared the olive-drab shirt across his shoulders. "You mind if I go back to Houston now?"

Jack left the broken badge on the operator's desk and followed Lebrun into the terminal. The agent's men sat propped against the walls. Jack put more weight on his left leg, walking without a limp or any pain. *¡Extraordinario!* He said, "I've been doing a lot of thinking about that, Lebrun."

"Yeah, Jack? And what do you think?"

"I think you can go to hell." Jack pulled his derringer from a pocket and shot Lebrun between his pale eyes. He turned away as Lebrun's men scrambled for their guns.

Jack looked out at the waving, rustling grass of the prairie. He barely felt the agents' bullets push him into the void.

CHAPTER 42

C arlos stopped the train at several points near sprawling ranches, or *haciendas* that looked promising. Between twenty and fifty farmhands and their children departed at a time. There was no way to know if they would be hired, or for how long, but at least they had a chance.

As the sun set, Carlos stopped trusting their luck on the cleared track. Since only two dozen of them were still on board, they voted to abandon the train after passing through Beeville, halfway to Laredo. After they unloaded, Oscar filled the firebox and Carlos opened the steam valves and they clambered off. By the time the boiler ran out of fuel, the train would've chugged through Freer and coasted to a stop on the Nueces Plains, north of its intended destination.

They camped on the prairie. In the morning, Jacie hiked back to Beeville with Oscar and Hector, both of whom could drive, and bought three trucks to hold everyone. Carlos remarked to Daniela, "From now on, let's always travel with an heiress." They reversed course, heading east, just in case Immigration pursued them.

Carlos also included *"curandera"* in his list of necessary traveling companions. During the journey, Letty oversaw his recovery, monitored Daniela's pregnancy, and kept everyone healthy. She'd even embalmed Pedro's body in the caboose, using her own recipe since this wasn't a custom of her foremothers.

The caravan drove to Corpus Christi. Daniela's sisters and families lived there, and Oscar had read about expansions to a large port and some early successes in oil exploration, so there could be jobs. On a promontory south of the city, they discovered a Mexican cemetery with headstones dating back more than a hundred years. The graveyard overlooked the Intracoastal Waterway and, beyond the breakwater, the slate-blue Gulf of Mexico sparkled. In between was a long barrier island called Padre.

"Perfect," Carlos said, and unloaded the cypress monument onto which he'd carved an epitaph. The letters didn't line up exactly right and the chisel had not been the ideal tool to use for carving, but he was satisfied he'd done his best. Daniela stood beside him as he proofread his work. He said, "I don't think I made any mistakes."

"It is perfect, just like this spot. Pedro would be honored."

César dug the grave while the others pulled up weeds and tall grass and righted crosses that had fallen. The wind nibbled at a cone of dirt beside the oak coffin Jacie had purchased for their friend's remains.

Carlos, Oscar, and two other musicians lowered the casket with ropes. Pulling the hemp out from underneath made a wailing pitch that pierced deeply and brought hot tears. The party of fugitives bowed their heads. Carlos asked for God's blessing on the hallowed ground, on Pedro's soul, and on the souls of his own family and friends. He gripped a handful of dirt and dropped it onto the coffin, ready this time for the parting.

Everyone used their hands to fill in the grave and the wind rounded the top. When Carlos pounded in the cypress monument, a seagull squawked and ascended. It circled over them, a flash of white and black against the deep blue sky, and flew toward Padre.

The band took up the instruments the Websters had recovered from the colony, and *El Mariachi Santa Cruz de Guadalajara* performed their most solemn *tragedías*, the perfect way to say goodbye.

*

Carlos enjoyed bantering with his sister-in-law and her family, with whom they lived for the moment. After supper, Daniela handed Esmeralda Camelia to Carlos and they went for a walk. He cradled their plump, month-old miracle of sparkling brown eyes, ready smiles, and musical sounds. "Esme," he whispered to her. She rewarded him with her full attention for a few seconds before her gaze wandered. Daniela's hand was warm in his, and the balmy evening breeze carried smells of spring flowers as well as the fish-and-diesel tang of Corpus Christi Bay.

The *barrio* bustled on Saturday evening. Families window-shopped, the husbands walking ahead, smoking, dressed in suits, denims, or overalls, and their wives trailing in small clusters with children in tow. Men on their own congregated on the street corners, flirting with the women who passed in pairs and trios. The fortunate gents with money sauntered into the social clubs and dance halls or walked to night-shift jobs. There was no sign of *la migra*, but Carlos and Daniela carried their papers at all times.

Daniela had forbidden him from seeking an after-Mass job on Sundays. She'd told Carlos he worked too hard repairing trains in the railroad roundhouse, that she didn't see enough of him. Following services at Sacred Heart of Mary, she had planned a full day of socializing with their friends that would require a walk around the city.

Her itinerary would start with a visit to Letty and César's. They lived beyond the western outskirts so César could work on a nearby ranch and the *curandera* could explore the countryside and harvest the local roots and herbs. After Letty's midwife skills helped deliver the baby girl, Daniela had named her as Esme's godmother. Esme seemed partial to Letty, who demanded to see her goddaughter as often as possible and announced that she would impart her many skills, prompting Carlos to invent a nickname for their little witch-in-the-making: "*Brujita.*"

On the east side of the city, Oscar's musicians and their wives lived in scattered apartments within a dozen blocks of one another, near the port where most of them worked. The bandleader lived close to his job, working alongside Carlos in the rail yards; he'd promised to accompany them on their Sunday visits. Jacie could be found wandering among the cafés and shops along the bay or, as likely, organizing impromptu math and English lessons for the *barrio* kids. Somehow, Oscar always seemed to know where to locate her.

As they strolled, Carlos pointed out the rainbow glinting in an oily puddle, thinking of the Ten of Cups. He said, "Let's visit Pedro now since we won't have time tomorrow."

"Did I try to fit too much into our day?"

"Just so long as there'll be time for us—I haven't shown you all of my secrets."

South of the city, they walked along the forty-foot bluffs that soared above the water. He pointed out to Esme the fishing boats trolling around *Padre.* Daniela gave her the names of the purples and oranges in the sky above them as their daughter's eyes reflected the colors of the gathering clouds lit by the sunset. Another storm was coming.

They crossed the stone border of the old cemetery. Out of habit, they pulled a few weeds and inspected the grounds. Pedro's gravesite had settled and begun to look a part of its surroundings. They'd decorated it during the last *Día de los Muertos fiesta* with marigolds and cockscomb, *papel picado,* marzipan skulls, and the food they'd enjoyed with him: corn muffins and apples.

Carlos read again the cypress monument he'd improvised:

PEDRO RODRÍGUEZ
1885-1930
Revolutionary & Man of Peace
Philosopher & Man of Action
Father & Man of God

Daniela said, "I'm so proud of you. You're a poet on top of everything else."

"Only because of the notes you keep leaving for me."

"No, it's you. Maybe that's your destiny."

Carlos said he'd rather stay with *mariachi*. He and Oscar were assembling an even larger band.

"You could learn to read and write music next," she said.

"You'll teach me?"

She laughed, a sound like shells tumbling in the surf, and Esme cooed and smiled in response. "I'd need a teacher myself, but I could study along with you."

"*Bueno*," he said. "Then it's my turn to melt the chocolate."

The afterglow in the west silhouetted Daniela and Esme. Mother shielded daughter from a freshening wind as they started for home. With luck, they could get back to the city before the rain started. Carlos thought they would make it.

EPILOGUE

No lloro, pero me acuerdo. *"I do not cry, but I remember."*

The seeker's story is not done. It is never complete, for there are those who will forever continue to seek.

Such as you.

Your choices are set before you. And what you will find, you already know is there. Your fate is written in the time gone by. What followed from your willingness to act? Why have you allowed others to act upon you? Understand rather than judge and you will know the answers to your questions.

The bravest thing you may do is not to look ahead to the future; it is to acknowledge the past.

I do not cry, but I remember. "No lloro, pero me acuerdo."

Your destinies lay before you. Are you ready to proceed?

AFTERWORD

I have an abiding love of history and a fascination with "secret history"—the facts seldom taught in schools or discussed in the media. The 1920s through 1940s always have been of particular interest to me: the movies, the music, and the hardy people who whooped it up after winning one world war, struggled to survive the hardscrabble decade that followed, and then marshaled their reserves and won a second world war. Greatest Generation indeed. I wanted to write about them, but not cover the same ground others had.

In 2002, while researching Depression-era histories, squatting in the stacks of the Roswell, Georgia public library and surrounded by old books, I stumbled on a footnote that mentioned the forced repatriation of immigrants and Mexican-Americans during the late 1920s and throughout the 1930s. I'd never heard or read any such thing before. One citation led to another, and eventually I discovered a few scholarly books published by university presses that covered the topic in more detail.

Here's what I found:

At the start of the 20ᵗʰ century, the U.S. government, state governments, and business interests encouraged Mexican immigration to fill the need for cheap labor on farms, in factories, and to expand the network of railroads. A mere nickel bought an immigrant a visa for legal residency, until entry rules became stricter in 1924.

Then came the Great Depression. To make room on the welfare rolls for white Americans and free up scarce jobs, perhaps as many as two million people of Mexican ancestry were expelled from the U.S., either at the point of a gun or through other means of intimidation. Probably a million were American citizens. Maybe sixty percent of those citizens were children. Crammed onto trucks and trains, they were shipped to Mexico, which often sent them to their southern states, as far from the U.S. as possible. The photograph on the cover of my novel was taken by the Mexican news journal *La Opinion* on August 17, 1931 and shows a repatriation train about to carry hundreds of immigrants and American citizens to Mexico.

Most of the American children did not speak Spanish, and many of their parents had lost their fluency. The Mexican government placed them in poverty-stricken towns and plantations where no one spoke English. The only way they could return home was to have someone back in the states find and send birth certificates, other documents proving citizenship, or unexpired visas. Then all they had to do was travel a thousand miles back to the border, usually on foot. When World War II began, some of the repatriated men received draft notifications, forwarded from their former U.S. addresses, ordering them to report for duty and fight for the country that had expelled them. It sounded like a nightmare to me—and started me thinking about the backstory for a potential novel.

Two of my favorite books are *Les Misérables* and *The Grapes of Wrath*. In the former case, it's because of the decent hero being pursued by the relentless, self-righteous lawman. In Steinbeck's classic, I admired his use of an omniscient narrator who made occasional appearances to give the reader the broader perspective of events—things the Joads would have no way of knowing—which ratcheted up the tension as you now anticipated the tragedy that soon would befall the family. With the repatriations in mind, I combined my favorite elements of both novels to tell the story of stalwart Carlos Moreno and his relentless pursuer Texas Ranger Jack Diego/Donati, with María the fortuneteller providing the omniscient overview. I completed the novel in 2003, had a couple of near-misses at publication during the years that immediately followed, and am gratified to see the book at last in print thanks to my *Hardscrabble Road* publisher, Deeds Publishing.

Occasionally, a story about the repatriation makes the news: men and women now in their 80s describing their ordeal to journalists and documentary filmmakers. However, the tragedy has never come to the attention of most Americans, including those of Mexican heritage, even after the state of California passed the "Apology Act for the 1930s Mexican Repatriation Program" in 2005. Senate Bill 670 states, in part:

CHAPTER 8.5. MEXICAN REPATRIATION

8720. This chapter may be cited as the "Apology Act for the 1930s Mexican Repatriation Program."

8721. The Legislature finds and declares all of the following:

(a) Beginning in 1929, government authorities and certain private sector entities in California and throughout the United States undertook an aggressive program to forcibly remove persons of Mexican ancestry from the United States.

(b) In California alone, approximately 400,000 American citizens and legal residents of Mexican ancestry were forced to go to Mexico.

(c) In total, it is estimated that two million people of Mexican ancestry were forcibly relocated to Mexico, approximately 1.2 million of whom had been born in the United States, including the State of California.

(d) Throughout California, massive raids were conducted on Mexican-American communities, resulting in the clandestine removal of thousands of people, many of whom were never able to return to the United States, their country of birth.

(e) These raids also had the effect of coercing thousands of people to leave the country in the face of threats and acts of violence.

(f) These raids targeted persons of Mexican ancestry, with authorities and others indiscriminately characterizing these persons as "illegal aliens" even when they were United States citizens or permanent legal residents.

(g) Authorities in California and other states instituted programs to wrongfully remove persons of Mexican ancestry and secure transportation arrangements with railroads, automobiles, ships, and airlines to effectuate the wholesale removal of persons out of the United States to Mexico.

(h) As a result of these illegal activities, families were forced to abandon, or were defrauded of, personal and real property, which often was sold by local authorities as "payment" for the transportation expenses incurred in their removal from the United States to Mexico.

(i) As a further result of these illegal activities, United States citizens and legal residents were separated from their families and country and were deprived of their livelihood and United States constitutional rights.

As of 2013, none of the other participating states or the federal government has ever apologized or sought to make restitution for the illegal repatriation activities.

"No lloro, pero me acuerdo."

ACKNOWLEDGMENTS

I wrote this novel before *Hardscrabble Road*, more than a decade ago, and made every rookie mistake, from bombarding my patient wife Kate with early drafts that never should have been shared with anyone, to bloated narrative and purple prose.

My original critique group—Mark All, Kathleen Boehmig, Mike Buchanan, and John Witkowski—had to endure the worst of it. They introduced me to Christopher Vogler's *The Writer's Journey: Mythic Structure for Writers*, an invaluable resource, and contributed countless other ideas that made the book better.

Then, a decade later, the newest incarnation of my critique group helped me polish the work yet again. Thanks go to Sweta Bhaumik, Josh Bugosh, Emily Carpenter, Suzi Ehtesham-Zadeh, Jane Haessler, JD Jordan, Tom Leidy, Chris Negron, and Fred Whitson.

Their comments reminded me that a creative work never is truly complete—it always can be improved. That might argue for never publishing anything, but there comes a point when the author needs to be shoved aside so the work can be shared with the world. That's where the professionals at Deeds Publishing come in: thank you, Bob, Jan, and Mark Babcock.

One of my favorite wits, Oscar Levant, said, "Imitation is the sincerest form of plagiarism," so thanks too to Victor

Hugo, John Steinbeck, and all the other greats I stole from, either blatantly or inadvertently.

And, on the topic of plagiarism, I'm also going to steal from myself, cribbing the final paragraph from my *Hardscrabble Road* acknowledgments. I'm not sure I can express my gratitude to readers of my books any better than as follows:

My deepest thanks to my readers. It's the ultimate leap of faith for you whenever you devote precious time and money to enter a world of someone else's devising, counting on being entertained at the very least, and maybe desiring a stronger emotional connection to the characters and the story. There are countless other ways you could've spent your resources, so my sincere hope is that you thought this adventure was worth your investment.

-George Weinstein
Roswell, GA
August 2013

AUTHOR'S BIO

George Weinstein is a writer and a Vice President at AAL, a consulting and educational services company based in Atlanta, Georgia. In 2012, his first adult novel, *Hardscrabble Road*, was published. His work also has been published locally in the Atlanta press and in regional and national anthologies, including *A Cup of Comfort for Writers*. In addition, he is the author of a novel for children, the motivational adventure story *Jake and the Tiger Flight*, written in 2008 for the nonprofit Tiger Flight Foundation, which is dedicated to the mission of leading the young to become the "Pilot in Command" of their lives. He wishes that there had been such an organization in Laurel, Maryland, where he misspent his youth.

George is the former President of the Atlanta Writers Club (AWC) and former everything-else there too. Having run out of term-limited positions for him, in 2012 the AWC Board bestowed on George the lifetime title of Officer Emeritus, which means he can never leave. Not that he would, but it's nice to be wanted. In his copious free time, George runs twice-yearly writers conferences for the AWC, bringing agents and editors to Atlanta to educate club members about the craft and business of writing, giving them a shot at representation or outright publication, and helping them to avoid the myriad mistakes he's made in his writing career. The AWC was established in 1914; George was established only a few years later. He has a self-portrait in his attic that looks like hell.

Read excerpts of George's work, book club questions, and more on his website:

www.georgeweinstein.com

CPSIA information can be obtained at www.ICGtesting.com
Printed in the USA
LVOW13s0752081013

355843LV00002BA/2/P